Thomas Twining, Richard Twining

Selections from Papers of the Twining Family

A sequel to 'The recreations and studies of a country clergyman of the 18th century' - the Rev. Thomas Twining

Thomas Twining, Richard Twining

Selections from Papers of the Twining Family
A sequel to 'The recreations and studies of a country clergyman of the 18th century' - the Rev. Thomas Twining

ISBN/EAN: 9783337227296

Printed in Europe, USA, Canada, Australia, Japan

Cover: Foto ©Andreas Hilbeck / pixelio.de

More available books at **www.hansebooks.com**

THE
TWINING FAMILY

PRINTED BY
SPOTTISWOODE AND CO., NEW-STREET SQUARE
LONDON

PRINTED BY
SPOTTISWOODE AND CO., NEW-STREET SQUARE
LONDON

SELECTIONS FROM PAPERS OF THE TWINING FAMILY: A SEQUEL TO 'THE RECREATIONS AND STUDIES OF A COUNTRY CLERGYMAN OF THE 18TH CENTURY,' THE REV. THOMAS TWINING, SOMETIME RECTOR OF ST. MARY'S, COLCHESTER.

EDITED BY RICHARD TWINING

> I pity the man who can trave from Dan to Beersheba and cry, ''Tis all barren!'——and so it is ; and so is all the world to him who will not cultivate the fruits it offers"
>
> STERNE, *Sentimental Journey*

LONDON

JOHN MURRAY, ALBEMARLE STREET

1887

PREFACE.

SOME few years since I was induced to publish a small volume of selections from the correspondence of my great uncle, the Rev. Thomas Twining, formerly Rector of St. Mary's, Colchester.[1]

Enquiries have since been addressed to me from various quarters, for a further contribution from the papers under my charge.

[1] In one or two critiques on the former volume it was remarked that more might have been said of Thomas Twining's work as a parish priest. On that point I may avail myself of the present opportunity of observing that the book was not intended to contain ' annals of the parish,' or of the rector's ministrations therein ; neither should I have felt myself competent to have treated of that part of his character. I would, however, refer to a passage in my grandfather's prefatory memoir of his brother :—' In the performance of all the duties of a clergyman, particularly of the most important duties of the minister of a parish, he was exemplary' (p. 4) ; and also to the following lines in his epitaph (p. 13) by Dr. Parr—a man not wont to flatter—

> Pietas erga Deum pura atque sincera,
> Si quidem honesta de natura ejus opinione
> Stabilique in Christo fide potissimum nixa est,
> Et cum summa in omnes homines benevolentia
> Nunquam non conjuncta.

More could hardly have been added to the force and value of such words.—R. T., 1886.

In order, therefore, to satisfy such demands, I have put together the present selection from our family journals and letters.

It will be seen that it bears less upon the public events of the period, and, over and above its literary element, brings out more conspicuously the records of that propensity for travels, at home and abroad, which has been handed down in our family through several generations.

The principal tours of which my grandfather has left notes or journals are as follows :—

1772. To the Land's End.

1775. The New Forest and Isle of Wight.

1775. Yorkshire, Northumberland, and the border-country of Scotland, returning· by the English lakes and midland counties.

1779. North Wales.

1781. Flanders and the Rhine to Frankfort.

1783. 'Maidenhead Bridge' and South Wales.

1785. North Wales.

1786. Paris and Tours (Loire).

1788. Rotterdam, Göttingen, and the Hartz.

1790. Carlisle, Solway Firth, Dumfries, Glasgow, and Blair Athol.

1793. 'Maidenhead Bridge,' New Forest, Isle of Wight, and Arundel.

1797. North Wales.

On his earlier home-journeys my grandfather was wont to travel on horseback, with a groom, saddle-bags, &c. ; later on, when accompanied by my grandmother or any of their children, in a low phaeton, with a pair of ponies, among whom 'Poppet,' 'Skipjack,' and 'Sly-boots' are recorded as special favourites, while occasionally a lady's horse, ' Juliet,' (another favourite) was in attendance ; and so, in that leisurely enjoyable fashion, they traversed the country, from John O'Groat's House to the Land's End. Each age, as it passes, may be said to have its own particular advantages, and certainly among those of the eighteenth century may be reckoned the moderate pace of life as compared with that of the present day.

In the next generation my father did not fail to keep up the travelling traditions of the family, as the following list will attest ; viz. :—

1800. To Edinburgh, on horseback.
1814. Flanders and Aix-la-Chapelle.
1819. Paris.
1827. The Netherlands, the Rhine, Switzerland, and Italy, returning through France.
1834. North Germany, Hanover, and Brunswick.
1839. Luxemburg, Treves, Munich, the Tyrol, Vienna, &c.
1844. Berlin, Dresden, Prague, Munich, Stuttgart, Metz, and Rheims.
1852. Paris and Chartres.

The last-mentioned excursion was made (with companions) when my father was in his eightieth year—renewing the recollections of his younger days with unabated enjoyment. It may be thankfully added : ' His eye was not dim, nor his natural force abated.'

His next brother, Thomas, also, during a distinguished career in the East India Company's Bengal Civil Service, at a remarkable period in the history of British India—embracing the victories of Sir Robert

Abercrombie, Lord Lake, and General Harris, with the fall of Seringapatam, the death of Tippoo, and the public services of the Wellesley family—did not omit to avail himself of the opportunities which it afforded him for visiting many interesting scenes in that country, and, as will be seen further on, with signal advantage

RICHARD TWINING.

1886.

Note.

For several particulars of the Twinings in olden time, the family are indebted to the kind researches of the Rev. W. H. G. Twining, of St. Stephen's, Westminster, at the Record Office, and among Parish Registers in Gloucestershire.

CONTENTS.

a

PAGE

PAGE

 ## CONTENTS.

APPENDIX.

SELECTIONS

PAPERS OF THE TWINING FAMILY.

FAMILY ANNALS.

THE family of 'Twining' appears to have had its origin in the county of Gloucester, in and around Tewkesbury. About two miles north of that town is the village of Twining, the name having been derived, as it is said, from two old Saxon words denoting two meadows, on the borders of a river there formed by the junction of the Severn and the Avon. The ferry is called 'Twining's Fleet.' The neighbourhood was remarkable for the fertility of its lands, and was the seat of numerous monasteries and abbeys. Of one of the latter—that of Winchcombe—a 'John Twining' is recorded as having been the abbot, under the pontificates of Sixtus IV. and Innocent VIII., in the reigns of Edward IV. and V. and Richard III. (A.D. 1461–1483). A wise ruler and a learned man, he raised his abbey to the rank of a university.

The name of Twining was probably taken from

the land, as was often the case in other parts of England. On the dissolution of the monasteries the name of Thomas Twining is amongst those who were pensioned off from the monastery of Tewkesbury, and many records of the same name are found between that period and the close of the seventeenth century. In 1651 a John Twining was accused of assisting in the defence of the garrison of Evesham against Cromwell, for which he was twice imprisoned and part of his property confiscated.

No distinct record has yet been found of the circumstances which led Thomas Twining, my great-great-grandfather, at the commencement of the eighteenth century to migrate to London, where he seems first to have taken up his abode in St. Giles', Cripplegate, and from whence he founded (*circa* 1710) the business of a tea-dealer at Tom's Coffee House in Devereux Court, Strand; the same which has been carried on and extended by his descendants[1] to the present day. It seems, however, not improbable that

---

[1] *Succession in Business, Devereux Court, Strand.*

1. Thomas Twining, born in 1675, in the twenty-eighth year of
   King Charles II., Founder 1710
2. Daniel Twining, his son and successor 1741
3. Richard and John Twining, sons of Daniel . . 1771 & 1782
4. Richard, George, and John Aldred Twining, sons of Richard
   1794 & 1818
5. And so to their sons and grandsons to this date . . . 1886

Early in the eighteenth century Thomas Twining built Dial House, Twickenham, and from that date to the present the family have continued to live there and in other places in that part of the Thames valley.

he may be identified with the 'Thomas Twining' whose name is recorded on a board in the parish church of Painswick as a donor of 5*l.*, in 1724, to the parish schools then founded. He was a freeman of the 'Weavers' Company' in the City of London, a circumstance which would seem to connect him with the wool trade, at that time flourishing in Gloucestershire, but from whence it afterwards drifted into Yorkshire. The same may account for the migration of many members of the family to other homes, but if, as is said to have been the case, that little Saxon village on the Avon sent forth in its day brave warriors to the Crusades, and, in an after age, supplied men who risked their lives and possessions in the cause of 'king and country,' we may humbly hope that the good seed then sown may long continue to bring forth fruit abundantly.

R. T.

1886.

———————

A FAVOURITE ODE IN LATIN.

The Reverend Thomas Twining to his Brother Richard.

ODE

AD JULIAM NAVIGATURAM.

Vix tristis dubiâ luce rubet polus—
Circum cuncta silent ; solus ego his vagor
    Incerto pede sylvis,
      Et mecum vigilans amor.
Crudelis fugies, Julia ? turbido
Te credis pelago ? nos fera dividens
    Inter sæviet unda, et
      Venti spes rapient meas ?

B 2

> Sic me, sic poteras ludere credulum?
> Sic promissa cadunt? ipsa tamen time! et
> Venti fallere nôrunt
> Nec servat pelagus fidem.

Colchester, May 2, 1778.

Dear Richard,—'Tis not mine, I assure you; would it were; I had much rather have written it than Horace's '*Galatea.*' Finding myself at my bureau here with pen, ink, and paper temptingly before me, and just one quarter of an hour to spare, I can't help treating you with this morsel, 'Donarem poteras, &c.' I might have sent you chickens or a green goose, &c., but I believe you will be better pleased as it is.

> Gaudes carminibus; carmina possumus
> Donare et pretium dicere muneri.

Your affectionate brother,   T. T.

CAMBRIDGE SAPPHICS.—THE RETURN OF SPRING.

The Rev. T. T. to R. T.

Fordham, April 19, 1781.

Dear Brother,—If I am to *amuse* myself what pleasanter employment can I find than that of talking with you? I have many things to say, and am absolutely *obæratus* in the way of epistolary debt to you; *over head and ears* in debt as we say: *quasi, ære alieno obrutus*, the word always conveys that idea to me. I shall begin to pay off, but at my leisure, and by dribbling remittances, as it shall suit my indolence or my *industry*, without paying the least regard, Sir, to your reproaches about *stretch*-work, short lines, and letterlings. I hold that no correspondence can be comfortable without perfect liberty. I have often been deterred from writing a letter by the obligation I have felt myself fettered with to fill a certain quantity of paper. Give me liberty to write three lines or three pages, I sit down with alacrity, and it almost always turns out that I write three pages ; for to *write* a long letter is nothing : all the pain is in the intention, or rather in the obligation. But you and I are agreed about all this : ' Scimus ; et hanc veniam petimusque damusque vicissim.' And now to exemplify, I *take leave* to break off and take a walk in my garden. The weather, since our removal, has been delightful. I am thankful for it ; for already air and exercise, together with that delicious and inexplicable complication of pleasurable feelings *that a return to the country at this time of the year* always gives me—all this has already done me much good. My cough is almost worn out, and Mrs. T. flatters me that I begin to *plump* again. In a week or two more I shall *bloom* like Mr. Rafter.[2] I ride or walk every day, and am as much in the air as possible. This is good for me though bad for Aristotle ; but he is a peripatetic, and will forgive me. My wife cries, ' Why do you take so much pains ? You are never satisfied.

---

[2] Mrs. Clive's (Kitty Clive's) brother. He lived with his sister at Twickenham, and sometimes appeared on the stage, with, however, but scant success.

Nobody else would take half the pains you do. When you have done a thing, why do it again ?' &c.— Ma foi, elle a raison.

The readers of these days are too indolent to deserve laborious writers. I think it will not be amiss if I abridge my labours and consult my health.

But now as we have been talking of 'the pretty spring time,' and its charms, and as you wished to see my sapphics, I must treat you with

ODE

IN REDITUM VERIS:

quam Cantabrigiæ olim, alieno jussu, haud sponte suâ,—invitâ Minervâ, iratisque Musis omnibus, — ingenio denique qualicunque vehementi capitis dolore obtuso, sibi vix vi expressit extorsitque T. T.

' *Demorsos sapit ungues.*'—PERS.

Iam retro cedit pede non libente,
Horridum nimbis caput involuta,
Alterum mundi latus imperata
      Visere Bruma.

Nuncii veris Zephyri, tepente
Arva mulcentes recreata flatu,
Æolo longi requiem laboris
      Affore monstrant.

Cui repentino Boream tumultu,
Heu nefas ! sceptrum expuisse adorsum
Vidimus nuper furere et recluso
      Carcere ventos.

There you have your revenge. I have no comment to make save that 'mundi latus,' though it sounds English, is Horatian ; that the last stanza is an elegant allusion to a very high wind we had lately had ; and that my ear naturally led me to the strict observance of my *ex post facto* sapphic standard. My metre and my Latinity is all I can defend. The subject was *set* us. We were also to write a prose theme and hexameter verses on this sentence of Sallust: ' Animi imperio, corporis servitio magis utimur.' I will e'en give you my hexameters because they did me a little more credit and have some meaning in them; (*April* 20) for they say what is certainly true in general, (in spite of now and then a ——) that there is not a more *likely* preservative against bodily rebellion than a turn for literary pursuits and an habitual relish for intellectual enjoyment. And so

> ' Animi imperio, corporis servitio magis utimur.'

[But here I take a ride ;—*corporis imperio !*] Æolus rather too busy.

> Scilicet excelsâ cæli demissus ab arce
> Est nobis animus divinæ particula auræ
> Mens, cognata polo, et supremi nescia fati.
> Hæc alto insignis solio, sceptrumque tenebit,
> Corporeamque reget justo moderamine molem ;
> Nempe animi imperio est utendum, corpore sano
> Verior ex adyto vox nunquam prodiit ; omnes
> Agnoscunt, vatemque stupent divina canentem.
> Vera omnes laudant pauci laudata sequuntur ;
> Est sanè, est animi imperium ; sed carcere clausum
> Corporis, alarum magno molimine vix ad
> Auras cognatas interdum surgere nixum
> Illico deturbat custos oculatior Argo
> ' Atque affligit humi divinæ particulam auræ '—
> Quin age—tu diram hanc tandem superare Chimæram
> Aude, nec cedas turpi formidine victus.
> Artibus ac studiis animus munitus honestis,
> Si semel excelsam doctrinæ advenerit arcem
> Imperium accipiet proprium acceptumque tenebit.

Pray, Sir, observe how my numbers express the struggle of the poor soul to rise ; but don't observe the 'carcere clausum ' for fear the commentators will be puzzled to reconcile it to what follows.

EXTRACTS FROM JOURNAL OF A TOUR IN FLANDERS AND ON THE RHINE BY RICHARD TWINING, WITH SKETCHES OF LIFE IN SPA, &c., 1781.

It is mine own, compounded of many simples, extracted from many objects ; and, indeed, the sundry contemplations of my travels.

As You Like It, act iv. sc. 1.

August 1, 1781.—To Margate with my wife and Mary[3] ; so full of Continental ideas, that nothing inferior to the lovely Kent, with its Thames, its Medway, its hops, woods, and hills could have attracted our attention.   The road, though by no means new to us, was still entertaining ; the fields were filled with reapers, the weather was delightful, and, in short, everything conspired to put us in good humour upon the day of our departure.

At Margate a glorious bustle in order to secure the necessary accommodation on board of our packet. It is often pleasant, though sometimes unpleasant, to feel upon small occasions what other people feel upon great ones.   I should have been sorry to have ex-

---

[3] Their eldest daughter, aged eleven, afterwards Mrs. Powell.—R. T., 1886.

changed my sensations, though they were founded in ignorance, for those of a man who was hackneyed in such expeditions.

A packet was to sail in the evening, but, as we had travelled upwards of seventy miles by land, we . were unwilling to encounter our passage on the great sea till we had been refreshed by a night's rest. In the night the wind was very high, and it shook our apartment, which was fully exposed to its fury. Happy were we to think that we had declined taking our passage in the vessel which was then tossing about.

Thursday, August 2.—The *vast* undertaking which we had in hand prevented laziness, and we rose early. Having had our baggage searched—after a certain .fashion—by the Custom House officer, and having provided ourselves with a cargo of provisions, we went on board. About half-past eleven we got under weigh, and the wind, of which there was exactly enough, was as fair as possible. ' Prosequitur surgens a puppi ventus euntes.' We had rather a motley collection of fellow-passengers, though with a great part of it we had the utmost reason to be satisfied. With one party especially we soon became well acquainted. It consisted of four Irish gentlemen. Colonel Townshend, his son, another Mr. Townshend, a clergyman, and the Honble. Mr. St. .Leger. Two of them were Etonians, and I verily believe that a comfortable conversation about school affairs kept off for some time that abominable plague, sea-sickness, which, having once found its way amongst us, spread like a true pestilence with the utmost rapidity. A curious couple occupied a chaise which was strapped on the deck : a mulatto, as ugly as mortal man could well be, and his very handsome white wife. She was sick to death ; he, sitting by her side, was gnawing a mangled fowl. It was impossible not to smile at this Othello's awkward and apparently unacceptable attentions to his fair Desdemona. Perhaps I may be a little too severe upon this hairdresser (for such was his profession), and, to say the truth, I was inclined at that moment to think ill of every man who could eat ! Our passage, however, was as pleasant, or rather as little unpleasant, as a passage of that kind can well be, but after all *land* voyages are the most agreeable. Not a morsel of the noble cargo of provisions with which, like ignorant sailors, we had provided ourselves could we touch. It was then that, for the first time in my life, I could cry out :

Nec jam amplius ullæ
Apparent terræ : cœlum undique, et undique pontus.

There was something sublime in this lack of land to persons who, like Æneas and his companions, had been accustomed to coasting voyages only.

The bell which called the good friars to their midnight prayers welcomed us into the port of Ostend. When we landed the gates were shut, and we had to wait about half an hour close to a vile moat before we could get the keys from the commandant. The well-stored interior of the wooden horse could not have panted more eagerly for admittance than did the provisionless passengers who stood knocking at those closed gates of Ostend. I began to fear that the cruel Governor had given orders, 'Ne recipi portis aut duci in mœnia possim,' and that it would be our fate to pass the night on the quay. The gates were, however, at last thrown open to us, and our ship's crew proceeded in a body to the same inn, the 'Maison de Ville,' where we had another long waiting job. We wished to have got rid of some of our companions, as we foresaw that one house would not be able to accommodate so large a party ; but it was in vain. They all clung together, and when the uproar which we made brought forth a sleepy servant, there were between thirty and forty candidates for beds. After a treaty of tedious length we procured seven, and from these we agreed that the mattresses should be taken, and that they should be spread upon the floor of the *salle-à-manger*. The whole family had by this time got up, and exhibited a scene which was entirely new to us and beyond description entertaining. It was the first Continental feast with which our inquisitive eyes were treated. In the kitchen was a tall meagre man, who in less than a quarter of an hour prepared for us a very good hot supper. It was most diverting to see this *Parmegiano-ish* cook fanning the fires with a lady's fan, which he waved backwards and forwards with wondrous grace. Honest Alexander, our nankeen-jacketed waiter, flew on our first appearance to the *salle-à-manger*, where the cloth was already laid, and removed the silver spoons and forks from the table ; our motley group may have been thought to justify his suspicions.   The daughter of our landlord and her two maids prepared, whilst we were supping at one end of the long room, the beds on the floor at the other.   The daughter was dressed in the French taste with a vast cap flying out from each side of her head ; her attendants in the close caps of Flanders formed a fine contrast to their elegant mistress. Though these lowly beds did not appear to be very inviting, yet want of rest made them so acceptable that some of our companions were eager to turn into them the moment supper was over.   A lady was among those who passed the night in this humble way ; and I could not but admire the readiness with which she submitted to this somewhat trying arrangement. She had, however, a husband to protect her.

Friday, August 3.—As it was late before we got to rest, we did not rise early, nor was it material, as Ostend may be seen in a short time.   It is now a thriving place, having been lately declared by the Emperor a free port, a vast change since 1757, when, by order of the Empress-Queen Maria Theresa, commerce between the maritime towns of Flanders and England was cut off, although the packet boat passed with letters as usual.   Ostend and Nieuport were then, by permission of the Empress, garrisoned by the French.   It seems as if Ostend had been taken at enormous expense out of the sea, from which it is protected by vast banks, upon which the safety of the neighbouring level country must depend. Since the Emperor formed the design of improving this place, and of allowing to its inhabitants all the advantages of commerce of which it is capable, a plan has been arranged for removing the bastions and a great part of the present fortifications, thereby procuring land for building. Ostend was fortified in 1583 by the Prince of Orange, sustained a siege of more than three years against the Archduke Albert, was taken by Spinola, in 1604, after its reduction to little more than a heap of ruins, when it surrendered upon terms. In a curious account of this siege it is asserted that the sound of the firing was heard in London. The Hôtel de Ville was destroyed during the siege in 1706, when the town was taken by the Allies. It was surrendered to the Emperor by the Barrier Treaty in 1715, besieged by and given up to the French in 1745, when Louis XV. made his entry. In 1722, Charles V. established an East India Company there, suspended in 1727, and entirely suppressed in 1731, owing to commercial jealousies of the English, Dutch, and French.

BRUGES.

August 4.—It was with considerable difficulty that we got ourselves and our baggage to the barque for Bruges before its departure. At length, however, we got on board. This boat was intended for market people, so that we had some excellent figures on board, such as one had often seen on canvas. The country too was such as Flemish painters had made familiar to us—reedy and flat, with corn here and there in niggardly patches, and cold-looking willows scattered about. Some houses were seen in a detached uncomfortable way, and, a long time before we reached it, a steeple at Bruges. Our water scheme ended between 9 and 10 A.M., and we had a walk of about a mile to our inn.

Bruges is a large city, with some good streets and good houses. The great market-place is a fine square. In it are two large buildings, magazines for merchandise. The town clock is in the tower of one of them. That tower was struck by lightning, and its upper part is at present remarkably ugly. In Bruges are many canals. The trade of the place has been much injured by that of Antwerp and Amsterdam, nor does it appear to have any chance of recovering its former prosperity. Bruges was bombarded but not taken by the Dutch in 1704, submitted to the Allies in 1706, after the battle of Ramillies, but was surrendered to the French in 1708. Louis XV. entered it in 1745. . . . I had a letter to a lady in the Convent of the English Augustines, and we were all desirous of obtaining a glimpse of conventual life. I was doubtful, however, whether I could with propriety introduce a party of eight persons (Colonel Townshend and his party were travelling with us) upon such an occasion ; but the *lady* portress, to whom I applied for advice, assured me that my friends would be welcome —and when she found that I was acquainted with her kinsman, Sir William Jerningham in Norfolk, she seemed to forget the letter I had put in her hands, and, like Joseph, asked me straightly of her kindred. Whilst we were talking with great earnestness through a small grate, the lady opened the door, and forth came a smart, well-dressed man, who proved to be the dancing-master to the nuns' school for young ladies, whereon I was asked if we had any thoughts of leaving our daughter behind us, and their excellent plan of education was pressed upon us as an inducement.

At length, however, and I believe with reluctance, the good portress took her leave, and we were shown upstairs into the visiting parlour. This is a small room with a grating across the middle of it. We waited there at least half an hour, for all letters are carried to the Superior of the convent, and, if the contents are lawful, they are then delivered to the lady to whom they are addressed. The shutters to the grating being thrown open, the nun to whom I had a letter, her sister, and the Superior of the convent appeared. They were all women far advanced in life. Before taking our leave they showed us the chapel, a small, neat structure with a handsome marble altar. The paintings were of no merit. We also visited the churches of S. Ann and S. Walburg, the latter belonging to the Jesuits, of considerable size, and handsome in its style and dimensions. It was built *circa* 1640. The cathedral church of S. Donat is an ancient structure. In this church was buried the famous Van

Eyck, the discoverer of the art of painting in oil, for which his memory has been deservedly cherished. One of his earliest paintings in oil is also preserved here, and his claims to high distinction are recorded in a Latin epitaph. In the church of 'Notre Dame' are the tombs of Charles the Bold, and of his daughter the wife of the Emperor Maximilian. They are of bronze gilt, of surprisingly beautiful workmanship.[4] The best thing in the church is a sculpture of 'The Blessed Virgin and Our Lord,' by Michael Angelo. The arm and the hand of the Virgin are really astonishing. I had not the least expectation of seeing such a noble work of art in Flanders. It would have contented me even if I had travelled as far as Italy in search of the works of Michael Angelo. It is said that the Earl of Leicester offered 4,000*l.* for it, a large sum in those days. This sublime work was captured on board of the ship by which it was sent to its intended destination, and the cargo being sold at Amsterdam, a native of Bruges purchased the piece of sculpture, of which the value was not known, and presented it to this church.

In the church of S. Sauveur, above the entrance to the choir, is a marble sculpture of the deity by Quellyn. In this figure, which is extremely venerable, is great dignity and great expression, though one cannot help wishing that painters and sculptors would confine their labours to imitable subjects ; for the praise,

---

[4] They were concealed during the French occupation, and so saved from removal by Bonaparte.

which was bestowed upon Phidias for his famous Jupiter, can never be bestowed with propriety upon him who endeavours to represent the deity of the Christian world. Quintilian, speaking of Phidias' Jupiter, says, "Cujus pulchritudo adjecisse' aliquid etiam receptæ religioni videtur, adeo majestas operis Deum æquavit.' It seems, indeed, that the ideas of this wonderful sculptor were almost too sublime for subjects inferior to those with which the gods of the heathen furnished him, for according to Quintilian—' Phidias tamen Diis quam hominibus efficiendis melior artifex traditur,' and Seneca says, ' Non vidit Phidias Jovem, fecit tamen velut tonantem ; nec stetit ante oculos ejus Minerva, dignus tamen illa arte animus et concepit Deos et exhibuit.' It is, indeed, somewhat difficult to conceive how an effect which would justify such praises could be produced by a statue of ivory, richly ornamented with gold, and of those materials did the Jupiter chiefly consist. Phidias, however, was not confined to such materials. He worked in marble, which must, one would think, have afforded a better opportunity of displaying his vast abilities ; but he seems to have derived the principal part of his fame from the Olympian Jove and the Attic Minerva, which was also of gold and ivory. The Greeks, who were undoubtedly good judges of sculpture, would not have admired and praised them so highly if they had not possessed distinguished merit. With the taste of modern times a Jupiter of ivory and gold is perhaps as nearly on a level as would be the vociferous eloquence of a Demosthenes.[5]

August 5.—The barque, which conveys passengers to Ghent, left Bruges at nine A.M. It contains excellent accommodation for at least a hundred people and enjoys a high reputation. Indeed, I may say, it is one of the best inns in Flanders. On the day of our expedition sixty-three persons dined at the 'first table,' and there is a separate mess for second-class passengers. The dinner is served at separate tables. Our party of eight had a table to ourselves, and an excellent dinner of two courses and a dessert, with various wines, was served with the utmost regularity, the charge both for the passage and the dinner being extremely moderate.[6]

August 6.—We were much delighted with the large and handsome city of Ghent. The streets and houses seemed all of them to be good. A shabby

[5] The mellow tint which age has given to the statues in the Elgin collection is nearly that of ivory, and approaches closely to that pale flesh-colour which is observable in many of the best old oil-paintings, though these last have probably lost some of their original colour. I conclude that ivory is not a bad material; the gold was probably applied only to the ornamental and supplemental parts—the steps, pedestal, throne or seat, parts of the dress, and the mechanical parts of fastenings and support. The Grecian orator was no doubt 'vociferous,' i.e. *loud*, because he addressed a large assemblage in the open air. Garrick and his brethren of the buskin must have been loud or not audible, but it was an excellence of their art, without injuring the range and flexibility or impairing the more delicate modulations of the human voice.—D. T., 1848.

[6] I enjoyed an exactly similar experience in 1830, in the ante-railway days, but later on the barque was ruined by railway competition—more's the pity!—R. T., 1886.

building was nowhere to be found. Our surprise was akin to that of the honest Tityrus when he found that Rome so far surpassed his own city.

> Verum hæc tantum alias inter caput extulit urbes,
> Quantum lenta solent inter viburna cupressi.

Ghent is intersected by the Escaut, the Lys, the Lièvè, and the Mœre, besides canals. It has some twenty-six parish churches besides the cathedral, and more convents than any city in Flanders. The church of S. Bavon, not spoilt by an organ in the middle of it, is wonderfully magnificent. The choir is surrounded by small marble chapels, ornamented with pictures and containing many interesting monuments. The doors of the chapels are usually of brass richly worked. The general effect of this grandeur, or at least the effect which it had on me, cannot be described. I had never seen anything in this style. The principal altar is really sublime. During our stay in Ghent we were. for the first time witnesses to the arrival of people travelling post. We heard a monstrous noise, but could not conceive its cause. At last the postillions appeared, cracking their whips most furiously till they reached the inn, thereby giving stunning notice of their approach. As soon as they arrived, to our great entertainment they jumped out of their enormous jack-boots.

August 7.—We were now to bid adieu to water conveyances, and, as the country through which we were to pass was new to all of us, we agreed to travel leisurely through it. We hired three coaches with a pair of horses to each : such lumbering vehicles have not been seen in England this century. The traces were of rope, our coachmen were decorated with bags or pig-tails, and, thus equipped, we set off in merry mood for Brussels. We proceeded with the deliberation which became velvet-lined and velvet-cushioned conveyances along a strait *pavé* to Alost, where we dined. The country at first was bad, but it improved towards Alost. The crops were chiefly oats or clover. We saw some tobacco. Trees were planted on each side of our road. A triumphal arch erected in honour of the Archduchess, the Emperor's sister, who is appointed to the command of the Low Countries, still remained. We saw the Emperor's *haras* or stud. It contained above fifty horses from different countries, some of remarkable strength, and a few very handsome. The Emperor gives a truly royal encouragement to the improvement of the breed of useful horses in his dominions.

August 8.—Brussels.—This city boasts of considerable antiquity. It goes back as far as the year 900 for its origin, though it did not obtain the title of city till 1040. The French bombarded it in 1695 for forty-eight hours. The keys were delivered to the Duke of Marlborough in 1706. It was besieged by the Elector of Bavaria in 1708, but relieved by the Duke of Marlborough. The inhabitants of Brussels dine at an early hour, and between dinner and the time for going to the 'Comedy' they frequently ride or walk in a place of public resort a little way out of the gates. In compliance with this fashion we ordered our coaches and drawled along the paved Avenue till we were quite fatigued. An airing in Hyde Park is less dull. We returned to drink tea at 'Vauxhall,' and to go from thence to the play. The play-house is rather small and intolerably dark. The Archduke and the Archduchess were present, but they were veiled by the general obscurity. From the imperfect view which I obtained the Emperor's sister appeared to be a well-looking woman, between thirty and forty years of age. The performers were far from capital. The accommodations at our inn were excellent. In the great hall, in which we dined, were, if our land-lord's tale may be credited, the original designs of the Blenheim tapestry.

August 10.—We were so well satisfied with our deliberate mode of travelling that we agreed to proceed · in coaches with a pair of horses to each. We left Brussels soon after breakfast. The country improved considerably, and though it could not boast of bold-ness it was not without some pleasant undulations. The cultivation was excellent. At some distance on our left we saw the lofty Tower of Malines. The approach to Louvain was very good. Some hills, high when compared with any rising ground that we had seen for a considerable time, now presented themselves to our view. Louvain, formerly, I believe, the capital city of Brabant, is extremely old. It is situated on the river Dyle, which runs into the Scheldt and thereby forms a communication between Louvain and Antwerp. Its principal trade is in beer. The university was founded in 1426. It consists of several colleges (I believe above forty), and has a good public library. Charles V. is said to have been brought up at Louvain. From Louvain to Tirlemont the country is less pleasing, and the perpetuity of strait road is most fatiguing. Tirlemont, where we slept, is a long straggling town with a spacious market-place.

August 11.—We travelled along a *pavé* without trees through a wonderfully fertile country, passing on the left the city of Tongres and a palace belonging to the Prince of Liège. We should gladly have deviated from the high road for the sake of visiting Tongres, the Atuatuca of Cæsar, but the unwieldiness of our equipages and an approaching storm obliged us to give up the excursion. It was at Atuatuca that the Romans sustained a considerable loss under L. Aurunculeius Cotta and Q. Titurius Sabinus ;[7] here also Q. T. Cicero was left with a command, and had nearly experienced the fate of his predecessors. The whole account of what passed in the neighbourhood of Atuatuca and in the country of the Eburones (the Liégeois) is extremely interesting, particularly of the attack which the Germans, who crossed the Rhine to assist Cæsar, made on the Romans who were left in Atuatuca. Well might Cæsar exclaim: 'Hic, quantum in bello fortuna possit, et quantos afferat casus, cognosci potuit.'[8] It is said that many remains of antiquity are still to be found near Tongres, but the

---

[7] See Cæs. *Comment. De Bell. Gall.* vi. 31. [8] See vi. 34, *ad finem.*

general plan of our journey would by no means admit of our searching for them. Pliny speaks of a fountain which was, I believe, in the neighbourhood: 'Tungri civitas Galliæ fontem habet insignem, plurimis bullis stellantem, ferruginei saporis : quod ipsum non nisi in fine potus intelligitur.' Some accounts say that this fountain was destroyed in 1468 and re-established in 1700, but, according to others, the description of Pliny relates to the Spa Spring.

The approach to Liège was good, though we enjoyed the sight for a short time only, for the clouds which had been gathering around us during the last half-hour now poured such torrents of rain upon us that the prospect was entirely shut out, 'immensum cœlo venit agmen aquarum.' Our carriages were quite unable to resist so violent an attack. The rain was accompanied by much thunder and lightning. The storm, however, was too furious to be of long duration, and in the afternoon we were able to walk about the beautiful environs of Liège, and to enjoy after the excessive heat of the morning the comfort of a refreshed atmosphere.

This country was formerly inhabited by the Eburones : [9] 'Civitatem ignobilem atque humilem Eburonum.' They were, however, the cause of considerable difficulty to Cæsar, who aimed at their utter extirpation.[1] 'Cæsar ad finitimas civitates nuncios dimittit : omnes ad se evocat spe prædæ, ad diripiendos Eburones, ut stirps ac nomen civitatis tollatur.' His

[9] Cæs. *Com.* v. 28.　　　　[1] *Ibid.* vi. 34.

wish appears to have been nearly completed, though not till 'the *German*, the rod of his anger, the staff in whose hand was the instrument of his indignation,'[2] had made a formidable attack upon the Romans themselves. According to Cellarius, Atuatuca was included in the territory of the Eburones: 'In Eburonibus cis Mosam (nam major pars inter Mosam et Rhenum erat) Atuatuca Castellum, post Tangri nunc Tungern dictum.' And yet Cæsar mentions the Atuatia and the Eburones as if they were distinct people. This indeed Cellarius allows, and consequently supposes that the Atuatia had nothing to do with Atuatuca.

Cluverius supposes that the Atuatia, having conquered their neighbours the Eburones, built a fortress in the country which they had subjected, and that this fortress was named after the victors. The commentators on Cæsar are not all of this mind. Ortelius says that Atuatuca was the capital of the Atuatici.

The principality of Liège carries on a considerable trade with the United Provinces, being, in point of situation, closely connected with them, part of it being a fertile country and other parts containing mines of lead, iron, and coals. Liège suffered greatly by the wars of the seventeenth century, and to some extent in the eighteenth also. It was taken by the Duke of Marlborough in 1702. The French entered it in 1705 but did not master the citadel. Till 1718 the Dutch kept a garrison there, when by the Peace of Utrecht

---

[2] Lowth's *Isaiah* x. 5.

the possession of it was surrendered to the troops of the Prince of Liège. The ecclesiastical principality of Liège appears to be one of the best pieces of preferment of the Church of Rome. There are in this establishment above seventy Trefoniers, a title corresponding to that of canons in other religious foundations. These Trefoniers must be of noble birth and must bear a certain number of quarterings in their arms. The Prince is chosen by themselves out of their own society. He has a clear income of about 25,000*l.* per annum, which in such a country is immense. His troops, consisting of nearly a thousand men (a modest army!) are paid by the States. The States are composed of two bodies, the clergy and the nobles forming one and the commonalty the other, so that the government bears some resemblance to that of Great Britain. The States raise money and frame laws, which receive the sanction of the Prince. He has the power of declaring war. The principality has its courts of judicature, an appeal lying from them to the superior courts of the Empire, for whose service the principality furnishes its quota of troops. Several English and Irish families reside in Liège owing to the college, in which the sons of many Roman Catholics are brought up. The city is large, old, and ill-built. The walks on the bank of the Maese are extremely pleasant, and command a view of the mountains which surround the lovely Vale of Liège. Upon various parts of these mountains are houses, abbeys, churches, and other buildings, and the mountains themselves are frequently cultivated to their summits. Upon their sides are hanging woods and extensive vineyards, the first I had ever beheld. The Maese is a fine river and worthy of the valley through which it flows. Cæsar gives the following account of this river :[3] 'Mosa profluit ex monte Vogeso qui est in finibus Lingonum,[4] et parte quadam ex . Rheno recepta, quæ adpellatur Vahalis, insulamque efficit Batavorum ;[5] in Oceanum influit.'

Sunday, August 12.—We left Liège early in the morning. The view from the hill, soon after we quitted the city, was wonderfully fine, and succeeding so quickly to the insipidity of Flanders, we were in excellent order to relish its wild charms. In the vale is the city of Liège, with its scattered suburbs decorated with many churches. The Maese also contributes its share towards the beauty of the scene, and the whole is encompassed by magnificent and well-clad hills. It is not without reason that Liège is called the ' Paradise[6] of Priests.' A large building belonging to the Benedictines is remarkably conspicuous, and has from such a distance the appearance of a palace.

Spa is chiefly situated in a narrow valley inclosed by lofty hills. Regularity does not appear to have been consulted in the smallest degree, and in consequence the streets of Spa do not possess many

---

[3] Cæs. *Com.* iv. 10.   [4] Langres in Champagne.   [5] Betuive ?
[6] 'Ob amœnitatem deliciasque varias paradisus sacerdotum nuncupata.'—CHIVER.

attractions to those who are in the midst of them ; but ascend the hills, and look down upon this wild little town with its white straggling houses, and you will probably regard this seat of health with admiration. In almost all public places there is a certain uniform way of spending time ; a certain plan contrived for bringing people together and for preventing *Ennui*, that never-failing companion of the solitude of the Gay, from making his approach. At Spa, time moves with great rapidity : but with equal regularity, and very nearly according to the following system. Between the hours of six and seven the company assemble at the Pouhon Spring, which is situated in the middle of the town, and, having taken the prescribed quantity of water, they proceed either to the Sauvinière or the Geronstère Spring—two springs which are at the distance of about a mile and a half from the town and from each other. There is a walk belonging to each, that at the Geronstère is the most frequented. Some people take the whole circuit and drink of the three springs ; but more, I believe, confine themselves to the Pouhon and the Geronstère. This ride is usually performed by those persons who have not their own horses and carriages upon the small horses of the country, which the neighbouring peasants bring every morning to the market-place near the Pouhon Spring, and people of the first fashion—ladies as well as gentlemen, or rather princesses as well as princes— are willing, for the sake of convenience and safety, to be carried by these scrubby-looking animals. From these morning expeditions the company return about ten, and breakfast either at Vauxhall or in their own apartments. The rest of the forenoon is spent, when the weather is not intolerably hot, in riding, walking, or visiting. I must, however, except those—and their number is great—who devote even this portion of the day to gaming. During our stay at Spa the heat of the weather was so excessive as frequently to enforce rest. Dressing and dinner being despatched, the evening entertainments take place. There are balls four nights in the week and plays the other three. When the plays are over the company meet in the assembly rooms at the Redoubt ; and the gaming tables furnish employment—for it deserves to be called business rather than play—as long as money and spirits last. The English have the character of being excellent friends to Spa, and the reason which is alleged for their being so entertains me. It is asserted 'que les Anglais buvent ces eaux pour se désaltérer, quand ils ont bu beaucoup de vin.' There may be some truth in this ; but it is observed that the English do not drink so plentifully of the water, whatever they may do of wine, as those of other nations. Gaming appears to have attained its summit of perfection, or rather of imperfection, at Spa. There is scarcely an hour in the day in which tables for hazard, pharaoh, trente et quarante, and biraby may not be found holding out their temptations to the unwary. The night also is spent in the same manner, and it is no unusual thing for the party to continue together till four or five in the morning.

Thus do many people seem to apply to themselves the poet's reflection upon the youthful Sarranus :—

felix, si protinus illum
Æquasset nocti ludum, in lucemque tulisset.—*Æn.* ix. 337.

The impropriety of the application must be often experienced.

. . . The rides and walks about Spa are wonderfully fine : especially to those persons who are nothing daunted at ascending and descending lofty hills by rugged paths. The most frequented ride, which is the circuit of the springs, is the least entertaining, for that part of the mountain which separates the Sauvinière from the Geronstère is, in itself, barren, nor does it possess an advantageous point of view for the surrounding country. The first morning that I took this ride I lamented that the ground over which I was to travel very often was the least productive of entertainment ; but in a few days I began to be reconciled to the circumstance, and even to be glad that the company of Spa occupied in their daily excursions the dullest hill, and left those which were more picturesque to be enjoyed in peace by the lovers of such scenes :—

Ut mihi devio
Rupes et vacuum nemus
Mirari libet.

The variety of scenery about Spa is so great that it will by no means admit of accurate description. It seems as if Nature, apprehensive that her character might suffer from the insipidity of Flanders, was determined to give in this country an ample proof of her creative powers. Mountains are seen on every side varying in shape and feature. Some may boast of the rich garniture of fields and woods, whilst others exhibit large tracts of land on which the curse of barrenness seems to have been pronounced. Narrow valleys and deep dark glens may be discovered from many parts of the rising ground, and the cheerful town of Spa is frequently a most pleasing addition to the scene. Villages and even single houses are rare; but still a few, and perhaps if only the beauty of the landscape be considered, enough, of each are to be seen. Immediately at the back of the town is a mountain, of somewhat difficult ascent, the sides of which, as well as the summit, are clothed with trees. Through these trees are cut walks, deserving from their charms to be much better frequented than they are. Spa is seen to great advantage from hence, and there is something extremely comfortable in viewing from this quiet region the scene of tumult and dissipation beneath. Not far from these walks is a part of the mountain which boldly thrusts itself forward, and affords a most noble prospect. . . . Among the more distant excursions is that to the Cascade of Coo, about two and a half leagues from Spa, in the humble territory of the Prince of Stavelot. We sat off one morning after breakfast accompanied by a peasant, who travelled on foot, by way of guide. We crossed the barren mountain, which separates the Sauvinière from the Geronstère, and soon afterwards entered the dominions of the ecclesiastical Prince of Stavelot—dominions of which the principal produce appears to be prospects. We had scarcely quitted the principality of Liège when we descended into a green valley in which were many comfortable . inclosures. As we mounted the hill on the further side of the valley a most sublime prospect presented itself to us. The mountains became more and more grand, and seemed to grudge the space which a small river gliding at their feet required. The scene changed, and changed for the better, almost every step we took on our way to the village of Coo. The small huts of this wild place. had poured forth their numerous inmates to receive us, and we were soon so completely surrounded by women, children, and dogs as scarcely to be able to stir. It was easy enough to discover what the women and children wanted ; but the dogs puzzled me. We were, however, speedily told that these miserable animals were intended for our entertainment by being thrown into the cascade. Having arranged that the dogs might be allowed to remain in peace, and that we might be suffered to proceed without such a train of beggarly attendants, I sat off with the priest of the parish, to whom my guide had introduced me, to take a view of the cascade. It was whimsical enough that this cascade, which was the only thing that we went to see, was the only thing which was not worth seeing. The river is one of those streams which is trifling in summer. but extremely formidable in winter. It winds along

the valley till it reaches the humble village of Coo ;
from thence it takes a circuit of about three miles,
when, having travelled round a beautiful mountain, it
arrives once more at Coo, where at that point at
which the two parts of the river approach nearest to
each other is the cascade : a fall of about twenty feet.

Upon the mountain which the river surrounds
stands the village of Coo, with its little chapel raised
up on high so as to be a beautiful object. In this
humble locality our guide, the priest and schoolmaster
of the place, spends his winters, the same being probably rendered less uncomfortable by the gratuities
of visitors in the summer. For the trifle which we
gave him he was extremely thankful, and courteously
invited us to take some refreshment. This, however,
we declined, and, having distributed sundry small
coins among the crowd of needy petitioners, we proceeded by a picturesque road to Stavelot.

I should mention that, after all, the poor people
would not forego the customary episode with the
dogs, some of them being thrown into the current,
which in a moment sucked them to the bottom. Our
reverend guide, however, assured us that the animals
were so used to it as scarcely to regard it, a view of
the operation which one could only hope they might
be willing to confirm ! The King of Sweden, having
visited the waterfall during his sojourn at Spa, was
treated — or rather, it is said, treated himself — to
a cow, which, poor thing ! being less expert at the
business, perished in the fall.

In our ascent of the mountain we frequently turned about, to look back at the charming Coo and its store of beauties: 'Respicio, et quæ sit circum me copia lustro.'

Stavelot is a small town—a fit capital for such a principality. It has several churches and a large building, the residence of the Prince and the canons. The monks choose an abbot out of their own society who is called Prince of Stavelot and Malmedi (the latter from a small town not far from Stavelot), has sovereign power throughout his own territories, and, though his income is not more than 5,000*l.* per annum, his rank in the empire is superior to that of his richer and more powerful neighbour the Prince of Liège. It is not necessary that the Prince of Stavelot should be of noble birth. It is, on the contrary, by no means improbable that the dignified prelate may be the son of a cobbler, or that his relations may occupy very humble stations in the town of Stavelot. After dinner I walked to the castle, partly to enjoy the view and partly from curiosity to see a prisoner who was said to be confined there. A young man about twenty years of age came about seven weeks before I was there to Stavelot. The horses which had conveyed him from Aix-la-Chapelle returned thither immediately, so that he was left at the inn without either horse or servant, and, as it afterwards appeared, without money in his pocket. He assumed the title of baron, and was in his behaviour so much the man of fashion that he was invited to dine with the

Prince.   After having spent about a month in the place he was taken up for killing game, and, not giving a satisfactory account of himself, was committed to the castle, and had been kept there ever since in close confinement.   He still asserts that he is of good family, and that he has written to his parents to inform them of his situation.   In England we are apt to complain of the severity of our game laws, but they appear to be at least preferable to those of the arbitrary ruler of Stavelot !

In my way to the castle, I began to consider whether I might with safety request admission, or if in so doing I might not give offence and become a companion to the unknown baron.   Relinquishing, however, any such considerations I knocked boldly at the gate.   It was opened by one of the most miserable-looking soldiers I ever beheld.   The poor fellow had not, indeed, any sign of a soldier except his musket and a stentorian voice.   The Prince of Stavelot is said to have a dozen such as a guard to his mountainous dominions.   Falstaff raised a less ragged company ! The sentinel offered to convey my petition to the commandant, who shortly appeared in his nightcap and slippers, and informed me, with great civility, that it was not in his power to admit me to the castle.   I told him that the beauty of the situation had attracted me, and he immediately re-quested that he might be allowed to conduct me to the ruins which adjoin the castle as affording as good a view as from the castle itself.   The prospect which

they commanded was not extensive ; but the view
of the valley and Stavelot reposing in it was very
pleasing.   I asked the commandant if he had any
prisoners in the castle.   He said two common people
were in confinement, but did not mention the baron,
and I did not pursue my inquiries any further.

To an Englishman the country about Spa is
classic ground, for there he may say with the gentle
Rosalind,

> Well !   This is the forest of Arden—

though we were by no means disposed to reply with
the clown,

> Ay, now I am in Arden, the more fool I.   When I was at home I
> was in a better place ; but travellers must be content.

In my frequent rambles about the woods I thought
of the good duke and his train—of Rosalind and her
fair companion—and fancied that under such an oak,

> whose antique root peeped out
> Upon the brook that brawls along the wood,

the melancholy Jacques lamented the fate of the

> poor sequestered stag,
> That from the hunter's aim had ta'en a hurt,

or that in such a place the good Orlando appeared
with his drawn sword to demand food for that

> old, poor man,
> Who after him had many a weary step
> Limp'd in pure love.

It was most pleasant to indulge thoughts of this
kind, and I found that my relish for a play, which I

had always admired, was considerably increased by reading it on the scene of action. Notwithstanding the neighbourhood of the gay Spa, and the great alteration which time has wrought in the Forest of Arden, this part of it is still so wild and retired, that anyone, pacing through it, may easily persuade himself that he is on the very spot which Shakespeare has immortalised. It appears from Cæsar's account of the Forest of Arden ('Silva Arduenna') that it was then of a vast extent—'ingenti magnitudine per medios fines Trevirorum [6] a flumine Rheno ad initium Rhemorum [7] pertinet;' and, speaking again of the same forest, he says : 'Quæ est totius Galliæ maxima, atque ab ripis Rheni finibusque Trevirorum ad Nervios [8] pertinet, millibusque amplius D in longitudinem patet' (Lib. vi. 29). It seems that the learned have differed about the extent of the forest, and some affirm that instead of reading 500 in the passage I have just quoted, we should read 50 ; but, as Cellarius very justly observes, a forest of only fifty miles in extent would not deserve to be called the 'largest forest in Gaul.' Tacitus says, 'petebantque saltus, quibus nomen Arduenna,' so that he does not confine the appellation of Arden to a single forest. It is, I think, reasonable to suppose that in the time of Tacitus this vast forest had been considerably diminished, and that it could no longer boast of such an extent as Cæsar attributed to it. The parts which

[6] Duchy of Treves.   [7] Rheims in Champagne.
[8] About Hainault.

were allotted to cultivation probably increased, and, consequently, those which were wooded became more and more separated from each other. Tacitus probably included all these detached forests under the one name of 'Arden'; but anyhow I am more inclined to read in Cæsar 'quingentis' than 'quinquaginta.' It may not be necessary to understand it in the strictest sense as an actual measurement, but as an endeavour to give in round numbers an idea of that vast forest, which reached from Rheims in Champagne to the banks of the Scheldt.

. . . Spa is called, with great propriety, the Coffee House of Europe or Europe in miniature. People of all ranks and from all parts of Europe come to this place. On a ball-night the rooms exhibit the most motley scene which can be imagined. The ladies in general paint amazingly. Some cheeks are fiery red, whilst others exhibit various tints of purple, and, in short, there is scarcely a tint bordering upon red which may not be discovered, except that inimitable 'blood-red,' which Nature exhibits and which Englishmen are prone to admire. Some ladies powder their frizzled heads with brown powder, which had anything but an attractive appearance, especially when, as was the case with one young lady of high rank, the hair was suffered to hang about her ears like a schoolboy's, without the smallest propensity to curl. Indeed, when some of these painted and powdered ladies have entered the ball-room, one has stared, much as

Alphonso did when *his* painted ancestor stepped
forth with terrific strides from the canvas.

The method of ladies riding on horseback in male
fashion is also somewhat strange to English eyes.
Though there was a time when the queens on the
Continent rode in that manner, yet the use of a side-
saddle in England appears to have been owing to
the example of Queen Ann, daughter of a king of
Bohemia, who introduced it to this island in the reign
of King Stephen. The society at Spa included,
however, some foreign ladies of high rank, who
seemed to know the difference between an awkward
reserve and a masculine boldness, between the polish
of good breeding and the tinsel of affectation.

There were some visitors at Spa who may be
thought to merit a word or two of particular description, and, in the first place, Prince Henry, brother of
the King [9] of Prussia. He is, I believe, allowed to be
the ablest general now living, for besides his consum-
mate military knowledge, he possesses a large share
of prudence, and of that necessary part of valour,
discretion, the want of which has sometimes drawn
his illustrious brother into serious difficulties.[1]

Prince Henry is an elderly man, of about sixty
years of age, of low stature and by no means of
distinguished appearance. He has a strange cast in
his eyes, so that it is difficult to know at whom or at

[9] Frederick the Great.

[1] The King of Prussia, it is said, owns that he has committed *many*
mistakes in war, Prince Ferdinand a *few*, but his brother, Prince
Henry, *none*.

what they are directed. One would not at first sight imagine how great a soul dwelt in such a body ; and yet, after a little examination, one may discover traits of superior ability. In his behaviour is that sort of affability which one would wish to meet with in a man of rank. During my stay at Spa I had the honour of being introduced to the Prince. The ceremony consisted in leaving three cards at his house— one for each of his Highness's chamberlains, and in being led by one of those gentlemen along a crowded ball-room

> Tentaturum aditus et quæ mollissima fandi
> Tempora—

and, after my name was announced to his Royal Highness, in exchanging bows. This ceremony enabled me to go to the public breakfast which he gave. The cards of invitation were in the name of the ' Comte de Oels,' his Highness's travelling title.

The Princess of Orange and her daughter came to Spa for a few days. The Princess, who appears to be about thirty-five years of age, is a niece of Prince Henry's. She is rather tall and of dignified demeanour, and before she had the smallpox, which has somewhat disfigured her, is said to have been extremely handsome. The Princess moved about with great state : to wit, a coach and six, a phaeton and pair, and several servants of the Prince of Liège, besides servants and horses of her own. When going to the Geronstère on horseback her Highness was preceded by two running footmen, several gentlemen, a lady, and servants accompanying her on horseback, with the phaeton and coach following. Her Highness rode in the French style, sitting across the horse. She travelled under the name of La Baronne d'Ameland, and in that name the cards of invitation to her Highness's public breakfast were issued. The Princess her daughter appeared to be about twelve years old.

The Duke and Duchess of Aremberg were at Spa. The Duke possesses a noble fortune, not less, as I was told, than 60,000*l.* per annum. He is a young man and very highly esteemed. It is sad to say that as he was shooting, not many years since, with the English resident at Brussels he had the misfortune to lose his sight by a gun accident. He bears this severe stroke with the utmost fortitude and even cheerfulness. He rides and sometimes dances, but I could not help fancying that, even during those hours of diversion, a shade of melancholy was perceptible, and I am sure my own inclination to gaiety was always checked when I saw him. The Duchess is one of the most pleasing women I ever beheld. Though her features are very good she is by no means a striking beauty; but the sensibility and good-nature which are clearly displayed in her countenance will scarcely permit one to set about an examination of features. She does not possess (I feel persuaded that I may speak confidently) a grain of pride or affectation :

> Illam quidquid agit, quoquo vestigia movet,
> Componit furtim, subsequiturque Decor.

What a lovely contrast to many Spa ladies ! I was

assured that the Duchess really was as amiable as she appeared to be, and when I thought of her, I lamented still more the misfortune of her husband. They were married before the Duke met with his sad accident, and have one daughter.

The Princess Dowager of Stolberg, 'née Princesse de Horn,' was an object of our daily interest. This lady is mother to the ' Pretender's ' wife and to the wife of the Marquis de Jamaïque, son of the Duke of Berwick. It would be a difficult matter to pronounce upon her Highness's age under the mask which conceals it, and how shall I describe that face—

quam vidimus ipsi
Sanguineis ebuli baccis minioque rubentem.

The Princess of Ligne was another striking figure in the Spa world, short and stout, and very vigorous in action and manner. Her Highness used to ride about the streets on a Spa hack (on a side-saddle), urging it up the steep *pavé* as fast as it could go, and laughing and talking incessantly.

Prince Charles of Ligne, a son of this lady, seemed to inherit a large share of maternal characteristics, as regards inelegance of deportment and simplicity of manners.

There was not anyone at Spa upon whom I looked with greater astonishment than the Marquis de Busca, Archevêque d'Emèse, Nonce Apostolique à Bruxelles. I had expected to find a nuncio a grave, dignified ecclesiastic, but I was mistaken. This nuncio was about fifty years of age, tall and corpulent, with a fair, smooth, smiling countenance, but with eyes of sinister expression. No man talked more or laughed louder than he did, and as for the laugh, it was as simple as ever mortal was made happy with. By way of external distinction he wore his hair dressed in a round curl, a black patch, like those on the wigs of English Judges, covering the back part of his head, and a cross of gold hung at his breast. He played at cards morning, noon, and night, his favourite game being whist.

I now come to the most splendid of all splendid men, the Baron de Haindel, a Strasburg nobleman. He had an elegant, Paris-built chariot, an open chaise, a set of coach-horses and saddle-horses, a head-coachman with enormous whiskers, an under-coach-man, a boy, a negro, and a running footman. There were two ladies in his suite singularly attired—one of them in the dress of a Circassian. The men were perpetually exhibiting themselves in the eyes of the public, either on foot or on horseback, and the ladies, conspicuous alike in dress and behaviour, were wont to appear in the rooms, even on ball nights. The running footman and the 'black' were perpetually changing their dresses. Sometimes they were habited like Turks, sometimes in silk or cloth with a profusion of gold about it, or in white, or nankeen. Then they had amongst them watches enough to set up a shop. The scrap of a boy had two (the minimum number !), the black had three, with chains hanging down to his knees. I do not exaggerate when I say that we used frequently, as we were sitting in our room, to hear the clatter of this man's watch-chains as he passed along the street. When the Baron went out in his chariot and six he was preceded by the 'black' and the boy on horseback, and the running footman, with his plumed cap, stood behind the carriage. When he moved about the town in the evening, his running footman went before his chariot with a flambeau. Sometimes he rode on horseback, one of the reins to his own bridle being of gold lace. Whether in a carriage or on horseback the Baron always went at the most rapid rate. He never went out without endangering the lives of those who walked through the streets. When he rode on horseback he deigned not to take the least care to avoid those who were unfortunate enough to be in his way, though the servant who followed at some distance used to bawl out, that the streets might be cleared for his furious master. I have seen people escape as it were by a miracle. This remarkable man usually appeared at the rooms in a sort of linen coat, white waistcoat, and white breeches, the waistcoat adorned with a double row of buttons composed entirely of diamonds and amethysts, and on his hat he had a diamond button and loop. Thus it is that riches beget folly, and are full often deemed a sufficient excuse for it:

meæ
Stultitiam patiuntur opes.—Hor.

Let it not, however, be imagined that such people have a monopoly of the Forest of Arden. Many estimable men were to be found in it. The Abbé Raynal bears the highest character as a grave, sensible, enlightened ecclesiastic, a man, I should say, of about sixty years of age.

Monsieur de Bertin, with his *cordon bleu*, made his daily visit to the Geronstère. He is a heavy-looking man in countenance, and one would hardly, judging by his looks, have thought him qualified to conduct the affairs of such a kingdom as France.

The Viscountess d'Oudenarde, who was with the Duke and Duchess of Aremberg, is a very handsome, distinguished-looking woman. I think I have seldom seen beauty, good-nature, and dignity more happily united than they appear to be in her person.

La belle Grecque was usually allowed the palm of beauty. She was a native of one of the Greek islands, where she captivated and married a French officer. She is certainly very handsome, and has the finest black eyes I ever beheld. It was said by those who were acquainted with her that her manners were most bewitching.

Amongst the English visitors were the Duke and Duchess of Richmond, the Duke and Duchess of Chandos, Lord and Lady Villiers, Lady Derby, Lord Cholmondeley, Mrs. Armitstead, &c.

We missed, much to our regret, a sight of the Emperor,[2] having been just too late for him both at Brussels and Spa. His Majesty seems to have been

---

[2] The son and successor of the Empress-Queen Maria Theresa.

particularly fond of the English, and to have paid great attention to them, and his sister the Archduchess is said to be equally attached to them.

The Emperor travelled with a very modest suite, a general, a physician, and two secretaries forming his whole train.

The Duchess of Chandos, who is said to have a privilege of saying almost anything to anybody without offence (a privilege seldom allowed except to those who are remarkably sensible or remarkably foolish), is reported to have asked the Emperor 'why he did not marry'? He told her that he did not know where to go for a wife. Thereon the Duchess recommended the Princess Royal of England. The Emperor thought her too young. 'Oh! not at all,' replied the Duchess. 'I am many years younger than the Duke, and yet we live very happily together.' But there is 'another objection,' said the Emperor, 'our religions are different.' The Duchess answered that 'nowadays nobody attended to religion in matters of that sort.' The Emperor smiled!

There were some musical people at Spa, and in the first place Signor Pacchierotti. He is not only an incomparable singer, but also a sensible, modest, and agreeable man. I used to be frequently with him; and, as he is extremely desirous of improving himself in English, he desired that we might always converse in that language, and that I would tell him if he used any improper word or phrase. Whenever I did so he was very grateful. 'Mr. Twining' (he often addressed me in the third person) 'does inform me with so much humanity.'

Mr. Pacchierotti had two concerts during his stay at Spa. He sang charmingly, but was not well accompanied. On one evening he sang in a private apartment to Prince Henry, who was prodigiously pleased with him, and the signor was no less pleased by the Prince's request.

So much for particular description of the Spa Company : there were 'multi præterea, quos fama obscura recondit.'

Those who choose to have a numerous acquaintance at Spa may easily obtain it, as the last comer pays the first visit, and, according to the custom of the place, there is not the least impropriety in calling upon an entire stranger. Exclusive of these visits 'en personne,' for which purpose every person has special cards printed, a fresh arrival is always announced by cards which the bookseller sends to every family in the place : and when any person quits Spa he sends circular cards 'pour prendre Congé.' On Monday, September 3, we took our leave of Spa, not without the blessing of one of the Capuchins who, according to custom, attended our departure.

．　　．　　．　　．　　．　　．　　．

．

AN EPISODE FROM THE AMERICAN WAR, 1781.

At our inn (The 'Roi d'Angleterre') at Aix-la-Chapelle we made the acquaintance of Major Parsons, a very agreeable man, who had seen much service in

America. He received two wounds at Bunker's Hill and made the dreadful march from Philadelphia to New York. This march lasted eighteen days, during which time his division, which was, unfortunately for him, the last, was in motion from one o'clock in the morning till six in the evening. The heat was intense, and they were perpetually harassed by a powerful enemy. The Major declared that several of his men went raving mad as they marched, and they died soon after losing their senses. The ammunition, baggage, &c., which they had to defend extended twelve miles, and though they would gladly, in order to avoid the 'letalia tela diei,' have travelled by night, the apprehension of falling into some ambush prevented their doing so. One evening, after a dreadful march, they reached the banks of a river, on the opposite shore of which was a redoubt; they could not perceive anyone in it. Two countrymen crossed the river in a boat and told them that the enemy had been there two days before, but that they had left the place. The wearied army now thought that an interval of comfortable rest might be obtained. The Colonel and the Major pitched their tents and the other officers and the troops prepared some kind of shelter for themselves with branches of trees, when, just as the Major was going to his tent, a smart fire began from the redoubt: the tents were in an instant swept away, and the Major and his men had no chance of saving their lives but by throwing themselves flat upon the ground and

lying there till the fire of the enemy began to abate.
Then they got up and ran to a hollow way, which
afforded them some protection. It now rained hard,
and they were forced to pass the whole night in this
miserable condition, seeing, on the surrounding hills,
the numerous fires of the enemy. The Major had
not yet recovered from his wounds and the great
loss of blood which they occasioned. As he was
returning from America, quite a cripple, his vessel
was blown about by a terrible hurricane, within sight
of the Lizard, for three weeks. They expected to
have reached their port in a few hours, when the wind,
continuing its violence, shifted to another quarter, and
he was carried out to sea for three weeks more.

LA TRAPPE.

After a visit to a Trappist monastery near Düsseldorf.

A popular and somewhat sensational history of
the 'Abbé de Rancé,' the founder of the Trappist
order, not being of much authority and differing from
that given by Marsollier, who wrote a long and
fatiguingly circumstantial history of De Rancé, now
rather a scarce book, I was induced to extract from
it such anecdotes as I thought best worth remembering. The institution had excited my curiosity long
before I had an idea of visiting one of the abbeys of
La Trappe.

Armand Jean de Rancé, born in Paris, January 9,
1626, was descended from a good family. Cardinal

de Richelieu was his godfather. His father originally
intended that he should be a Knight of the Order of
Malta ; but as Armand discovered in his infancy
unusual abilities, a much better education was bestowed upon him than commonly falls to the share
of those who are destined to the profession of arms.
Upon the death of his elder brother he took Orders,
and before he was eleven years old preferment was
showered upon him in abundance. He applied himself more closely than ever to his studies, and had
made considerable progress in the Greek and Latin
languages before he had completed his twelfth year.
At this early age he published an edition of Anacreon
with a Greek commentary, and also a French translation of the same author. Upon the death of his
mother, to whom his behaviour had always been most
dutiful, and indeed his disposition in general appears
to have been remarkably amiable, his manners became
less strict, and he partook of the usual gaiety of youth.
Notwithstanding this circumstance he continued his
studies, and applied himself diligently to philosophy,
theology, and, amongst other pursuits, to judicial
astrology. In the year 1652, he finished the regular
course of his learning. His father died soon afterwards. De Rancé was then about twenty-five years
of age, and, being in possession of a noble income, he
led a life of pleasure which was not quite suited to
his profession. It was about the year 1657, when he
had reached his thirty-first year, that he began to be
dissatisfied with his mode of life. Amongst other

circumstances which led to serious reflections and his consequent reformation, a dialogue which passed between himself and a shepherd is mentioned by his historian. The poor man bestowed many commendations upon his employment, clearly preferring it to the more distinguished offices of the rich, concluding his speech with the following words: 'Qu'il ne voudrait pas quitter la terre pour aller dans le ciel, s'il ne croyait y trouver des campagnes et des troupeaux à conduire.' De Rancé was also much affected by a remarkable escape from a gun which was discharged at him. Whether these were the real causes of the change in his conduct or not, he made from this time a rapid progress in his scheme of reformation, and in 1660, his elegant and somewhat intemperate plan of life was converted into a course of frugality, or rather of mortification and voluntary indigence. He felt the impropriety of his former conduct; but was, during a short interval, irresolute as to his future. According to his own account, he knew not what the Lord wanted of him. In order to satisfy himself on that important point, he consulted some bishops, and other persons of superior piety, and, listening to their advice, he relinquished by degrees his private fortune, and all his benefices except the Abbey of La Trappe, which seems to have been the object of his preference, because, from its poverty and the wretchedness of its situation, it was best suited to his scheme of mortification and retirement.

To this dreary spot he withdrew in the year 1662,

but, to his great disappointment, he found his abbey in so ruinous a condition, and its brethren so ignorant and undisciplined, that he almost despaired of restoring either to any tolerable order. His wishes were, however, at length accomplished ; but this was no sooner the case than others arose, and he seemed determined not to stop while it was possible for him to take another step in the thorny road of self-denial. In the year 1663, having converted the abbey, which was 'commendataire,' to an abbey 'en règle,' he bade adieu to the world, and took the religious habit. . . . De Rancé, who was then in his thirty-eighth year, was not satisfied with such ordinances as had hitherto been observed by this order ; but he prevailed upon those of his abbey to adopt such as were more rigid. They unanimously agreed to deprive themselves of wine and fish. Eggs were rarely allowed, and meat only in cases of extreme necessity. Particular hours were also allotted to labour.

In the year 1664, the Abbé was deputed, much against his inclination, to conduct an affair at Rome of considerable importance to the Church. Monastic rules were less strictly observed than they used to be, and the Cistercian monks, in particular, who were, according to their original institution, subject to the most rigid laws—laws full as rigid as those of La Trappe were afterwards — pleaded strenuously for some indulgence. There was no reason to imagine that such indulgence would be granted by the Pope ; and the French clergy, who were averse to the

measure, entrusted this weighty concern to the Abbé
de Rancé. He was furnished with letters from the
first persons in the kingdom, and was everywhere
treated with the utmost respect. This business was
not concluded until the year 1666, when the Abbé,
having made a long and, to him, irksome stay at
Rome, had the mortification to find that the cause
was decided against him. During the time of his
sojourn in Italy he made no abatement of the austerities which he practised in his abbey ; nor could
he be persuaded to allow himself such indulgences
as seemed to be necessary for his support in the
business which he was conducting. The wonderful
remains of antiquity in Rome he scrupulously avoided,
and indeed properly enough by one who thought it
was wrong to receive any pleasure from his senses.
To abstain from seeing was possible, to see and
not to be pleased was impossible. The Abbé was no
less eager to court unnecessary inconveniences. The
coldest weather could not induce him to wear gloves,
because they were contrary to the original institution ;
neither could the intense heats of Italy prevail upon
him to lay aside any parts of his coarse and cumbrous
garments. Upon his return to La Trappe he added
to the rules already established others far more rigid.
An entire seclusion from the world and a complete
ignorance of everything that passed in it, even of the
concerns of their own families, formed a part of their
plan. The allowance of food was limited to so small
a quantity that, considering its comfortless nature, it

seemed to be scarcely sufficient to support life through their long hours of prayer and laborious employment. Silence was also enjoined more strictly than ever, except when engaged in their devotions or when they had occasion to consult their reverend superior. Recreation of every kind was strictly forbidden. The Abbé himself conscientiously adhered to every rule which was instituted for the rest of the monks, and, indeed, his condition differed from that of his companions only in its being more eminently subject to labour and mortification.

The income of the abbey was almost entirely devoted to charitable uses. For themselves two ounces of dry bread were frequently the daily support of a man who was engaged for some hours in the most fatiguing employment. But those things which, from a principle of conscience, they denied to themselves, were, on the like principle, bestowed upon others. All strangers were received into the convent, and during their stay, which often lasted several days, they were provided with food and lodging, and were most diligently attended by the monks. A profound silence was, however, observed both by the fathers and their guests, and the more conspicuous was the poverty of the visitors, so much the greater zeal did it call forth. As a proof of the meritorious manner in which these services were performed, it is said with great seriousness that the monks waited upon their most wretched visitors with as much joy and attention as they could possibly have evinced if our Blessed

Lord Himself had appeared among them. It is asserted that upwards of 6,000 strangers were entertained in the monastery every year during the presidency of the Abbé de Rancé.

The mortifications and austerities which were with such marvellous constancy practised at La Trappe were followed, as might have been expected, by 'various diseases and sundry kinds of death.' All, except those who had the greatest reason to be alarmed, were alarmed, and entreaties and arguments were not wanting to induce this apparently perishing society to abate its rigours ; but in vain. Urged by many such solicitations from without, the Abbé consulted the whole community, and, with one single exception, they all declared that the severity of their rules by no means equalled the enormity of their sins ; and they resolutely rejected every suggestion of indulgence. Marsollier mentions, as a proof of the elevation of mind to which the monks of La Trappe had attained, the history of a suffering brother. The poor man was afflicted with a dreadful rheumatism, of which he forebore either to complain or speak till mortification had seized his shoulders and had already extended down the back. A surgeon was sent for and a terrible operation ensued. He endured the agony with the most apparent tranquillity, and when the surgeon and the Abbé exhorted him not to increase his sufferings by concealing them, he replied, 'Ah ! mon père, quand Dieu nous fait de si grandes grâces, peut-on se résoudre à s'en plaindre ?'

Our James II. is recorded to have paid many visits to the Abbey of La Trappe. Of one of these a circumstantial account is given, and the speech which the Abbé made on the King's reception begins thus, 'Sire! Dieu nous visite aujourd'hui en la personne de votre Majesté.' It appears that James, who was distinguished for greatness of soul, bore the loss of his kingdom with most becoming fortitude and resignation, and that his visits to La Trappe were very comforting to him. In short, those qualities and that conduct which were thought on one side of the Channel to render him unworthy of his crown, were deemed on the other clear evidence of his deserving it.

In the year 1695 the Abbé, who was then old and miserably infirm, resigned his command of La Trappe and became simply one of its most humble and most obedient members. Such, however, was the opinion of his superior piety and understanding that he was still consulted by his brethren and their new Abbé. De Rancé was now confined to the infirmary by continual and excruciating pains, which he endured with undeviating patience to the last moments of his life. It was with the utmost reluctance that he so far deviated from the rigid laws of his order as to make some small alteration in his diet, though it had become indispensable for the support of his weakened frame. He was at length mercifully released from his complicated sufferings, and died in peace in the year 1700, at the age of seventy-five.

THE DÜSSELDORF GALLERY.

I quitted the Düsseldorf Gallery with a far higher appreciation of Rubens and Vandyck than when I entered it. They are the heroes of this place, and I cannot perhaps find a better opportunity of recording a few anecdotes, or of offering with all due deference my opinion of their distinguished merits than the present. Italian masters seem to belong more properly to a Transalpine tour, when their productions can be viewed in a less sparing manner.

Rubens was born in 1577 at Cologne, to which city his father, who was of a respectable family at Antwerp, had retired. Rubens manifested his love of art at a very early age. He received instructions from Verhaecht, Van Ort, and Otto Venius. He was afterwards for some years in Italy, where he studied the colouring of the Venetian school with greater success than the antique spirit of the Roman school. The pure air of Italy seemed unable to dissipate the heavier atmosphere of his own country, and, notwithstanding the opportunity of studying the immortal works of. Raphael, he returned a true Fleming to Flanders. The Düsseldorf Collection affords abundant proof of his inventive powers and profound skill in the art of composition and the ' chiaroscuro ' in particular.

The Rubens Gallery in the Düsseldorf Collection is a room of seventy feet in length, and is filled with forty-six of Rubens's works, many of them of a very large size. I know not how to describe the effect which, when the door was first thrown open, such a blaze of colouring produced. I had never beheld such dazzling magnificence, and it was no easy matter to command composure sufficient for accurate observation. During his stay in England, where he resided in a political capacity, he received the honour of knighthood.; and having attained the age of sixty-three, he died in possession of the highest reputation and considerable wealth. Among his most celebrated disciples were Jordaens and Vandyck. The private character of Rubens was extremely amiable. His behaviour towards the ingenious but dissipated Brouwer affords a pleasing instance of his generosity and love of art. He not only exerted his interest successfully to obtain the liberty of that painter when he was in trouble, but furnished him with every necessary, and endeavoured, as much as possible, to make his merit known. Brouwer having returned, however, to a life of intemperance, died shortly afterwards, and Rubens, having heard that the body had been privately interred, and being desirous of showing one further mark of respect to the professional merit of his friend, ordered his remains to be taken up and reinterred with considerable pomp at his own expense.

VANDYCK.

Vandyck was born at Antwerp in the year 1599. Rubens, though not his only, was his principal, master. He visited Italy, where he studied with vast success those schools which were most famous for design, as well as those which excelled in colouring. In England we are most familiar with his portraits; but in the Düsseldorf Gallery I was equally delighted with, as astonished by, his historical pictures. His designs, though less copious than those of his master, are far more chaste. His colours, though not equally splendid, are infinitely more pleasing and natural. In point of taste, Vandyck clearly deserves the preference. He drank deeply at that fountain of antiquity which seems to have been ill-suited to the pallet of Rubens. After we have soared to such a dazzling height with one painter, it is inexpressibly grateful to repose with the other.

Vandyck met with great encouragement in England, and received the honour of knighthood from King Charles I.

Sir Joshua Reynolds had visited Düsseldorf a short time before I was there, and had expressed himself highly gratified.

The custodian of the galleries, as I found, was not unacquainted with the perishable qualities of Sir Joshua's colours, and had, as he told me, suggested to him the use of oil of poppies, as a vehicle for insuring stability to his charming tints. I do not know what degree of merit there may have been in such advice; but it cannot be denied that whoever might enable the great English artist to fix his colours would deserve well of this country.

A CHÂTEAU OF THE ELECTOR PALATINE.

September 13.—Between Düsseldorf and Cologne we visited a château of the Elector Palatine. It is of modern structure, having been commenced about twenty-five years since. It consists of a central building and two detached wings. In the centre is a hall—a plain room of good dimensions—and a large saloon with a dome, which reaches to the top of the house; near the top is a concealed gallery for music. This saloon is of marble. On each side of it is a drawing-room, a state bedroom, a dressing-room, and an ante-chamber. One set of apartments is for the use of the Elector, the other for that of the Electress. Each has a bath-room, and there is a private communication between their respective apartments. Upstairs the same equality of partition is observed. A drawing-room, a bedroom, and a dressing-room is allotted to each; and adjoining the apartments of the Electress is a bedroom and a dressing-room for her lady-in-waiting, and a room for her servant. On the Elector's side are similar rooms for the lord-in-waiting. There is much gilding in the principal apartments, and the floors are inlaid. The tapestry is not finished, nor are the mirrors put up. The Electress's state bed is a ponderous and very unattractive structure.

There is something pleasant in the idea of a prince and princess retiring, each with a single attendant, into a good country house; but it would not appear that in this case such retirement is inviting, as the

Elector and Electress rarely avail themselves of it, not confirming the Horatian saying—

Plerumque gratæ divitibus vices.

The wings contain the requisite offices and apartments for ten gentlemen and eight ladies. Each lady and gentleman has a drawing-room, bedroom, dressing-room, and a servant's room. There are underground communications between the main building and the wings. The gardens had no special attractions to English eyes: straight walks, canals (dry *beds* when we saw them), stone basons, cut hedges and formal arbours—the whole of limited extent and ill-kept. The Rhine flows within half a mile of the château, but is not visible.

On our journey onwards to Cologne in a very hot day, and over very bad roads, our horses were reduced to a foot's pace, and it was not until we had nearly arrived at our destination that our driver halted to give them some refreshment, when to our astonishment it was administered in the shape of nine successive pails of water, without a morsel of food !

COLOGNE.

Cologne, the Colonia Agrippinensis of the Romans, was situated in the country of the Ubii, a people who formerly inhabited the German side of the Rhine. They solicited the protection of Julius Cæsar, and were afterwards transplanted into Gaul by Agrippa.

Here they built an altar, the Ara Ubiorum, erected probably in honour of Augustus. Writers, however, differ as to whether it was at Cologne or Bonn that the altar was erected, and Cellarius thinks it was at neither one nor the other, but at some third place, some short distance from the Rhine. Some think, too, that the name Colonia Agrippinensis was derived, not from Agrippa who conducted the Ubii across the Rhine, but from Agrippina, daughter of Germanicus, wife of Claudius, and mother of Nero, who settled a colony on the spot.

Petrarch was at Cologne in the year 1333, and seems to have been surprised at finding so much urbanity and so many lovers of the Muses among the inhabitants of this barbarous city. He describes the ceremony of a lustration which was performed annually by the women, to avoid the evils with which the ensuing year might threaten them, and he concludes his account of it by saying, ' Happy people, who embark all your calamities on the Rhine, which conveys them to the English.'

The Rhine flowed within less than a stone's throw from the windows of our inn. We looked at it with delight as long as the daylight lasted, and when that failed every star in the firmament that could assist us generously did so. The inn windows were protected by prison-like iron gratings, every house not *within* the walls of the city being required to be so barricaded, it being contrary to military discipline that there should be ingress or egress through the windows.

Cologne is one of the Free Cities, and has a university, founded in 1388.

September 14.—From Cologne to Frankfort we travelled post for the sake of greater expedition, and found it both easy and pleasant. After leaving Bonn we met a carriage travelling post in that direction. It had four horses, ours three only. The drivers, as soon as they came up to each other, stopped, and without saying a word changed our three horses for the other four : a German custom, and, I think, a very good one. The exchange did not occupy five minutes, and that small loss of time was no doubt recovered as each set of horses travelled homewards. To ourselves there was the clear gain of one horse, to the horses the avoidance of half their intended journey.

RHINE VINEYARDS.

Vineyards on all sides, fenceless, yet not one of them cried out, ' Oh that I had a fence of the thorn and briar ! ' (Isaiah), for notwithstanding public footpaths frequently lead through the midst of the vines, yet no passers-by presume ' to pluck off her grapes.' The vineyards sometimes meet the woods halfway up the mountains, sometimes they are continued almost to the summit. ' Bacchus amat colles,' and what wonder if such hills as these should engage his affections. He has certainly culled out the best parts of the world for his habitation, scorning like the fickle Venus to ramble from the line to either pole.

Ergo rite suum Baccho dicemus honorem.—VIRGIL.

REIMAGEN.

A lovely winding road brought us to Reimagen—a different view of the old and undulating mountains behind us. Reimagen, at present a poor town, has probably seen better days, for it is distinguished in Roman story by the name of the 'Rigomagus.' The Obringa, a small river which flows into the Rhine at this spot, was considered as the boundary of Upper and Lower Germany. Instead of meriting such a distinction it ought rather to be classed with those numerous petty streams which, sensible of their own insignificance, wisely request the parental Rhine to escort them to the ocean :

> Viam qui nescit quâ deveniat in mare,
> Eum oportet amnem quærere comitem sibi.—PLAUTUS.

At Neuwied we found ourselves in the electorate of Treves. Germany is divided into so many principalities, electorates, and petty signories, that it is no easy matter for a traveller to know through whose territories he is passing. Within a few hours he may make many changes. Princes and electors, lay and ecclesiastical, abbots and abbesses, barons and burgesses, claim in their several States a power little short of absolute, extending to the promulgation of laws and to life and death. . . . The imperial eagle spreads his broad wings over all, so his power constitutes the final appeal, and in return for this he fails not to carry off in his talons some prey from every quarter. It has, indeed, happened, and it seems to prove a considerable defect in the German Constitution, that some of its component parts have been able to make a formidable opposition against the body to which they belong.[3]   Thus it is that the Elector of Brandenburg is a reasonable object of terror to his sovereign the Emperor, and the Elector of Hanover, though less mighty, has been able as an ally against his master to offer a serious opposition.   It is true that the princes do not derive their power merely from their electorates, but rather from the crowns of Prussia and England.   The source from whence they derive their authority is, however, immaterial.   That limb becomes too independent for the general welfare of the body which can say to the head, ' I have no need of thee.' The complicated position of some of the electors has subjected them to very awkward circumstances, and they have been obliged, as possessors of the electorate, to supply with contingents of troops the very army which, as sovereigns of another country, they have opposed.

COBLENTZ.

·The Rhine was once more to be crossed in a 'pont volant,' a water conveyance unknown in England. The contrivance is extremely ingenious, as by means of it a wide and rapid river is crossed in a few minutes without manual labour.   Indeed, the force of the

[3] This objection, after sundry modifications in the way of ' mediatising' the petty princes, has been effectually swept away by Prince Bismarck and his Imperial master in their creation of a German Empire in 1869–70.

stream, which according to the usual mode of navigation would render the passage difficult, tends in the present instance to remove all difficulty by communicating to the flying bridge the needful impulse. Thus Cæsar's bridge received advantage from the force of the current : ' tanta erat operis fortitudo, atque ea rerum natura, ut *quo major vis aquæ se incitavisset, hoc artius inligata tenerentur.*' It seems as if the Rhine was always to be celebrated for its bridges, leaving to other rivers the less sociable distinction of aversion to them. Cæsar was the first and the most eminent bridge-builder who exercised his talents upon the mighty Rhine. His account of that prodigious undertaking should surely accompany those who visit this part of the river, and when they see what a river it is, how broad and how rapid, they will think the Germans had good reason to suppose that it would protect them, even from the power of the Romans. They were, however, mistaken. In the course of ten days from the time of commencing this vast work, Cæsar convinced his enemies that they could no longer rely upon the watery barrier, and they were taught ' et posse et audere populi Romani exercitum Rhenum transire.' . . . . . .

Quitting our novel water conveyance we ascended the misty mountain, the mist preventing our seeing much of the vast fortress of Ehrenbreitstein. As we were winding up the mountain we overtook a boy with a basket of grapes on his shoulder. We would have bought some but he said he was carrying them to an uncle at Limbourg—a place above thirty miles from Coblentz—and could not sell any. He would, indeed, give us a few bunches. We accepted his present, and rewarded him amply by conveying him upon the box of our *voiture* to Montebour, which was half of his journey.

A GERMAN FOREST.

September 16.—Soon after leaving Hassel, a small town belonging to the Prince of Orange, we entered a fine undisturbed forest, ' multos servata per annos.' Upon emerging from it we saw a beautiful ridge of mountains before us wooded from top to bottom, and having admired its richness and wildness I took a little pocket Virgil in my hand to read now and then, as it were by stealth, a few lines. At last, however, it got a firmer hold upon me than I had intended, and my eyes had been fixed on the book for some time when, raising them, I became aware of a man armed with a musket being at the wheel of our chaise. Taken thus by surprise I stared and, perhaps, like poor Gil Blas under somewhat similar circumstances, trembled somewhat.   Before handing over my money, however, too liberally, I found that I had to deal with a friend and not a foe.   The man belonged to a party of armed peasants appointed to protect travellers through the forest, and he came to ask a trifle for his services.   We afterwards met several of these parties, and more picturesque groups I never beheld. It is by no means safe to pass through this forest by night.

In the daytime there is scarcely ever any mishap. We were now entering a part of the forest which promised to exceed anything we had seen ; but our expectations were for the second time laid low, yesterday's broken axle having been followed by a wheel coming off. Leaving the men assisted by some peasants to replace the wheel, we pursued our way on foot, penetrating into the most delicious forest I ever beheld. Its extent was said to be sixty miles, and it seems from time immemorial to have enjoyed an uninterrupted state of *Idleness* ('multos *ignava* per annos '). Trees of various ages, various shapes, and various sorts are placed in the most picturesque points of view imaginable. No thinness, not a spot where trees ought to be and where they are not—no glimpse of open country : but all forest. There is no *made* road —scarcely a tree sacrificed to the track ; but it keeps winding about in search as it were of space sufficient for its progress. The ground, too, is happily varied, rising on one side of the road and falling on the other. Every now and then some of the country carts appeared working their way with difficulty along the unseen track. Small groups of peasants, the forest guards, are frequently seen resting with their arms under an aged oak, or waiting by the roadside to receive us. The pencil of Salvator Rosa would have been happily employed on such subjects. Many of the trees, too, had already put on their autumnal tints ; so that the forest exhibited a charming variety of colour. Soon after emerging from these enchanting scenes—for the forest came to an end at last—we espied in the valley beneath us the tiny Maine.

At Königstein—a curious old town belonging to the Elector of Mayence—we changed horses and proceeded towards Frankfort. A forest, in a style quite different from that which we had lately traversed, was on the Frankfort side of Königstein. Beyond it a vast plain stretched out its huge length at our feet, with the city of Frankfort in the distance. If the Emperor of Germany and his warlike neighbour the King of Prussia should ever be inclined to make a fair trial of their strength, here would be a ' field ' capable of receiving their numerous armies. It is, however, to be hoped that the humanity of the Emperor and the old age of the King will prevent a contest which could scarcely fail to be more than usually bloody.[4]

The number of soldiers raised in Germany, or rather subject to the Powers making up the Germanic Body, is surprising. It is said that the Emperor could upon a short notice put 300,000 men into the field, that the forces of the King of Prussia exceed the number of 100,000 men, and that the Elector Palatine has 40,000. Nor is it only the Emperor and the Electors who have troops at command. Princes, much inferior in point of rank, may boast of armies

[4] It was reserved for the nineteenth century, after the wars of Bonaparte and, later on, after the Prusso-Austrian and Franco-Prussian contests, to witness changes far in advance of those here faintly foreshadowed.---R. T., 1886.

by no means contemptible. The free cities have their
military establishments, and each petty seignory affects
to raise a guard for its defence.

.   .   .   .   .

FRANKFORT.

We entered Frankfort in thunder, lightning, and
rain. It was the time of the great fair, and almost
every inn was full. At last we succeeded in getting
apartments at the top of a palace-like inn —' L'Empereur.' The ' Castle ' at Marlborough is nothing to
it.[5] At the ' Empereur ' many families of distinction
were lodged. There was a *table d'hôte*, at which
fifty to sixty persons dined every day and almost as
many supped. They also sent out several dinners,
and yet the house was free from confusion, and
waiters were always at hand to procure whatever was
wanted.

The theatre at Frankfort is not so good as such a
city merits ; it is, in fact, only a large room fitted up
for theatrical purposes. A new theatre is in course
of erection. During my stay I saw a comedy,
a tragedy, and an opera, but the most popular part of
the performances is the ballet. Here as elsewhere I
am afraid the age of dancing will flourish at the
expense of acting and singing. The London opera-
house was crowded last winter not with those who
went to hear music, but with the amateurs of dancing.

[5] What would the journalist have said to the ' Grand ' and ' Métro-
pole ' hotels of the present day ?—1886.

Indeed, the opera was under the direction of a ballet-master, music merely filling up the intervals, so completely had the two arts changed places. I hope it may be in the power of Pacchierotti, who is engaged to sing next winter in the Haymarket,[6] to restore his profession to its proper place. I fear, however, that if Pacchierotti should sing and Vestris dance the latter will be the greater favourite.

> Segnius irritant animos demissa per aures :
> Quam quæ sunt oculis subjecta.

.   .   .   .   .   .

FRANKFORT FAIR.

Whenever we walked out the fair was a never-failing source of entertainment, and of temptation also. The principal business of the year is transacted during the two fairs, each of which lasts above three weeks. Of these no idea can be formed from those humble fairs with which England abounds. To the German mart goods are brought from almost every part of Europe. Each merchant hires a shop or stall where the articles of his traffic are exposed for sale in the most tempting manner. The Maison-de-ville is parted into several alleys of shops nearly resembling 'Exeter Change.'[7] The market is filled with covered stalls, and amidst these, people of all ranks, in endless variety of dresses, are continually passing to and fro. Amongst the buyers was an

[6] At the opera-house in the Haymarket.
[7] A place of which all recollection will soon pass away !—1834. All but lost to memory in 1886.—R. T.

American [8] merchant. The shopkeepers at the German towns for many miles around Frankfort lay in their stocks at this prodigious market. Frankfort is one of the free imperial cities. It is fortified and of considerable extent. It contains evident signs of antiquity, many of the houses being extremely old and several of the streets very narrow, but there are also noble streets and excellent habitations. The street in which the principal inns are situated is wide and long, and its houses are well built. The ' Redhouse ' (*Maison-rouge*), is almost equal in size to a palace. The Emperors of Germany are crowned in the ancient cathedral. The quay is a scene of great animation, the chief commodity which causes the bustle being Rhine wine, of which vast quantities lie about.

.   .   .   .   .   .

THE JEWS' QUARTER.

Frankfort contains about 80,000 inhabitants, of whom 20,000 are Jews : to these a particular part of the city is allotted ; and they are locked up in it every evening. Their hours of confinement begin at 5 P.M. in the winter and 8 in the summer, and if after those hours any Jew is found out of his quarters, which are secured by gates, he is subject to a considerable penalty. On Sundays they are totally confined. The married Jewesses are obliged to wear a particular sort of cap (a less becoming one could

[8] Apparently a rare spectacle in 1781.

scarcely be devised) to distinguish them, and partly, perhaps, to prevent their forming any connection with Christians. The Jews are so numerous that measures of caution, though they have at first sight the appearance of severity, may have been found or thought to be absolutely necessary. Till they have the same legal privileges as the rest of mankind it may be impolitic to trust them with the same power, for one cannot suppose that they would resist any opportunity of ridding themselves of their present marked subordination. It is strange[9] that so numerous a people, many of them residing in the most polished parts of Europe, should neither enjoy an equality with their fellow-creatures, nor have, to all appearance, the most distant prospect of acquiring it. They certainly have, as Shakespeare says, ' organs, dimensions, senses, affections, passions,' and such of them as have had the benefit of a liberal education have in general reaped full advantage from it.

.   .   .   .   .   .

The Government of Frankfort is Protestant, but there are a vast many Roman Catholics in the city, who are allowed the free exercise of their religion. The magistrates are chosen for life ; about twenty to thirty of them who are of the first class have the principal management of public affairs. The magis-

---

[9] Still more ' strange ' that in this enlightened age, when the emancipation of the Jews has been so honourably completed in England, such a violent anti-Semitic feeling should have manifested itself in several parts of the Continent !—R. T., 1886.

trate must be chosen from those burgesses who were born in the city. No stranger can be admitted to the rank of a burgess unless he either marries the daughter of a citizen or engages to do so whenever he enters into the holy state. At the Red-house (*Maison-rouge*) there is a large room called Vauxhall, where concerts and balls are held. We went to one of each. At the concert the band was but moderate. Signora Taddi, who was in England a few years since, was the first singer. She has a voice of great compass and power; it would have been heard to greater advantage in a Grecian amphitheatre than in a concert room.

At the ball we saw a vast many princes and princesses—three princesses with whom we fell in love at first sight. They are the daughters of Prince George of Hesse-Darmstadt, brother to the reigning Prince. One of them is married to her cousin, the hereditary Prince. Her sisters Augusta and Charlotte were with her; there is a fourth sister married to Prince Charles of Mecklenburg, brother to our Queen.[1] The three Princesses who were at Frankfort are charming women—tall, handsome enough, and possessed of countenances brimful of good humour. Princess Augusta, whom we most admired, has been talked of for the Prince of Wales.[2] She has the most dangerous dimple I ever saw. If the Prince would

---

[1] Queen Charlotte, wife of George III.

[2] The Prince of Wales, afterwards George IV., was declared 'of age' in 1781.

make her a good husband I wish he would marry her : if he should marry her and not make her a good husband, I shall not be much inclined to swear allegiance to him. The mother of these Princesses and also the hereditary Prince were also at Frankfort. Among the Princesses was one of the Nassau family, who honoured Mrs. Twining with a short conversation. Our daughter, who was dressed in the English style, with her hair curling on her neck, attracted the notice of many people. Colonel ——, in whose company we had been dining, and who had been remarkably civil to us, insisted on introducing her to the Princesses of Nassau and Hesse-Darmstadt. Prince Frederick of Hesse-Cassel was at the ball. He was a middle-aged man, son to an aunt of the present King of England.[3] The Prince of Salm-Salm and the Princess of Nassau-Houssein were also there.

A NOVEL DANCE.

I was engaged in looking at these fine people when a gentleman and lady came whirling by and had almost overwhelmed me. I could not imagine what they were about. I had scarcely extricated myself from the danger with which they threatened me, when another and another couple came twisting by in like manner. I found on inquiry that this was a favourite German dance called a waltz, and is performed in the following manner. The lady and

---

[3] George III.

gentleman stand face to face. The gentleman puts his arm round the lady's waist, and with the other hand he gets firm hold of her arm. You would at first think they are going to wrestle. Thus prepared, and the gentleman having got so good a purchase upon the lady, they begin to spin round and round with a velocity which would have made me giddy in half a minute. Whilst they turn in this manner they make the circuit of the room, resembling, 'si parva licet componere magnis,' the double revolution of the planet on which they danced. So attractive an example did not fail to find imitators, and seven or eight couples soon joined in the whirl. They reminded me, as soon as I had recovered from my surprise, of Virgil's top simile, ' stupet inscia turba.' Now and then the roundabout motion ceased for a minute, but then the dancers kept in action, just as chairmen [4] do when they are stopped at a crossing.

.   .   .   .   .   .

We had some letters of introduction at Frankfort, and they procured us much kind attention and hospitality. We were invited to dine with Mr. Gogel,[5] one of the principal merchants in Frankfort. He deals more largely in Rhine wines than anyone else

[4] Sedan-chairmen.

[5] Mr. Gogel, the head of the old and highly respected firm of Gogel, Koch & Co., bankers and merchants. In 1827 and 1830 two succeeding generations of our family received the same cordial attention from Mr. Gogel's successors. During an inspection of the enormous cellars belonging to the firm, extending under one or two streets, I tasted in 1830 the same old· 'aulm' of hock which my grandfather had tasted in 1781. It was kept as a curiosity.—R. T., 1886.

in the city, and has acquired a good fortune and the highest reputation. We were entertained in a way which, in point of elegance, exceeded anything I had seen. Dinner was served at 2 o'clock, when twenty-five guests of different nations sat down to a sumptuous repast. On leaving the drawing-room, which was hung with beautiful tapestry, the gentlemen gave an *arm* each to a lady, it being more fashionable in Germany to *arm* than to *hand*.

On the following evening we were entertained at supper by another very considerable merchant, M. Brevillier, who gave us a magnificent entertainment. The dishes and wines were handed round in like manner as at Mr. Gogel's dinner.

FIELD-SPORTS.

Game is very abundant in Germany, and it is not withheld from the lower ranks of the people by game laws similar to those of England. Strangers, indeed, as the unknown Baron at Stavelot experienced, are not allowed the free use of a gun ; but, though the peasants are permitted to sell hares and partridges in the public markets, they are not, upon the whole, more exempt from grievances than the peasantry of England ; and they must, *e.g.* patiently submit to the destructive ravages of a wild boar, without presuming upon any account to destroy him.

> Is modo crescentes segetes proculcat in herbâ,
> Nunc matura metit fleturi vota coloni. —OVID.

Hunting is a favourite diversion with the Germans. The Prince of Darmstadt pursues it in a truly royal style. I was assured that his Highness has 700 horses for the chase and 1,000 hounds. There are sometimes 200 to 300 people out, besides peasants, perhaps in all near 1,000 persons. Wild boars are to be met with in abundance. They are quiet unless provoked by a particular noise, when they immediately fly at their assailant. During the great hunting parties the Prince sometimes desires one of the company to bring him such a boar. The person, who is thus *favoured* with princely notice, quits his horse, draws his hanger, and, supporting it against his knee, sets up the offensive cry. The enraged animal immediately turns upon him and commences the engagement. The art consists in presenting the hanger in such a manner that the beast may rush upon it and fall dead at the victor's feet. If the assailant is not expert, but suffers the animal to escape at the first onset, his situation becomes extremely critical. Young men are said to practise upon tame boars, who are easily provoked to the attack.

.   .   .   .   .   .

HANAU.

Hanau is a small town, not ill-built, with a good 'Place' and 'Place d'Armes.' Little did I suspect as we drove up to the inn that a tall, handsome man at the door, in a laced coat, was the landlord. He had been, it seems, in the Prussian service, and, having acquired a comfortable fortune, he quitted it and preferred to continue the old inn, which his father and mother had kept before him, and so to have an opportunity of seeing a variety of people, rather than to live as a private gentleman and see scarcely any-one. He keeps a superb coach, a phaeton, four coach-horses, saddle-horses for the road and hunting, pointers, &c. He is accordingly treated by his guests as a gentleman, and interchanges salutes on either cheek with such of them as are worthy of that distinction. He invites his company to partake of the pleasures of the field with him, and offers to furnish them with horses gratis: though if they should wish to hire carriages or horses he announces that he has good ones to let.

September 21.—Homeward bound. Among the various sensations which I had never experienced before this journey, were some which I may properly call ' home ' sensations. I do not recollect that travellers vouchsafe to mention them ; perhaps they originate in undue timidity. They are elegantly ex-pressed by Ovid, who excelled in *nature* as well as in fiction.

Subeunt *illi, fraterque parensque* ;
Huic cum *pignoribus domus* et quod cuique relictum est.

These sensations were sometimes productive of pleasure ; sometimes of uneasiness : of pleasure when the idea of again meeting those who were dear to us prevailed ; of uneasiness when the thought of the distance by which we were separated from them was predominant. But though the prospect of returning home was grateful to us, yet we had received so many kind attentions during our stay at Frankfort, and had spent our time so pleasantly, that we left it not without reluctance. The unsettled state of the weather, however, and the near approach of the equinoctial gales, warned us to turn our faces homewards, and our good friend Mr. Platz having very obligingly procured for us an excellent boat, we embarked on Friday morning, the 20th, in company with Mr. Livingstone, an American gentleman, whose acquaintance we had made at Spa, and whom we had afterwards met at several points of our journey. Our barge was extremely commodious, containing a very good cabin to dine in, two sleeping cabins—one with two beds and the other with one bed—a servant's cabin, and a kitchen. We laid in a stock of cold provisions and, in short, everything that was necessary for the voyage, including a basket of splendid grapes. By the side of our barge was a large boat which contained our two carriages, my crazy German vehicle being certainly more fit for a water excursion than another journey by land. The Maine was about as wide as the Thames at Windsor, but it was usually very shallow and of a red, unpleasant colour. The banks were in general low and uncultivated. At a distance on the right were some mountains. As soon as it became dusk we cast anchor and passed a pleasant, quiet evening on the gentle Maine. We had charged our watermen not to get under weigh in the morning until it was fairly light, and of that we had sufficient notice by the noise which attended their departure. We turned out in time to see Hochheim, the district from which the famous wine of that name is produced, soon after which the red waters of the Maine united themselves to the sea-like flood of the Rhine, though they flow together for some distance before they become completely mingled. As we approached the antique towers of Mayence and its neighbouring hills, the sun burst forth and illumined the scene.

> oppositas nitidissima solis imago
> Evicit nubes, nulláque obstante reluxit.—OVID.

At times, however, vast masses of shade from the fleeting clouds were seen moving over this magnificent landscape.

We now returned to our boat, big with expectations of interest from our water excursion. . . . We had some rain, but the sun broke through the clouds from time to time, and exhibited the sublime objects which surrounded us to great advantage. Conceive then this noble river, clear and rapid, and rich in islands 'modicas insulas circumveniens,' as Tacitus says of it—its vine-clad slopes and numerous castles reduced by time to the most picturesque ruins. We may suppose Drusus to have been their founder, as, according to Florius,[6] he built fifty castles upon this part of the Rhine. Biberich, the palace of the Prince of Nassau Houssein ; the Rheingau, with its vine-

---

[6] Lib. 412.

yards, and Caub its limit, were passed. in succession, and at Bingen we found good accommodation for the night. Bingen, though a small town, makes no inconsiderable figure in history. It was called by the Romans 'Binguim.' The modern town is on the right bank of the Nava or Nahe; the old town was on the left. It appears, from Tacitus,[7] that a bridge had been built over the Nahe at this place. New walls were added to the old town by Julianus Cæsar.

Additæ miratus veteri nova moenia vico.[8]

September 23.—We rose early and embarked once more on board of our barge, on our voyage to Coblentz, which, weather permitting, we hoped to reach in the evening. I could not have thought it possible that the views of this day should have been still more captivating than those of the preceding, but they really were. The mountains approach nearer to each other, and are, for some distance, so close to the river as scarcely to leave room for even a villaget. The vines being unable to find any ground which is by nature either level or only *moderately* steep, are forced to be planted upon terraces supported by low walls. The river thus contracted rushes angrily along. Rocks sunk in the channel increase its fury 'Occulti pateris luctamina saxi.'[9] The navigation requires great care.

<hr>

[7] Hist. lib. iv. 70.
[8] Auson : and see Ammius Marcellus, lib. xviii.   [9] Ausonuis.

A WHIRLPOOL.

Bacharach! Our observations were suddenly interrupted and we were not a little startled by a monstrous noise overhead. What can be the matter? We are driven into a wrong channel, and the master of the boat is frightened out of his wits! To stop is impossible, and one could clearly perceive sunken rocks and a most threatening channel. But we are safe through it! As the men were endeavouring to get to the right of an island, they were driven by a sudden squall to the left. During our peril they comforted us by saying that if the boat should be staved in, which, in its headlong rush, it certainly would have been if it had struck on a rock, we might escape to shore in the small boat, a contingency which we were thankful to escape, and we all partook of our captain's joy when we re-entered the right channel.

RHINE TOLLS.

The various princes who possess territories on the banks of the Rhine exact a toll from the vessels which navigate it. These tolls are so frequently repeated that the Rhine cannot afford such advantages to commerce as it would otherwise do. The King of Prussia has, among others, a claim upon the navigation—a very heavy one it is said to be. In this way are the beneficent intentions of nature counteracted! Caub, St. Goar, Rhinefels, on the mountain behind it, successively excited our admiration. Never had we seen anything so fine! Am I ever repeating such expressions? It is that at each new bend of the river we are ever feeling an increase of pleasure which prompts me to use them.

At one spot a rich and distinct rainbow was no inconsiderable addition to the scene. It reached some way down the mountain. I remember seeing the like beautiful effect in Scotland. Here it was quite a classical picture :—

Aut flumen Rhenum, aut pluvius describitur arcus. [1]

.   .   .   .

We soon came in sight of the Castle of Ehrenbreitstein at a distance. On our journey up the Rhine we had passed it on a misty morning ; now a fine setting sun exhibited this vast pile of building to the utmost advantage. The scene was wonderfully magnificent.

At Coblentz—the 'Confluentes' of the Romans, and supposed to have been one of the stations fixed on by Drusus[2] for the security of the Roman province in Gaul—we repaired to our old quarters.

September 24.—Here we took leave of our Rhine barge, and pursued our homeward route by land. The weather had changed so much since we were last in our open carriage that I thankfully availed myself of Mr. Livingstone's considerate offer to convey Mrs. Twining, who had scarcely recovered from an illness on our way, and our daughter in his

[1] Horace.   [2] See Cellarius and Cluverius.

English post-chaise, while I and his servant, an intelligent and most attentive companion, travelled in our German *calèche*.

.   .   .   .

The vintage had begun, and we saw cartloads of fine ripe grapes moving along the road. As we passed by, the good peasants came running up to our chaise with a handful of fruit for us, not waiting for, and evidently not expecting any *douceur*. We went into a house to see the process of bruising the grapes, &c., but the people were not at work. We saw, however, the various utensils and great casks filled with mashed grapes, 'plenis in lintribus uvas'— passing by the remaining part of the description—

> Pressaque veloci candida musta *pede.*

.   .   .   .   .   .

At Andernach we changed horses, and once more lost a wheel. The damage, however, was soon repaired, and we proceeded by the old and lovely road through Reimagen to Bonn.

September 25.—Thence on the following day to Cologne without let or hindrance. We were too late to see the tomb of the three kings and the treasury at the cathedral; but we *did* see, to our infinite satisfaction, the famous picture of the Crucifixion of St. Peter by Rubens. He painted it for the city in which he was born. The saint is crucified with his head downwards; the body is contracted, and this contraction is painted with astonishing skill, and the picture, both as regards drawing and colouring, is indeed a masterpiece.

The cathedral consists of two parts of a very fine Gothic building, viz., the choir and the western tower. The nave, which should have connected them, was never finished. This is a pity, for it would have been a noble building.[3]

And now we were to turn our backs upon the lovely Rhine ; it was, when we set out, the chief object of our expectations, and it has now become the chief object of our affections. Some of those charms, which we have beheld with such great delight, I have endeavoured to describe, in the hope that the description will so far answer the design with which it has been written, as to assist our recollections when we may be disposed, by our own fireside, to repeat the passage of the Rhine.

September 26.—At Bercheim we changed the horses which brought us from Cologne ; but, instead of good ones, got, for my carriage, a very bad pair. They soon dropped into a walk, and soon after that entirely knocked up. A neighbouring village furnished us, at a cottage—there not being any inn—with some hard-boiled eggs, to which the *curé* added a bottle of wine, and there we rested until a pair of return horses took us slowly to Juliers, where we arrived at 10 P.M.

September 27.—To Aix-la-Chapelle, returning to our favourite inn. There is a tradition that the warm

---

[3] In the next century it has been seen in its completeness, thanks to the liberality of the King of Prussia.—1886.

springs of this place were accidentally discovered by
Charlemagne, his horse's hoof sinking into one of
them, and the spot is still pointed out in 'Charles's
Bath.' This tale bears some resemblance to Ovid's
account of the famous Helicon—

> Dura Medusæi quam præpetis ungula rupit.
> .   .   .   .   ˙ Et Pegasus hujus origo.⁴

BATTICE.

At quite a small village about half-way between
Aix-la-Chapelle and Liège we dined, and the *table
d'hôte* afforded us a very good dinner, consisting of
two courses and a dessert. I do not recollect having
been at a single inn on the Continent which has deviated from this polished custom. The vulgar phrase,
' Sir ! you see your dinner,' appears to be peculiar to
our island, for abroad no dinner is ever, in this sense,
seen. Our dessert consisted of eleven dishes, though
there were only six persons at table.

Between this village and Liège we crossed the
Maese, a fine broad river, by a bridge of boats, to a
large shoal in the centre of the stream, and thence to
the opposite bank in a ferry-boat, which the current,
assisted by a strong rope fastened at such a height
that a small boat might have sailed under it, conveyed
over.

LIÈGE TO LOUVAIN.

September 28.—At the *table d'hôte* supper at Louvain, the landlord took care to inform us that we were

⁴ *Met.* v. 257 and 262.

to sleep in the same room which the Emperor[5] had lately occupied. He amused us with many anecdotes of our august predecessor, and spoke of him in the highest terms. It was not, however, by our landlord alone that the praises of the Emperor were sounded. He seems to be generally beloved by his subjects, and to bid fair to merit the title of 'Pater Patriæ.' We were told that his Majesty always sleeps on a straw mattress, which he carries with him. His own valet, whose fidelity he highly esteems and often praises, sleeps upon a little bed placed at the outside of his chamber door. As to his plan of living, the Emperor said of himself, 'Je ne bois que l'eau ; et je ne mange qu'à vivre.' His affability gains him many friends ; and the desire, which he constantly shows, of contributing towards the welfare and happiness of his subjects cannot fail of securing their affections.

MECHLIN.

An elegant though not a large city, fortified as well as its great neighbours. The cathedral, finished in 1411, is a venerable and noble building, with a lofty tower and a fine set of carillons. Mechlin is situated on the Dyle, and, like every city in the Low Countries, has had its share of calamities. In 1572 it was sacked during three days by the Spaniards under the Duke of Alva, name of evil omen ! In 1578 the troops of the Prince of Orange destroyed the

---

[5] The son of the Empress-queen Maria Theresa, and her successor on the Imperial throne on her death in 1780.

churches and convents near Mechlin.   In 1580 it was
sacked by the English under Colonel Norris.   In
1718 there was a great insurrection.   In 1746 it was
abandoned by the Allies and taken possession of by
the French.   The misfortunes of this country might
indeed be traced much further back : for when it was
inhabited in the time of Cæsar by the Menapii, it
suffered many of the miseries of war.   ' At Q. Titurius et
Lucius Cotta, legati ' (the Dukes of Alva of that day !)
' qui in Menapiolum fines legiones duxerunt ; omnibus
eorum agris vastatis, frumentis succisis, ædificiisque
incensis ' &c.[6]

ANTWERP.

September 28.—Nature had made the approach to
Antwerp as easy as possible ; but art has contrived to
make it, to an enemy at least, very difficult of access.
The city itself is altogether the most elegant we had
seen.   After a circuitous route through the streets, our
driver not knowing his way, we turned suddenly into
the Place de Meir, and I cannot express the admiration
we felt at the first view of this the noblest part of
noble Antwerp.   We rejoiced to find that our inn
was situated in it.   On Sunday afternoon the gay
world of Antwerp drove up and down the ' Place,'
their coaches drawling after one another in the style
of Hyde Park.

The Emperor on his late visit to Antwerp gave
much encouragement to the hopes of the oppressed

Cæsar.

citizens of once-more enjoying the benefit of a free trade. . . . When he viewed the large and now almost useless warehouses of the city, he exclaimed, 'I see what Antwerp has been and what it may be.' He encouraged a subscription for an East India trade. The sum which he named was nearly equal to 200,000*l.* sterling,[7] and the subscription was completed in a single day ; it already bears a profit of four per cent. The inhabitants would gladly have doubled the sum ; but the Emperor thought it prudent to begin moderately. Three ships are to be sent to China in the spring, and three to the coast and bay. A whaling fleet is also to be sent to Cape Horn. . . . The East India trade will, I fear, prove prejudicial to us by stocking that market to which our smugglers resort. At the last sale of teas in Antwerp, an inhabitant of Dunkirk bought all the fine green teas (Hysons) for his English trade.[8]

The 'Marquisat du Saint-Empire,' in which Antwerp is situated, is one of the seventeen provinces. It comprehends only the City of Antwerp and its territory.

The Scheldt is a truly commercial river, broad, deep, and tranquil. It was called by Cæsar, Pliny, and others ' Scaldis,' by Ptolemy 'Tabuda.'

[7] A modest sum compared with the requirements of the present day !—1886.

[8] This apprehension was fully justified. Until Mr. Pitt brought in and carried the ' Commutation Act,' the tea trade in England had fallen to a very large extent into the hands of the smugglers. From that moment smuggling, so far as tea was concerned, was virtually extinguished.—R. T., 1886.

But let us turn from the consideration of those blessings and miseries which commerce and war have formerly shed upon this city, and consider those numerous productions of art with which it is stored. Antwerp has reared a numerous family of painters ; and, like grateful children, they have amply recompensed her for her care.

In Mr. Van Lancker's collection are several remarkable pictures by Polemburg, some of the best I have seen of that master. I have sometimes thought that his figures are too highly finished for his landscapes, the different parts of his pictures not seeming to unite well.

Polemburg was born at Utrecht in 1586, and, travelling to Rome, was so much struck with the works of Raphael that he attempted to imitate his grace, especially in his studies of the nude.[9] It is scarcely possible, however, that his imitation could produce any considerable effect whilst he confined himself to landscape-painting. Instead of annexing, as far as he might be able, the grace of Raphael to designs which bore some resemblance to those of that greatmaster, he used them so as to interfere to some extent with the uniformity of his landscapes ; for in the midst of rural scenes, evidently not of the paradisiacal age, nude figures grouped with art, and exhibiting in their attitudes the grace of Raphael, are

[9] In a small, highly finished picture of the Nativity by Polemburg which I have, the figures are decidedly more of the Flemish type.— R. T., 1886.

evidently out of place. But though Polemburg may have been deficient in judgment, one may venture to say that the generality of Dutch painters would not have succeeded so well in such an attempt as he did. His works were much esteemed by Rubens, and he met with considerable encouragement in England from King Charles I.

.   .   .   .   .   .

ANTWERP CATHEDRAL.

The cathedral is a large though not an elegant pile of building, though I would except the steeple, which is more elegant and of more exquisite design than any other which I remember to have seen. It contains a large number of pictures, among which the 'Descent from the Cross' by Rubens never fails to attract the first attention. It is, indeed, a noble composition ; though I am not sure that I did not derive more pleasure from his smaller picture of the Crucifixion at the Church of the Recollets.

The 'Assumption of the B. Virgin' by Rubens is a fine picture, great in design and admirable in colour, every part in harmony.

THE EXCHANGE

contains a fine, strong portrait in a singular style by Cornelius (or Martin) de Vos, a very striking portrait ; also an excellent one of Quintin Matsys by himself. Although we were pretty diligent in visiting both churches and private collections, our stay at Antwerp was much too short to do them full justice. If we should repeat our visit we should be disposed to confine ourselves to a few of its most celebrated pictures.

BRUSSELS.

September 30.—Leaving Antwerp in the afternoon, we did not arrive at Brussels until after the gates were shut, and had to wait above an hour in the rain before, after much entreaty and a fee, we gained admittance. On these occasions it is the fee alone which can ensure success.

Nec verbis victa fatiscit
Janua, sed plenâ est percutienda manu.—Tib.

We stayed only one day at Brussels, during which we visited the choice collection of pictures·belonging to M. Danvot, the banker. It is·indeed one to live with. He was good enough to accompany me and talked of painting with great enthusiasm, though, perhaps, like most enthusiasts, not without a certain degree of prejudice. . . . .

October 1.—On the following morning we left Brussels, and proceeded through Alost to Ghent. A road which nearly tired us the first time was not likely to be interesting the second. We should, however, have travelled to very little purpose if we had not been able to find entertainment from the good things we had so recently seen. We had only to follow the example of the oxen who were ploughing

by the roadside, and who we may imagine to have
found comfort in their wearisome journey by the
thought of the store which they had treasured up in
better hours.

October 2.—At Ghent we bade adieu to wheels,
which we did without regret, and entered on board
of the barque for Bruges.   But, alas! it was neither
the same barque nor the same company that we had
met before, when we made our first voyage upon this
capital canal.   The barque was something worse, the
company much so.   The goddess of discord seemed
indeed to rule this day.   An ill-behaved, though well-
dressed, young man offended and quarrelled with
several of the passengers.   Unfortunately I was the
most opposed to his wrath, which was to be appeased,
as soon as we landed at Bruges, by an appeal to the
long sword, which he carried at his side, so that, as
we proceeded, I might well say, with Tibullus—who
could not hate fighting more than I should—

> forsitan hostis
> Hæsura in nostro tela gerit latere.

The company were unanimously against this man
of war, but could not prevail upon him to acknowledge himself in the wrong; till at last his younger
brother, a modest and well-behaved young man, convinced him of his error, and then he declared himself
an advocate for peace, tendering his hand (a very
dirty one, by the way!) in ratification of the treaty.
Before we parted, two other gentlemen quarrelled and
abused each other heartily, and we afterwards heard

that two Englishmen had been taken into custody in consequence of a quarrel at Ostend.

October 3.—We went on in the common passage-boat to Ostend. The wind was so unfavourable for our voyage to England, that we were apprehensive we should be detained on the Continent longer than we wished. We spent the afternoon in walking about the town, in viewing the soldiers, who were levelling the ramparts in order to make room for new buildings, and in looking at the vast quantity of shipping, and the amazing bustle of commerce, of which Ostend may now boast. · There surely is not a more thriving place in Europe!

October 4.—Though the wind was still unfavourable, there was so little of it, and the weather appeared to be so much settled, that we determined to take our passage in a fishing-vessel which was about to sail for England. We dined at the *table d'hôte* with a very large company. There were three English officers, who were to travel by land towards Minorca, and who were to endeavour to throw themselves into that place. They seemed, however, to think that they were bound on a fruitless expedition. At 3 P.M. we went on board, and were in motion before we perceived that the sky bore rather a threatening appearance. The wind was against us, and we passed between the wrecks of two ships which had been lately thrown upon the coast—

Et laceras nuper tabulas in littore vidis—Ovid

so that we felt somewhat discouraged. It was, how-

ever, too late to retract; and before we were clear of
the harbour we took to our berths, and there remained
till we reached Margate. In the night the sea rose
considerably ; so that the passengers generally—my
late foe of the Ghent barque inclusive—were afflicted
with the *maladie de mer.* Our vessel was of the short
broad-beam build, and rolled about in the true tub-
fashion. We had reason to fear that we should have
to endure this miserable situation for thirty-six, or
possibly even for forty-eight, hours. In the morning,
however, we were comforted by being told that the
wind had come about in our favour, and that we
should probably arrive in port about 3 o'clock. We
did so ; and, after a passage of twenty-four hours,
landed, pale, begrimed, and thankful, upon Margate
pier. The next day—for we were too much fatigued
and travel-stained to proceed that evening—we set
off for London and home.

'COMMENTS ON HIS BROTHER'S TOUR OF 1781.'—
ADMIRAL PARKER'S VICTORY OFF THE DOGGER
BANK.

The Rev. T. T. to R. T.

Fordham, Sept. 2, 1781.

Dear Brother,—As my mother tells me that a
packet goes to you every Tuesday and Friday, I
cannot resist the temptation of taking a little corner
in the next conveyance, just to let you know how I go

.¹ See preceding extracts from Journal.

on, and to thank you for your Brussels and Spa letters, which were most acceptable. You are very good ; better, candour obliges me to own, than I fear I should be to you in a similar situation ; I, who find myself unaccountably indisposed to letter-writing from the moment that I turn my back upon my own inkstand, though only for a little *home* excursion. Upon *foreign* ground ! Ah ! my brain would be in such a fermentation of curiosity, and my time so swallowed up by staring and sleeping, and staring again, &c., that I verily believe I should be unable to give my friends any other satisfaction than that of now and then a *date* and a T. T. to certify my *existence*. But without further waste of paper let me first tell you that I continue very comfortable, my nights *seldom*, now, interrupted by nervous freaks ; my spirits, above all, prodigiously mended. I even write, now and then, a line of Aristotle. But when he begins to give me trouble I spurn him from me and run into the garden. I drown my difficulties and puzzles in my pond, as Horace drowned his cares ' in mare Creticum.'

Your letters tell me enough to make my mouth water for your journal, which I shall be impatient to lay hold of when you return. I got down my great map the other day and took a trip after you. But these Netherlands, these Pays Bas, always bother me. I never know what they are, nor where they are, nor to whom they belong, nor when I am in Germany, when in Flanders, when in Holland, &c., for which I suppose you despise and pity me heartily. When you return, your first sentence in every company will always begin, ' When I was in Flanders,' or ' When I was upon the Continent, &c., &c.' Well, my comfort is that, bating vineyards, I can match you for beautiful scenes, and hills decorated with woods. As for mountains, I want a line to be drawn—at what precise height do hills and mountains commence? Have you forgiven me my unthinking enormity of a *three-sheet* letter? It cost one shilling to London, as my mother, with some gravity, informed me. I hope the family will recover it : I will never be guilty of such a piece of *étourderie* again. The rest of my Yorkshire expeditions will keep till your return. Your Spa letter to me and to my mother both arrived while she was at Colchester —so each has seen each, which was clever. By this time you have seen and heard, I imagine, *our* account of the battle with the Dutch. We make *them* superior in number of ships, guns, &c. ; they, *us*. It seems clear that we had the advantage in the fight ; by their *own* account their damages much exceed ours : *one* man-of-war sunk, more men killed, ships more damaged, &c. It has been said that they lost more than one ship, but it is not confirmed. Admiral Parker has got great credit and all his captains.[2] The King paid the fleet a visit on its return, shook hands with and thanked the Admiral in public, &c. The Dutch fought well. 'Twas the only fair old-fashioned

[2] Admiral Parker's battle with the Dutch off the Dogger Bank, August 5, 1781.

H

sea-fight of *this* war. I wish the Dutch fought *with* us, not *against* us. The combined fleet from Cadiz is now certainly gone for Minorca. The papers say they have passed by Gibraltar. Now adieu. Yours affectionately,

T. T.

AIX - LA - CHAPELLE. — PACCHIEROTTI. — SIR JOSHUA REYNOLDS.

R. T. to the Rev. T. T.

Aix-la-Chapelle, Sept. 6, 1781.

Dear Brother,—I do not believe that a better letter ever entered Spa than that which I received from you the other day, nor do I believe that any person at Spa ever received more pleasure from a letter than I received from yours ; and is it possible that you could desire Jack not to send it if he thought it would put me to much expense? Why, Sir, it was like Virgil's desiring that the Æneid might be destroyed. But it is well for mankind that, though Virgil and yourself were cruel enough to make such requests, other people were wise enough not to comply with them. Having thus vented my displeasure against the idea of withholding your letter, I proceed to thank you for writing it. It is worth while to get a great way from home on purpose to relish, in the utmost degree, communications of this kind. Do not imagine that because you are as far from me as I am from you, that you are therefore qualified to judge of my sensations. In the first place I ought, before our situations could be in the least degree similar, to write as good a letter as you have done. Now I do hereby swear that I will never do such a thing. But, after all, it makes a wide difference whether a man is at home, or a great way from it.

You will see by the date how far *I* am from home. The imperial eagle is still my protector. We stayed at Spa a few days longer than we intended ; for a complaint (which was almost universal) attacked my wife ; some people were very bad with it. We moved hither as soon as we could, being impatient to get out of a place which has been, during the chief part of our stay there, remarkably unhealthy. We have in this town excellent accommodations ; and we have found a physician, a pupil of the celebrated Boer-'haave, who is particularly successful in his treatment. Already Mrs. T. is much better than she was ; and Dr. Le Join assures me that she may, with the utmost safety, pursue her journey in a few days. I hope he is a true prophet. Mary and myself have been very well.

I have not yet visited the Maison de Ville here ; but we talk of going thither to-morrow. It is a most celebrated building, upon account of the peace which was concluded there in 1748. I wish I could make as good a peace there now. I have not yet been able to find Mr. Kucklehorn. I scarcely know whether you are in jest or in earnest when you desire that I would present your compliments to him ; but if he should come in my way, I shall certainly do as you bid me.

Mr. Pacchierotti was at Spa. He and I were quite 'thick.' We rode together frequently. He drank tea with me, and has promised to visit me at Twickenham. He is a very sensible. and a very modest man. He is engaged at the Haymarket next winter, and is, I suppose, by this time in England. He wished to let the winter come upon him by degrees in that climate. He had two concerts at Spa, and trust my poor ears when they assure you that he sung charmingly.

. Sir Joshua Reynolds was here a few days ago ; I believe he is gone on to Düsseldorf. I should like to meet him in the Gallery there. It may possibly be so, for he will scarcely hurry away from such a collection.

I will endeavour to write another letter to you soon. If you should be quite in the humour to send a few lines to Devereux Court in a short time after you receive this, Jack can inclose them in a letter to Brussels. A confirmation of the good account which you gave of your health will make me very happy.

When Mrs. T. read your letter, she immediately cried out : 'And will you continue your journal ?— will you ever attempt description after this ? ' 'What would you have me do ? ' said I. 'Is no man to write, unless he can write as well as my brother does ? '   Your affectionate brother,

R. T.

HIS BROTHER'S RETURN.—ARISTOTLE.

The Rev. T. T. to R. T.

Fordham, Oct. 19, 1781.

Dear Brother,—I was delighted to hear that you were all safe upon English ground ; as much delighted as if I had told you so immediately, which, methinks, I ought to have done, and yet why ? Would not you be sure enough of it without my telling you ? Therefore I will say no more ; I even repent of having begun something like an apology. What have you and I to do with ceremony and etiquette, and the *minikin* duties of civility and *bienséance* ? Your little letter was worth a good deal to me ; for I was in some pain about you from the windy weather we had had. And so now you are at home, sleeping in your own bed, and indulging by your own fireside ; and seas, and mountains, and buildings, and all the *outlandish* sights you have seen are floating in your brain, like a vision. I often amuse myself solidly by *re*travelling, in imagination, my Yorkshire travels. The colours, indeed, soon grow faint, the outline ill-defined, and the picture interrupted by many vacant and blank spots, like the page of a book when one has been staring at the sun. But there will always be enough left to be pleasant. This will much more be the case with you. People in general are not sensible of the advantage of laying into the mind a *fresh assortment* of ideas. Some philosophers have held that *ideas* are the essence of the soul, that it is nothing but a bundle of ideas.   If so, a man has as much more soul than his neighbour as he has more ideas.   I have gone on with my transcribed and revised translation of Aristotle, bit by bit, till it is brought within two chapters of the end.   I don't relish the idea of throwing away all my pains. By far the worst is over.   Note-writing will be amusement.   I promise you it shall be *that* or nothing, for I have learnt the value of life and health.   Was it not comfortable in a degree you never felt before to arrive at *home*.   Did you fall down and kiss the shore of your native land, like Ulysses, and other ancient heroic travellers?   Did not you enter your garden at Twickenham with Catullus in your hand?

> Quam te libenter quamque lætus inviso !
> *Vix mi ipse credens* Thyniam atque Bithynos
> Liquisse campos, et videre te in tuto.

Did not you feel the joy—

> cum peregrino
> Labore fessi venimus larem ad nostrum,
> Desideratoque acquiescimus lecto?

That little thing ad Sirmionem Peninsulam is delicious. If you have not read it since your return, make haste. Now, I begin to call for books.   Is there not a parcel due to me?   You did not pick up a Victorius upon the Continent?   nor a *chien lion* I fear !   I long for your journal with intense longing !

Your affectionate   T. T.

MAIDENHEAD BRIDGE.—LARGE FAMILY PARTY.

The Rev. T. T. to R. T.

Fordham, July 26, 1782.

Dear Brother,— I thank you for your remembrance of me at Woodstock. I suppose the sign of your *auberge* put you in mind of the bear, your elder. brother, 'confiné par le sort dans un bois solitaire.' I allude to a bear of La Fontaine's that I always admired, as somewhat related to myself. He is worth your looking at, I assure you. ' L'ours et l'amateur des jardins ' is the title of the fable.

Upon my word, a goodly, party, and the rear well brought up by Mr. George T., though ' last, not least.' Your children suck their father's love of travelling with their mother's milk. Among the many good things of the golden age neither you nor I shall ever reckon it one, as Tibullus does, that there were then *no roads* (Lib. i. El. 3) ; no, nor that there was no riding on horseback, and *no doors* to their houses. Nor, for my part, do I care much about the honey that trickled from their oaks ; for I think it a nasty thing, and I desire nothing better from an oak than its form and its shade. As to *swords* and *wars*, &c., there, indeed, the whole family will agree. By trying, thus, to be very witty and ingenious, I have told you that I am *well*. I thank God I have had no return of my fever that deserves mention since I wrote to you last ; we hope it has taken its last leave. But, whether well or ill, I can brook nonsense ; therefore never curb your fancy. I thank God *this* disorder is nothing like that dispiriting one that persecuted me last summer, and held death continually before the eyes of my imagination. It was the very 'slough of *despond.*' My appetite is good, and generally my spirits ; and (to keep to Spenser)

> All the night in silver sleep I spend,
> And all the day to what I list I do attend.

(' Oh ! he has been reading Spenser, I see !') It looks like it, but it is not so. They are two lines that long· ago pleased me (all but *silver*,[3] which is rather queer), and stuck in my memory. (Here's parenthesis with parenthesis, a thing I delight in.) Upon my word, I have made, I fear, a pleasant blunder above ! as sure as I am alive the slough of despond is not in *Spenser* but in *John Bunyan* ! I would not give a farthing for myself if I did not blunder now and then.

By this time your travels are over. I hope my sister is, or will be, the better for the trip. Your party was a charming party,[4] but r—a-ather of the largest. The famous saying of old Hesiod, that ' half is more than the *whole*' ($\pi\lambda\acute{e}ov$ $\H{\eta}\mu\iota\sigma\upsilon$ $\pi\alpha\nu\tau\acute{o}s$, you can *read* Greek, sir ?) is to nothing more appli-

---

[3] But Virgil, you know, calls the sleep of death *iron* sleep, and Homer brazen sleep ; why not Spenser the sleep of life and health, *silver* ?

[4] A large family party to ' Maidenhead Bridge '—then, as still, a favourite place of resort. After a sojourn of some days at the pleasant inn there, they extended their tour, stage by stage, until they reached South Wales !—R. T., 1885.

cable than to a numerous party. But, alas ! I forget
that I am a bear in a wood. As to the lines of Ovid
you would have been a very clever fellow if you could
have made anything of them. I imagine, by this time,
you have found they should be

nec adhuc spectasse *per* annos
Quinquennem poterat Graiâ quater Elida pugnam.

Heinsius corrected them so *at his peril.* I won-
dered what the passage could mean, went into
Keymer's shop and looked at a Mattaire, where I
found the passage as mended by Heinsius. When
I got home my Variorum told me all. Why do
you pester yourself with such vile editions ? I remember a blundering Horace that used to plague
you, which I hope is burnt. Are there no pocket
editions but what are as hard to get into the head as
they are easy to get into the pocket ? It is very true
what Montesquieu says, that a neglected garden is an
insupportable thing. I thought, when I came hither,
that I would only consider my garden as a field, and
all would be well. But it was the abomination of
desolation, and I could not bear to walk in it or look
at it, nor Mrs. T. At last we have got it mown, and
you can't think how I enjoy it. There was a sort of
moral turpitude in letting the grass and weeds grow
in a garden that hurt my conscience as well as my
eyes. Have you read Miss Burney's 'Cecilia' ? I
have not yet, but I have got it ready. *Five* vols.
rather fright me, but there are no notes, references, or
difficulties to stop one in such reading, which is cer-

tainly a great comfort. I have not thought of Aristotle since I came hither, nor read much ; but only got my books ready for reading by dusting and wiping off the winter's mould—a new way of using books which I recommend to you as good bodily exercise. Adieu.

Yours affectionately,   T. T.

I received the hymn to Ceres ; and, what was odd enough, just before I received it from Mr. Parr, with some marginal 'pot-hooks' of his in Latin, and I shall return it with more pot-hooks of my own. I may tell you more of it another time. There are two translations, one by ——, which I have ; poor poetry and worse criticism, at least as to Greek, in which he is very deficient. The other, I *believe*, is by Hoole, but I have not yet seen it ; I should suppose it the best. Have you read or heard any account of Hayley's poem on epic poetry ?

HIS BROTHER'S JOURNAL.--PUBLICATION.

The Rev. T. T. to R. T.

Fordham, Oct. 12, 1782.

Dear Brother,— . . . . I *have taken the barque for Brussels* long ago, and am now at Spa, swallowing water, prospects, cascades, nay, gaming tables, dishevelled ladies, and whole mountains, &c. You afford me much entertainment, and Mrs. T. almost as much. Why *almost* ?—because she cares not about your pictures, nor your geography, nor your history. She is glad when prospects and human creatures return ; and indeed these will, of course, be *most* amusing to *all* your readers. The rest is rather for your own recollection. I read of an evening to Mrs. T., so do not travel post. And why *should* I? I by no means wish to be at the end of my journey : nay, in *such* a journey, whether literal or figurative, *all* is end : we are arrived wherever we find ourselves. When I have read your volume in this way, I shall run it over by myself, and make any remarks that may occur to me. May I pencil your liberal margin, or shall I take a sheet of paper? Upon my word you might, if you were not such a squeamish fellow, make an amusing publication —PUBLICATION, PUBLICATION, I say—of your journal. I don't pretend to say it would do in the state it is now in; written, I am sensible (though some of it, by-the-by, extremely *well* written), without the least view of this kind. But I see you turn pale, you are a Twining mind and body. I laughed exceedingly at your caution about asking questions concerning that poor prisoner at Stavelot Castle. All the while you were walking about the ruins, I saw your humane curiosity peeping out, and then hastily drawing in its head when it thought Monsieur le Commandant would see it. Your feelings in the forest of Arden are after my own heart, &c. But no more at present of these matters. My only intention when I snatched up this paltry half-sheet this morning was to tell you that I continue well, and to thank you for the green book.[5]

<hr>

[5] The Journal in green binding.

What a voluminous and painstaking journalist! I
hope you are going on apace with your second tome ;
don't let your ideas catch cold.[6]

Yours affectionately,   T. T.

ARISTOTLE.—HIS READINGS.

The Rev. T. T. to R. T.

Colchester, Oct. 27, 1782.

Dear Brother,—As you say you shall be anxious
for a line, I write you a line just to assure you that
nothing could be better received than your apologetic,
explanatory epistle, for which I make my bow. But
how could you possibly have any anxiety, or doubt,
about its reception ? Your Georgical MSS. did not
escape me, or rather, your intention in sending
them ; but I did not see them till after I had written
my letter. No, I shall not make you so ill a return
as to let you hurry me, or bother me. My time here
is indeed pinched up to a mere nothing ; and there
seems no medium between throwing my Aristotelian
barbouillages into the fire (a thing I have really, at
times, almost wished I had the resolution to do), and
giving them all the time I can find. But inclination
sooner or later *will* make its way, and summer gives

[6] The responsibility for printing for the first time some copious
extracts from the Journal rests upon the present editor. The manu-
script is contained in two stout quartos, and amply justifies the favourable opinion which is expressed in this letter of its descriptive powers
and comprehensiveness.—R. T., 1886.

me time for all things. I write now merely to remove
your anxiety. You shall hear again e'er long.

What can you possibly mean by talking of the
expecting world, when the two doctors Forster and
Parr, the two doctors John and Richard Hey, the
one Doctor Burney, and the *learned* and *busy* R. T.
are all that I know of who are acquainted with my
design? Oh, yes, and Elmsall, whom I had forgot.
I fancy, Sir, you are treating me with *ironing*, as Mrs.
Slipslop says.

I am still in *Platonic* health.

Yours affectionately,   T. T.

N.B.—My *present* readings are Plato, Aristotle,
and Tom Jones.

JOHN PHILIP KEMBLE IN 'HAMLET.'—AN EARLY CRITIQUE.

Richard Twining to his Friend John Hingeston[7]
(an Extract).

Isleworth, Oct. 4, 1783.

I paid a visit the other evening to our old spot—
the pit passage—and occupied my identical place in

---

[7] 'John Hingeston.'—This excellent man was one of the firmest
and most attached friends of our family. He was a bachelor, living in
New North Street, Red Lion Square, from whence he was a frequent
visitor in Devereux Court and at Isleworth. The hours for dinner and
tea were early in those days, but those of business were late, and the
latter meal was habitually taken in the counting-house at an old-
fashioned table, which turned up on a hinge and stood against the wall

the pit.   My wife was with my brother and sister in the boxes.   I wanted to see and to pass my critique upon Mr. Kemble, and, therefore, begged permission to go into the place of critics.   I am too far advanced in my letter to attempt a full account.   I will only say that he is by much the best Hamlet I have seen except Garrick, who yet remains without any chance of an equal.   Kemble will, I think, improve.   He has a very expressive countenance, a good figure, and a strong yet melodious voice ; but whether it will endure much exertion I doubt.   His action is often good, and yet often bordering upon affectation.   I think there is sometimes a want of manliness in him ; but this may be awkwardness or timidity.   His ' Angels and ministers ' was too much laboured.   He died ill ; but the closet scene was a most capital piece of acting, or rather of *non*-acting ; and the charge of secrecy was exquisite.   It is a long time since I have seen Shakespeare's plays upon the stage, and, however heterodox it may appear, I will frankly confess that several passages in the play offended me mightily. It has, however, myriads of charms to make amends for its defects ; yet one could not help wishing the defects were done away. . . .   R. T.

---

during the day.   When the tea-things were set out, and the worthy old bookkeeper heard Mr. Hingeston's familiar footstep, it was a signal to put the kettle on.   That quaint old table held its place in the counting-house, and was used for the same purpose fifty years afterwards when my father and I used to return to work in busy times after dinner.—R. T., 1886.

DISSERTATION ON POETICAL IMITATION.—DR. FORSTER'S CRITICISMS.

The Rev. T. T. to R. T.

Colchester, March 7, 1784.

Dear Brother,—This is merely to announce a packet by to-morrow's coach, containing your Virgilian MS. which I forgot to put into the last, R. Hey's dissertation on gaming (for I have now written to him), and, lastly, my dissertation on poetical imitation. I brought it to town with me last winter, but you had no time—it would mortify me too much to suppose you had no inclination—to read it. I am in no hurry for it. If you will give it a perusal and tell me what you think of the *whole*, and anything that strikes you particularly as to *particular* parts as wrong, obscure, &c., I shall think myself obliged to you. As I have had large remarks from Dr. Hey and Dr. Forster I need the less desire you to stop at little defects in language. Whether it seems to you *clear* and *right* is what I principally wish to know. Take your own time. I send you Dr. F.'s scrawls upon the dissertation, not to give you the trouble of any remarks upon them, but only to show you what a comfortable literary friend and Aristarchus I have in him.

> Eager to praise, yet resolute to blame,
> Kind to my *work*, but kinder to my fame.

Modesty, perhaps, ought to have prevented my showing you the praise he gives me in one or two

places.   I know very well what to allow for the
partiality of a friend.   I lower his *praise* into *approbation*, and then I may own without scruple that his
approbation is encouraging to me.

Yours affectionately,

T. T.

TOUR IN NORTH WALES WITH DR. HUGHES.

Richard Twining to the Rev. T. T.

Llanfwrog, July 17, 1785.

Dear Brother,—After my long silence, a letter
from me, even if it came from a well-known place,
would probably be a matter of some surprise to you ;
but a letter, dated from an unpronounceable village in
the sweet Vale of Clwyd, was what you could by no
means have expected.   Perhaps you will scarcely
believe, for I can scarcely believe, that I am so far
from home.   The case is, I both longed for, and
really required, a little relaxation, and the only way
to obtain it was to fly from those calls of business to
which I am, and I believe ever shall be, subject whilst
I am in the neighbourhood of London.   My friend
Hughes,[8] who is a most excellent travelling companion,
strongly urged my accompanying him to his native
vale ; his friends too gave me irresistible invitations, and
Mrs. T——, who would not have been able to travel
with me this summer, promoted the plan.   And so,

---

[8] Afterwards a D.D. and Canon of Worcester, and afterwards
Canon Residentiary of St. Paul's.

yielding to entreaties, which were, as you know, seconded by certain natural propensities, I took a place in the Chester post coach. It carries only four persons. Hughes, an aunt, and a nephew [9] of his, were my fellow-travellers ; so that we had the coach to ourselves, and felt the *incommoda* of a stage as little as possible. Near Stony Stratford I got on the box, and had a view of Passenham. I was sorry that I could not call upon Dr. Hey, but stages, like time, will stay for no man. Dr. Hey and Mr. Elmsall, who knew that I was to dine that day (last Monday) at Stony Stratford, very civilly walked over to see me. Mr. E. said he had left you perfectly well, after your rambles. From Stony Stratford we passed through Daventry, which 1 had seen, to Dunchurch, which I had not seen. From this place I branched off, with poor Thomas,[1] to Rugby. Mr. James [2] was a perfect stranger, and I felt, as well as Thomas, that we were in a land of strangers. Mr. James had a little formality, a little unnatural attention about him, which did not, at that instant, quite accord with my feelings. Having left Thomas at Rugby, we proceeded to Coventry, where we slept a short sleep of three hours, and submitting ourselves once more to a rumbling stage coach, we passed over Sutton Coldfield Heath, a most dreary spot, and through Newtown, Whitchurch, and Wrexham, to Mr. Newcome's

[9] Thomas Newcome, afterwards Rector of Shenley, Herts.
[1] His son Thomas, afterwards in the Bengal Civil Service.
[2] Head-master of Rugby.

at Gresford.   Mr. Newcome is Hughes's brother-in-law; he has the living of Gresford, and a charming living it is, not merely in point of income, but also of situation.   It contains hills and valleys in abundance, plenty of wood, and some water.   Mr. N. has a large family and a good parsonage-house, and he is a very entertaining and sensible man.   I saw some sweet places in the neighbourhood of Gresford, and particularly Mr. Yorke's at Erthigg, which is a lovely spot finely tumbled about by nature, and happily improved by art.   We left Gresford on Friday, and dined that day at Llangollen.   The ride from Ruabon to Llangollen is capital.   The road forms a terrace above the Dee, which winds amidst most noble mountains.   The scene is perpetually varying, and perpetually improving.   At Llangollen we drank tea with Miss Butler and Miss Ponsonby, who are noticed in one of 'my silly blue books.'[3]   Their house and garden are much improved since I was last at Llangollen.   In the evening we came by a very mountainous road to this place, the residence of Hughes's mother.   It is situated near the inland end of the sweet Vale of Clwyd, the pride of this country. I believe you have heard me talk of my scale of counties.   I had given the upper place to Denbigh-shire, and it deserves it.   We are going this afternoon to Cotton Hall, Mr. Salusbury's, and as quickly as Welsh hospitality will permit, to the mountains of Carnarvonshire.   Snowdon is our grand object.

[3] A phrase of Mr. M. Grey's.

Whether he will be accessible or not is a matter of some uncertainty, but if we cannot reach his summit, we must endeavour to comfort ourselves with the waterfalls, and the romantic scenery in his neighbourhood. In the course of our tour, we hope to get a few dips in the sea.

Your affectionate brother, R. T.

NORTH WALES (IN CONTINUATION).

R. T. to the Rev. T. T.

Isleworth, July 20, 1785.

Dear Brother,—I suppose you have heard of my safe return from the Welsh mountains. It is fitting that you should also have some account of my expedition to them: and here it is.

My letter from Llanfwrog conducted you through the hospitalities of Gresford, and the lovely Vale of Llangollen, to the more celebrated Vale of Clwyd. Having spent a few days with Mrs. Hughes at Llanfwrog, and surveyed the beauties of the Ruthin end of the vale, we proceeded along the vale to Cotton Hall, Mrs. Salusbury's. Here we slept two nights. During our stay we made an excursion to Llewanny, the seat of the Honourable Mr. Fitzmaurice, brother to Lord Lansdowne. This gentleman has an estate of 17,000*l.* a year, and only one son ; and yet he has plunged himself into a business which might make even a tradesman tremble. He is a bleacher

of linen.   The buildings which he has erected, and
the machines and apparatus which he has placed
in them, are really astonishing.   He has a shop in
Chester, at which he sells his linen when it is bleached.
The dwelling-house is a large but irregular building,
containing a noble hall, in the true antique style, with
galleries, a huge chimney, great beams, and weapons
of all sorts stuck around it.   I like a room of that
sort.   It carries one back to ages long since past.
The other rooms, though good, do not accord with
this feudal hall: they are in modern guise.   Mr.
Fitzmaurice very civilly invited us to eat turtle with
him.   I met the 'over-credulous Mr. Pennant' at
Llewanny.   As we were both of us going to Colonel
Myddelton's we rode, and, indeed, spent almost the
whole morning together.   I was glad to meet a man
whom I had read and heard much of.   He was brimful of Welsh information and very communicative.
He kindly gave me an invitation to Downing, which
I wished to accept, as his collection would, I know,
have afforded me entertainment ; but a man who goes
into Wales and means to accept all the invitations
which come in his way must not be limited in point of
time as I was.   From Cotton Hall we made an excursion to Llanrhaiadr, which belongs to Mr. Parry, an
old schoolfellow of mine.   He married the handsome
Miss Thomas, of Cambridge.   Here I was obliged to
refuse another good dinner.   Mr. Parry's is an excellent house, in the midst of the Vale of Clwyd.   We
breakfasted at Colonel Myddelton's, at Gwynanog.

This is, altogether, better worth seeing than any place which I met with in Denbighshire. It is not so highly ornamented as Mr. Yorke's at Erthigg, but it is much more wild and picturesque, and contains a much greater variety of scene. Some parts are completely retired, others command a noble view of the Vale of Clwyd, with Denbigh and its venerable castle. I could not help saying to Hughes, 'I wish I could show my brother this spot.' Colonel Myddelton immediately turned round: 'Bring him next summer; I have plenty of beds and shall be heartily glad to see you both.' I assure you he was in earnest, and so was I.

It was a hard job to get away before dinner, but we were obliged to be resolute, and so we posted along the vale towards the sea, which we made at Abergele, paying another visit in our way, and crossing a noble bridge of a single arch near St. Asaph. The scenery near this bridge is charming. Abergele is a Welsh bathing-place, and a poor place it is. It is situated under some high cliffy hills, which with some difficulty we scrambled up, and were amply rewarded for our pains. We scrambled down again, and refreshed ourselves with an evening dip in the sea. In the morning we breakfasted with Mr. and Mrs. Yorke. They have two noble houses in the county, one at Erthigg, the other at Duffrynally, but, for the sake of bathing, they were crammed into a mere dog-hole at Abergele. Mr. Yorke invited me to Erthigg, as he was going thither in a few days; but, alas! it could not be. From Abergele we went to Conway. The approach to Conway—go which way you will—is noble, but from Abergele it is beyond description charming. There is everything which ought to be, and everything in the precise place in which it ought to be. We dined at Conway, called upon Mr. Holland, walked over his Arcadia—which has merit, notwith-standing the affectation of its name—and proceeded to Bangor. This is one of the finest rides in Wales, along the stupendous pass of Penmaenmawr, and by the side of the Straits of Menai. Did you ever roll great stones down precipices ? If not, you cannot conceive what a fine effect they have, bounding and dashing, till, with a horrid crash, they reach the bottom, and fly into a thousand pieces. It is a sublime sport, and played to great advantage upon Penmaenmawr.

I was once in my life guilty of *passing by* the Vale of Aber. Let no man repeat such a sin. This time I went up the vale. It is narrow, mountain-fenced, watered by a rapid stream, which you cross by a true Alpine bridge, and terminated by the union of those mountains which had been on our right and on our left. ' But the river, what becomes of that ? ' Why, just at the point of union it comes, *sans* hesitation, from the mountain's brow to the pool beneath. There I sat, and I verily think that I never enjoyed a water-fall more. When we turned our back to the waterfall we saw the whole length of the vale, and at the end of it the sea. Mountains were perpetually thrusting themselves forward into the vale ; but they never came quite so far as to shut out a remnant—a liberal remnant—of the sea. Live objects are good in a landscape. On the very edge of the mountainous precipice a horse was feeding. You would not have changed places with him for all beneath the sun. In the valley a dozen milkmaids were tripping along, each with a little wooden milk-pail upon her head ; add to all this the characteristic goat. We entered a miserable-looking hut, but internally it was clean and comfortable. We found a young woman in it, the mother of six children. The goats were at the door, and she gave us a draught of milk which was fit for the best prince that ever ruled the principality. We contrived too to get a blessing, which I would not change for the Pope's. From Aber to Bangor we were entertained with the rejoicings at Beaumaris on the opposite shore of the Straits. The eldest son of Sir Hugh Williams came of age on that day, and in the evening bonfires were lighted in great abundance along the coast of Mona, and quite on the point of the promontory. These fires sparkling up one after another [4] and reflected on the waves, had a very pleasing effect. The present Bishop of Bangor has made considerable additions to his palace since I last saw it. He has a large private fortune ; so has Mrs. Warren's sister who lives with him ; and they do a world of good.

The walk from Bangor to the Straits is beautiful, and we took it, not merely for the sake of its beauty, but also for the sake of a dip in the briny Straits.

[4] Written before Scott's *Lady of the Lake.*—D. T.

Whenever the sea was within onr reach we ran to it like a brace of Newfoundland puppies.

After breakfast we walked to Bangor ferry, the great Irish ferry, and crossing it we got into a coach with a couple of genuine Irishmen. They entertained me prodigiously, partly by telling wonderful stories of a Mr. McDermot, a famous sportsman who leaped stone walls of six feet in height, with his head towards the horse's tail ; the horse always resting in his passage across the top of the wall ;[5] and partly by their boasted preference of the country about Dublin, to anything which was to be seen in Wales. They had a stroke, too, at the reverence which a Welshman bears to pedigrees. We parted company and hired a chaise to carry us to the famous copper mines at Paris mountain. It is said by the learned that the Romans discovered and worked these mines. They now yield an immense income to their owners ; and they afford a very curious sight to strangers. It is a sight, too, seen without difficulty, which is not the case with mines in general, for here the mine resembles an enormous gravel-pit ; nor is it necessary to descend into it in order to see the various operations which are being carried on. This mine is worked at so much less expense than the Cornish mines that it almost threatens their ruin. Great pieces of the rock which contain the ore, are blasted by gunpowder. These pieces are wound up in buckets from the bot-

---

[5] Many Irish hunters purposely strike the walls with their hind feet as they go over, to increase their impetus.

tom to the top of the pit, and here are broken into still smaller pieces, the mere stone being thrown aside and the ore sorted according to its value. In this operation of breaking ore many hundred people are constantly employed. It is exactly like breaking sugar except that it is somewhat more noisy, and that the fingers of the breakers are protected by iron cases. The best pieces are sent immediately to the smelting houses near Liverpool. Inferior pieces are burnt in kilns upon the spot. The smoke from these kilns is not only very disagreeable but also very pernicious, and the owners of the mine pay a considerable sum to other landowners in the neighbourhood for the damage which is done by the smoke. The water which is found in some parts of this mountain is so strongly impregnated with copper that, if a key or any piece of iron is held in this water for a few minutes, it comes out with a face of copper. The black smoke and the red dust which are perpetually flying about the mountains convert its inhabitants into the queerest kind of blackamoors you ever saw. A female so disguised works here, dressed in man's apparel, and she protects herself most manfully, not fearing to attack, in the way of good sound boxing, any mortal upon the ground. The smallest attempt at gallantry immediately incurs her powerful displeasure ; nor has she ever been known since she has inhabited the mountain, to deviate from the strictest rule of decorum. When affronted, instead of calling like a weak woman upon man for protection, she puts in warlike form the weapons with which nature has provided her and cries out :

> Respice ad hæc : adsum dirarum ab sede sororum :
> Bella manu letumque gero.

She is also, like Alecto, a lady of great travel, for she first put on man's attire—I do not say—' FURIA- LIA *membra* exuit '—to accompany a young gentle- man abroad. In another instance the heroine of the mountains resembles the infernal goddess ; for, like her, she is furnished with her crooked horn.

> cornuque recurvo
> *Tartareas infundit aquas.*

From the Paris Mountain we saw very distinctly the Isle of Man. We returned to Gwindu and thence to Bangor ferry ; we crossed by moonlight and slept at the ferry-house. The skirts of Angle- sea, towards Carnarvonshire, are beautiful. They are well cultivated and well wooded, and command the best view of the Straits, as the Carnarvonshire mountains form a noble background. But the in- ternal part of the once celebrated Mona is miserably flat, stony, and naked ; not even the withered trunk of a druidical oak is to be seen. It is said, however, that this island produces corn enough for the whole principality. The cattle are certainly much larger than in any other part of North Wales. We set off the next morning to Carnarvon ; it is a delicious ride. As soon as we had breakfasted we went on horseback to Llanberis Lake ; it lies at the foot of Snowdon. Mr. Hughes, a clergyman, who lives at

Carnarvon, accompanied us. The approach to mountains is almost always fine ; the approach to such mountains as Snowdon is specially so. We got into a curious boat, and were rowed by a more curious boatman to the end of the lake. At the end of this lake is a second, and upon a projecting hill, which parts them, are the ruins of an old castle. This is the view of Snowdon which Wilson has taken, and it is sublime indeed. More wild scenery I have never beheld. We saw goats in abundance, and we exchanged a mutual stare. We made an attempt to row back to the Carnarvon end of the lake, but our labour was lost. The wind and the waves prevailed against us ; so we got out of our boat, and scrambled by a very queer and mountainous path to our horses. It was altogether a first-rate expedition : the crescendo of mountains as we went up the lake pleased me as much, I think, as any crescendo of sound can have pleased you. Our new companion was a quiet, entertaining man, and well acquainted with the country. He had ordered dinner at four, to suit our excursion ; it was, however, half-past five before we returned—but it was no matter. We were too hungry to attend to the exact degree of roasting or boiling, and Mrs. Hughes received us with forgiveness, and so all was well. We would have made our bow after tea, but it was not to be received. Between tea and supper we walked under the walls of the city, which are washed by the sea. I do not recollect any city-walls which afford such a walk. The next morning

we turned our backs upon the Straits, having first
bathed in them, and not far from the spot where the
Romans crossed under Suetonius Paulinus—I should
have told you that when we were in Mona we read
'Caractacus'—but the scenery belied, rather than
assisted, the poem.   Well, having, as I said, turned
our backs upon the Straits, we proceeded upon hired
horses under the guidance of a *valet de place*, or, in
plain English, a Welsh guide, towards Snowdon. We
travelled about eight or nine miles upon the Beddgelert
road.   It was not new to me, but it was still entertaining ; and we had the satisfaction of seeing, as we
approached the monster, that his head was unencum-
bered with clouds.   At the lake we dismissed our
horses and our Carnarvon guide, sending them on to
wait for us at Beddgelert, and with a new and Snowdon guide we began the formidable ascent.   It was a
hot day, but I am, you know, patient of heat.   We
made frequent pauses in order to catch both breath and
prospects, and at each pause we were sure of an addition to our prospects. Anglesea and the promontory
of the Great Orme's Head by degrees opened themselves to our view, till at length we saw every part of
them. Our sea prospect became more and more extensive ; and those mountains in the neighbourhood of
Snowdon, and which appeared, when we were in the
plain, as formidable rivals to it, were now become,
to use the prophetic phrase of our guide, 'mere bee-
hives.' Snowdon is rich in lakes. They are of different
sizes, different forms, and of different heights.   Some

extend, like rivers in the valley, and some appear above half-way up the mountain. At one time I saw eight of them. Near the summit is a spring ; more pure water cannot surely be found. It was as clear as crystal and as cold as ice ; and, notwithstanding the cautions which had often been urged to me in the world beneath, I ventured ·to fall prostrate and to take a refreshing draught. The genius of the mountain protected me. This spring is not above ten minutes' walk from the summit ; but e'er we had performed half this journey we saw a small cloud rising as it were out of the sea. It was in itself a noble sight. It increased in size and came moving majestically towards us ; but it evidently portended the exclusion of all other objects. Nor was it long before it arrived, bringing with it to us, who had so lately been in a state of dissoluble heat, the chill of December. We put on our great-coats and sheltered ourselves, as well as we could, behind some stones which were piled up on the very summit of the mountain. This cloud did not, like that one which overtook me at Plinlimmon, drench me with its waters, but it was rather like iced smoke. Sometimes it completely excluded every object ; at others it let in upon us for a few moments the lakes and the valley which surrounds the mountain. We waited about half-an-hour ; but as the clouds were evidently disposed to collect more abundantly, rather than to disperse, we gave up the point. We had contrived to be amused and merry, but it was impossible not to be bitter cold. That we might see as much of Snowdon as possible we had stipulated with our guide that he should take us down on the Beddgelert side. He had, indeed, told us that it was not a very good way; but he got us upon the very ridge of the mountain, with a most horrid precipice on each side, before he told us that he had not been that way these forty years. The least slip, the least failure of the unequal ground on which we trod, must have been fatal. All beneath was perdition. Hughes, who followed me, exclaimed, as we were in the midst of the Pass, that he could plainly perceive by the hunch on my back that I was thinking of my wife and children. I believe he was right. Hughes, who is mountain-bred, declared that it was like walking upon the edge of an upright pewter plate. The rest of the descent, though often steep and jarring to the frame, was not perilous. We found, however, that we had undertaken a much longer walk than we were aware of, and that Beddgelert was a long way even from the bottom of the mountain. It was in vain to retract, and so we e'en accinged ourselves to the labour; and after a mountainous walk of six hours we arrived, with appetites which were far less satisfied than our limbs, at the humble inn of Beddgelert. I had particularly desired to have some mutton for dinner, and our good old landlady (she put me vastly in mind, both now and upon my former journey, of poor Mrs. Eastmond) had roasted for us such a hock of mutton as you never beheld.

.She apologised for it by saying it was the only mutton in the parish. We accepted her apology, and laughed not till she had quitted the room. Our hunger sharpened our teeth, and what we could not chew we washed down with ale, which the old lady had brewed in October last, against Sir Hugh Williams' son came of age. As the mutton was the worst so the ale the best which I ever tasted. It was certainly meat and drink, and as it began to rain hard and we had eight or nine miles to ride to a bed, I trusted that it would prove good clothing, and so it did for it either kept me dry, or made me indifferent to the wet, which is much the same thing. If you remember any part of the 'silly blue book' which I filled when I was last in Wales, you must certainly remember the warm praises which I bestowed upon Pont-Aber-Glâslyn and the ride from that bridge to Beddgelert. It is most magnificent magnificence. The devil threw up this bridge. The mountains on each side of it surpass his productions. It soon grew dusk, and it soon grew dark. I could see enough to remind me in some places of what I had seen before, and to make me wish in others for more light. In feats of horsemanship I was far more courageous than Hughes. He got off and walked down most of the hills. It rained, and he foresaw that his saddle would get wet; but he said it would make him stick the faster when he got on to it. I have been so much accustomed to ride down steep and bad hills, that I now entertain but little apprehension about them.

The next morning it was Sunday morning; we walked to Mrs. Griffiths', and had a good view of the Vale of Festiniog. It is a charming little vale — green, and watered by a nice winding stream, and its boundaries are mountainous, and in many parts wooded. It was the favourite vale of Lord Littleton. The ride from Tan-y-bwlch to Maesunyodd, the house of Mr. Nanney, was entirely new to me, and it was exquisite. We ascended by a very winding road the steep and wooded mountain on the side of the vale, and having crossed the mountain, we came to a lake which we travelled by the side of. The boundaries of our road were a mountain and a precipice: at the foot of the precipice was the lake, and from the end of the lake we had a view of the sea.

The congregation of a Welsh village, waiting in the churchyard for their pastor, put me in mind of Fordham. Not, Sir, that Fordham is like a Merioneth-shire village; far be it from me to affront it by such a comparison. But it was in Fordham churchyard that I first beheld such an expecting congregation, and a similar sight never fails to remind one of your parish.

Mr. Nanney's house is, I suppose, one of the best in Wales for affording a specimen of true Welsh living and true Welsh hospitality. His name was Wynne, but he changed it for the name of Nanney. An estate was his recompense. So that now there are a Mr. and Mrs. Nanney and six young sons and daughters, who having been born Wynnes are still so.

His house appears to be small, such as promises one or, at the most, two spare beds. We were therefore surprised to find in it, by way of sleeping company, Miss Griffiths the heiress, Miss Jackson, Miss Jones, Miss Evans, Mr. Evans—*Parson* Evans (for so he was announced), and Mr. Pugh. Was it not a jolly society? We proposed going before dinner, but this was not to be heard of, and after dinner, when our merriment increased, we were strongly solicited to stay all night. In that country nothing is deemed impossible in the way of accommodation, and I doubt not but that the ladies would have slept all together rather than have turned away any part of the company for want of a bed. It was not necessary to use much entreaty to prevail upon us to prefer Mr. Nanney's house and its merry inhabitants to a miserable and dull inn at Harlech. We therefore yielded, and without any further ceremony one of the beds which were allotted to us was carried through the hall in which we were sitting. In this country gentlemen live at such a distance from each other that they can seldom pay a visit and return home the same day. I wish you could have seen Parson Evans. He was about fifty, dressed in a blue coat, and his dark hair hung straight about his shoulders. I saw *a man in a blue coat* (for that was my definition of him) walking towards the house, and was surprised to hear Mr. Nanney exclaim ' Here comes Parson Evans!' The esquire gave him a hearty but rough welcome. Mrs. Nanney, who seemed to manage this unmanage-

K

able family in the pleasantest way possible, received him in a more polished manner, and the parson himself returned to each of them the most genuine Welsh smile. He did not say much, but the English which he did bestow upon us, was delivered with the whine of his native language. Mr. Nanney, who probably knew that his reverend guest looked forward to the pleasures of the evening, when the pipe men retire into the little parlour, said to him, 'Well, old *Limekiln*, we shall raise a fine smoke by-and-by.'

After supper, when the ladies were gone to bed, we went into this little parlour, and it did indeed smoke like a lime-kiln.

A material alteration has certainly taken place in this country within these few years respecting drinking. I did not see the least propensity to excess in any house in which I dined. When I called for a second glass of ale at Mr. Nanney's he very civilly told me that he thought I had better drink wine, for the ale was stronger than I was aware of.

On the Monday morning we were to proceed by Harlech to Monmouth, and I proposed to the younger part of our family that they should accompany us. This proposal was much relished, and soon acceded to, as soon, at least, as we declared that we must go, for we were pressed to make a longer stay, and to dine on the Tuesday, with Miss Griffiths at Tan-y-bwlch. How you would have laughed if you could have seen our party to Barmouth. Twelve horsemen and horsewomen scampering up and down hill and galloping over the sands as if we were bewitched — some ladies without their hats, one without her shoe. We stopped on our way to see Harlech Castle. Its situation is very fine. It stands like Gibraltar, upon a rock, which is inaccessible on the sea side ; its broken walls command a fine prospect. We stopped also at a summer-house which Mr. Nanney has built upon the cliff a little beyond Harlech ; it has a very extensive sea view. At Barmouth we added two more young ladies to our party : and I think it was, when complete, such a party as this humble seaport had never beheld. The memory of us, as of a prodigy, will, I think, remain for some time. It was nearly dusk before our friends took leave of us. They did so with pressing invitations for us to renew our visit. The moment they were gone Hughes and I stripped and had a most luxurious dip in the sea. Now you will perhaps exclaim 'what a day of riot and folly!' It may be so, and yet I will confess to you that it was to me a very pleasant day, and I believe there was not any man in the company who was more young and boyish and who 'played the fool' more than myself. If Wisdom should frown and tell me that as a *père de famille* I ought to be more discreet I can only reply, in the language of my friend Hughes, '*Nous sommes pauvres mortels.*'

The next morning we rode to Dolgelly. It is a charming ride. I had often been told that when I was last in Wales I ought to have gone all along the vale between Llangollen and Dolgelly, and I had been taught to repent that I had not done so. I wished now to correct my error, and Hughes readily came in to my proposal of doing so. Our road was, for some way after we quitted Dolgelly, very picturesque—a narrow valley, with wooded banks, and the vast mountain of Cader Idris.

From Drws-y-Nant we passed a dreary kind of heath, and were rewarded by a view of Bala Lake. It is the most extensive lake in the Welsh world, being three miles long. We travelled beside it to Bala town. This lake is bounded by mountains; the river Dee runs through it; and tradition says that the waters of the river never mix with those of the lake.

Bala is a town of consequence with respect to Merionethshire, but of no consequence upon a larger scale. Hughes met his old nurse at it, who declared that she had often whipped him; and to make him some amends she gave us a leg of excellent Welsh mutton. We sent for a barber, and in came a tidy Welsh woman. Hughes, who was the most eager to be shaved, was afraid. I, who am much more stubborn, beard and all, than he is, sat down; and she shaved me most dexterously.

We expected to meet with a chaise at Bala; but it was not worth one. We were obliged, therefore, to go another stage upon our Carnarvon horses, which were scarcely equal to so long a journey. At Drudw, where we slept, we found a house almost filled with Welshmen and Welsh uproar. If we had been five minutes later, the house would have been quite filled, a circumstance which would by no means have suited either our horses or us.

The next morning (for what signifies the day of the week or the day of the month), we got once more into a post-chaise, to the great comfort of my fellow-traveller. We passed through Corwen, Dr. Pretyman's sinecure, on our way to Llangollen. This is a charming vale, possessed by the Dee, and formerly containing the residence of that genuine and turbulent Welshman, Owen Glendower. This vale improves near Llangollen, but it is still finer between Llangollen and Ruabon, so that I saw, when I was last in Wales, the finest part of it.

From Llangollen I went, for the third time, by Vale Crucis Abbey to Ruthin and Llanfwrog. We were welcomely received upon our return by Mrs. Hughes. Our absence had not been long, but it had been so full of adventures and entertainment that, to me, it seemed to be much longer than it really was. It is often said that when time passes pleasantly, it appears to pass quickly; but this is not constantly true. Time seldom passes more pleasantly with me than when I am upon an excursion; and yet the quick succession of pleasant circumstances which have often occurred in the space of a few days, have made them appear to me almost as long as weeks which have not been half so pleasantly spent.

I passed two or three days more at Llanfwrog, making an excursion to Major Kenrick's. Hughes's elder brother—an East Indian—came to Llanfwrog when we were in Carnarvonshire, and nothing would content him but a dance; so he gave one at the Cross Keys at Ruthin. Dances do not occur very frequently in this part of the world, and they are, consequently, the more valued. We had a good party, and danced as if our exercise was to last for some time. It was past one before we got to bed, and a little after eight I bade adieu to Wales; nor did I stop, except to change horses, till I reached Isleworth —thirty-five hours' perpetual whirling. At the end of the first hundred miles I felt rather tired; but 'vires acquirit eundo' was my motto, and I was quite stout when I got to Isleworth. The iron bridge over Coalbrook Dale, and Coalbrook Dale itself were the principal features in my return. The scenery of this dale is suggestive of the lower regions—furnaces blazing and smoking, abrupt rocks, quantities of coal and iron, the bustle of a seaport, and black figures innumerable. I did not see half what I ought to have seen; but with the half that I did see I was wonderfully pleased.

I passed through Bridgnorth and Kidderminster in the dark, got to Worcester at sunrise, and so through Oxford to Isleworth.

Well, it was a noble excursion!—of which I have given you a hasty, and, I fear, almost unintelligible, account.

———————

PARIS.—ITS STREETS, ETC.

Richard Twining to the Rev. Thomas Twining.

Paris, August 17, 1786.

Dear Brother.—Neither the Duke of Dorset's secretary nor my old school-fellow Mr. Eden, yet know that I am in the French capital. I am therefore scarcely to be deemed your Parisian brother. But as I merely wait for my *voiture* (Oh, that you could see what a gig it is!) and have curls as big as the biggest black pudding you ever saw, I hope you will treat the beginning of my letter with some degree of respect.

I find one great comfort that I did not look for at Paris. It is that both Mrs. T. and myself may do just as we like. We may dress just as if we were at Isleworth ; nor have I at this moment sustained the least alteration, except in the above-mentioned curls, and this morning my own English servant has done my hair in *plain English.* Furthermore, we may walk, even in the streets. I had been told that it would be shocking in the uttermost degree for Mrs. T. to be seen on foot, and bad enough even for me. It is no such thing. The streets, it is true, are intolerably dirty, they are also narrow, there is no foot-path, and the carriages, which are numerous, drive most rapidly ; so that walking, though it is not a service of disgrace, is certainly a service of inconvenience, and even danger. The day after my arrival a gentleman took me with him in his cabriolet. We were no sooner seated than he set off, full trot, without paying the least attention to the crowd of foot-passengers. The servant who was behind the cabriolet frequently called out as we flew along, '*hurri!*' and to the attention and good lungs of this man, and to the good ears and alacrity of those to whom his cry was addressed, was the safety of the foot-passengers entrusted. If any man had attempted to drive in this manner in our capital he would soon have had a stop put to his career.

The paintings in the Palais Royal, those which are intended for the Louvre and the Luxembourg Gallery, are all undergoing a thorough repair. I am not only concerned that I cannot see them now, but I tremble, as I always do, for the effects of a thorough repair. M. Bougeon, who has a choice collection, is dangerously ill, and two other amateurs are in the country with the key of their cabinets. Do not, however, imagine that Paris is destitute of amusement. On the contrary there is so much to be seen and so much to be done that, from morning till night, we have been in a state of perpetual staring and employment. Without a map it would require a twelvemonth's residence to become acquainted with the numberless streets of this city. They are in general short and narrow. And those which are streets of trade do not make the gallant appearance of trading streets in London. In those parts of the city which are inhabited by people of fashion are hotels which in grandeur far surpass anything that I have known in London. But even those do not appear at the first view equal to many in the West end of our city. The reason is that all these grand hotels stand back, and are built round courtyards. It is impossible in a letter to do much more than name what we have seen. The first spectacle that we went to was the French Comedy. It was very brilliant. The play was the 'Marriage of Figaro.' It was well performed ; one woman, in particular, was charming. I found, however, that my ears would not readily accommodate themselves to French rapidity. The Italian Comedy, as it is called, but a French comedy, as we found it to be, was less striking ; but I was nearer the stage, and if I could have seen as well as I heard, I should have been much entertained. I was, however, seated at the back of a green box ; and was perpetually subject to the intervention of wide-spreading hats and caps. On Tuesday, which was a fête, we went to a spiritual concert at the Tuileries. *My* opinion of a concert is not, you know, worth much, but it is backed by better opinions. In London it would have been deemed a very moderate concert. The best thing was a concerto on the violin. A solo on the hautboy was most un-Fisher-like indeed. Yesterday morning I was most highly entertained at the King's Library by seeing some coloured drawings, and such a representation of the library of the Vatican as would have delighted you. We saw, at the same time, the collection of busts and statues of the celebrated sculptor, Houdon. He was sent to America to take the likeness of General Washington. In this collection were busts

of many princes and of the most distinguished authors.
Diderot was amongst the number. As far as I have
been able to discover, Diderot is not prized by the
French.   D'Alembert was there, and Buffon.   We
walked last night in the king's botanical garden.   In
a large house which stands in this garden Buffon
resides.   I have been twice at Notre-Dame.   It contains many paintings, and is a fine building.   Upon
the fête day we heard a symphonie in this church,
which was crowded with people.

Your affectionate Brother,   R. T.

FONTAINEBLEAU.—BANKS OF THE LOIRE.—TOURS.

R. T. to T. T.

Tours, August 28, 1786.

Dear Brother,—I must give you a little letter from
the banks of the Loire. As to the dimensions of it
(the letter) they are fixed by my *valet de place*, who
maintains that this is the right paper.

I have about me strong river propensities, and
long before I reached France I felt a strong desire to
visit the banks of the Loire. Fontainebleau was
nearly half-way to them, and served as an additional
inducement for me to undertake the journey. So,
with difficulty, I wrested myself from the temptations
of the gay capital, even upon the eve of the Festival
of St. Louis, and here I am. The Loire flows before
my window; and, within a few yards, is a noble

stone bridge of fifteen arches. They manage these matters very cleverly, for the bridge is as level as the road which leads to it, which, I ought now to tell you, is perfectly level. There is a novelty in the appearance of such a bridge, and to those who are to go over it there is an evident utility; but, says Mrs. T., and she is right, a level bridge is not the most picturesque of bridges.

Oh! what a dismal place is Fontainebleau! You never saw such a pile of melancholy magnificence. Perhaps we saw it to some disadvantage, for it was filled with workmen. The king and his whole court are to make a grand voyage to this antique palace early in October. You would think it impossible that the apartments could be ready for him, but when the king utters his decree nothing is impossible. The men now work from five in the morning till twelve at night.

The Gâtinois (go to your map) is extremely fertile, but as flat as a pancake and as insipid as fertility can be. Orleans consists of two very different parts, the old and the new. The old is ancient indeed. The new, consisting principally of a long and wide street and a noble bridge across the Loire, is extremely handsome. My wife would perhaps say that I speak too highly of it; but she was so unmercifully bitten at Orleans that her testimony of this city should not be implicitly received. I failed not to notice the statue of the Maid of Orleans. What a jumble! When the Loire is in good condition it must, I think, be as wide at Orleans as the Thames at Westminster bridge ; but, at this time, the river is unusually low, and much of that which should be water is sand. From Orleans to Blois we travelled through a country of almost perpetual vineyards, the Loire frequently appearing on our left. I must own, however, that my expectations have not been fully answered. The banks of the river are tame, often poor, and I have long been convinced that the product of vineyards is much better than the view of them. We have many, many rivers in England that are better worth travelling by than the Loire. And yet this river is the pride of France; this country is called the 'garden,' the paradise of France. The situation of the bishop's palace at Blois is really fine. It overhangs the town and river in a right lordly way. From Blois to Tours we travelled the whole way along the far-famed levée on the banks of the Loire. But this levée is for all the world like one of the best fen dykes. Such an artificial elevation is a poor business. Now and then we had a view of the winding river that was good, but, till we got to Tours, none that was fine. The appearance of Tours, which is not called so in vain—for it has many towers—is really fine. Its bridge of fifteen arches is a capital object to travellers. It was Sunday when we arrived, and as soon as we had secured our delicious quarters we posted to the Mall, which is reckoned the finest in Europe. You cannot think how the French delight in such walks. The climate makes shade desirable. The Mall was decorated with all the beaux and belles of Tours ; and it was the best walk, and the best ornamented walk of the kind I have ever seen. My dislike of avenues, which perhaps as my friend Hingeston tells me, I carry a little too far, probably prevented my enjoying the pride of Tours as I ought to have done. In our way hither we stopped to see Chanteloupe, the celebrated seat of the late Duc de Choiseul. But in this place, and in Chantilly, expense smothers taste. Gilding, gilding, nothing but gilding. The principal street at Tours is spacious and regular ; and, altogether, this is the most lively and the best situated of all the French cities that I have seen. Just as we entered it we overtook a good priest, in his priestly garb, riding upon an ass. It is a beautiful evening, and I must walk, so good-night.

R. T.

ENGLISH SOCIETY IN PARIS.—MAJOR MONTFORD.

R. T. to T. T.

London, Sept. 29, 1786.

Dear Brother,—I must give you a few lines, *en attendant* my journal. I ought to have received your letter at Paris ; 'but so it was,' as the *Major* says, that I found it in Devereux Court. The advice it contains would, perhaps, have done me good. In all honesty I say, *perhaps* ; for amidst the unforeseen and almost irresistible temptations of Paris, it is a hard matter to be wise. Some parts of your advice were conditional, and indeed I should not have had an opportunity of following them completely ; for though an Englishman when he goes to France may determine not to keep English company, it may not always be in his power to associate, as he could wish to do, with the French. You shall hear how we managed in this respect.

It was my intention when I left England to spend only a few, a very few, days at Paris, so that I did not procure letters of introduction to any French families. It was not, therefore, surprising that I did not visit any. And, to say the truth, though you will probably abuse me for it, we spent our time so very pleasantly at Mr. Sykes's that I felt not a wish to go elsewhere. We were always expected at their table. They have all French servants ; they live wholly in the French way, and our party was occasionally enlivened by French company. Above all Major Montford was almost constantly with us. He is an Englishman by birth, but has been many, many years in the French service ; he is now a major of 'the Invalids.' He knows everybody and everything, and is, as his friends laughingly tell him, fond of talking and of telling long stories. In the course of my travels, I have never met with a man who was so willing to give information and who gave it in so pleasant a way. He saw that I was curious and he fed my curiosity. If we went out upon any scheme, and our party was too large for one carriage, the Major and I were sure to be packed together ; and sometimes—I may say usually—by ourselves. The ladies used to say that we were only fit to be together. In consequence of our inseparability I am sure I obtained many anecdotes which, though seemingly of small import, were, to me, highly gratifying. Another good thing was that I could ask him anything. Though he is a Roman Catholic and the King's servant, I could venture to speak both heresy and treason ; and without the least dread either of the Inquisition or the Bastille. It was no small addition to my pleasure that the Major in his conversation spoke at least as much French as English. He was better than a master to me. I hope I shall, one day or other, have an opportunity of introducing you to the Major.[6] Be not frightened at him because he wears a red coat, for I promise you he is of a peaceable spirit. His figure is almost the caricature of a Frenchman ; a tall thin man with spindle shanks and a head of hair frizzed and powdered to the life. Many a walk have I had with him ; but I never knew him put his hat upon his head. You would like to accompany him about that vast building, the ' Hôtel des Invalides.' ' *Mon père,*' says he to the very aged men ; ' *mon frère,*' to those about his own age. He is merry, very gallant to the ladies—but you must see him—we are to correspond, without names, that treason may be admissible ! His sister is principal of a convent at Bordeaux. I had a capital evening with an Academician and his wife ; more of this

---

[6] The Major, after the Revolution, came to England, and had often a place at my father's table. –R. T., 1848.

anon. Mr. Sykes has a French gentleman in his family, with whom I used to get French conversation almost every evening. As to out-of-door matters, my curiosity took tolerable care of me ; but if I were to go to Paris again I think I could manage better. Oh that we could but contrive to go together ! The journey is nothing, and I am sure you would be delighted beyond measure.

Your affectionate brother,   R. T.

HARWICH PACKET.—FELLOW-PASSENGERS.—THE BRILL.

R. T. to T. T.

Rotterdam, July 18, 1788.

Dear Brother,—I will at least begin a letter to you ; whether I shall be able to finish it or not, will depend upon the punctuality of a Dutch merchant who is to call upon us and to show us the lions of Rotterdam. In an affair of mere pleasure, of unprofitable service, I think it probable that a Dutchman will not be perfectly punctual.

We left Harwich at 3 o'clock on Wednesday with as fair a wind as could blow and about as much of it as could be desired. We were remarkably fortunate as to the duration of our voyage ; for in a very little more than seventeen hours we were at Helvoet. The last three hours were motionless hours (I speak of the vessel), and I got upon the deck, drank tea, and recovered

rapidly. At Helvoet we had a sort of second breakfast, and then we proceeded in downright waggons and
over a most rocky road to the Brill. The motion of
this vehicle was ill-suited to my tender state. At the
Brill our motley crew parted. We had indeed the
most straggling cargo I ever embarked with. We had
Dutch, German, Italian, Jew, Persian, and English.
We had a man who had been far into the Mogul
country, and who still wears his Armenian habit.
We had another who had been seven times at An-
tioch, where the Gospel was first preached. He had
been at Ephesus, where St. Paul preached to the
Ephesians ; at Rhodes, where the famous Colossus
stood ; at Egypt, 'cum multis aliis locis.' I am afraid
that my Latin will almost bring the statue of Erasmus
which is just before the house into my room. We
had also an Italian physician—first physician, as he
said, to the Prince of Monaco—and another Italian,
with his two servants—one of them he called his
chamberlain. I never saw such a set. The Brill
is very striking to an Englishman on account of its
neatness. Here we hired a boat to carry the Rotterdam part of our passengers to Rotterdam, and we arrived there a little after 3 P.M. so that in a little more
than twenty-four hours we got from Harwich to Rotterdam. Such a passage is not often made. We
joined three gentlemen, whom we have been with
ever since by intervals, each following his own pursuits. Novelty of appearance is most delightful to
such a staring kind of traveller as myself, and at Rot-

L

terdam I have had my fill.   It is unlike anything I have
ever seen.   The view from the tower of the great church
is extremely extensive and in its way entertaining.   It
is not climbing merely to look over a few streets, but
over a whole country with all its towns, country houses,
canals, peat-pits, &c.   The Bombjhees is upon the
side of the Maese.   Large houses and a row of stately
trees before them.   The Maese is a wide river offering an abundance of commercial advantages, which to
a Dutchman are, I dare say, preferable to the romantic scenes of the Rhine.   I called upon one merchant,
whose first question was 'Avez-vous des affaires de
négoce?'   I said 'Non, le plaisir seulement,' and he
proceeded accordingly as if nothing particular was to
come of it.   He came up to me upon Change, and
when I mentioned Mr. Gogel, of Frankfort, he remarked, 'C'est une maison très solide.'   Our coach
waits to take us to the environs.   To-morrow we are to
dine with a gentleman at his country house.

Your affectionate brother, R. T.

THE HAGUE. — STRONG ORANGE PARTY FEELING.—
HAARLEM.—MR. HOPE'S HOSPITALITY, &c.

Richard Twining to John Hingeston.

Amsterdam, Aug. 1, 1788.

.   .   .   .   .   .

From   Rotterdam   we   went   in   a   Treickschudt
through Delft to the Hague. . . .   At the play we

saw the whole family of Orange. We are all of that family. You would laugh if you were to see our hats loaded with orange-coloured ribbons and cockades. We saw also the magnificent room at the House in the Wood. At Haarlem we spent a day and heard the organ. I have often wished you were with us, but never had a stronger wish of the kind than in Haarlem Church. Even my ears authorise me to say that it is a wonderfully fine organ, and that opinion is confirmed by ears far more to be relied on than mine.

We saw Mr. Hope's house in Haarlem Wood. It is a prodigious building. I should have told you, that you may laugh at us, of our having been locked into the great church at Haarlem, and of our being obliged to attend to a Dutch sermon, which lasted at least an hour and a half.

Upon our arrival at Amsterdam we were somewhat roughly attacked, because Hughes had inadvertently buttoned his great-coat over the orange ribbon which was in the button-hole of his under-coat. I never was more heartily frightened. But we got out of our scrape tolerably well. We went to North Holland, dined at Saardam, and drank tea at Broek. These places are perfect curiosities to an Englishman. . . . We have met with much civility here. Of this, too, you have probably heard already. You will doubtless esteem it a huge condescension if my wife takes any notice of you on her return, after having been handed about and complimented by the Prince

of Tour and Taxis.[7]   I assure you I am duly sensible
of the honour which she does me in bestowing upon
me, now and then, a little attention.   On Wednesday
we dined at Mr. Hope's.   He treated us sumptuously.
Wednesday is always his public day.   In the evening
we went to the Subscription Theatre.   None but
subscribers, or those to whom they give tickets, are
admissible.   Yesterday we were invited to dine out,
but we declined it.   In the evening we met a large
party and supped at Mr. Hope's.   He invited us to
his house in Haarlem Wood on Sunday, but we must
be off.   It is not yet finished, but is as much talked
of as a palace of the Prince of Orange. . To-day we
dine with a principal merchant, and sup with the
British Consul ; so that you see we have our hands
full, and I am to call upon Mr. Hope between the
two visits.   We have been at Amstelveen, where the
Prussians gained their decisive victory, and at the
famous sluice of Muyden.   We had a charming view
of the Zuyder Zee, and a whole fleet of ships upon
it. .. . . .

Many thanks for your kindnesses to the boys.[8]
I experience your kindness when I am present, and
I hear of it when I am absent. . . . .

Yours most sincerely,   R. T.

[7] In 1827 my father and sisters were at Frankfort, when on the
death of the Prince of Tour and Taxis a service was held in one of the
churches at which all the postilions attended, the prince having been
at the head of the ' Poste aux Chevaux.'—R. T., 1886.

[8] Mr. Hingeston was the delight of the younger generation—ever
ready to study their happiness, taking them to ' the play,' or what not.

BRUNSWICK.—GÖTTINGEN.—THE ROYAL PRINCES.—
PROFESSOR HEYNE.

R. T. to T. T.

Göttingen, August 14, 1788.

Dear Brother,—I will begin a letter, though I shall probably be called off before I have made much progress in it.

There are travellers who think all things, except very great things, beneath their notice, and who, when they get to an inn, will be contented to rest peaceably in it, and to write and read, and to seem as indifferent to all things as if they were actually at home. I am not a traveller of this description. Nay, I run into the very opposite extreme; and I feel as if everything that I had not seen was really worth seeing. From me, therefore, but little should be expected, whilst I am travelling, in the way of correspondence. To give, in some cursory way, notice to one of the family of our well-being and well-doing, if so the case be, and to have the important intelligence communicated by that one to all the rest, should be sufficient to ensure us from censure.

In such ways you have probably heard of us frequently. One short letter I wrote to you soon after we landed, and I wrote a long letter to Dr. Forster [9] from Brunswick; and now to continue as it were that letter under the notion that the two letters will be common to both.

---

[9] Rev. Dr. Forster, Colchester.

I think I concluded Dr. F.'s letter by saying that we were going to an opera, and afterwards to a masquerade.   They were given by the Court.

The singing was not the thing that I went for, nor is it, you know, the thing that I understand.

I went to *see,* and I saw the Duke and Duchess of Brunswick, the hereditary Prince, the Duke's brother and sister, the Dowager Duchess, the Princess of Prussia, and a tribe of courtiers.   I liked to see the conqueror of Dutch patriots—a set of people whom I abominate heartily.   The Duke looks as if he could drive thousands of them, by his mere word of command, to seek for refuge in their miserable canals. The Duchess is so like the King, her brother, that if she were dressed as he is she might almost pass for him, unless, indeed, her greater circumference should betray her, for she is very stout.   The hereditary Prince is much such another young man as our young Princes.   The Dowager Duchess is a well-looking old lady.   The Princess was elegantly dressed, and by the help of her feathers and diamonds she looked better than I could have thought any dress would make her look.

The Duchess and the Dowager Duchess came in chairs, the rest of the party in coaches.

The chairmen, instead of long great-coats, had short postilion-like jackets, and they wore high caps with a black thing lolling from the middle of them. The livery-servants walked abreast before the chairs. I wished the theatre had been better lighted ; but all foreign theatres are dark. The masquerade was at the Redoute, another and a larger theatre.

A floor was laid over the parterre and stage, and there the masks were admitted. There were five tiers of boxes all filled with spectators.

The Duke's box is in the front of the stage, and occupies nearly the whole front.

There the Duchess and the Court appeared unmasked. The house was brilliant as to lights, and it was altogether a striking sight, though, as to the mere masquerade, it was the tamest and shabbiest thing I ever saw. There was not one handsome dress—there were many dresses that were ordinary to the last degree—and not one grain of anything like wit or fun.

We left Brunswick on Tuesday morning, and slept that night at Seesen.

The country was fertile, woody, and hilly, and consequently entertaining. I did not at all expect to find anything so good in this part of Germany. The Elector of Hanover and the Duke of Brunswick have right fair possessions. Our inn at Seesen must not be included in this description, for its outside was fouler than the outside of any inn you ever beheld. The inside was a little, yet not much, better. To make the matter worse, it was crowded with travellers, so that many a German was lodged upon the floor. *We* got beds.

The first stage, from Seesen to Nordheim, was more mountainous, woody, and picturesque than any

we had travelled, but it was withal excessively rough
—so rough that it broke our carriage.

'Stop! stop!' cried Joseph; 'one of the "necks"
is broke.' What neck? thought I. It was one of the
necks of a double crane-necked perch.

I verily thought that we were rendered immovable;
but a strong rope and a little dexterity secured us to
this place; so here the injury can be easily repaired.

Göttingen is not a large, but it is an old and
shabby-looking, place. This morning ·I had a high
and first-rate treat. I heard Heyne deliver an hour's
lecture. His subject was ancient paintings. His
language was, unfortunately, German. You cannot
think what a disposition I felt to be attentive; and I
could now and then discover, by the affinity of the
German language to the English and French languages, and by the introduction of a Latin word
or two, what part of his subject the professor was
engaged in. A gentleman who accompanied us eked
out this scanty knowledge by answering very readily
any questions that I put to him. The whole set of
lectures will comprehend many subjects of antiquity.
In that of ancient paintings he has hitherto made but
little progress.

Yesterday he dwelt chiefly upon the *al fresco*
paintings, and the art which the ancients possessed of
preserving works of this kind, even when they were
very much exposed, for a considerable length of time.
The lecture was delivered in the public library. It
was attended by about ten students. Heynĕ (for the

final *e* is pronounced with a catch) is about your size—not quite so tall. He is forty-nine. He is very active. He almost ran along the library to and from his chair. He is a very plain man, to which plainness his squinting materially contributes. His articulation is not distinct. His manner is extremely animated. He seems to be all *esprit*. He frequently folded his arms, and nodded his head in a way which puts me much in mind of Dr. Burney.

August 15.—I could get no farther yesterday. Now for a *bit*—and it will be but a bit—of continuation. The Princes [1] invited us all to dine with them yesterday. Hughes and myself went. Mrs. T. declined the invitation, as she understood there would be a large party of gentlemen, and that she would be the only lady. The party consisted of Prince Ernest, Prince Adolphus, Colonel Maberly, Colonel Linsincke, three other gentlemen who attend the Princes, Mr. Dornford, an Englishman, Hughes, and myself. Prince Adolphus sat at the top of the table; then Hughes,[2] then Prince Ernest, and then myself. A pleasanter dinner, and a dinner of more perfect ease I never was concerned in. An abundance of eating kept us till about 4 o'clock. We sat down to dinner at 2 o'clock. We then had coffee.

We saw the library before dinner and the museum

---

[1] Prince Ernest, Duke of Cumberland and King of Hanover; Prince Adolphus, Duke of Cambridge, sometime Viceroy of Hanover.

[2] Dr. Hughes was Preceptor to George III.' three younger sons at Kew and Windsor.

after dinner.   Prince Ernest would send the coach for
Mrs. T., and so she was drawn by a pair of prancing,
long-tailed 'creams' such as draw our sovereign
lord the King when he meets his great Parliament.
And the coachman was so bestriped with gold lace
that his back dazzled us as we went along.   The
library is a remarkably good one.   The books are
numerous and well chosen, the room in which they
are placed is spacious and handsome, and the rules of
the College render the library as useful as possible to
individuals.   Any student upon making application
to a professor may have any book that he pleases at
his own lodgings.   Having seen all that was to be
seen at the library and museum, and having returned
the visit of a gentleman who had called on us, Mrs. T.
went to the inn; and the Princes and some of the
gentlemen who attend them walked with us round the
ramparts.   Hughes and I supped where we had dined.
A professor, the assistant of Heyne, and another gentleman were added to our party.   The name of the
professor was something like 'Boule,' but I cannot
catch German names with any degree of certainty.
We broke up a little after ten, but not till the Princes
had made me promise that I would endeavour to prevail upon Mrs. T. to dine with them to-day.   We
breakfasted this morning with Mr. Dornford.   We
met a clergyman from Claresthal, a town in that wild
country the Hartz; a gentleman, a German, who
assists Mr. Heyne in index-making and so forth; a
physician, Mr. Loftus, the son of Lord Loftus, of Ire-

land, his tutor, and I think two other gentlemen ; Mrs. T. was of our party.

At 11 o'clock Mr. Dornford, Hughes, and myself paid a visit to Mr. Heyne. He was in his outward study, which he quitted to receive us in a sort of ante-room. In his inner study, which we went into, is a bed. He is a married man, and has one son and two daughters that I heard of. How many more he may have I know not. Our conversation was principally about the Princes. I found an opportunity, however, to inform him that I had a brother who meant to publish very soon a translation of Aristotle's Poetics. I was going on, but the little man, who seemed glad to receive any literary information, said, in his quick way, 'And with a long commentary ? ' I replied, ' Yes, a very long one.' He said he was glad to hear it, for a work of that kind was much wanted. I met him afterwards at the Princes' house, and a few words more passed upon the same subject.

I rather fancied that these short conversations might dispose him to be more desirous of getting your book than he otherwise would have been. This professor Heyne is a surprising man. He was a weaver. At the age of about 29 he commenced his life of study. Till that time he did not know that such a person as Horace or Virgil existed. From the time his studies commenced he has been indefatigable. It is the custom of this country to rise and to begin to study at 3 o'clock in the morning. The general law of the library and the direction of all matters which concern it are left entirely to Heyne. This part of his duty makes it necessary for him to engage in a very extensive correspondence to every part of Europe. He reads three or four lectures every day. The distribution of prizes (something like exhibitions) is entrusted entirely to him. He has to examine and adjudge. Besides this, there is a seminary of which he has the entire care, and at this time he has the occasional examination of the Princes. You may suppose that circumstances out of the common established form of business will frequently occur, in consequence of which the great director Heyne must be consulted. These are all public occupations. His private studies and private literary labours are such as seem sufficient to occupy every part of any man's time. He has a new edition of Virgil almost ready for publication. He showed us the volumes that are already printed. There will be many engravings in this edition. Prince Ernest has promised to send a set over for me by the King's messenger as soon as the work is published. In my way from Mr. Heyne's I called at Dietrich's. He is the Payne of Göttingen, but his shop is not like Payne's. The booksellers here keep scarcely any books but such as are in sheets. One cannot travel comfortably along the shelves as one does in London. The shop seems as if it belonged to a stationer rather than a bookseller. I have made but a very few purchases ; but I have settled matters with Dietrich in such a manner that, if I should at any time want to get books from Göttingen, I may do so without the mediation of Elmsley, whom Dietrich is as much dissatisfied with as you can be.

We all dined with the Princes. Mrs. T. was placed between Prince Ernest and Prince Adolphus. I was stationed as before by the side of Prince Ernest. Captain Linsing was on my right : a very entertaining man. Professor Fischer was the only gentleman, except the usual attendants, who dined with us. Mrs. T.'s apprehensions of ceremony and of the awkwardness of being the only lady were soon removed. Nothing could be more easy or pleasant. The manner of conducting a dinner in this country is admirable. There is not any of that bustle or confusion which attends almost every large dinner party in England : everything proceeds quietly and methodically. The only thing that any person sitting at the table helps to, is soup. Every other dish is handed round in its due course by a servant. If the dish requires any carving, the servant takes it to a side table, carves a small plateful of it, and hands that plate about to every person at the table. If it is a dish that requires no carving at all, the dish itself is handed about ; so that, in the course of the dinner, you are sure of having the contents of every dish presented at your elbow, and you may either take or reject, as you please. The Germans eat of a vast variety of dishes. At the Princes' house the wine was not set upon the table, as it usually is ; but it was called for, as in England. The servants always wait till the dessert is finished ; Colonel Maloeta then draws (in a snug way, though it did not escape my

observation) the napkin from his button-hole ; this
is taken by Prince Ernest as a signal for rising.   He
handed Mrs. T. into the adjoining room, where we
had coffee, after which the Prince again handed Mrs.
T. to her, or rather to his, carriage, for he very politely sent his prancing ' creams ' for us.

Before we went away, he made us all promise to
dine with him again to-day.   It is the Duke of York's
birthday.   He asked me to sup with him last night,
but I made my excuse.   Sufficient for the day was
the good thereof.   We were engaged to drink tea
with Mr. Loftus, the son of Lord Loftus, of Ireland,
and with Mr. Clarke, his tutor.   He is a clergyman.
They very obligingly had asked such persons to meet
us as they thought we should best like to see, and
particularly some ladies, that Mrs. T. might not
remain without female acquaintance.   A word or two
about those of the party whom I could at all make
out.   As I think it well worth while to see everything,
I shall conclude that you will think it worth while to
hear everything.   Professor Tring, his wife, and three
or four daughters.   Professor Tring is sub-librarian.
Whatever title a man has, his wife bears the same, only
with the feminine termination, which is I believe *in*, so
that it is Professor Tring, and Professorin Tring, and
it is highly necessary to give the lady her title.   Miss
Schlözer was the principal object of our curiosity.   She
is about nineteen or twenty, the daughter of Professor
Schlözer.   Her father has taken particular pains with
her, and she has made an uncommon progress in her

studies. She understands seven or eight languages, is deep in natural philosophy, has applied herself even to anatomy. She is musical withal, has travelled to Italy, and is at the same time a workwoman, and acquainted with domestic business. She has received her Doctor's degree, after having been regularly examined by the famous Professor Michaelis. The most curious part of the story is, that her bust is placed in the public library! But to proceed with our company. Baron Speck and his tutor. He is a student; his estate lies on the finest part of the Rhine, near Bingen. Mountains for the sublime, vineyards for the benefit of his pocket. I could not help looking at the young baron, as if he were more picturesque than other men, because his estate was more picturesque than theirs.—Dr. Crichton,[3] a Scotchman, a very modest, sensible young man; I like him vastly. There were three or four other young men, whom I could not well make out.

Our party broke up about eight. Mr. Dornford spent the evening with us. This morning we received and paid visits. I have called upon professors whose names I cannot remember; at Dietrich's I had a good lounge. We went again to the public library, and saw some very good prints. The collection is numerous, and the time that we could bestow upon it was insufficient. We dined with the Princes, and in addition to their usual party met Dr. Züss. I know

---

[3] Afterwards Sir Alexander Physician to Emperor of Russia. He was living in London in 1856.

not how these good people spell their names. As it
was the Duke of York's birthday, a particular kind of
glass [4] with a cover to it was handed about. The
person to whom the glass is first given holds it out
to the person who is to drink next. That second
person takes off the cover and keeps it till the first
person has emptied the glass, and till it is brought to
him filled with wine. He then puts on the cover, and
holds the glass forth to the next drinker. This ceremony is repeated till the glass has gone round. We
eat mutton cutlets, French beans, smoked pork (a
thing they call *würst*), and pickled herrings all at
once. Is it not a curious mixture? I promise you
it is a very good one.

We had again a pleasant day. I was only concerned at our not being able to hear Heyne's Latin
lecture upon the laws of Sparta. He sent to a friend
of ours an invitation to Hughes and myself. It was
a Latin invitation, and he mentioned the subject.

The Prince's preceptor promised to take us in good
time. But, alas! the lecture was over as soon as the
dinner. I have had the satisfaction of hearing that
Heyne knew how the case really was, and therefore
threw no blame upon us.

After dinner I went again to Dietrich's, and to a
map shop, and to the riding house, where I saw the
Princes and their party prepare for an afternoon's
ride. Prince Ernest says that his principal delight is
in riding. He wished me to tell him how much it

* The Loving Cup! familiar to the present age.—1885.

would·cost to keep a pack of hounds in England. Prince Adolphus asked if I did not supply the E. I. Co. with tea. Upon my return to the inn with Mr. Dornford, I found two of the daughters of Professor Tring, Mr. Loftus, and Mr. Clarke with Mrs. T. When their visit was over, we took a walk upon the ramparts. Mr. Dornford and Dr. Crichton have been with us this evening. The Princes asked me to sup with them, but I declined it; and they have also invited us to dine with them to-morrow, but this we shall be obliged to decline, for Hughes, Dr. Crichton, and myself are going into that wild country, the Hartz, to see the King's silver mines. As it will probably be an expedition of considerable fatigue, without any such sight as will make a lady amends for so great an exertion, Mrs. T. is to remain in Göttingen till our return. She is to be introduced to-morrow to Mrs. Heyne, and to some other ladies; and on Monday she is engaged to the learned Miss Schlözer. Mr. Heyne has promised to give me a list of such of the Leipsic or Göttingen books as are best worth our having. I hope to see him again upon my return from the Hartz. I have not mentioned Prince Augustus.[5] He has been for some time extremely ill, and is still far from recovered. I sat an hour by his bedside. He was in high spirits, but I believe he talked more than·he should have done. His physicians visited him whilst I was in the room. I heartily wish him well, for he is a young man, of

---

[5] Prince Augustus, Duke of Sussex.

M

whom those who are the best judges speak highly. And now, good-night, for it is late, and I must be up early. If you knew how much my time was taken up by circumstances which engage my curiosity you would excuse the blunders with which my letters may abound.

.Your affectionate brother, R. T.

GERMANY.—THE HARTZ.—RAMELSBERG.—DESCENT OF A MINE.—A TURKISH BATH..

R. T. to T. T.

Isleworth, Sept. 18, 1788.

Dear Brother,—

My last letter to you was from Göttingen, was it not? But I think it was before I had made an excursion into the Hartz, the Hercynian Forest. A part of it belongs to our King as Elector of Hanover, and he has some mines in it, silver mines as they are called, though I think by a *mineral* license or bounce, for out of a hundredweight of ore they do not get more than half an ounce of silver. But they get other things that are worth having ; such as copper, lead, vitriol, &c. It is a wild country, abounding with fir forests, with firs of such a height that, when you are near and upon a level with the ground they spring from, it is breakneck work to look at their heads, and yet sometimes, in travelling over the mountains, I looked down upon the tops of these tall

firs in the valley. We slept at Clausthal. It joins to
Zellerfelt, and, taken together, they form a big-looking
and a most odd-looking town of, I suppose, a mile and
a half in length. It is in the midst of our King's part
of the Hartz, and is wholly possessed by those who are
concerned in the mines. The houses are all of wood,
even to the roof, and as wood is cheap and paint dear
scarcely any part of any house is painted. We had a
letter of introduction to Baron Töcbra, who showed us
his museum, and abundance of civilities, and treated
us with some excellent tokay. We went down one
mine at Clausthal. Hughes had never been in a
mine, and he made his descent in fear and trembling.
He declared that he enjoyed the sight, but I believe
his joy was at the greatest height when he found
himself safe above ground. Nothing, he said, should
tempt him to go into another mine. He embraced,
and held fast by, that most genuine principle of anti-
curiosity, that having seen one mine he could have a
very good idea of all other mines. Neither my
curiosity nor that of Dr. Crichton, who accompanied
us, could be contented with our prebendary's doctrine,
so he returned to Göttingen, and the Doctor and I
proceeded to the Ramelsberg, near Goslar. The Baron
had assured us that this mine was infinitely better
worth seeing than that of Clausthal, and he very
civilly sent a note over the evening before our
excursion to it, that everything might be prepared for
our seeing it to the greatest advantage. You cannot
think what a civil, what a *pleasantly* civil, man this

Baron was. He sent us about in his own carriage to see the smelting-houses and all the above-ground operations at Clausthal.

And so the Doctor and I proceeded to the Ramelsberg. The road was so very mountainous, so very stony, and so very bad, that we were advised by all means to leave our own carriage behind at Clausthal, and to proceed in one of the rough vehicles of the country. And how do you imagine they contrived in the midst of all these difficulties and dangers to drive and to manage this carriage of ours ? It had four wheels and was open in front. It was drawn by two stout horses, one before the other. The driver rode sideways, without saddle, upon the first horse, whose bridle he never touched. The shaft horse, upon whom we seemed most materially to depend, was left to his own discretion. Nobody held him, nobody was within reach of holding him. We concluded, however, that all this, which certainly seemed strange to us and not a little perilous, was *done according to the custom of the country*, and therefore we acquiesced, and it all did vastly well, and we arrived safe, after a fine wild ride, at the Ramelsberg. To avoid a considerable *détour* in our carriage, which had shaken us so much that we were glad to quit it, we walked a walk that afforded us a singular kind of view. We crossed a hill of moderate height ; it was as green as living grass could make it. The grass was separated by hedges, and the hill was altogether sufficiently *finished*, even for the most finished scenery of this country. On one·

side were mountains, some of them clothed with firs,
on the other side, and near, was all the 'infernal' scenery
of the Ramelsberg, all the horrid apparatus, and all
the incumbent barrenness and desolation of a mine.
In front, the little green hill on which we stood
sloped gradually into the sombre town of Goslar.

At Ramelsberg we found everything prepared for
us. Preparations had also been made for Hughes,
but, alas ! he was not of our party, which I was, and
still am, sorry for, as he lost a sight which was far better
worth seeing than any other in the mining way I ever
beheld. . Having seen the works upon the face of the
earth, the various machines which are made use of, and
some neat models of them, we took—all habited like
miners as we were—to the ladders. I must do all the
ladders which I met with in the Hartz the justice to say
that they are much more strong and secure than those
in Cornwall. Our whole descent was about six hundred .
feet. We walked along a curious passage or gallery
which extended above a thousand feet. The walls and
roof were in many places dyed most beautifully by the
vitriol. Green icicles, for so they seemed, hung above
our heads. At the side of our gallery were occasionally
openings or caverns. In all the copper mines that I
had seen the rock had been blasted by gunpowder,
in order to pursue and get at the vein of ore. At the
Ramelsberg the rock is of such a nature that, when it
is hot, it is easily knocked down by the help of crows
and hammers. This mine then is worked by fire. In
the first cavern that we visited we found the pile

exactly in the form of a funeral pile (see Kennet, &c.) prepared for lighting. The torch was applied to the dry billets and in a few minutes all was in a blaze. The height of the cavern was about eight feet. The flame spread over the roof; it was like a great reverberatory furnace; I never beheld such mad ungovernable fire. We were quickly forced to quit the cavern and to get to some distance in a passage which looked into it. It was a sublime sight. Having viewed one or two other caverns of, what is deemed, moderate heat, we were asked if we would choose to proceed to heat in the extreme. I always choose to see everything, and Dr. Crichton's curiosity seemed to equal mine, so on we went. Having proceeded some way we arrived at two benches. We were desired to sit down, not for the sake of rest or refreshment, but to be well inured to the heat of *that* spot, that we might be able to bear the greater heat which was to come. We stopped there till we were parboiled, till every corporeal sluice was set ajar. Being thus qualified, we continued our walk till we arrived at the ultimate object of our labour. It was a cavern far hotter than any we had passed through. The men who worked in it, and, indeed, almost all the men who worked in any part of this mine, were naked excepting a leathern bag, as an improvement upon the fig-leaf, and a leathern flap to protect them *à posteriori*, when they might have occasion to sit down upon the hard rock. These poor men seemed to be in a state of absolute dissolution. Each man had a knife fastened to the girdle of his flap, and with it he occasionally scraped off the rivers of sweat (for it would be absurd to describe such streams by the delicate phrase of perspiration) which poured from the crown of his head to the soles of his feet. I had nothing to do but to stand still and look on, and yet they were not 'big, round *drops*,' which 'coursed one another down my *innocent* nose,' but a good, continued *sweat-course*, which in its progress received ample augmentations from every pore in my body. The miners were employed in knocking down, with iron crows and hammers, those parts of the roof and sides of the cavern which had been sufficiently loosened by the fire. There was something frightful in this employment, when one considered the load of mountain which was above us, and which they seemed, as far as it might be in their power, to endeavour to bring about our heads. It appeared impossible to know how far the effects of the fire might have extended, what already loose parts of the rock might be above those which the fire had loosened, or, in short, how much every stroke of the crow or hammer might bring down.

The miners continue below and at work for eight hours at a time. I inquired what they had to drink, for it was evident that such copious discharges must be copiously supplied. The answer was 'Nothing but cold water.' I saw one poor man, in his most liquefied state, squat down and drink lustily out of a barrel of cold water. The water that they drink is kept at some distance from the cavern in which they work, it would otherwise soon be too hot to afford them any refreshment.

Having satisfied our curiosity, and having really endured almost as much as we were able to endure alive, we returned to our quondam resting-place that had been heated, so we might be cooled by degrees. There we had leisure to ask questions. The pay of the miners per week is regulated, so we were told, by the quantity of work which they perform. We were assured that they lived to a good old age, yet I rather suspect that instances of longevity are rare. The children of the miners are, at first, employed above ground, in preparing and washing the ore, &c.; at about the age of fifteen they are admitted into the mine, where they are set about the least trying and least laborious part of the work, till by degrees they are admitted to the hot honours of the burning caverns. And, I warrant you, the little black rogues reckon eagerly upon every advancement, that they exult when they quit the fair light of the sun to accompany their fathers into the regions beneath.

We stopped in one cave that was larger than the rest. It was of a circular form ; its diameter was, I suppose, about one hundred feet. The roof was supported by three or four large pillars, that had been left out of the solid rock. Our conductor placed some of his naked men, with uplifted torches in their hands, against different parts of the wall of this cavern, so that the whole was illumined, and in the most characteristic way possible. It was a scene that would have delighted the soul of Salvator Rosa.

Your affectionate brother,   R. T.

(IN CONTINUATION.)

Isleworth, Sept. 20, 1788.

Dear Brother,—I believe I left you in the Ramelsberg ; and unless you have a *goût décidé* for mines, which I do not suspect, you will be glad to get above ground. I had prudently provided myself with a complete change of linen, which, charged as the linen was that I had on, was a real luxury. Our good guide had also taken care to have some slices of *würst* (an excellent German dish, a sort of huge sausage made of something like highly smoked ham), and a glass of wine ; so that we soon recovered from the fatigue of our descent. We then made our bow, paid our fee, and crossed the green hill to our carriage. We dined at Clausthal, and returned to Göttingen. It was past two in the morning before we arrived there, and as we had been up at four the preceding morning, you will readily conceive that both the Doctor and myself were somewhat tired.

Mrs. T. had not accompanied us. It was not an expedition for ladies ; and as she was by no means without acquaintance at Göttingen, and she had her own attentive Joseph with her, I had no doubt but she would pass the two or three days that we were

likely to be absent pleasantly enough ; and so she
did.   She would have declined dining with the.
Princes, but the good Colonel urged her going in so
kind a way that she knew not how to refuse, and
the whole party behaved so as to prevent her wanting
such support as Hughes or myself might have afforded.   One day, when she was not well enough
to go out, the Colonel requested she would send to
the Princes' table for soup or anything she might
like.   I mention these things because they are such
instances of real attention and kindness as are not
often met with in a strange country ; and not to
have been pleased with them, and not to have
pleasure in remembering and mentioning them, would
be abominable.

Mrs. T. drank tea one afternoon with Professor Tra-
ber and his lady.   There she met the Princes, and Mr.
Dormer, the minister of Clausthal, and his wife and
daughter.   Another afternoon she drank tea with Mrs.
Heyne ; and a third afternoon she had a party of professors' ladies and daughters to drink tea with her,
amongst the rest the learned Miss Schlözer.   She drank
tea one afternoon with Mrs. Schlözer.   Nor were
beaux wanting ; for besides the gentlemen of the
Princes' establishment, Mr. Dornford, Mr. Loftus, and
Mr. Clarke were always ready to render any service
in their power to the English lady.   When Mrs. T.
drank tea with Mrs. Heyne, she did not see the.
professor.   Mrs. Heyne said she seldom saw him, except at meals.   She said also that, much as he had to

do, he scarcely ever appeared, even in the smallest
degree, tired. He usually gets up and begins his
studies at four; never later than five. Upon my return from the Hartz I paid my *prendre congé* visits;
amongst the rest, one to Professor Heyne. I had,
indeed, resolved, if it were possible, to see him again
before I left Göttingen. I found him at home, and
had a most comfortable conversation with him. My
principal object was, to find some fair opportunity of
talking a little more about you and your work, and I
succeeded to my utmost wish; and now you will perhaps ask, as my wife always does upon similar occasions, 'Well, what did *you* say? and what did *he*
say?' But I really cannot tell you in the identical
words that passed what either of us said. I spoke
favourably, yet modestly, of you. I felt a zeal and
an affection which seemed to engage his attention;
and, indeed, I told him to remember that I was
speaking of a brother. I concluded by requesting
that he would give me leave to send him a copy of
your book as soon as it was published. He thanked
me, and has told me in what manner I may send it.
He was happy, he said, to have made my *connoissance*.
I was happy to have made his; and so we parted.
As to my promise of sending him your book, I should
readily - do, you see?—give it to him upon his own
account; the respect that I have for him would easily
carry me so far.. But the truth is I felt another inducement to make the promise and the present.
Though Heyne is not the man whose judgment is to

be biassed in any blamable way by what any other man says or gives, yet almost everything may be seen in a more or less favourable light, and perhaps every man is disposed at particular times, and in consequence, it may be, of seemingly trivial circumstances, to form more favourable opinions than he would do at other times, and under other circumstances. And I think it is possible that the circumstances under which Heyne will now open and read your book will be more favourable than they would have been if he had never heard either of your name or your book till, it might be, some time after the publication, when chance threw them both together in his way. But if all this should be an absurd fancy of mine, yet it is at least certain that Heyne may now have an opportunity of reading your book sooner than he otherwise would have done. If he reads, I am confident that he will approve—nay, no affected modesty—and if he approves, as he corresponds with learned men in every country in which they are to be found, and probably has a more extensive correspondence of this kind than any other man in the world, who is so likely to make your book known in the world as Heyne? Besides, when I send the book, I shall write to him. If you should wish me to say anything particular to him, I can say it. Or if you should wish to correspond with him yourself, I fairly can, and readily will, introduce you. And now I shall only add that I hope you will approve, or at least not disapprove, what I have done.

.Heyne produced Dr. Parr's preface, with the portraits, dedications, &c., in the original twelve-shilling publication. He said that Dr. Parr must have read a great deal; and that he seemed to have a wonderful memory, and a great aptitude in bringing together, and aptly tacking together, such passages from the different authors he had read as at any time suited his purpose. But it was evident that this was not the sort of writing, not the sort of Latin, that Heyne most prized. He applied to it the epithet *consu.* He smiled, too, at the enigmatical vowels at the bottom of the dedications; though of the dedications themselves he thought very highly. And now we will for the present take leave of Professor Heyne. I will not suppose that you have had too much of his company, or that you would have wished me to suppress any anecdotes relating to him.

I think I have not yet introduced you to Professor Lichtenberg. He is deformed, but a great beau. I found him in a long morning-gown, and *coiffé à merveillé.* His head is out of all proportion to the rest of his frame; and with his great face he makes the prettiest, softest smile you ever saw. On his chair he always has a pillow or cushion, which affords him relief. He is Professor of Natural Philosophy, and I was assured that he is an excellent professor, and particularly expert at experiments. Not like good old Mr. H——, whose experiments always failed; and then, when he would account for their failure; his tongue failed. If I wanted to give any person who had never seen a litter a complete idea of a complete litter, I would take him to Professor Lichtenberg's rooms. A great variety of apparatus was spread about in the most improbable and accidental way possible ; and all those common pieces of furniture which usually have places and uses assigned to them seemed to be applied, by the professor, to all uses indiscriminately, and to have an equal right to all places. Again, the professor is a man of infinite humour. Fun is his delight. He is the author of the 'Dissertation on Hogarth's Cuts' in the little German almanack that I sent you. He speaks English tolerably well, and was extremely civil. It could scarcely be in return for any service that we had rendered him ; for though one of the hydrometers which we carried over (you know Hughes would look at them at Fordham) was intended for him, we contrived to break both of them, or, at least, both of them were broken, before we reached Göttingen.

For reasons both of convenience and policy I shall here make an end, for the present, of all travelling information. I cannot conveniently proceed, just now, in the history of my progress ; and satiated, as you must be, with the literary intelligence, the *fried tripe*, of Göttingen, it would be impolitic to set before you the insipidities, the mere *boiled leg of lamb*, of Cassel.

I shall be glad to receive your preface. I will read it ; I will say what I think about it ; and I will return it. As you have pleased both yourself and

Dr. Forster, it is not very probable that I should find anything to criticise. I have no objection to your title-page. You say 'with notes on the translation and on the original.' Do you put the translation first because the notes are principally on the translation, or to gratify your *ear*? It might, otherwise, be thought better and more modest to put the original first. Abroad, notes on the original will be more catching, more inviting, than notes on the translation; and it might therefore be well to prevent the abroaders from imagining that notes on the original have only the second place. Thus have I told you, in one breath, that I have no objection to your title; and in the next, if not in the very same breath, I come forward with something like an objection. You have it, however, just as it occurred.

As to your personal description, I scarcely know what to say. That *I* dislike the additions of rector, vicar, and so forth, is most certain. A.M. at the end of a name that is not already known in the literary world may do good. It is a proof that a man has been in the way of getting knowledge, of qualifying himself for literary labour; and I think it probable that, in your case, such an addition might do good abroad. It cannot do harm anywhere: I say *in your case*, because your name, though it is sufficiently known amongst the learned men of this country, is not, I apprehend, much known amongst those of other countries; and therefore it may be as well to appear with the little testimonial of A.M. You are

A.M., are you not? Mr. Mason's name has been known, in *his* way, even from his youth upwards ; so that he might have left out even the little addition which he makes use of. Mr. Potter's translations are, I conceive, calculated, more exclusively than your translation, for the readers, both learned and unlearned, of this country.

There, I think I have now answered those parts of your letter which required an answer. To do this is like paying a debt, balancing an account, starting clear with the world.

My brother John and his wife set off yesterday, *viâ* Tunbridge Wells, for Margate. They have very good-naturedly taken Richard [6] with them. He has been extremely attentive to business, and I was glad that so promising and proper an excursion came in his way. The *first* thing of its kind is usually (provided it be of a good kind) delicious. It would have delighted you to see what a high idea Richard entertained of this, his first journey. He embarked, as if he had some hereditary and decided *goût* for travelling. He studied Paterson's 'Road-book' as if the way to Tunbridge had been hard to find. I hope they will have good weather. My good friend, John Hingeston, is at Margate ; and I have not a child, from John to Mary, who is not glad to be where John Hingeston is. [7]

Hughes is keeping his residence at Worcester. I

---

[6] An early and pleasant testimony to my good father's diligence in business and relish for a well-earned holiday.—R. T., 1886.

[7] See notes pp. 109 and 148.

have had two letters from him. In his first letter he says, 'A residence at Worcester, *sans famille*, is a dull business. There is a brother prebendary here, however, who gives me dinners and suppers.' In his second he says, 'I have been ordering a dinner for the minor canons. I wish you could see me order a dinner.' If Hughes had no assistance, it must have been a curious dinner indeed.

Brother, you may remember that Dr. Forster promised to pay me a visit at Isleworth, after our return from foreign parts. You may remember, too, that when I mentioned your accompanying him, you said not absolutely nay. Mark, then, what I have to propose, and communicate the proposal to the good doctor.

My brother John and his wife will probably spend the month of October at Margate. During their absence I must be confined to town, and therefore my proposition goes over to November. I propose, then, your coming to us with the doctor in November. Be not afraid of the sound of that month. I have plenty of wine in my cellar, and a good stock of coals in my coal-hole, and I warrant you shall find Isleworth as warm as Colchester. You cannot plead Aristotle against me ; and, in short, I hope you will not find anything to plead, but that, in your reply, you will answer roundly for Dr. F. and yourself, 'We hope to be with you early in November.'

And thus ends my long batch of scribbling. Let it serve to convince you that, when I feel somewhat

N

disengaged from the cares and attentions of business, I am happy to renew that sort of correspondence and intercourse with you which proved one of the greatest comforts of the more leisure part of my life.

My wife and Mary join with me in love to my sister and yourself. Mary thanks you for your letter, and for the trouble which you have had about her translations. But she will thank you more at length herself. She is now reading some of Voltaire's tragedies; and I· mean that she should read some of Racine's and Corneille's. I suppose she cannot go amiss?   Your affectionate Brother,

R. T.

(IN CONTINUATION) GÖTTINGEN.—PROFESSOR HEYNE.
—DOROTHEA SCHLÖZER.

Sept. 22, 1788.

I had just finished my account when I received your letter; and I will here answer that part of it which relates in any way to Heyne. I am much pleased to think that I have prepared the way for your writing to him. You will see that I have already mentioned such a thing, and, indeed, I wished with a hearty wish that the opportunity might not be lost. As to the gift of the book, I care not a farthing, from any pecuniary consideration, whether you give it or I give it; but there are better reasons than golden reasons for your giving it: your insisting upon your right as author of the book to supplant me in my promise

of giving the book, would alone serve as your sufficient introduction ; and perhaps, as the book will be
some time in getting to Göttingen, you may as well,
when all is printed and ready, send Heyne's copy before you publish to the world in general. And yet
there may be objections against this, though I do not
see them. Heyne reads English, but he does not
speak it. Our conversation was in French, but he does
not speak good French ; or rather, he does not pronounce French well. Your letter must certainly be in
Latin. I am glad I bought the very book which you
wished I should buy. You see there are three volumes.
I read, and was much pleased with some of the dissertations in the first volume ; and I fancied that I saw
some things which touched your work. I have a
notion that I dog's-eared the bottom corners at those
places. You will observe that these volumes are
amongst the books which I meant you should some
time or other return : for I have not put *T.* before Twining ; but I beg you would now put the
T. and keep the books ; and you can lend them to
me, which will do just as well. I would, indeed, have
bought two sets at Göttingen, but I had already as
many books as we could well carry, or as I thought the
officers would allow me to bring in without the pass
of a regular entry. Besides, I have paved the way
for a correspondence with Dietricht.

Miss Schlözer is, I assure you, a well-looking young
woman ; not a beauty, indeed, but animated and
pleasing. I described the Irish bishop's daughter,

though I could not recollect her name, as a sort of counterpart to Miss Doctor Schlözer.

I suppose you have received a box of books, &c.; and it may be as well to say a word or two about them. If I should repeat anything that I have already said, you will pardon me; for you know I write much, and usually in a hurry. I beg you would keep the Apollodorus; I think you had not that book. And the *Dramaturgie*, which I picked up by chance in a bookseller's shop at Lille; in which shop I had an amusing conversation with a spruce abbé and another Frenchman. I know nothing about the book; but it seemed to be full of Aristotle, and Diderot, and so to be in your way. If it should be *only* in your way, away with it. Keep also the dissertation on Greek poetry, which also I know nothing about; and 'L'Ami de la Maison.' Pulter's 'History of the Göttingen University,' in German, and two German almanacks, are to be used as recreations during your study of the German language. Lichtenberg's 'Account of Hogarth's Prints' may possibly make a good lesson for you. I have another portrait of Miss Schlözer, so keep that which I have sent to you. Heyne's 'Opuscula' I have already desired you to add to the T. T. list; so put a T. to it; or if you write Thomas at full length, it will, you know, be, as you say it ought to be, Thomas *Tandem* Twining. You see I am in a silly mood. Let that convince you I am better. I have sent my own purchases, as I thought you would like to look at them. Indeed, I brought over the first three volumes of Heyne's new edition of Virgil, as I thought you would wish to see it as soon as possible. There is a new preface and much new matter. The fourth volume and the cuts are not ready; but Prince Ernest has promised, when they are ready, to send them to me. You will see what a shabby thing a bookseller's catalogue is in Germany; and a bookseller's shop is the most uncomfortable thing imaginable. Everything is in sheets ; it looks like the shop of a stationer. I bought the Encycl. des Enfans for the children ; but I saw, after I had bought it, that the editor had been kind enough to convert the errors of the Reformed Church into the orthodoxies of the Catholic. Not that it much signifies, as it is not a book to glean religion from. The list of publications at Göttingen and Leipsic was written by Heyne on purpose for me ; and though his handwriting is not famous, yet, inasmuch as it is *his* handwriting, I value it. I should have bought a few more books from Heyne's list if I had well known what to do with them. If there should be any that you much wish for and that you cannot get in England, I will open my correspondence with Dietricht. The paper about *West-feld* was stuck up when I was at Göttingen. I read it through a grate, and was vastly pleased with it. It was written by Heyne, though it bears another name. Is it not admirably well done ? If the young man is made of penetrable stuff it must do him good. Mr. Dornford saw how much I was delighted with this small composition, and he very obligingly procured me a

printed copy of it, and also a copy of the learned
Michael's testimonial in favour of Dr. Schlözer.   There
are two portraits—one of Lavater, and another of
Professor Blumenbach.   To conclude, there is a sort
of farewell memorandum card written and signed by
Miss Schlözer.   She has a book, a sort of album, in
which her friends write or draw something, and sign
their names.   Heyne appears in it, and several other
professors.   Some, a few, seemed to quote aptly ; the
greater part, as might be expected, but indifferently.
Miss. S. took Mrs. T. in most completely.   She said
she would send her her book.   Mrs. T. thankfully acquiesced, imagining this learned lady had published
some book which she meant to give her.   The next
day the book came, and soon afterwards Miss S.,
who, I believe, expected that both Hughes and myself, as well as Mrs. T., would join the throng.   Hughes,
however, declared that he would not for the world
do so silly a thing.   Not that he has any objection
to silly things in general, but this struck him as
being of inadmissible silliness.   As H. did not write,
I did not.   If he had been silly, I should have been
silly.   I should have felt the necessity of being so.[8]
Mrs. T. could not escape, for the word of promise
was gone forth ; and Miss S. gave her to understand
that the exchange of remembrance, in form of a card,
was ready for her.   And so Mrs. T. is to live in manu-
script with the mighty Heyne.   I will be bound to

---

[8] 'Birthday books' and solicitations for autographs were evidently
not in vogue in the last century.—R. T., 1886.

say you long to know what she wrote. It was no more than this : '" Remember me "—Ghost in Hamlet,' and her name. I had almost forgot Heyne's servant. He is a fine steady old boy, who has lived with him this long while ; and he fashions in wax and sells small heads of his master. I am told that he sometimes hits them off tolerably well. I would have bought one, but that which I saw—and he had no other—was utterly unlike. 'We are very busy, sir, with our Virgil ;' 'I believe our Virgil will be out in a month.' Such is the language of Heyne's trusty servant.

Prince Ernest (for I give you anecdotes, since you seem to like them, just as they occur, without re-spect of persons)—Prince Ernest undertook to show us a most beautiful walk. Of the walk itself I cannot say much. The country all about Göttingen is unen-tertaining. The spot to which we walked was really worth seeing. It had a picturesque wildness about it that is not often met with near habitations upon the Continent. The objects were a spring, which rose amidst some overhanging trees, and a mill which the spring was soon strong enough to turn. Our party consisted of the two princes, two of their gentlemen, Mr. Dornford, Hughes, and myself. Prince Adolphus, who is so stout that he does not easily keep pace with his brother, hung back with me. He caught hold of my arm (is it not a fine ennobling thing to have a prince with his star take hold of one's arm ?) and talked with unceasing rapidity till we reached Göttingen. He told me that he hoped to serve in the cavalry, and therefore he wished to see as much as possible about horses.   That he had lately been present at the operations of docking, nicking, &c., and of all these operations he gave me a circumstantial account. Prince Ernest gave Mrs. T. a bottle of attar of roses. I gave him one of Gray's mirrors, with which he was much pleased.   And I am to send Prince Adolphus a steel watch-chain ; and to procure for Prince Augustus, who is a young mineral collector, a specimen of tin ore from Cornwall.   Before I came away I was invited to pay the princes a visit next summer—a thing that I am not very likely to do, unless, forsooth, you should correspond yourself into such a regard for Heyne that you must needs go to Göttingen to see him ; and with you I would go anywhere.   I believe I have often given you fair reason to conclude that I had almost done with Göttingen and everything belonging to it. I have said 'Before I conclude,' 'Before I quit Göttingen,' and so forth ; and yet after such phrases I have, as it were, started afresh.   You divines are apt to treat your congregations in this way ; and as you expect to be forgiven, forgive.

From Göttingen—there, I am actually off—we went to Cassel, which is said to be the handsomest town in Germany.   The ride to it is capital—I believe better than anything we had seen.   Near Minden (Hanover Minden, not the battle Minden) the country was something like our Henley.

' PREFACE TO HIS 'ARISTOTLE.' [*]

The Rev. T. T. to R. T.

Fordham, Oct. 22, 1788.

Dear Brother,—As time is too precious to be wasted in repetition, I shall refer you for my thanks to the packet which you will receive, containing no less than five sheets of scribble, and all about this poor mangled preface of mine.

> Look ! in this place ran Elmsall's dagger through :
> See what a rent the envious Forster made !
> Through this the well-beloved Richard stabbed, &c.

Well, it is all for its good.

> Per damna, per cædes, ab ipso
> Ducit opes animumque ferro
> Non Hydra secto corpore firmior, &c.

But while I think of it let me tell you that Hey and Elmsall have not seen my preface, as you seem to think. I only consulted them as to some particular bits that would come within a letter. I gave Elmsall a sort of table of contents and the '.Pye' passage. To Dr. Hey I sent the ' P.' passage and the F. page ; he made no objection to either, except the jingle between ' abilities' and 'utility,' which I think I can remove without hurting the passage. . . .

In what you say about ' my ' fame you express exactly my own feelings ; and I believe you say the very

---

[*] I have inserted this letter and the following one to show what pains were taken to send out the ' Aristotle' in the best possible form—not a point, however minute, escaping attention.—R. T., 1886.

truth.. I certainly, therefore, shall keep to ' his.' As to the addition of ' formerly fellow of,' &c. &c., you do not see it in quite the right point of view, at least not in that view in which Dr. Hey advises it. It is not meant to do me *honour*, but as mere *distinction* ; to answer the question, ' What T. T. is this ? ' There are numbers who remember Twining of Sidney, and some of them, perhaps many, would be more likely to buy the book for knowing who wrote it. This is certain, that if I could add anything by way of distinction, individualisation, &c., this addition would answer best. But at present I do not think of adding it. What I should mean as mere description might appear to a reader to be a boast, and then it would be as silly a boast as you think it. I hope you received the index safe. A fine fat index, is it not ? Rather plethoric, I fear; but that is a fault on the right side. . . .

I have been in doubt as to motto or no motto. I have thought of several Greek mottoes that are too quaint or obscure, or something. At last I hit upon a passage in Ammonius's Commentary on a work of Aristotle that would certainly pass, with Greek folks at least, as pat and proper ; it is one by a famous Aristotelic commentator, and it describes what an Aristotelic commentator should do. . . .

Your affectionate Brother,

T. T.

THE LAST TOUCHES TO 'ARISTOTLE.'—A VISIT TO
HARTLEBURY.—BISHOP HURD.—MR. MASON.

R. T. to T. T.

Isleworth, Oct. 25, 1788.

Dear Brother,—I should not answer your last letter
—and a most excellent letter it is—so soon if I had not
worked myself up to fancy that I *do* care about the
manner in which Hurd may be indicated. As soon as
I read your letter I differed from my worthy ally[1] in
the 'Pye' cause, and I agreed with our adversarian
doctor[2] that it ought to be 'Hurd, bishop.' Still I
thought it a matter of no great consequence ; and
having, as you justly say, made a serious attack upon
the main body, I was unwilling to thrust at that little
outwork, the index. But I have seen Hughes, and
consulted him as the bishop's friend. He inclines to
'bishop,' and I have looked at the title to Hurd's
Horace, where I find 'By the Rev. Mr. Hurd.' If,
now, you allude, in the place to which you refer, to
anything in Hurd's Horace, you ought, I think, to
give him either the title which he had when he
published his Horace, or that which he has now.
To take, as it were, the intermediate title of 'doctor'
seems to be wrong. You will say, perhaps, that
though he is bishop he is still doctor. But he is
not to be called doctor. Custom is, I conceive, so
strongly on the *bishop's* side in the present question

[1] Dr. Forster.   [2] Dr. Hey.

that I think I may venture to assert not a single man would object to 'Hurd, bishop,' except Mr. Elmsall, whose objection you have raised by your question. But 'Hurd, doctor,' will, if I am not mistaken, strike many as improper. The bishop himself would say to himself, 'Why should he describe me so?' and as you have in some respects opposed his opinion, it seems advisable to give him that appellation which he and his friends would like best, and which will cost nothing. And now I am on the subject of the Bishop of Worcester I will give you some account of his lordship from Hughes' letter. I am sure it will entertain you. He says, 'I have spent two pleasant days at Hartlebury (the bishop's palace near Worcester). Mason was there yesterday. I had known nothing of him before except by fame ; and "what can you know now?" you will say. I know that he is a maintainer of his own opinion, if he thinks he is right, though in opposition to a bishop. We had one or two disagreements between them on literary matters. The bishop was describing the sound judgment of some author. "Judgment, my lord," quoth the poet, "you are not serious?" "Indeed but I am, Mr. Mason." "I have read his book," quoth the other, "but I could never see any judgment displayed in it." The bishop drew his nose to the sharpness of a razor. I wish you may know that keen look. I knew it exactly. They got to Isaac Barrow next. "What a prodigy that man was, Mr. Mason !" "A clever man, my lord, but no prodigy." "You are hard to please,

Mr. Mason." "I mean," replied Mason, "that there were better writers of his own day than Barrow." "Ay! where will you find one?" "Why, what think you of Jeremy Taylor, my lord?" "Ay, ay, you are right there; but Jeremy Taylor was such a man as half a dozen ages don't produce. Jeremy Taylor was such a being as Shakespeare, and, if he had written plays, could, no doubt, have written as good." The bishop told a story of an old gardener he once had, who would never gather a particular pear before Old Michaelmas Day. It was well told; but his lordship went on, "You see how custom supplies the place of reason." "That's a good story, my lord (saith old Caractacus), with a bad moral." "I mean," says the bishop, not much pleased, "that such customs are almost always founded on experience of their utility." "Now, my lord, you mend your position." We had some good-humoured repartees, too. I was asked "who preached at Kew now?" I answered, "My lord, it is the same man that was curate to Mr. Bellamy, a Mr. Cow, a Scotchman, who married Dr. Wollaston's daughter, but I believe he has changed his name to Cowie, or something like it, to please his wife." "Why, Cow is a comical name for a lady," quoth the bishop, "or for a preacher either." "We had a Bishop *Bull*, my lord," says Mason, "but no *Cow* that I recollect." "But Cow comes from Bull, Mr. Mason, and he should have traced a pedigree." "Yes, and so does Bull from Cow, for the matter of that; but this won't do in heraldry any more than in grammar, my lord ; you have heard me quote the old English grammarian of Beverley on the nature of plurals:

> Two kinds and kindreds both from kind do flow,
> As cows and kine do each proceed from cow ;

but not a word is said of bulls, you see."

'"Ha, ha!" you should have seen the bishop laugh, and cry, "Very well indeed, well indeed, Mr. Mason! our dissertation has brought out some good poetry." "Tom of Beverley, I assure your lordship, was no bad poet if his subject had been a better one. As it is, I suppose his verse is as good for the honour of the English language as the 'quæ genus' or the 'propria quæ maribus.'"'

I am sure that will please Dr. Forster, who is, I know, a warm admirer of those grammar poems, which are so happily calculated to facilitate the study of the Latin language. Hughes adds, 'Mr. Mason told me he had never been near the Anglesea coast, which I was surprised to hear.' A few years ago Hughes and I read 'Caractacus' in Mona and at the foot of Snowdon. We fully thought that Mason as well as Caractacus had been there before us. . . .

I attend your packet, which shall be returned without delay. The index is full, but surely it is all the better for that; an index in which one cannot find what one ought to find is like a direction post without any writing on it. One turns to it in full expectation of being sent forward comfortably, and lo! all is disappointment. The index reads against the French critics. I suppose the fact is, Aristotle was not the right kind of author for them ; that he required more laborious investigation than French critics are apt to bestow.

It is quite possible, nay, probable, that before this letter reaches you the proofs of the index may have been returned to Mr. Day. I can only say that, till I came hither, I did not mean to write at all ; and before I came hither the post was gone. Many things that I have to say to you must remain unsaid till another time.

Your affectionate Brother,

R. T.

MAIL COACH TRAVELLING.—FRENCH LIBERTY, 1789.

Richard Twining to John Hingeston.

Bitteswell, Aug. 30, 1789.

Dear Kingston,—You see I lose no time in thanking you for your letter, which was thrown over the garden wall scarcely an hour ago. That mail coach is a delicious thing ! I mean to those who live at Bitteswell, not to those who travel in it. It comes by every morning a little before nine.[3] Mr. Powell has a bag with his name upon it. His letters are put into the bag whilst they are changing horses at Lutterworth, and the guard, for the sum of one guinea a year, throws it over the wall as he goes by. He blows his horn as soon as he enters the village (at the turnpike gate), and out we all scud in quest of

---

[3] A journey of about thirteen hours from London.

news.[4] Is not this comfortable ? I tell Mr. Powell he will not spend a guinea more wisely than that which he gives to the guard. Then the hour at which the coach arrives is the most convenient possible—just at breakfast. About two or three o'clock the mail returns, and the guard blows his horn again, and takes back the bag with any letters it may contain.

.   .   .   .

I cannot comprehend what the 'Liberty Boys' of France are about. It seems to me as if that country never enjoyed less liberty than at present. That any fellow should have the liberty of hanging me if I do not wear a cockade is a sort of liberty that is not much to my fancy. Under the most rigid exercise of the monarchy I might have lived in or passed through France without hazard, if I had been prudent. Now no amount of prudence would really ensure safety ; a fit of caprice or a blunder might send one to the fatal lamp-post. This spirit of resisting authority seems to be extending itself, and one can scarcely tell where to find symptoms of monarchy except in the republic of Holland.

Mary[5] is much better than she was. The rest of the family are quite well. We dined yesterday with Squire Dicey of Claybrook, the adjoining parish, and a right hospitable squire he is.[6] To-morrow he is to

---

[4] The same practice prevailed until mail coaches were superseded by railways.

[5] Mrs. Powell, his daughter.

[6] The Dicey family lived there for several generations, and have

dine here. We are going this afternoon to return visits. On Tuesday I believe we shall set off for home, where I hope we shall find you well. Do I not write worse than usual? It is owing I suppose to the gilt edge of my paper. 'Do you think we shall ever be able to prevail upon Mr. Hingeston to come to see us at Bitteswell?' is a question that has been put to me. My answer always is, 'I should hope so ; but he is apt you know—and it is the only fault he has—to be ceremonious.' I suppose you have heard from my brother of my downfall? It was not that gentle scramble upon the knee with which your horses now and then treat you, but a thundering overset—such as might have been felt, I conceive, at the Antipodes.[7]

Yours sincerely,   R. T.

VISIT TO DR. PARR.

R. T. to T. T.

Isleworth, Sept. 10, 1789.

Dear Brother,—Here I am alone, and so for a renewal of our correspondence.

Richard [8] and I called upon Dr. Parr in our way

---

been as much distinguished for scholarship and high talents as for social qualities.—R. T., 1886.

[7] I was riding by my father's side between Coton House and Lutterworth, when 'Flounce' fell as if she had been shot.—R. T., 1789.

[8] My father's visit to his former schoolmaster, when Dr Parr

O

from Warwick to Birmingham. I think I have told you that Richard accompanied his mother to Bitteswell ; but I believe I have not told you that in order to show him a little of the world and to give him an indulgence which from his good behaviour both in and out of business, he really deserves, we made a circumbend by Coventry, Warwick, Birmingham, Stratford, and Oxford. The doctor was 'walked out ;' his maid entreated us to 'walk in,' as she said she was sure she could find him in a few minutes. Out she sallied ; but soon returned without the doctor. She then rang a great bell which was loud enough for a church bell. In a few minutes in came ' Jack,'[9] running at a great

was head-master of the High School, Norwich, in 1779.—R. T., 1885.

In February 1824, my father received a letter from Dr. Parr, of which the following are extracts :—

' *Samuel Parr, Hatton, to Richard Twining, Old Boy at Norwich School.*

' The name of Twining has long been endeared to my mind by the intellectual and moral excellences of the persons to whom it belonged. The accomplishments and good sense of your mother will never be forgotten. I have likewise to recall the taste, the wit, the erudition, and the numerous virtues of Thomas Twining (the "country clergyman"). I gladly recognise *Richard* as my old and worthy pupil at Norwich. . . . I am now in my seventy-eighth year, and have little chance of visiting the capital again ; but if you or any one relating to you should bend your course towards Warwickshire, do not be content with giving me a hurrying morning call—take your dinner and your bed at my parsonage. Remember me to your justly-esteemed father. I pray God to bless you. Adieu !

' I am truly your well-wisher and obedient humble servant,

'(Signed) S. PARR.'

R. T., 1885.

[9] The Doctor's pupil.

rate, to know what was the matter ; and at no great
distance behind came the doctor, who had evidently
answered the bell as quickly as he could. His figure
was excellent ; he had on a waistcoat or jacket of
the rough great-coat kind of stuff of which footmen's
jackets are made nowadays. The colour was the
footman's colour. Nothing clerical about it. But
then the doctor had black stockings and breeches and
a wig—which, though it was reduced by age, was still
a great wig—and a sort of dignified hat, the sides of
which were bent back on the crown. Such was the
doctor—heated and out of breath ; but he was right
glad to see us, and we were most hospitably received.
Mrs. Parr and his daughters were from home. Jack,
one of his pupils, was with him, and a Doctor Taylor
—a young and silent Scotchman. The doctor insisted
on our partaking of his dinner, and he did all but insist
on our sleeping at his parsonage. It was a capital
day. But surely he is one of the strangest men that
ever lived.[1] He soon attacked me as a ' Pittite.' ' I
hate Pitt,' says the doctor. In his library, which is
an excellent room, and excellently well filled, is a
portrait of Fox, and also the Bellenden prints of Lord
North and Mr. Burke ; and the Bellenden Fox is in
his dining-parlour. His cane is hung up to show the
blue and buff ribbons with which it is ornamented.
In one corner of his garden is a small summer-house
with a chimney smoking, and there the doctor sits

[1] See Appendix. Imitation in Greek of Theophrastus's characters
written playfully by Sir William Jones and sent by him to Dr. Parr.

and smokes, and there he trims ministers and bishops.
The walls would be white if they were not covered
with all sorts of odd prints, particularly, as he says,
prints of impostors ! We had much conversation together, and as a great favour the doctor showed me
his unpublished letter to Lord Warwick, 'the best
thing,' he says, 'he ever wrote and much more severe
and much better written than anything from the pen
of Junius.' He begged me to read Junius as soon as
I got home to see if it was not so. He made me read
his letter while he stood over me. He forgot his pipe,
and rose on tiptoe and seemed almost to burst with
delight when I came to his favourite and most severe
passages. There was somehow or other a freedom in
the doctor's manner—a friendship which encouraged
me to express a wish that he would give the world
something better than perpetual invective. I owned
his powers in this way ; but from him something better
than the best invective might reasonably be looked for.
He said no ; he would never write on any subject of
general literature ; that he merely sought amusement
for himself ; and that the world had no claim upon
him. He did not know but that he might have some
claim on the world. He seemed pleased at what I
had said, and therefore I ventured to add that if, instead of taking so warm a part in politics as he had
done, he had done what he was certainly so well able to
do in the way of general literature, there was not any
party in the kingdom which would not most readily
have taken notice of him, and from which he might

not have received important preferment. He took this well : and, however the zeal of party may at times reconcile him to his position, yet I cannot help thinking that if he could act his part over again, and no public declaration stood in his way, he might be induced to proceed with more moderation and prudence. Doctor Parr inquired most kindly after you, spoke most highly of you, drank your health ; but—he has not yet read your book.' [2]

Your affectionate brother,   R. T.

ELECTION AS AN EAST INDIA DIRECTOR.

R. T. to T. T.

Isleworth, Jan. 19, 1793.

Dear Brother,—I thank you for your congratulations.[3] I continue to receive them from various quarters.

Mr. Devaynes, the chairman,[4] a man who knows his own interest as well as most men, and looks as

[2] Dr. Parr *did* read it, however, later on, as appears from a letter which he wrote to Richard Twining, dated Feb. 26, 1817, of which the following is an extract :—'You ought to publish what I wrote to you. I repeat the word "*ought*," for I never shall be quite at rest as matters stand, and you can never speak too highly of my regard for your brother and my respect—I had almost said admiration. If there be in my letters to you any strong expression of the instruction and delight which I received from his *Aristotle*, pray communicate it to me. I shall like to bear a direct and luminous testimony to the transcendental merits of that work.'

[3] On his election as an East India Director.

[4] Of the East India Directors.

much after it, declared to a friend of mine the day after the ballot, that he was very glad the question [5] was carried.

I had occasion to see the deputy-chairman on Friday, and to show him a letter which I meant to send to the Court of Directors. He took me by the hand very cordially, and said my 'conduct throughout had been very correct,' and he told me he would deliver my letter himself, and say to the court what he said to me. He added that he was very glad the question was decided as it was.

.   .   .   .   .   .

I have every reason to think, and I certainly am very glad of it, that I never stood better with the Court of Directors than at present. I may have a good deal of trouble as to framing the bye-law. It rests, however, with the Court of Directors to point out the mode of framing it. . . .

For my part I will continue to do everything that I think I ought to do in the matter.

.   .   .   .   .   .

R. T.

[5] His motion against 'directors' trading to and from India. It was a matter of great satisfaction to my grandfather that after he became an East India director he received from those among his colleagues, whose interests were most seriously affected by that motion, many cordial proofs of their regard, and the fullest recognition of the uprightness of the principles by which he had been actuated in bringing it forward. It was a proceeding requiring no slight exercise of courage as well as ability to bring it fully before the Court of Proprietors, and to carry it on to a successful issue.—R. T., 1886.

HOME TOUR.—STRATHFIELDSAY.—RYDE.—FRENCH
ÉMIGRÉS PRIESTS AT WINCHESTER.

R. T. to Rev. T. T.

Arundel, June 16, 1793.

Dear Brother,—Having first thanked you for your
very excellent letter, which found me upon my
rambles, I will give you, in a cursory way, some
account of those rambles. They have done us all
good. My wife's spirits are better than they were;
though she is frequently very low, and I fear will be
so for some time.[6] I have been queer and uncomfortable since I have been out: so much so, that, if I had
consulted my own wishes, I should have returned
home. But I was very desirous of proceeding, for the
sake of others, and I am persuaded that I have been
the better for doing so.

We stayed at Maidenhead Bridge a fortnight.
My mother came down to us; and my brother John
and his wife, and Richard, paid us two visits. Though
I have spent so much time in that country, I never go
to it, without discovering some new proofs of its loveliness. I think there is no country altogether so
desirable to live in. We were fortunate enough to
procure a key of Lord Inchiquin's grounds, so that
we could ride or walk, under or through those rich
hanging woods, which I dare say you have observed,
on your right, as you crossed the bridge. That
country does not abound with extensive views; one

---

[6] From distress at the death of her daughter Emma.

seldom sees anything, but what one can see well. A great view does very well, now and then ; but views of moderate dimensions afford me much more pleasure, especially at a time when the mind wants composure. Scenes of rural nature do, indeed, afford me a peculiar kind of pleasure ; and they have often occasioned in me that sort of religious feeling, which you describe so well and with so much animation. But I must get on.

From Maidenhead Bridge we went to Reading, and from thence to Basingstoke. All this was high, turnpike-road travelling, and good for little else than to lead one to something better. We contrived, indeed, to quit the high road, to pass through Lord Rivers's park at Strathfieldsay ; and it was an entertainment and a relief to us.

At Winchester we saw the cathedral and the college—usual sights. We also saw the unusual and melancholy sight of the French priests, who live in the King's House. There are about six hundred of them. I had much satisfaction in bringing forth my little stock of French, to converse with such as came in my way. We saw several of them in the chapels which they have fitted up. We visited one of the apartments in which they sleep. There were two gentlemen in it, praying. I apologised for disturbing them. They were glad to hear their own language, and would fain have introduced us to their Superior. But I understood that he was often much affected at the sight of strangers. We met several parties of

priests as we walked about the city, and they always
pulled off their hats to us. Some were in the cathedral, during the time of service. I was showing one
of them the statue of William of Wykeham, which
was given to the college by Colley Cibber's father.
He asked me at what time William of Wykeham
lived. When I told him, he replied that our religion
was not then separated from theirs. All these things
are, it is true, of small consequence. But I could
not even see, much less speak to, a French priest in
such a situation, without thinking of a number of
circumstances, which made everything relating to him
appear of great consequence.

We spent nearly two days at Southampton—a
place which has been much improved of late. It is a
handsome town, surrounded by a charming country.
From Southampton we went to Lyndhurst. We
were then in the midst of the New Forest. We
spent one day in riding about the most wild and most
forest-like parts of it. I never spent such a *forest*
day in my life. We had a good guide, who carried
us quietly to choice spots, and left them to make
their fair impressions. We embarked, at Lymington,
for the Isle of Wight ; sailed to the Needles, the
stupendous cliffs of Freshwater, Yarmouth, and
Cowes ; and, which is wonderful for me, all this
without my being sick. The weather exactly suited
me. We passed two days most pleasantly in the Isle
of Wight. I had been there three or four times
before ; but I was not aware of its loveliness. There

is *such* a road, under the cliffs, on the south side of the island ! It hangs about half-way between the summit of the cliff and the sea-shore ; and between the road and the sea the ground is broken in the wildest manner imaginable. We were much struck with a small house which we saw. It belongs to Sir Richard Worsley. We desired to look at the garden. A labouring man, to whom we expressed our desire, said he would call the French gardener. The French gardener came, and, without opening the gate, attempted to ask, in English, whether we had an order for admission from Sir Richard Worsley. I really could not understand him. But I spoke to him in French, and he immediately applied the key to the keyhole, and said not a word more about his master's permission. He showed us everything, and was full of conversation and of civility. There is not a soul about the place who can speak a word of French, and he can scarcely speak a word of English ; so that he was right glad to enjoy the blessing of conversation— a blessing to all conversible beings, but, I take it, particularly so to a Frenchman. Sir Richard Worsley has a mind to try if he cannot have a vineyard in that mild and sunny part of the island ; and he has imported the Frenchman to cultivate his vines. I believe I got more out of the Frenchman than Sir Richard will do.

When I got to the seaside, at Ryde, and saw a great swell, and the wind much against us, I was in a huge fright; for I really suffer a vast deal from sea-sickness. Contrary, however, to my expectation, I had one of the finest sails I ever had in my life. The quantity of wind steadied the boat, and we sailed through the waves without any of that up-and-down motion, which always harrows up my soul ; and there was a fine fleet of men-of-war at Spithead, and of Indiamen at the Mother-bank. We spoke the 'Dublin,' and invited Francklin,[7] who is one of her officers, to sup with us at Portsmouth. He did so. I was very anxious to hear about the 'Ponsborne'[8] (Thomas's ship), which he had just left at St. Helena. She met with a very mortifying accident there. When she arrived at St. Helena, she found a considerable number of Indiamen, with their convoy. These ships were to sail for England the following day. It seemed possible, and but just possible, for the 'Ponsborne' to get her water on board, time enough to accompany them. In order to do so, it was desirable to anchor near the shore ; and indeed, the usual and best anchorage was occupied by the ships already off the island. Unfortunately the 'Ponsborne' went—to all appearance very gently—rather too near the shore, and she struck upon a rock. Her striking was scarcely perceived by any person on board. But those who were on board the other ships saw her strike. They immediately sent off boats to her assist-

---

[7] Captain Francklin, of the East India Company's service, an old friend of the family.

[8] The 'Ponsborne' was the ship by which his son Thomas had taken passage to St. Helena on his way to Calcutta in May 1792.

ance, and, by great exertions, saved her. She had a hole in her side, which a man might have crept through ; and she had soon nine feet of water in her hold. I am assured, however, that before the ships sailed, on the following day, they left the 'Ponsborne' in perfect safety ; and that, in about two months, we may expect to see her.

Thomas received so much civility from the captain and officers of the 'Ponsborne,' that I have good reason to be interested about them ; and the news of the accident which the ship had met with, worried me sadly.

At Portsmouth we saw the dockyard. Elizabeth and Ann were much entertained. From Portsmouth we came by Chichester and Arundel to this place (Worthing), merely for the sake of seeing Mr. Haynes, who was here alone, and not well. This is a very stupid place indeed. I do not find fault with it because it does not abound with company, but because the coast is flat and insipid, and the sea destitute of ships.

My good friend, Mr. Hingeston, has, from motives of mere kindness, accompanied us all the way.

I have received a few lines from Thomas ; they were dated in January. He sent them by one of the officers of the 'Ponsborne,' and he forwarded them to England. They were merely to acknowledge the kindness which he had received from that officer. This was like Thomas, who is remarkably attentive. I expect more letters as soon as the regular packets are delivered. This short letter implies, however, that Thomas was well; and so, you may be sure, it was highly acceptable to us.

There are two inns at this place. One (where we are) is kept by Mr. *Hogsfleshe*: the other, at the opposite corner, is kept by Mr. *Bacon*!

Your affectionate brother,
R. T.

LOVE OF HIS FAMILY.—CAUTION AGAINST OVER-WORK.

T. T. to R. T. (Extract).

Colchester, April 25, 1797.

. . . . I have received a letter this very morning from Thomas.[9] He calculates that he and Daniel shall arrive here on Thursday evening. Everything has been ready for them for some time. I shall be very glad to see them, and don't imagine that their visit will be ill-timed or in the least inconvenient on account of my not being so well as I should be. Their company will cheer me; though poor Thomas's departure from me can be only melancholy—it is little to be expected that we should ever meet again. One *bit* of your last letter gave me great pleasure—need I specify? I hope you will *more* than 'fancy for a few minutes' that you may be able to settle a plan of more leisure and comfort to yourself. · If you allow, as you do allow, that although you *can* do what you

---

[9] His nephew, about to return to India.

have done, you *cannot* without having reason to expect
that you shall suffer for having done it, then I say
you are not, properly speaking, *able* to do it, and it is,
properly speaking, *necessary* that you should *not* do it.
But, good and sound reasoner as you are, you always
argue falsely and sophistically upon this *one* subject.
Are you affronted now?   I think I could prove what
I say.   Say fairly at once that it is *for the good of
your family that your life should be shortened*, and I
will argue with you no longer.   Daniel,[1] in a letter I
had from him some months ago, touched this subject
in a way which touched me.   I fully intended to have
told you what he said ; but from time to time forgot
it, and now, to my great mortification, I cannot find
the letter, though I have hunted for it repeatedly.
But I may lay my hand upon it one day or other.   He
is a most excellent lad, head and heart ; but these
rare things are no rarities in your family.   I have
thought it very unfortunate that we have been kept
asunder so long, that I have not had the pleasure of
seeing any of the family under my roof for so long a
time ; but I hope times will mend, and opportunity
be more civil ; and I hope *I* shall mend, for there is
great room for it.   I wish you and Hughes would come
as you talked of. . . .

T. T.

---

[1] His nephew, then at Pembroke College, Cambridge.

ON PRAYER AND THANKSGIVING.

T. T. to R. T. (Extract).

Colchester, Oct. 12, 1797.

.   .   .   .

About *thanksgiving* we are agreed. . . . Bishop Butler has written better upon prayer than anybody. ' Prayer, he says, ' is a dutiful direction of the mind to God as present;' and he thus explains the scriptural expression of praying always—praying without ceasing —giving thanks in everything, &c.—' that is,' says he, ' to be frequently and habitually turning our minds to God.' Again, ' to say or read over any composition in which these pious sentiments are expressed, to do this with humility and reverence in our outward deportment : this is the *form* of prayer ; but prayer itself consists in really directing, or endeavouring to direct, our minds to God in the manner of which such form is expressive,' &c. In *social* worship *words* are necessary, and posture is of some consequence ; but in private and personal devotion there can be no occasion for either. Sometimes I am led to put my feelings into a few extempore words, for *forms* I never use by myself. When I have lifted up my wishes or my thanks to God, with a strong feeling, and a proper reverence and humility, though in *perfect* silence, without uttering a word, I reckon that I have prayed. . . .

T. T.

THE 'CHESTER HEAVY.'

R. T. to the Rev. T. T.

Bitteswell,[2] April 30, 1798.

Dear Brother,—I really pity the man who cannot ride in a stage coach. I got into the 'heavy Chester' on Thursday morning at six o'clock, and before eleven at night I was supping in this room,[3] and Ann,[4] myself and Jonathan,[5] did all this, not to mention breakfasting, dining, and tea-drinking for 4*l.* 9*s.* 6*d.* Ann and I had the good luck to have only one companion, a young man, perfectly quiet and accommodating, so that I and my leg did as well as possible. We were joined at meals, indeed, by a young officer, who was an outside passenger. He was a foreigner, though now in the Irish service, and had served a campaign or two in Flanders, and had been at the bloody battle of Jemappes. We carried his cutlass in the coach ; but he told Ann that she could do more execution with her eyes! And so, I do assure you, our journey went off very well, as well as if we had come down in a more costly way. . . . But I was very near not coming to Bitteswell at all. I had, as usual, a good many things to do the day before we

[2] For some of its many attractions, see Appendix.

[3] Ninety miles in seventeen hours !

[4] Ann Twining, his daughter, afterwards lived at Bitteswell, and died there Sept. 24, 1865, in her eighty-seventh year.'

[5] Jonathan Landers, his old valet. He afterwards lived in Devereux Court for many years, where he retained his duties as 'hairdresser,' 'powderer,' &c., on his former master's arrival from Isleworth.

were to set off; and therefore I determined not to attend a parish meeting,[1] concerning military matters. My brother and Richard were to attend, and I thought two Twinings would be enough to bring any warlike plan to perfection. But there was reason to apprehend that some persons in the parish would endeavour to bring the business forward in an improper way, and the messenger came to beg I would attend. I did so, was called to the chair, and had to preside in a hot room and at a noisy meeting, till almost eleven at night. I had no doubt that this would bring on a bad headache. I went to bed at twelve, told the clock, one, two, and three, and as I then felt quite ill, I determined to stop the coachman as he went downstairs, and to send him to Devereux Court, to let George know that he must accompany his sister. But between three and four I fell asleep, and when I was called at five, felt so much refreshed, and the morning was so fine, that I resolved to undertake the journey. My faculty of sleeping in a carriage was of some service to me.

Mr. Powell, who has had a bad winter, is quite recovered. Mary is as gentle and as orderly as ever, but she is far from strong. She has rather frequently small ailments; but I hope she will get the better of them as she grows older.[7] . . .

Your affectionate brother,   R. T.

[1] In our old parish of St. Clement Danes.

[7] That hope was happily fulfilled. Mary Powell lived at Bitteswell throughout her long life, honoured and beloved till the year 1875, when she died at the age of eighty-two.

P

In the year 1792 my uncle, Thomas Twining,[8] hav-ing received his appointment through an old family friend, Mr. Parry, then an East India Director, to a writership on the Bengal establishment, proceeded at the early age of sixteen to Calcutta. Having a fondness for mathematics and a special gift for the acquirement of Eastern languages he was placed on his arrival in India in the financial department, and was soon pro-moted to be head-assistant and acting sub-accoun-tant-general, as well as commissioner of the Court of Requests.   His health, however, at that time far from strong, suffered greatly from the strain which the duties of those appointments involved ; and he was obliged, after struggling against it for some time, to leave Calcutta for a healthier climate up the country. It was then that the Governor-General, Lord Corn-wallis, thenceforth his constant friend and patron, proposed appointing him assistant to the Resident of Santipore, 'of whom he spoke very highly, saying that it was the situation he should give to his own son under similar circumstances.'

Accordingly, on July 17, 1794, Mr. Twining took his departure from Calcutta in a budgerow,[9] joining, as had been arranged, the flotilla of Sir Robert Aber-cromby, the Commander-in-Chief, in his voyage up

---

[8] Thomas, second son of Richard and Mary Twining, was born on January 27, 1776.

[9] A budgerow is a large pleasure-boat with two spacious rooms (a sitting- and sleeping-room) surrounded with Venetian blinds. It is contrived for sailing or rowing, having a high mast for mainsail and topsail, and twelve to sixteen oars.

the Ganges,[1] a fleet consisting of more than forty sail, besides a large number of merchant boats, availing themselves of the convoy, at the head of which sailed the two noble pinnaces of the Commander-in-Chief—the one for his Excellency's habitation, and the other for his receptions at dinner and other purposes. At the first mooring-place Mr. Twining had the honour of joining the circle at the Commander-in-Chief's table at dinner, receiving from his Excellency, whom he then saw for the first time, a most cordial greeting, and the heartiest invitation to be his guest daily during their voyage, telling him to dismiss the cooking-boat which he understood he had brought with him, as he would have no occasion for it. From that time Sir Robert Abercromby continued to be one of my uncle's kindest friends.

In the course of the voyage they visited Plassy and inspected with the deepest interest the scene of Clive's great victory over Serajah Dowlah in 1757.

Passing through the Sorly Nullah, or small stream of Sorly, the fleet arrived at the main stream of the Ganges—the sacred mighty river. Its effect upon the crews will be best described in the words of the Journal:

'The impatience of the seaman to see again his native land is not greater than was the anxiety manifested by the Hindoos of the fleet to behold the Ganges. Half a mile farther the object of all this enthusiasm became visible over a point of land we

---

[1] Or Hooghly, the Calcutta branch of the Ganges.

were to pass.   In an instant a clamorous expression of joy pervaded the whole fleet; everyone raised his hand repeatedly to his head, and some bent and touched the deck in sign of humility and respect. The magnificent appearance of the great river, now fully open before us, and the strong effusion of pious feeling : not, certainly, towards the stream itself, but towards the Power which bade it flow—towards that Being Who holds the waters of the earth in the hollow of His hand, formed altogether one of the most impressive scenes I had ever witnessed.   I was deeply struck with the wonderful grandeur of this vast river, and could feel no surprise that the early inhabitants of these first-peopled regions—'the poor Indian, whose untutored mind saw God in clouds, and heard Him in the wind'—should have regarded so sublime an object with superstitious reverence, and that such impressions should have passed to their descendants.   As I stood upon the deck of my boat, now arrived at the head of the nullah, the width, rapidity, and agitation of the prodigious mass of water rushing by, formed a spectacle truly grand, and though I have since beheld other remarkable scenes, I recollect no one which impressed me with more surprise and admiration than the first sight of the Ganges.   The Ganges here, at this season, was so wide that objects upon the opposite shore, and even the line of the shore itself, were not distinctly visible. . . . This noble river had already flowed a thousand miles through the plains of India and was yet 400 miles from the sea. Its depth was sometimes more than thirty feet, and its course was at the rate of seven or eight miles an hour. In its progress it had been joined by eight rivers as large as the Thames.'

Passing through the province of Behar, to which magnificent district Mr. Twining was some years afterwards appointed by the Marquis Wellesley, they proceeded to the great city of Patna—through a district 'comprising the country between the limits proper of Bengal and Benares and the royal districts of Rhotasghur and Shahabad—of which Sasseram was the ancient capital, and the fortress of Rotas the defence—and Tirhoot and Sircar-Sarum ; the two latter on the opposite side of the Ganges. The name of this unrivalled country implies its charms : it is called Behar, a word signifying, " Spring," the poetical season of India, as of other countries :

'" Come, lovely Spring, ethereal mildness come !" is the song of all nations.

'On October 7, after a voyage of two months and nineteen days they arrived at Futtighur on the western bank, 580 miles from Calcutta, and the limit of Sir Robert Abercromby's voyage up the Ganges ; and so ended "a most delightful excursion."'

The Journal then proceeds :—'Finding that the General meant to take the field himself, I expressed a desire to accompany him, to which he assented ; but upon my applying to the commissary-general, the latter said that it was impossible to allow me either

tent or carriage, so pressing was the public demand.
I therefore determined to set out for Agra as soon as
the army should have marched for Rohilcund, and see
the Taj-Mahâl, the fame of which had long excited
my curiosity.   The general, who had often expressed
a desire to see Agra before his return to Calcutta,
approved my plan.   I informed him that if I succeeded in reaching Agra, I should probably endeavour
to extend my journey to Delhi.

On November 10, 1794, Mr. Twining and his company, with an escort of sepoys started for Delhi, *via*
Agra.

DELHI.—COURT OF THE GREAT MOGUL.

Dec. 2, 1794.

After breakfast I and my people were busily occupied in preparing ourselves for going to the imperial
residence.   The time fixed for my presentation was
12 o'clock.   At 10 the Khan (Sind Razy Khan) arrived with numerous attendants.   He was very handsomely dressed.   Our arrangements being made, I
mustered in the court of the palace such of my guards
and establishment as I had ordered to be in readiness
to accompany me.   They had done their best to remove the dust of the plains from their clothes and
accoutrements, and made a very respectable appearance.   I was dressed in white, and enveloped in a
very long orange-coloured shawl.   I had that morning
bought a magnificent pair of shoes or sandals curi-
ously worked with gold.   The toe advanced consider-

ably and having gradually diminished almost to a point, curled back over the foot with a high sweep, like a Dutch skate. Notwithstanding their size and costliness they were scarcely heavier than a pair of common shoes. They were, however, only fit to be walked with on a mat or carpet.

Soon after 11 the procession moved out of the great court of the palace, the Agra guard with their captain at their head taking the lead, the men following two and two at short distances so as to form a long line. About the middle of this I took my station on my little charger, Sind Razy Khan on a prancing steed being on my right, and my moonshee, also mounted, on my left. Behind me followed my palanquin. The people salaamed as I moved gently through the streets. Leaving the city by the Lahore gate we passed over a small plain, and at the farther side of it reached the high walls which enclosed the precincts of the imperial residence. The gates being opened, some officers stationed there conducted us through the usual great court of the elephants and a succession of other courts, in the last of which I was met by other officers whose more splendid dresses denoted their higher rank. Having dismounted and received and returned the customary salutations I was conducted to the hall of audience, a fine building which formed with its numerous accessory apartments one entire side of a spacious square. It was so extensive as to seem itself a palace. In this great and beautiful hall I saw the Shah Nusheen, or imperial

seat, and beneath it a beautiful turah of white marble
for the vizier of the empire to stand upon in the
presence of the emperor.   Formerly, when the Padshah appeared in this hall on great occasions, he sat
upon the celebrated peacock throne subsequently
removed by Nadir Shah in the reign of Mahmoud
Shah, and then the vizier stood below upon the marble
elevation above mentioned.

I was next conducted into the dewan khos, another ancient hall of public ceremonial, and still more
beautiful and magnificent than the preceding one;
but bearing more marks of modern spoliation.   This
splendid room was composed entirely of white marble,
as was the adjoining terrace and its two pavilions.
The columns of white marble which support the roof
of this beautiful divan are inlaid with the choicest
cornelians, displaying a degree of taste and art which
reminded me of the similar embellishments of the Taj,
and they were it seemed likely the work of the same
hand, since both buildings were erected about the
same time and by the same monarch.   The highly
sculptured roof, which rested lightly on these elegant
columns, was also of white marble embossed with
gulcarrys of the same exquisite workmanship inter-
mixed with decorations in gold.   A velvet cushion
was on the chabioturah;   and under a handsome
canopy, supported by massive pillars of silver was the
throne of the Padshah, covered with crimson velvet.

Whilst I was admiring these beautiful specimens
of Oriental magnificence, some officers of the palace,

sumptuously dressed in shawls, advanced and saluted
me, and said that the Padshah had taken his seat in
the turbeigh khaun, and was ready to receive me. I
accordingly moved forward, followed by Sind Razy
Khan and the moonshee, with the numerous persons
who had joined us, and soon came on a long and spacious terrace having a handsome colonnade on one
side, and on the other a garden. Towards the centre
of the terrace I perceived two lines of persons, apparently of rank, seated on a large carpet spread upon
the terrace opposite an opening in the centre of the
colonnade ; the opening being a spacious recess connected with the interior of the palace, with many persons in splendid dresses standing in it, and the emperor
seated in front of them. At the edge of the carpet I
took off my sandals and advanced alone a little beyond the first line of persons sitting, and turning to
my right I saw the emperor immediately before me.
He was seated on a low throne covered with crimson
velvet, and was surrounded by numerous persons standing ; some standing behind him in the divan, others
along the corridor on each side. In conformity with
the lesson I had received I now made three low
salaams. Casting a deliberate look around me I perceived that the extremities of the lines near me were
composed of very young men : the rows mounting
gradually towards the other end near the throne being
formed of persons considerably older. All were princes
of the imperial family—sons and grandsons of Shah
Allum, the reigning emperor. Their number, I under

stood, exceeded forty. I now advanced very slowly five or six paces, and then made three more profound salaams, after which I retreated backwards to where I had stood at first. There I made three low bows as before and then advanced slowly, followed by Sind Razy Khan and the moonshee, till I came close to the aged monarch, who sat erect in the Oriental fashion. Large cushions of silk lay on each side of him and behind him ; but he did not seem to rest upon them. Even at seventy-one years of age he looked the tallest and stoutest of all present. Altho' prepared to see him blind, as he was, the appearance of the Great Mogul upon his throne in such a condition was an extraordinary and distressing spectacle, especially as his affliction did not proceed from accident nor arise in the course of nature, but was due to an act of most inhuman barbarity, committed by one of his subjects. There was, however, nothing repulsive in the emperor's appearance, nothing being perceptible but a depression of the eyelids. Upon his right hand sat Mirza Acbar, his eldest son and heir to his throne, the junior princes being ranged in the two lines in front according to their rank and ages. Among the great personages standing about the throne I perceived my acquaintance Shah Sahib, the governor of Delhi.[2]

My moonshee now gave me a piece of fine muslin folded into the size of five or six inches square.

---

[2] Mr. Twining had, by desire, paid his respects to the governor on the preceding day, and had been received with the utmost courtesy and distinction.

Putting this on my right hand he placed upon it five gold mohurs, equal in value to about 8*l.*, and I then held it towards the emperor, who, being informed of what I had done, stretched out his right hand and laid it on my offering, after which the treasurer of the palace advanced and took the gold from the cloth. The moonshee, who was my treasurer on the occasion, now put three gold mohurs on the muslin, and I presented them to Mirza Acbar, who himself took them. In the same manner I offered smaller presents to as many others of the padshaizados as the resources of my exchequer would permit, for all the Padre Juvenal's [3] gold and silver too would have been exhausted if I had presented offerings to all this numerous family! This immemorial custom of the East having been complied with, the emperor, speaking in Persian, enquired after my health, and in very obliging terms expressed his pleasure at my safe arrival at Delhi after so long a journey. I returned my acknowledgments for this condescension, adding that the fame of his Majesty and of his imperial house had reached the distant parts from whence I came. The celebrity of his virtues had inclined me to approach the seat of empire, where my reception into the august presence would ever be a source of

---

[3] Padre Juvenal, a Roman Catholic missionary at Agra, by whose kind assistance Mr. Twining procured a fresh escort of sepoys—the former one having desired to return to Bengal—and a further supply of money against his drafts on Calcutta. The Padre had availed himself of Mr. Twining's company and armed escort on his journey from Futtighur to Agra.

satisfaction to me in my own country.   I had, I said,
been the companion during a great part of my journey of a powerful general [4] who took a deep interest in
his Majesty's glory, and whose delight would have
been to reach the foot of the imperial musnud, but
that he would always hear with pleasure of the
power and splendour of his Majesty's throne, and had
now been fighting for his Majesty's prosperity, as
would probably appear by a letter with which I had
the honour of being charged for the presence.   The
emperor, holding forth his hand, received the letter
and gave it to Meer Gholab Khan, his head-moonshee,
to read.   It was written in the Persian language upon
highly varnished paper spotted with gold.   After de-
tailing the principal events of the late war, it offered
the General's congratulations to his Majesty on the
defeat of Gholam Mahomed the usurper of Rohilcund, and the conquest of Rampore, his capital.   The
emperor expressed his satisfaction at these events,
and acknowledged the General's attention in communicating them.   He then enquired after the
General's health, and desired that I would express
his thanks to him.   I returned my acknowledgments
and said I should soon probably have an opportunity
of communicating his Majesty's condescension to the
General, to whom it would be more pleasing than
victory.

The emperor now ordered his officers to invest

---

[4] General Sir Robert Abercrombie, the victor of Rohilcund and an
attached friend of T. T.

me with the imperial khelaut, upon which I expressed my thanks and withdrew—retreating backwards between the two lines. Having repeated the three salaams I walked to the spot where I had left my sandals, and, putting them on, was conducted along the terrace to an apartment not far from the extremity by which I had entered. Here I was invested with a long splendid robe of muslin, richly bespangled and embroidered with gold. It covered me entirely and reached down to my golden sandals. A turban of fine gold muslin, many yards in length, was wound round my head. A handsome scarf of white muslin, worked with gold, and ending with deep fringes of gold, was placed on my shoulders and reached almost to the ground. Another long piece of muslin, also embroidered with gold, was wound round my waist, forming a broad thick girdle over the robe and under the scarf. My moonshee, much to his satisfaction as well as my own, received a handsome green shawl. I was now reconducted to the Presence, where I found everything in the same order as before—the Great Mogul sitting among his family and chief officers. Again taking off my sandals at the edge of the carpet I repeated my three obeisances, and then advanced through the avenue of princes to the throne. The emperor, informed of my approach, addressed me thus :—'Your visit has afforded me much satisfaction. The communication of the victory gained by the General is an attention that pleases me. Make this city your residence for a few days, such being your desire, or longer if you please. You will view dances and entertainments which will be exhibited before you in Shah Sahib's palace and garden. You will now walk about the fortress and see everything. Your feast will be supplied from the Presence.' I replied :—' May your Majesty be blessed with prosperity and health !' and then withdrew backwards as before, bowed three times at the extremity of the two lines, and retired.

.   .   .   .   .   .

After a minute and interesting detail of the wonders of Delhi and its vicinity, the Journal proceeds :—

' I received a further communication from the palace ; it related principally to the Commander-in-Chief, but also regarded myself. In addition to the marks of satisfaction which I had already received from the Emperor, Sind Razy Khan now brought to me his Majesty's permission to wear a seal or other ornament inscribed with his name and the date of my visit to the Presence.

.   .   .   .   .   .

As the departure approached, the objections to the road I was about to take across the plain and through the great forest of Secundra were again represented to me ; but I had found that in travelling, as in other situations, when embarrassments occur, the means of overcoming them generally present themselves ; and I was unwilling to return without seeing, if possible, General de Boigne, whose fame was spread through Hindostan.

In the evening, twenty-one fine sepoys, armed with matchlocks and sabres, arrived from the Governor. I immediately gave orders for marching at daybreak.

My party consisted of fifty persons including the moonshee and myself.

* * * * * *

AN ADVENTURE IN THE DESERT.

Dec. 7, 1794.

SOON after dusk one of my men came to tell me that a party of horsemen, apparently Gonjers, the ·worst tribe of banditti, was meeting us. Fearful as it is there is something noble in the name 'Mewatty,' for courage commands a sentiment of respect even in unlawful actions, when not allied with cruelty. The Mewatty is always the bold, and often generous, assailant ; he is the 'Macheath' of the desert. Gonjer, on the contrary, implies nothing but systematic craftiness and unsparing barbarity ; and communicates no impression but terror and dismay. He is the 'Schinderhannes' of the plains of Hindostan. My sepoys, though too brave to manifest alarm, were not the less sensible of the real nature of our situation.

I was in my palanquin, and, I believe, nearly asleep, when the report was brought to me. I slipped my sword-belt over my shoulder, put my pistols in the holsters, and mounted my little charger to prepare for defence. But I soon found there was no time for this ; for the horsemen were now close upon us, and their numbers, I saw, were greatly superior to our own. One resource alone presented itself. It was one which, however indefensible when not necessary, the preservation of my party seemed to justify. Drawing my long orange-coloured shawl over my head, I was at once transformed into a sirdar of the country. This, however, alone would be no protection to us. At the same time, therefore, I ordered the red cloth on the top of the palanquin to be let down over the sides ; and I told the captain of the guard to reply, when challenged, ' Padshahuka harem-kee bibee-sahib' ('a lady of the imperial seraglio'). The head of the cavalry reaching us, the commander called out, in a surly, uncivil tone, ' Khe-hy ?' (Who is there ?') The captain of the guard replied, ' Padshahuka harem-kee bibee-sahib,' and passed on. The chief of the banditti, arriving opposite me, leant forward on his horse and looked earnestly at me, and then at the palanquin, giving me, as he passed, a cold salaam, which I returned, but without either of us saying anything. Many of his men addressed themselves in rather a taunting manner to mine ; but I desired the latter to make no reply, and to leave the horsemen the greater part of the road, which, indeed, they were fully disposed to take. Disappointment, probably, was added to their natural roughness, for there was an insolence about them which I had never seen before among the natives of India, and I was afraid, as the two lines brushed each other, ours nearly shoved out of the road, that their rudeness would be too much for the patience of my spirited sepoys. They evidently wished to provoke a pretext for attacking us. Preserving, however, a perfect silence, and a reserve which accorded with the nature of our charge, we safely reached the extremity of their long line. Excepting the greater length of their spears, and their incivility, I could perceive nothing in their appearance to distinguish them from the Mewatties we had seen before reaching Agra ; but the jemmadar of the governor's men informed us that they were all Gonjers out on a marauding expedition, and were then probably in pursuit of a caravan we had met in the morning, and of which they would make an easy prey, for their numbers could not, as well as we could guess, be less than a hundred and fifty to two hundred men—well mounted and armed. The moonshee was not deficient in courage, but his frequent recurrence to this adventure showed that it had made a deep impression on his mind. For myself, I could not but consider it fortunate that, having fallen in first with a party of Mewatties and then of Gonjers, I had escaped from both.

VISIT TO GENERAL DE BOIGNE.

At the next station, on their road to Coel—then the head-quarters of General de Boigne, a soldier of fortune, a native of Savoy, who, after innumerable difficulties, had, at thirty-five years of age, won his way from being a prisoner of the Maharajah Scindia to be the generalissimo of his armies—the travellers had agreed, on the urgent advice of one Hosim Khan, 'a very respectable and intelligent man,' to strengthen their escort by the addition of ten well-armed sepoys, their route that evening passing through a district of bad reputation ; but so it was that they traversed a desolate tract of country, intersected by deep ravines, very favourable for ambuscades, rendering a considerable détour necessary, or at least advisable, without having seen any living creature or scarcely even a blade of grass, and late at night arrived at Chandoos in safety, though not without considerable difficulty in finding their way in the darkness of night. In the hospitable quarters of General de Boigne my uncle remained for several days, receiving the most cordial and gratifying attentions, listening to the general's frank and full narrative of his extraordinary career, and accompanying him on his elephant to inspect the army under his command, the same consisting of a regiment of cavalry, three brigades of infantry, amounting to nearly twenty-five thousand men—of whom the greater part were armed with muskets and bayonets, the remainder with matchlocks—together with a park of artillery of 120 guns. The General having insisted on furnishing an escort of his own men for the remainder of the journey, the sepoys from Delhi, and those last engaged, were sent back, retaining only the guard, who had orders from the Governor of Delhi to accompany Mr. Twining to Futtighur. At the same time the General earnestly invited him to turn aside from the nearest and usual road, for the purpose of visiting an Englishman, a very accomplished man and an intimate friend of his, to whom the sight of a countryman would be particularly agreeable. The history of this singular visit shall be told in the words of the journal.

'VISIT TO MR. LONGCROFT.

' My escort had never been so respectable as now. It consisted of forty-seven excellent soldiers. I rode all the afternoon with the captain of General de Boigne's party, a fine intelligent man, who spoke with pride of his general's campaigns, and amused me with stories of the Gonjers and Mewatties. . . .

' At five in the afternoon, a village, built apparently on a sandy protuberance which rose above the general level, appeared before us towards the horizon, and General de Boigne's guard informed me that this was the village at which the English gentleman lived. I could feel no regret at coming out of my way to spend a few hours with him. . . .

' As I rode up the gentle acclivity of the village street at the head of the party, I observed that our numbers and military array drew the inhabitants from their houses ; but the chief of the escort informed them that it was a traveller going to pay a visit to the " Feringhy Sahib," or foreign gentleman. Having cleared the village, we turned a little to the left, when high mud walls with a strong projecting gateway appeared as a small fortress before us. This was the residence of the General's friend. Upon arriving at the gate we found it closed ; nor was there anybody outside.   We heard, however, some bustle within, and concluded that our arrival had been observed.   The captain of the guard knocked and, explaining who we were, desired admittance.   The only answer from within was that the gate could not be opened.   Further explanation was given, but the same answer was returned.   I then took the General's note from my pocket, and delivering it to one of my servants, directed him to thrust it under the gate, and to request that it might be taken to the Sahib.   In a very few minutes the gate was opened, and we marched in. Some armed people were under the deep arch, and against its walls I observed swords, shields, and matchlocks sufficient to equip many more.   After passing a few low buildings, probably occupied by the servants and garrison, I came upon the area of the fort, and in the middle of it I saw a small bungalow.   Dismounting at the edge of the verandah, a servant conducted me across it, and raising a curtain suspended before a doorway showed me into a spacious but extremely dark room.   I had not been half a minute alone when I perceived a tall thin figure advancing through the obscurity towards me.   Although the solemn gravity of his manner, his dress, and everything around me brought the idea of a hermit to my mind at the moment, it was at once dispelled by a certain peculiar charm in his language as he took me by the hand and gave me the kindest welcome.   If his appearance seemed to correspond with the dreariness of his abode, his expression was that of a man of education and of the world. He regretted my detention at the gate, but such a visit, he said, was most unusual, and the appearance of my horsemen and soldiers had led to measures of preparation which the state of the country rendered indispensable. He immediately placed a small room, servants, and cold water at my disposal, and, finding that I had not dined, ordered dinner to be prepared. On my rejoining my host in the dark hall he asked me if I should like to take a short walk. Upon my replying that I should much like to see his indigo works, he said that they were very near, and that we would walk to them. Turning to the left under the wall of the fort, we descended the eastern declivity of the eminence on which the village stands, and at the bottom of it arrived at the indigo works. They consisted of a long range of vats or tanks about sixteen feet square and six deep, constructed of substantial masonry, and covered with chunam, or fine mortar. In front of this line was a second range, somewhat smaller, and so much lower as to admit of water running into them from the bottom of the upper range. The indigo plant, a shrubby bush about three feet high, raised from seed sown in the spring of either the current or preceding year, being cut in the rainy season, is put upon hackeries drawn by bullocks, and carried to the factory, where it is placed and pressed down in the larger vats, and there remains covered with water all night—or for a longer or shorter time according to the age of the plant, the quality of the water, or the state of the atmosphere. Thence it is drawn off into the lower vats and descends to the bottom, forming a blue slime or mud. The water is then run off, and the blue sediment or indigo is formed into cubical cakes by means of little frames or moulds, and being packed in strong oblong chests finds its way to the markets of Europe.

'As the evening closed, my host observed that it would not be prudent to remain out longer, adding that even in the daytime there was little safety beyond his walls, and that his continuance at Jellowlee would be almost impossible but for the known protection of General de Boigne. The General, he said, had lately promised him a small cannon. On re-entering the bungalow things were greatly changed. The gloomy hall had disappeared, lights were on the table, a cheerful fire blazed on the hearth, and a dinner, which was far from requiring the apologies my hospitable host made for it, was placed before me, and, as he addressed me in my own language, I could, but for the turbaned servants who waited upon us, have almost fancied myself surrounded by the green fields of our common country instead of the arid plains of the Doab.

'Passing by much conversation on his personal and domestic affairs, I will relate a story which he told me as we sat before the fire to a late hour.

'" One afternoon not long previous to your visit a party of Pindarees, a third tribe of robbers, came down suddenly on the village of Jellowlee, and were making their way through it to attack my castle, taking with them such plunder as the poverty of the villagers afforded. These, however, fought with great bravery, retreating up the village step by step, and at length succeeded in arresting the progress of their assailants near the top of the street. There the conflict became very obstinate, and many were killed on both sides. The assailants numbered about three hundred. · While, however, the two parties were thus engaged, one of the villagers, having marked the leader of the enemy, ran round, and, coming up in the rear of the Pindarees, speared their chief in the back ; whereon the party, dismayed by the loss of their leader, retreated down the street, and I, who was waiting the result of the action, within hearing of every shot, escaped.

' " The Pindarees having reached the bottom of the street wheeled to the right, and passing the indigo works, galloped off. Plunder and desolation marked their way to the Ganges. There they turned to the north, and followed the course of that river to Anopshur, a military post in the kingdom of Oude, where there was a detachment of the Company's troops under the command of Colonel Robert Stuart, for the protection of the nabob's territories in that quarter. The colonel was taking his morning ride when the Pindarees came up. Galloping between him and the cantonments they cut off his retreat, made him prisoner, and carried him off. They kept him in their troop many days, and finally took him across the Jumna to a country to the north-west of Delhi, not far from the dominions of the Begum Somroo. This princess, hearing that an English officer was prisoner in a neighbouring state, lost no time in interceding for his release ; and further, having provided the ransom demanded and sent the required sum, Colonel Stuart arrived at the court of his benefactress, by whom he was treated with great consideration till she had an opportunity of sending him in safety to his own station."

'In this manner India and, with greater interest, England afforded the subjects of our conversation till the fire was nearly burned out, and till it became necessary to terminate this delightful intercourse by preparations for my journey in the .morning, being obliged to decline my host's pressing invitation to remain longer with him. As it was my intention to start at daybreak, I preferred to sleep in my palanquin placed in his verandah, and there we bade adieu. There was at that moment a friendly, or rather an affectionate anxiety for my safety that struck me, and his last kind words, before returning across the hall to his own room, were a promise to send a messenger after me in the morning if he should hear of any Mewatties being abroad. At daybreak I felt my bearers raising my palanquin to put it on their shoulders, and heard the great gate open for us to pass out. General de Boigne's cavalry turned to the right, on their return, by my desire, bearing my letter expressing my satisfaction with their services, and the gratification which his introduction to his friend had afforded me, and we went in the opposite direction, nearly east, the same route as that which the Pindarees had taken. At sunrise I had mounted my horse, and we had completed about twelve miles, when one of my escort descried a messenger running as from Jellowlee over the ridge we had passed. It was evident that he was holding up his hand as a signal for us to stop. I hastened, however, the people across the stream, and desired them to place the palanquins along the bank opposite the ford, so forming a parapet behind which the sepoys could load and fire to advantage in case of need.

'The messenger was now approaching with a letter in his hand, and receiving it from him, I found it to be as follows :—

'"My dear Sir,—On reading over again this morning the note you brought me from General de Boigne, I am led to think that your name, instead of 'Tiveny,' may be 'Twining,' in which case I shall have much reason to regret not having made this discovery sooner, since, if my supposition be correct, you are the brother of the young lady who gave her hand to my nephew, Mr. Powell.[5] I beg you will favour me with a line to relieve my suspense.

'"Yours very truly,

'"THOMAS LONGCROFT."[6]

---

[5] The Rev. James Powell, of Bitteswell.
[6] Mr. Longcroft was also my mother's uncle.—R. T., 1886.

'Great indeed was my surprise. I immediately passed over the river, and wrote on the top of my palanquin a few lines to my discovered kinsman, expressing my deep regret that this extraordinary fact of a relationship between us had not become known during the pleasant hours I had passed in his company the preceding evening. I also expressed my sense of the kind reception he had given me, and my desire to commence a correspondence with him on my return to Santipore. I felt a desire to return to Jellowlee; but the time for my being at Futtighur was already very nearly expired, and I was unwilling to keep the sepoys of the Governor of Delhi much beyond the time I had mentioned as the limit of their absence. Mr. Longcroft's messenger accordingly returned up his side of the valley while I mounted the other, my mind most deeply occupied with the singular adventure which had just occurred. That Mr. Longcroft and I should have passed a whole evening together without discovering the near connection which existed between us was indeed extraordinary. How many circumstances, the mention of how many persons and places, would have revealed us to each other! Had I but asked him the common question, what part of England he was from, or had he addressed the same inquiry to me, the mention of Isleworth or Colchester would most probably have led to a disclosure. It was also somewhat surprising that, knowing his guest was attached to the Civil Service of the East India Company, he did not ask him if he was acquainted with a fellow-servant of the name of Twining. It was also singular that before leaving England I should never have heard his name mentioned, although I had seen several of his family and friends before my departure, especially his nephew, Mr. Powell of Bitteswell, and his sister, Mrs. Smythies of Colchester, and my uncle Thomas Twining of the same place.'

THOMAS LONGCROFT.

His family resided at Strand-on-the-Green, near to Kew Bridge, and were the neighbours and friends of the celebrated painter Zoffani. Thomas Longcroft was fond of painting, and hence arose a particular intimacy between Zoffani and himself. The great painter being about to try his fortune in Bengal said one day to his young friend, 'Tom, will you go with me to India?' He accepted the proposal, and *did* accompany Zoffani to Calcutta, and afterwards to Lucknow, where the court of the Nabob Asuph ul Dowlah was then in all its splendour. Zoffani was patronised, and no doubt liberally rewarded by that munificent patron of artists and the arts. He painted for him a celebrated picture, in which his Highness is represented at a cock-fight, accompanied by his court, and by Zoffani himself.

At this time, however, the manufacture of indigo was becoming an object of extensive speculation in India. It attracted the attention of Thomas Longcroft, and determined his future pursuit. He quitted

Lucknow, crossed the Ganges, and near a small de-
fenceless village, in the midst of desert plains and
tribes of robbers, he established himself in the fortified
habitation to which so singular a combination of circumstances conducted me. What could have induced
a man of respectable connections, of genius, taste, and
elegant acquirements, to bury himself in so cheerless a
solitude is a question I am unable to answer; but it may
probably have been the abundance and cheapness of
land in that thinly populated country, and the prospect
which it appeared to afford him of an early return to
the bosom of his family, and to the charms of his
native Thames—a dream, alas! never to be realized,
for he ended his days in the desert, without a friend
to receive his last wishes, without a Christian hand
to consign him to the earth, or a tree to shade his
grave.

Note.—After Mr. Longcroft's death a large collection of drawings of scenery and celebrated temples
in India, by his hand, were sent home, and are now in
the possession of and highly valued by his descendants,
both on account of their remarkable merit and their
singular history.

R. T.

For the above most interesting selections from
the journals of my uncle Thomas Twining I am
indebted to the kindness of his son, Thomas Twining,
Esq., of Perryn House, Twickenham, who has been

so good as to place them at my disposal, and I much regret that want of space has alone prevented my being able to make a larger use of their abundant materials. I cannot but hope, however, that at some future time they may be allowed to see the light *in extenso.*

R. T.

Richard Twining to the Rev. T. T.

London, April 1, 1800.

Dear Brother,—I send your sheet of Mr. Malone's Dryden, and also the copy of a passage in a private letter from the Marquis Wellesley to Mr. Dundas.[7] It was communicated to me in a very handsome manner by desire of Mr. Dundas. I know you will be glad to see this testimony of Thomas's good conduct, and to find that it does not escape notice.

Your affectionate brother,

R. T.

Extract from a private letter from the Marquis Wellesley to Mr. Dundas (from Calcutta).

'The customs were placed for some time under the management of Mr. Haldane, a member of the Board of Trade, who was principally aided by a young gentleman of the name of Twining in restoring order to the business of the Custom House. Mr. Twining has distinguished himself very much in this transac-

------

[7] Then president of the Board of Control.

tion ; he is at present too young in the service to be placed in the enjoyment of a salary adequate to his merits, but I shall take the first practicable opportunity of promoting him.[8]   In the meanwhile I have appointed Mr. Dashwood to the Collection of the Customs.   I can rely on his diligence and integrity, and Mr. Twining will act under him.'

With the above honourable testimonial in my mind it was with peculiar interest that I recently read in the biography of the late Sir Charles Trevelyan in the 'Times' the record of a distinction of the like kind, which he also, at the outset of *his* career in India, had so nobly won.

It is not to be inferred that in these successive instances of distinguished service there was any monopoly of the high qualities of strict integrity and firmness of principle ; but it may be truly said that it must have required no ordinary amount of ability and courage for those young men, in the dawn of their official career, with their scant experience, to have grappled with and denounced the abuses which they found around them ; and to each of them may be not unfittingly applied Horace's eulogy on Quintilius,—

[8] The Marquis Wellesley amply redeemed this early promise, and continued to honour my uncle with his confidence and friendship throughout his life.   Other members of the family, also, especially the late Lord Cowley, never ceased to bestow upon him similar tokens of interest and regard.—R. T., 1886.

> Cui pudor, et justitiæ soror,
> Incorrupta fides, nudaque veritas
> Quando ullum invenient parem ?—*Car.* i. 24.

> Oh ! when shall Faith of Soul sincere,
> And Modesty, unspotted maid,
> And Truth, in artless guise arrayed,
> Among the race of human kind
> An equal to Quintilius find ?—FRANCIS'S *Horace.*

R. T., 1886.

PLEASURES OF . A JOURNEY ON HORSEBACK.
ACTIVITY OF BUSINESS.

Richard Twining to R. T., jun.

London, June 28, 1800.

Dear Richard,—I hope you discover that it is a better thing to travel on horseback with a servant behind you and a great-coat before you—as our ancestors travelled—than to be pinioned and stewed in a stage-coach. But when I talk of the manner in which our ancestors travelled do not imagine that I mean our ' *nose*[9] fathers' of the Twining race. I believe that excepting your grandfather, who really *did* travel and was fond of travelling on horseback with a servant behind him, and your great-grandfather, whose mode of travelling up to town has never been ascertained, and is not, perhaps, worth inquiring into, the Twinings never presumed to travel at all. I am sure we ought to have a high respect for that most worthy man over the chimney[1] who transported our

---

[9] A joke on their hereditary adyantages in that feature !

[1] The portrait of my great-great-grandfather, Thomas Twining, the

family from the Severn to the Thames, and so made horsemen of us, and enabled us. to travel as you travel—that is, like a gentleman. I rejoice to find that you go on so successfully,[2] and we go on successfully here ; for we carry on a *roaring* trade,[3] though we neither weep nor cry out. Mr. Jones is now getting samples (here he comes) from chests which reach from one end of the warehouse to the other, and this

founder of our business in Devereux Court, *circa* 1710, said to be by Hogarth.   He is painted in the flowing wig of the period, and wears the gown of a freeman of the Weavers' Company.—R. T., 1886.

[2] My father was on a mission of business to Edinburgh, *viâ* Passenham (Dr. Hey) and Bitteswell.—R. T., 1885.

[3] ' A roaring trade.' Towards the close of the eighteenth and during the early part of the present century the tea trade had experienced a remarkable development through the operation of Mr. Pitt's Commutation Act in 1783–86. The title of that Act affords little or no clue to its object, which was to commute the heavy duty on tea (just about cent. per cent.) to scarcely more than a nominal one in comparison (an *ad valorem* duty of from 2½*d.* to about 6⅜*d.* per lb.) for a window tax. During the consideration of that measure by ministers Mr. Pitt did my grandfather the honour of inviting him to several interviews, at which the condition and prospects of the tea trade were thoroughly gone into. At that time fully one-half—some said two-thirds—of the trade was in the hands of the smugglers, and those dealers who recognised the duty of not encouraging such illicit practices were almost driven out of the field.   From the time of that Act becoming law the operations of the wealthy smugglers (chiefly in Holland) were speedily extinguished, and they have never revived.   They ' died hard,' and at the first periodical sale of the East India Company after the reduction of the duty their manœuvres succeeded in effecting a great rise in the cost prices of tea ; but the attempt was defeated by the disinterested conduct of the East India directors, cordially supported by the trade.

Subsequently, although under the exigencies of the French war the duty reverted to its former high level, and so continued until free trade to China led to an abolition of the *ad valorem* duty, the operations of the smuggler in tea were never resumed.

has been the case ever since you left us; so I shall make this over to George, who will, I dare say, have many things to say to you..

Your affectionate Father,

R. T.

A WEDDING DINNER.—'O HYMENÆE.'

The Rev. T. T. to his Nephew, Richard Twining.

Colchester, Saturday, May 14, 1802.

Dear Benedick,—I thank you for your letter, though it is but fair to own that I might not have had the grace to answer it so soon if you had not in your P.S. told me that you did not wish to hurry me about writing, and, in the same breath, given me to understand that you should expect to hear from me at Peasemore. Bravo! and so you shall; and I thank you for that spur at the heel of your epistle, which has made me suddenly jerk forward at this rate; for I am but a lazy post-horse, as two[4] persons at your elbow, to my shame, can testify. One of those persons, indeed, has something of the same infirmity himself—enough to make it not very difficult to him to forgive me. But the other—I believe she does not know what it is to be indolent (she has a good husband who does all that business for her); but, luckily for me, she knows as little, I believe, what it is to be angry. I must be allowed to be a tolerably

---

[4] Referring to Dr. and Mrs. Hughes. Dr. (then Mr.) Hughes had the living of Peasemore, and the Rev. Daniel Twining was his curate.

R

good judge of that, for I have tried hard to make her so (this is the apology oblique—'and the flattery direct,' quoth she).

Your account of yourself and your *compagnons de voyage* (both literal and metaphorical) furnished a very pleasant accompaniment to my breakfast.

I thank you for your thanks. I can only say that I was made very happy by all the parts that I performed upon the occasion,[5] and that I shall always recollect those few days with pleasure. The snug, quiet dinner in my little boudoir of a study (*où, pourtant, personne ne boudoit ce jour-la*) was a thing that I relished much. It is always pleasant when one can cheat ceremony and etiquette, and pluck out all the buckram from form and fuss. A true wedding dinner is a thing of some finery and *apprêt*. Our dinner could not be charged with anything of that sort, though it was not quite so free and easy as our friend Petruchio's. You did not say 'the meat was burnt,' nor call for 'the rascal cook,' nor 'throw the meat about the room,' &c. And I hope you do not yet find that you are a 'grumbling groom,' or that you want 'much alteration.' I think, upon the whole, you have been fortunate in weather. You have had sun to show things well. But a little more of the genial would have suited me better. Indeed, for these last two days we have been starved with cold. The thermometer yesterday was eight degrees lower

[5] My father and mother's marriage and wedding dinner.—R. T., 1886.

than the day before. Yet the sun shines, and it is
very good weather to look at from a window. You
say not a word about the Isle of Wight; but I take
it for granted that you have been there since you
wrote. It is odd that I have not the least recollection of Lyndhurst, though I remember very well the
forest scenery. I rather think that my father, who
loved short and out-of-the-way ways, did not take in
thro' Lyndhurst, but left it on the right. Apropos
to your asparagus, I ordered some for supper the
other night, in order to get thoroughly acquainted
with it, and to practise eating it. Ask my niece[6]
Hughes whether she does not think that a neat silver
guillotine, to cut off the heads of asparagus, would
be a pretty addition to the silver tongs, and silver
trowels, and other refined and knickknacky conveni-
ences of the age. I have just heard from Dr. Hey.
He says he has not been able to learn whether the
union[7] took place on the 5th or not; and that 'this
uncertainty has hitherto prevented his giving you
anything in the epithalamium way.' He will epitha-
lamise you in person, I suppose; for he sets out for
London on Tuesday next, to stay about a fortnight.
So you will probably catch a bit of him before his
departure. I shall send my glees to Devereux Court
for him. He says he wishes to receive them while
in town. Tell Eliza, with my best love, that all are

[6] A pet name for Mrs. Hughes.
[7] My father and mother's marriage at Colchester, May 5, 1802.—
R. T., 1886.

quite well at her *ci-devant* home.   But she will hear from her mother as soon, I believe, as you hear from me, for I gave Mrs. S. the direction to Peasemore yesterday.

Remember me kindly to your host and hostess; tell them my scruples about coming when their house is likely to be full.   But I will write soon.   And Daniel,[8] too—I use him very ill.   But he will forgive me. *Monday morning.*—I am sorry you have such cold weather.   We have ice every morning; French beans, potatoes, &c., are almost entirely killed.   What does *Farmer* Hughes say to this?   Mrs. Welch gives an account of the dear little Mary[9] that pleases us all very much.   I rejoice at your account of your fellow- travellers.   Bring them home the pictures of health— nay, the realities rather.   Ann did not look, or seem, well the day we parted.   My love to her; and I embrace the whole house.

Your affectionate Uncle,   T. T.

A MUSICAL GATHERING.—DR. HAGUE, CAMBRIDGE. DR. CROTCH, OXFORD.

T. T. to R. T., jun.

Passenham, Monday, July 26, 1802.

Dear Richard,—You have heard, I imagine, from your grandmother, that I arrived at this earthly para- dise (for such it is always to me) on Thursday, the

---

[8] D. T., then curate at Peasemore.   [9] Mary Powell, died 1875.

15th. I found Miss Missenden here; and on the Monday following came Dr. Hague from Cambridge, and Dr. Crotch from Oxford. Mr. Upton, who was to have been here, could not come. Another sort of engagement came across him—a voyage to Ireland to canvass for a borough there. Dr. Crotch more than supplied his place; as, besides his being an excellent violoncello, his accompaniment on the piano was a great treat. I have often had great enjoyment of music here, but never so great as now—particularly from our quartetts, which went better than any I ever bore a part in. I wished for you to have seen and heard a very extraordinary thing: a man, neither professing the instrument nor in practice, bowing with his left hand and fingering with his right, on a violon-cello strung as usual, playing the most difficult basses of Haydn as well, or nearly so, as any master. All so correct, so perfectly in tune, and giving so exactly the effect intended by the author! But his ear is so quick, and his knowledge of composition so good, that he really can play a passage, by the mere guess of musical instinct, with more effect than most other players do by rule, and teaching, and practice. I found him also a very pleasant little man, and I had particular satisfaction in conversing with him, and comparing notes with him, about the merit of different composers. We generally agreed pretty well in our notions; only I wish he was a little less pre-judiced in favour of Handel and the old school, and against modern music—against it in general, though a great admirer of Haydn. · He one day said to me that he wished Haydn had confined himself to instrumental music. There I ·could not agree with him, and I think I did succeed in softening him·a little by producing instances, and especially his exquisite canzonet, 'She never told her love,' &c., which he acknowledged to be capital. With Miss Sharp and Miss M. we made a little choir of six voices, and, among other things, sung some of Handel's choruses with more effect than I could have conceived, Crotch giving the pianoforte almost the fulness and effect of an orchestra by his powerful manner of playing. We also sung glees of all sorts, and among them my two new glees, which went vastly well ; and, as they pleased the critical nicety of Dr. Crotch, I may venture to think them passable. They have . the honour to be great favourites here. A young lady told me she was sure I must have been in love when I composed them. Several evenings our glees and catches after supper kept us up till between twelve and one. There's a jolly old uncle for you ! In short (as a man always concludes when he has been very long), I think I never had such a musical feast in my life. But—*sic transit gloria mundi*—Crotch went away on Saturday, and Hague departs to-morrow. I shall remain quietly here till Monday, August 2, dine at Hertingfordbury the next day, and probably stay there till the following Monday, August 9 ; then to my home, to which, thank God, I always return with pleasure and satisfaction. There

I shall stay, like a good boy, till the middle or end of September, when I hope to have a peep at St. Faith's,[1] and to find your mother much better, though I have just received a pretty good account of her from your father. Will you be so good as to get a dozen copies of my Aristotle put into boards, as usual, and send them to Messrs. Hanwell and Parker, booksellers, Oxford, by the Oxford waggon? You see I have been doing business, and have performed the part of my own rider at Oxford. N.B.—No duck[2] in all my journey.

My best love to your *chère moitié.* I hope she is well. If you would indulge me with only a few lines (for I know how busy you are in your father's absence), just to let me know how you all do—particularly your grandmother, of whom I have not heard anything for some time—it would be a regale to me. Wednesday, 28th.—Just as I had written the last words I was informed of all I wanted to know by an apparition, when I was sufficiently recovered from my surprise to have the use of my understanding. I dare not reveal any more; but it will be expounded to you, I dare say, ere long. And so, though I am always glad to hear from you, I think myself bound in conscience to release you from the necessity of writing to me, if you are too *affairé* to have time or inclination. Dr. Hey would have added something; but I have left so little room that, having several

---

[1] My grandmother's favourite cottage home near Norwich.—R. T., 1886. [2] His favourite dish at a country inn.

things to say, he will write to you soon.   Dr. H. and Miss Missenden desire to be remembered.   Oh, how sweetly she does sing! and all sorts of things at sight.   My love to all.

Yours affectionately,   T. T.

MEMOIR.

In the year 1764, William Preston, aged thirty-six, the son of an innkeeper at Burton, in Westmoreland, entered the service of Messrs. Twining, in the Strand, as bookkeeper.   His father was a most respectable man, and was highly esteemed in his native town. He had several daughters and the son of whom I write. Their parents had given them a sound, useful education, and they were a happy, united family.   William Preston used to tell in after-life how he remembered being called in as a youth to assist his father in waiting upon the Pretender, who came to their inn with his suite— male and female—in 1745 on their way to Derby. They were all in high spirits and very jovial, ordering in stoups of claret and making merry.   He also re- membered how changed was the scene when they again halted there on their return—a harassed, panic- stricken, shattered company, scarcely daring to stop for a hurried meal and needful rest.   There was no order- ing of wine then, but all was haste and confusion, so keen was the apprehension of the Duke of Cumberland and his troopers following up the pursuit.   In after years the father died and the family home was broken up. William Preston then came to London in search of employment, and the eldest daughter became housekeeper to a City merchant (a Westmoreland man) who lived with his family in one of the old-fashioned paved courts off Lombard Street. William had no difficulty in obtaining employment, and the brother and sister between them, by frugal, self-denying lives, assisted in the support of their younger sisters until they too were able to contribute by their industry to the family purse. It was not long after their arrival in London that William Preston entered upon the office of bookkeeper at Messrs. Twining's, and there he lived for thirty years, a faithful, devoted, and intelligent servant, unwearied in the discharge of his duties, content with a moderate salary, methodical and exact in his proceedings, indifferent to holidays, generous to others, frugal to himself, caring little for amusements, and adapting himself, as a matter of course, to the long hours of business which were then customary.

There is a story of him on record that during his long sojourn in London he had never ridden in a hackney coach, nor indulged himself in a vehicle of any kind save on one occasion, when, having started afoot in his Sunday suit to pay a visit to his elder sister in the City, it came on to rain, and he had to balance in his mind between the probable injury to his best coat and the cost of a sedan-chair. Deciding on the latter, he hailed the chairmen, and so proceeded on his way.   He had reckoned on being set down at the entrance of the court, and so making his way by a modest ring at the bell to his sister's housekeeper's room.   To his infinite dismay, however, the chairmen carried him straight up to the door of the mansion, and, before he could stop them or disentangle himself from the unaccustomed vehicle, they had announced his arrival by a thundering double knock.   He was distressed beyond measure, but was speedily relieved by the announcement that 'Mr. and Mrs. Oliver were not at home!'

The only indulgence which this worthy man allowed himself was an annual attendance at the meeting of the 'Westmoreland Society,' on which occasion he delighted to meet his old friends and neighbours from his native county, thankfully supported its objects in his own unpresuming way, and never failed to return home in good time without any infringement of the strictest rules of sobriety.   His functions in the Strand were by no means limited to the mere routine duties of a clerk : he was also the confidential friend of his employers, and took the warmest interest in their family affairs—advising with the senior partners, and ever showing himself the devoted friend of the younger members who were in training to take their place in the firm, and by whom his attachment was cordially reciprocated.   And so matters went on for thirty years, when, having seen more than one son of the younger generation introduced into the business, he felt that he might indulge his wish for retirement without inconvenience to his employers, and so determined to return to his native town and end his days there. The way to that arrangement was made smooth to him by his having laid up a sufficient amount of savings for a comfortable maintenance, and even to make a home for his sisters with the assistance of such contributions as they two were enabled by their industry to add to the family purse. To achieve this object, however, more effectually they decided on investing their united savings in the 'Short Annuities,' having persuaded themselves that they were not likely to outlive the term of their duration. As years went on, however, and their lives, passed in peaceful retirement with the benefit of temperate habits and pure air, were prolonged beyond their expectations, a certain sense of uneasiness crept into the little household, and the unwelcome idea obtruded itself now and then that, after all, they might outlive the 'Short Annuities,' and come suddenly from independence to poverty. On one of the several visits which Mr. Preston made to his friends in the Strand during the years of his retirement—visits which were returned by several members of the Twining family—the possibility of such a reverse of fortune was alluded to. The contingency was, in fact, one which had not been altogether lost sight of in the Strand, and it was at once a duty and a pleasure to his old employers to remove all doubt or anxiety on that score in giving him the assurance that in the event of their present income failing, its equivalent would be forthcoming during the lives of himself and his sisters. That was felt to be the least which such services as his deserved, and so the worthy man wended his way home in peace. His life was prolonged to the venerable age of ninety years, when (in 1818) he passed away in perfect ranquillity amid the respect and regard of all who knew him.

The above memoir has been compiled from records left by my grandfather on the death of Mr. Preston. I have added one of several letters which he afterwards addressed to the family, showing, as they all do, the unfailing interest which he continued to feel in all their concerns, domestic and otherwise, and affording, with a pleasant account of his simple habits of life, an amusing sketch of the difficulties of a stage-coach journey in those days between London and Westmoreland.—R. T., 1885.

A JOURNEY FROM LONDON TO WESTMORELAND IN THE EIGHTEENTH CENTURY.

William Preston to Richard Twining.

Burton, Aug. 9, 1795.

Sir,—I think it is now time to take up my pen, and to give you some small account of one of the most pleasant and agreeable journeys that I ever in my life experienced. I set out from the 'Angel' behind

St. Clement's, Saturday morning, at four o'clock, and got to Mrs. Lambe's door[3] as the clock struck nine in the evening, where I met with a most kind and friendly reception. I was treated in a manner like a brother or a near relation. I have no occasion to say any more, as you know the family so well, and must beg, when you write to them, to be kindly remembered. Mr. Lambe went with me to every part of the city; and indeed the buildings are most beautiful. He was very sorry that he could not accompany me to Bristol; but he would give me a few lines to a Mr. Chester, a druggist in Castle Street, to take a walk with and show me the city. I was rather disappointed on Monday morning, the coaches being all full; but by chance I met with a returned post-chaise. I had not gone five hundred yards till an officer came in, a very agreeable companion, and we very soon became acquainted. He told me he had been at Lancaster, Burton, Kendal, and every large town in the kingdom. He ordered the chaise to the 'Ship' in Small Street, near the Exchange. I made a promise upon the road to dine with him; but when we got to the inn, the dinner, or something like an ordinary, would not be ready till four o'clock. I could not wait so long. I got a mouthful of cold lamb and a glass of wine or two with him, and then we parted. I then went with my letter to Mr. Chester in Castle Street. I then met with another sociable companion. He walked all over the city with me, to the Hot Wells,

[3] At Bath.

and upon the rocks at Clifton. On our return we drank tea with his mother and sisters. I had not been five minutes in their company before the old lady remembered my face, being some time ago an inhabitant in Chancery Lane. At seven in the evening I set out in the mail, and very soon found that one in the company was going to Carlisle, and another to Dumfries. They both remembered seeing my old face in the handsome shop near Temple Bar. We got to Newport, I believe, in Somerset, about ten to supper, passed through Gloucester at twelve, and at four in the morning we had a sight of Foregate Street, Worcester. I immediately inquired after the coaches, and was told that they very often came there full ; that I might wait two or three days.

I was very easily prevailed upon by my good companions to go on with them to Birmingham. We got there at nine o'clock to breakfast, and as there was no mail any further, and being three in company, we agreed to take a post-chaise, and set out immediately. We dined at Stone, and got to a village called Winslow, about twelve miles from Manchester, at ten o'clock that evening. We were all of us glad to have a long night's rest, and did not wake till after breakfast in the morning. We were taken to the Bridgwater Arms Tavern and Hotel, Manchester. We were all of us very desirous of getting forward, but not one place to be had in the mail. My companions did not like the heavy coach, and then I left them. I dined in company at the tavern with thirty gentlemen. One of the company, whose face I very well remembered, asked me if I had seen Mr. Davenport of Twickenham lately, as he thought I was acquainted with him. He told me his name was C. Bromfield, and desired when I wrote to you that his name might be mentioned. There were two or three more in the company that I knew, whose names I do not recollect. As we had dined, I went to see Mr. Mayers; he accompanied me all the afternoon, and all over the town. I went to bed early, and set out again at five o'clock in the morning. I had then a companion who knew the 'Grecian' in Devereux Court very well. We got breakfast at an agreeable inn, the 'Swan,' at Bolton-in-the moors, where the passengers for Preston changed coaches and passengers that met us from Liverpool. I had not been long in the coach before I found an old acquaintance of my father's, and another—I believe he had been an old Scotch merchant,—who had travelled all over the kingdom for more than fifty years. We soon reached Lancaster, and stopped only then to change horses, and at half-past eight o'clock I got upon my native soil, and parted with my good company. I found my sisters very well, agreeably surprised to see me in such good health and great spirits. I have had the whole town, I may say the parish, to see me. I have sat down fifty times, and have been nearly two days in writing this poor and trifling epistle. With my best respects to your good mother, yourself, Mrs. Twining, your brother and sister, Mr. Richard, Miss Twining, and to every branch of the family. When you see Mr. Hingeston, pray let me be remembered ; likewise to Mr. Hennah and brothers, Mr. Jones and all of the household.

I am, sir, your much obliged and humble servant,

WILLIAM PRESTON.

P.S.—My sisters desire their respectful compliments to you, Mrs. T., and family, not forgetting Mr. Hingeston. You will be kind enough to let Mr. P. behind St. Clement's know that I am got well into Westmoreland. I told you I liked Bath, but I forgot to tell you that I liked Bristol much better.

Sir George Dallas to Richard Twining, jun.

St. Margaret's, Titchfield, Hants, Jan. 8, 1817.

My dear Sir,—With what sorrow I have read your excellent father's [4] dignified letter to the proprietary in the paper of yesterday I need not say to you, who are so intimately acquainted with all the grounds of that public and private regret which such a measure

---

[4] In the year 1816 my grandfather was visited with an attack of paralysis, and although he recovered from it to some extent, and his powers of mind remained unclouded, he recognised the importance of not attempting to renew his former course of active life, and his high sense of duty not permitting him to accept those offers of temporary relaxation and rest which his partners in business and his colleagues at the East India House so cordially and earnestly pressed upon him, he carried out his intention with characteristic firmness, and shortly afterwards resigned his seat in the direction and retired from business.— R. T., 1886.

must occasion among the proprietary and his friends.
That he has acted wisely there can be no doubt,
with those who know the purity and wisdom of his
mind ; and his friends and family must hope that in
thus detaching his mind from public affairs it will
not only prolong to them his valuable life, but enable
him, with unruffled serenity, to enjoy undisturbed
the evening of his amiable and well-spent life. I
rejoice most truly to think he is so much better, and
it will afford Lady Dallas and myself great pleasure
to learn that this amendment promises to continue
and to increase. While he lives may he be free
from pain, and preserve his admirable faculties ; and
distant be the period when he shall receive the reward
of his virtues.

I ever am, my dear sir, yours very truly,

GEORGE DALLAS.

RECOLLECTIONS OF A FIRST VISIT TO PARIS IN
1819—ÆTATIS 12.

In the summer of 1819 my father and my uncle
Smythies made an excursion to Paris, and I had the
happy privilege of accompanying them. Our summer
quarters had been fixed that year at Bognor, at that
time a very small, retired watering-place. I remember
the little difficulties which attended our journey
thither, the coach chartered expressly for our
family party, and sent to take us all up at the

S

door of my father's house in Norfolk Street, the 'scratch' team, the ostler, promoted, *pro hâc vice*, to the post of coachman, and the not unfrequent apprehensions of an upset on the journey. At one critical point, if I remember right, my father took the reins himself, and on a hilly stage some of us outside passengers dismounted to urge the miserable horses forwards by the stimulus of pebble stones. Thankful we all were to reach our journey's end in safety after a *very* long day. A few days afterwards my father and I started for Southampton, where my uncle was to meet us. My mother, and my sisters Mary and Elizabeth, accompanied us as far as Chichester, where we visited the cathedral. Thence they returned to Bognor, and my father and I pursued our journey to Southampton, deviating from our route to call on my grandfather's old friend, Sir George Dallas. At Southamptom we put up at the 'Dolphin,' and the next morning, as the packet for Havre was not to sail till 3 P.M., we filled up the interval by a sail on Southampton Water to Netley Abbey. At the appointed time we embarked on the packet, a well-appointed sailing vessel (no steamers in those days), arriving at Havre, after rather a rough passage, in twenty-eight hours, some portion of which was spent in beating about off the bar, waiting for water to take us in.

Havre was at that time a thoroughly French town, and not remarkable for cleanliness. The inns were mostly entered through the kitchen ; but although the smell of garlic did thereby find its way to the apartments upstairs, they were fairly clean and comfortable—at all events, sufficiently so to satisfy sea-tost travellers. As for myself, the novelty of the scene far more than compensated me for any amount of the odours peculiar to ' la belle France.' Then came one's first *table d'hôte*. What an 'experience' it was! what a mysterious and seemingly endless variety of dishes did it present! and what a contrast to Rugbeian roast mutton and rice puddings! Only think of a schoolboy's amazement at the ragoûts, fricandeaux, &c. &c., winding up with an invitation, after dipping bee-like in endless sweets, to partake of the familiar *gigot*. After dinner we went in search of my uncle, Thomas Twining, who, with his two sons, was at Havre at the time, and he took us for a drive along the banks of the Seine, Thomas, my elder cousin, riding on a pretty little Arab pony. From Havre we travelled *en voiturier* . to Rouen, by a beautiful road following mainly the right bank of the Seine, and there we stayed for a day or two to see that picturesque old city, with its noble cathedral, reminiscences of Joan of Arc, quaint old streets, ancient bridge, and beautiful suburbs. The evening view from Mount S. Catherine, outside the city, was enchanting.

From Rouen we went by the diligence to Paris, where we established ourselves at the ' Hôtel Nelson,' Rue S. Augustin, close to the Rue de la Paix. There we spent a charming fortnight, the weather splendid

—too hot for Uncle Smythies, but admirable for sightseers. Our *valet de place*, François, generally called a halt to look at something or other in the middle of some shadeless place, observing with a wicked smile on his face, when one of the party beat a speedy retreat, 'Ah! toujours à l'abri pour monsieur!' And how much we did manage to see in the time!—the Louvre, Tuileries, Père-la-Chaise, the Gobelins, the Luxembourg, Chambers of Peers and Deputies, Château de Vincennes, the scene of the poor Duc d'Enghien's murder, the manufactory of Sèvres, St. Cloud, Versailles, the latter on the fête of St. Louis, when the waterworks were in full play and the park crowded with company, the Trianons, great and small, with their interesting reminiscences of Marie Antoinette, Napoleon, and Josephine. Especially interesting, too, was a visit which we paid, by invitation, to breakfast with the Duc de Gramont, 'capitaine des gardes du corps' at the Tuileries. It was on a Sunday; and after breakfast and much talk between the duke and my father about Isleworth, Twickenham, and recollections of the days of the *émigrés*, the duke took us into a gallery or corridor through which the king, Louis XVIII., Monsieur the Count d'Artois (afterwards Charles X.), the Duke and Duchess de Berri, and the Duke and Duchess d'Angoulême and their suite passed into the Chapel Royal, whither we had the honour of following them, and were placed in a pew in the royal gallery to hear High Mass.

Montmartre and its telegraph occupied us another

morning, and various restauraunts and theatres in the
evening ; but as I was considered too young for daily
feastings and theatricals, I was sometimes left at home
for *potage au ris-purée* and a *côtelette de mouton*, followed by an evening stroll in the Champs Elysées,
where we disported ourselves at the ' Jeu de Bagne,'
i.e. mounting a hobby-horse, a swan, a dragon, or a
car *ad libitum*, and being whirled round, dagger in
hand, to dart at a ring suspended in the air.   To carry
it off on the dagger's point was to ride gratis !   Oh,
those were happy days !

The theatres were then in their palmiest condition, especially the Théâtre Français, with Talma
and Mademoiselle Mars.

Our route homewards from Paris was by way of
Dieppe and Brighton, sleeping one night *en route* at
a village inn, where we were stowed away on shelf
beds, one above another in the one room which did
duty as ' bedroom, parlour, kitchen, and all.'   The
packet boat was a very indifferent one, and the passage (by night) was stormy ; but it landed us safely at
Brighton after a twelve hours' passage ; and, after refreshing ourselves with toilet and breakfast at the
' Old Ship,' we pursued our journey *viâ* Worthing to
Bognor, where we had the pleasure to find ' all well.'

Soon afterwards I was due at Rugby, returning to
work with a famous store of new ideas—ideas as fresh
in memory now as when they were gathered more than
sixty years since.   R. T.

1886.

EXTRACT FROM THE 'GENTLEMAN'S MAGAZINE,'
MAY 1824.

Died, April 23, 1824, in his 75th year, Richard
Twining, Esq., at his house at Twickenham. He
received his education at Eton, but, in consequence of
the death of his father, remained there only till he
was sixteen, when he was called upon to undertake
the management of his father's business. This, however, was sufficiently long to determine in a great
degree the course and habits of his subsequent life ;
for he there imbibed that taste and love for literature
which he never ceased to improve, and which formed
an essential part of his character.

Equally skilful in the despatch of business, and
diligent in employing his leisure to advantage, whenever he could disengage himself from the fatigues of
London he hastened to his favourite retreat at Twickenham or Isleworth, to resume the study of the best
authors in Latin, as well as English, both in verse and
prose. Natural talents thus wisely improved, height-
ened as they were by a lively and enlarged sense of
moral and religious obligation, rendered him a most
pleasant companion, even to those who were more
exclusively devoted to learned pursuits. In whatever company he appeared, he never failed to attract
attention by the extent of his knowledge and the
politeness and urbanity of his address.

He ever acknowledged with the warmest gratitude
how much both of amusement and instruction he

derived from the affectionate intercourse and correspondence which subsisted between him and his elder brother, the Rev. Thomas Twining, of Colchester, the learned and elegant translator of Aristotle's Treatise on Poetry.

His letters were highly interesting and entertaining. On serious subjects they were forcible and affecting ; on lighter subjects they were humorous and playful. Even the smallest note upon the most trifling occasion received a grace from some happy turn of thought or expression. An unwearied activity of mind, an uncommon quickness of perception, a solidity of judgment, and a never-failing readiness to assist those who stood in need of his assistance, involved him in a multiplicity of business. His hours of leisure were by no means hours of idleness.

In the debates at the East India House he often took a prominent part. No man better understood how necessary it is that every public speaker should make himself master of his subject. Those who heard him perceived that he spoke from a cool and mature reflection. He was earnest only that truth and honesty and justice should prevail. He never went out of his way to attack others, nor repelled attacks with rudeness or acrimony. It was his chief wish and endeavour to soothe, to persuade, to conciliate. In .judicious choice and arrangement of arguments, perspicuity of expression, grammatical accuracy, freedom from all hesitation, redundancy, or embarrassed repetition, and in close and harmonious articulation, few have surpassed him in any assembly.

The high sense entertained by the East India proprietors of his integrity, ability, and valuable services, procured for him, in a manner peculiarly gratifying to him, a seat in the direction. The same zeal for the honour and prosperity of the Company, which had actuated him as a proprietor, still actuated him as a director, till that fatal disease, which rendered him incapable of regular attendance, and has now closed his earthly labours, determined him to resign a situation the duties of which he found himself no longer equal to discharge.

To this imperfect but faithful sketch, be it added, for the information of those who had not an opportunity of knowing him intimately, that he supported his long-protracted sufferings and decay of strength with that cheerful resignation to the will of God, and steadfast hope in Christ, which were the ruling principles of his active and exemplary life.

HIS 'GRAND TOUR' WITH HIS THREE ELDER DAUGHTERS, MARY, ELIZABETH, AND FANNY.—BRUSSELS.—WATERLOO.—NAMUR.

Richard Twining to his Sons.

Genappe, July 18, 1827.

My dear Sons,—When you consider that at this time last week we were rolling about in the vicinity of the Goodwin Sands, and that now we have crossed the memorable and glorious field of Waterloo, you will not be surprised at my finding but little time for letter-writing, or at my making 'joint stock' of this report of. our proceedings. I ought not to be in danger of falling asleep in writing with so many things in my head to keep me awake, though you may have a better excuse for a nap in reading the same. We are within about four miles from Waterloo, and in taking this opportunity of writing I can scarcely have any intention of exciting you to deeds of arms, for with two of you they are out of the question, and I don't think that there would be many advocates in favour of your turning soldier, William, in this piping time of peace; but, having had two or three very interesting hours in the neighbourhood of Waterloo, I would gladly give you a portion of the pleasure we have enjoyed, if it can be conveyed by the post. I believe I told your mother of our arrival at Antwerp. It is a most interesting city, and I was glad to see the cathedral again in possession of those splendid works of Rubens which the French had transferred to Paris, but which have been since restored to their rightful owners. Antwerp, like other places, bears the marks of Bonaparte's grand and decided ideas—witness the noble wet docks ('les Bassins') which he constructed there, and which will be a perpetual advantage to the city, seeing that previously, though placed on the banks of a fine river, and having often possessed very consider-able commerce, it had no dock into which a vessel of any size could enter. The churches, certainly, were not held by him in equal estimation, though he respected them more than Robespierre had done ('No great merit *that*!' you will say), and restored the exercise of religion, which had been suspended, publicly. *This*, and his relieving the citizens from many customs which were great restraints upon their trades, &c., soon rendered him popular, and reconciled the people to measures which suited his policy, but which they would otherwise have considered great grievances. At the time at which the battle of Waterloo decided his fate, and for some years before, he had accumulated a prodigious quantity of timber for shipbuilding (as I saw in 1814), and had contemplated the restoration of a navy, as that was one of his principal ports. But all these projects have vanished like 'the baseless fabric of a vision'! And now we will, if you please, turn to the more humble ones which we are realising. I mentioned the 'Concours' at Brussels, and fearing that the 'Poste' horses might be in requisition on Tuesday, when the king was expected to take his departure, I thought it best to proceed to Malines. Mr. Woodcock and his family were very near to us, and, indeed, they dropped Charles at our inn there, and he saw me at a distance; but, not meeting with our courier, could not learn the address of our party. As it turned out, we should *not* have been in any difficulty as to horses; but the getting forward answered entirely, as it gave us a comfortable opportunity of seeing the very nice archiepiscopal city of Malines, and took us to Brussels in good time to hear some of the prize players, the

bands of the neighbouring towns, &c. They performed on a stage erected in the park (the centre of
the most splendid *range* of buildings I have yet seen,
though London in its rapid strides may produce
equal architectural beauties) immediately opposite to
the Royal Pavilion. Thanks to a good-humoured
corporal, we got beyond the line to which *our* tickets
(the best we could obtain so late) would have admitted us, and we had a good view of the royal family.
The King and the Prince of Orange sat without their
hats during the performances ; and in the evening the
Prince and Prince Frederick, his brother, were walking about with very little ceremony at the entertainment which was given in the same park, or rather in
that part of it which is called ' Waux-Hall '—a grove
of considerable extent, intersected with walks, and
tastefully laid out. In one part is a building of large
dimensions for promenade, dancing, &c., which was
on all sides illuminated in the most brilliant manner ;
the small theatre was also open for the same purpose,
and there was a platform on which we saw some
Anglo-Belgian waltzes [5] and quadrilles, of which we
will say nothing. We did not stay for the fireworks,
as they were not to commence till midnight and my
prudent companions thought it better to retire at
eleven. Yesterday morning the Woodcocks came by
appointment and sat an hour with us. We then
resumed our business—I must beg pardon for so pro-
faning that word !—taking a carriage morning and

[5] No longer a novelty as in 1781 !—R. T.

evening to enable your sisters *à parcourir la ville sans se fatiguer.* The finest objects as specimens of ancient architecture are the Hôtel de Ville and the Grande Place, the former very highly ornamented Gothic, especially as to its lofty tower; and the latter exhibiting some curious old houses built by the Spaniards while the Pays-Bas groaned under their dominion. When we *drove* into the square that your sisters might take a sketch or two—for on foot it is quite formidable to be surrounded by such a crowd as a few minutes' work with the pencil will attract; they might have introduced more objects than they wished or expected, for two unfortunate fellows were undergoing punishment before the magistrates assembled at the Hôtel de Ville. They were fastened to posts on a platform—their time of exposition being nearly over —when, having been branded between the shoulders they were removed under an escort to be conveyed to the galleys and hard labour for a term of years. But, that I may not doom you to like penance, let me hasten to conclude our short but not idle visit to Brussels; where we ended with a good dinner (the *summum bonum* of travelling!) and a bottle of Chablis, price 3 frs. 50 c., which, being good and cheap, we made our beverage at the Hôtel Belle-Vue. I meant to have gone over the field of Waterloo with you, but I seem to be filling my sheet without so doing. It was a particularly interesting evening—indeed we had considered that the evening would be the best time, and no evening could have been better adapted to the scene which we beheld, assisted by the information of an intelligent guide who clearly pointed out the various objects of which one has so often read ; but of the real position of which I never before had so distinct an idea. At the village of Waterloo we had visited the church in which are inscriptions to many a gallant officer, and amongst them to Major Bean and Major Hodge. In a burial-ground near, a nephew of Colonel Fitzgerald was inspecting the monuments at the same time we were. On proceeding to the field we ascended the mound which has been raised to commemorate the battle. The height to the top of the gigantic lion which crowns it is 250 feet, and from the terrace you command a distant view embracing the whole field, which certainly is a very grand one, independently of the extraordinary events which have so gloriously distinguished it. We afterwards stopped at La. Belle-Alliance, where we had a bottle of wine which we 'got the better' of with the assistance of our allies— Mayor,[5] our guide, and the " Poste-Royale ! " ' I conclude this at Huy, the most delightful of all delightful places *hitherto*. I will only add that at Namur we made our *début* at the *table d'hôte* and behaved beautifully till, at the conclusion, a Dutch gentleman—who, with his wife, a pleasant lady and their son, a sharp, intelligent lad of twelve or fourteen, sat opposite us—the business of eating being at an end, joined in a conversation which was going on at a distant part of the table, and certainly I

* Their courier.

never heard anything so odd as his nasal, and hardly intelligible French was ; it might have passed muster, but when his son looked across the table with a broad grin on his face perfect gravity was out of the question, and our only hope was that he would not renew his oration.

I believe we shall disappoint the gay folks at Spa by not going there. From Namur to Huy our leader required all the efforts of his driver to keep him straight to his work. Nothing could be more eccentrict than his movements, the only instinct which never failed him being that which invariably took him, and ourselves after him, to the door of every place of refreshment on the road. Our driver was a comical old gentleman, in his grey camlet jacket, a cloth cap on his head, and a pair of blue-striped linen trousers, which formed a curious appearance between the boots which came above his knees and the aforesaid camlet jerkin. He reminded us of our countryman Dr. Syntax.

God bless you, dear boys :

Your affectionate father

R. TWINING.

A CONTINUATION.

Richard Twining to Richard Twining, jun.

Carlsruhe, Aug. 12, 1827.

' Elizabeth has written to your mother reporting

us, I believe, up to Darmstadt, including of course our visit to Schweinfurt[7] which had nothing of regret about it save its shortness, and I was sorry that the extent of our undertaking obliged us to be such misers of our time. It was delightful to feel how much pleasure we had it in our power to confer, and I am sure we received an ample portion of it in return. Had we stayed to realise a tenth part of the schemes which had been chalked out for us you might have seen us come back to our native land laden with Bavarian[8] honours; but as it is I fancy I must trust to our Court of Devereux for all of which I shall be able to boast. Our digression to Schweinfurt gave us nearly four days' extra travelling; but, putting aside all feelings of friendship, we had a great treat in much of the country through which we passed and in seeing Würzburg. Our driving twice through a forest of twelve to fourteen miles over an excellent road, going with a midday sun and returning in the early morning light, was very pleasant. I did not augur much pleasure from a German cross road to which we had

---

[7] The native place of our good old German friends, the Schramms, three brothers, Martin, Simon, and Christopher, and their two maiden sisters. They had just before retired thither after a long, diligent, and successful professional career in London as professors of music. They lived in Half Moon Street, Piccadilly, and Christopher, the youngest brother, played the violoncello with the Prince Regent. Three more worthy, simple-hearted creatures never lived!

[8] The King of Bavaria did them the honour to send a courier (no 'telegrams' in those days!) to express H.M.'s wish to see the Schramms'' English friends; but, unfortunately, they had already departed.

to trust from Aschaffenburg to Darmstadt.   Our first
five miles lay through a sand which seldom allowed us
to move beyond a walk ; but it was chiefly through a
forest of firs which afforded some relief to the eye and
a welcome shade, and at intervals we had other trees
to enliven the scene.   Our postillion started in the
sulks ; but *we* did not, and when at the end of the
stage I praised his horses as '*equit*' he nodded his
head, adding with a smile : ' *Et le postillon n'est pas
mauvais.*'   Indeed he *worked* hard, and walked for
no small distance.   Our next stage, however, was the
trial, for then we had a great deal of '*pavé*'—which, I
should think had not been mended within the memory
of man—and ruts and narrow lanes, and our third horse
was good for nothing.   However, we made our way at
last to the *chaussée*, and were by no means sorry to
pass through the stately streets of Darmstadt.   To
order dinner and to enquire whether there was any
' repetition ' of the opera had our first attention, and
although the latter was to begin at six· o'clock· and
we were not far from that hour I still hoped to partake of both.   Had I known that the performance (a
rehearsal) would be so short as it was we might have
gone while dinner was preparing.   Fortunately for us,
however, the Grand Duke commanded another drill
on the following evening, and then we saw him take
the lead of his excellent band, which reconciled us to
being obliged to forego ' *the thing*,' viz., the Darmstadt
Sunday opera. . . .

On our journey to Heidelberg we took in the

beautiful gardens of Schwetzingen, and were well pleased in passing an hour and a half in walking about them. They occupy 186 acres, and it is delightful to see how art has subdued nature in converting a plain of sand into as fascinating a spot as can be imagined. Distant mountains form a good object; but the gardens have no variety of hill within their own bounds. Still there is such a disposition of wood, water, temples, and statues as to reconcile one to the flatness of their surface. The gardens at Heidelberg are beautiful in a different way. *There* Nature formed the combination of mountain and river on a noble scale, and what art has added, and what art has destroyed, are in fine unison. The arts of peace during the reign of eight successive electors raised the noble palace which the art of war during that of Louis XIV. has converted into a pile of ruins, supposed to be the finest in Germany; and which, standing in the midst of the gardens overhanging the city, and commanding the beauteous Neckar, formed a delicious conclusion to our evening's ride. We had just been gazing at the famous Heidelberg Tun, which still exists—if such emptiness can be called existence—in the cellar of the castle, when coming suddenly on the terrace we beheld the sun making a most glorious set. It was, indeed, a splendid sight. The plain, of which we have seen more than most travellers care to see, is, with all its flatness and *determined* sandy soil, not without interest. Bounded on the east by the mountain range called the ' Berg-strasse,' and by the Vosges on the

west, there is every appearance of its having been formerly covered with water, though one is not bound to
vouch for the truth of the legend which ascribes the
withdrawal of the waters to the act of a magician, who
conferred that benefit on mankind in penance for some
misdeeds, the particulars of which were probably set
forth in the indictment. . . . At our '*table-d'hôte*'
to-day an English gentleman, long resident abroad,
told me of Mr. Canning's severe illness ; and he was
afterwards called to another part of the table to
receive the intelligence of his death.   Can it be true ?

LINES ON THE DEATH OF THE RIGHT HON. GEORGE CANNING.

Another of her statesmen gone—
Well may our country shed a tear
To see them carried one by one
    Upon the sable bier.
Oh ! let not party's struggling crew
Deprive *him* of the tribute due .
Who with such splendid talents blest
Seemed qualified to keep at rest ·
    Conflicting Powers.
Eton will long delight to praise
The brightness of his early days ;
And Oxford proudly place his name
Amidst her sons of noblest fame,
    Upon her loftiest towers.

R. T.

A SWISS PASTORAL.

Summiswald, Aug. 23, 1827.

Leaving Lucerne at 8 o'clock this morning we accomplished the journey to this place (thirty-three miles) in eleven hours, stopping for two hours and a half in the middle of the day at Zell for dinner, &c. We cannot travel fast now, as we have the same horses for several days together. We have now three, with a fourth when we have a hill to ascend, and they are to take us to Thun, where we shall leave the carriage and proceed to Unterseen either in a boat on the lake or by the little carriages of the country, 'chars-à-banc.'

You will probably not find Summiswald on the map, but it is a village on the way to Thun, leaving Berne to the right. Here we have a complete specimen of a Swiss inn. Nothing can be more clean, neat, and comfortable, and we have been much entertained with hearing two daughters of our landlord sing and play the pianoforte and guitar. They sang a number of Swiss airs and *ranz des vaches* extremely well, and in the most pleasing, unaffected manner possible. The piano was by far the best we have met with since leaving England ; and, indeed, we had quite a charming little concert.

M. T.

LAUSANNE.—JOHN PHILIP KEMBLE.—THE TÊTE NOIRE.

At Lausanne the travellers did not fail to visit Beausite, in memory of my father's old and valued friend, John Philip Kemble, who lived and died there after his retirement from public life ; and, after a deviation *viâ* St. Martin to Chamounix, crossed the Tête Noire to Martigny. At that time the passage was a difficult one even as a mule-path, and they found 'the mulets much more fatiguing than the horses,' of which they had had 'experience at Grindelwald,' and the saddles without any supporting rail 'as the others had.' Nothing, however, could be more 'interesting : a grand view of Mont Blanc at the end of the valley, and the wildest rocks and firs in the foreground, with complete staircases of stone, and such precipices ! On our way we passed the "Val de Bagne," from whence came that dreadful inundation in 1819. It entered the valley of Martigny, and rose nearly to the roof of the small church which we passed ; "mais heureusement les murs étaient bien forts, et repoussaient l'eau à l'autre côté, ce qui sauva le village qui est derrière l'Eglise. Ah ! mademoiselle, c'était un événement bien triste, une quinzaine de gens ont péri !" Vast masses of rock and stone still remain of the devastation that took place, and which the guide described to me.'

E. T.

THE SIMPLON.

Sept. 12, 1827.

We started from Brieg at 5 A.M., with seven horses, and soon began to ascend the stupendous road of the Simplon. Every time we turned a corner of the zig-zagged road the views seemed to get finer : such a magnificent terrace along the side of the mountain, hewn out of the rock, with beautiful stone bridges. The torrents which rush down the mountain are carried under the road in stone aqueducts. At certain distances from each other there are 'refuges' for the protection of travellers in case of their being overtaken by a storm or other accident. At the third relay we stopped for fresh horses, and though first on the road we had to wait nearly an hour whilst the horses were refreshed, as they do not keep nearly enough for the numerous travellers who pass at this season. Soon afterwards we passed through the first tunnel that is cut out of the rock, and came to a forest of firs, where an avalanche had, within a few years, destroyed a large number of trees as it fell into the deep ravine below. Before arriving at the second tunnel, we had a splendid view of the Jungfrau and a chain of snow-crowned Alps above, with the valley of the Rhone and the little town of Brieg, from which we had ascended about four leagues, below. We reached the summit at 11 o'clock, and then had a huge 'sabot' of wood, instead of an iron drag, on one wheel of the carriage for the descent of the pass. Huge as this

' sabot ' was, we wore out three of them during the descent. At 11.30 we arrived at the village of Simplon, and there dined—rather early, you will think ; but I assure you we did not think so after nearly seven hours of mountain air. After leaving this little village, which is surrounded on every side by mountains which crown the summit of the Simplon, it is vain to attempt a description of the awful grandeur of the scene. We passed through another arch, which is the largest and finest of any, with a torrent rushing over masses of rock at the side of but far below the road, till it comes to a precipice of enormous depth, over which it falls in a magnificent cascade. At each side are perpendicular rocks, between which there is only just room enough for the road and the torrent. We saw many more fine cascades and gorges between the rocks covered with immense firs. We soon arrived at San Marco, the first of the Italian villages, and soon after at Isella, where custom-house officers came forward on our entering the Sardinian territory ; but they were easily satisfied that we had nothing of contraband. On approaching the beautiful bridge of Crevola, we saw, all at once, the charming valley spread, as it were, before us ; the houses and churches in quite a different style from those we had left behind us—the former always white, and the latter with very tall steeples or ' campanile.' The inn, too, instead of wooden floors and outside galleries, had marble floors, and long windows opening on to a paved terrace, some nineteen yards square, with plants and statues round it, and an Italian sun shining upon that and the white houses, until one could hardly bear to look at them, it was so dazzling. Then at our tea, instead of the brown bread and honey of Switzerland, we had beautiful white bread, peaches, figs, and grapes. The vines are much prettier than in Switzerland, being all trained upon trellis-work, and the large ripe bunches hanging down inside. . . .

F. H. T.

R. T. to R. T., junior.

Milan, Sept. 18, 1827.

The different opinions which are formed respecting the *time* which various places require is very striking. We have been repeatedly told that this city was dull, and that two days would suffice for it. We have been pretty actively employed, and have seen much; but we leave much unseen, and as to dulness, amongst the people generally, there is a constant moving about the streets and squares; and, as to the higher ranks, the number of carriages on the corso on Sunday and the appearance of the opera reminded us of the park and our own opera. . . .

We ascended to the roof and tower of the Duomo, a building of unique beauty and magnificence. It is entirely of white marble, as white as if it had but just received the last touch of the chisel. Every niche within and without, the capital of every pillar, and the top of each pinnacle, is ornamented with a statue, and each one seems worthy of close examination. Within and without too, are basso-relievos of exquisite beauty, and endless numbers. The finest sight which the roof afforded was the view of the distant Alps, and certainly we have never had any view of Mont Blanc and Monte Rosa which gave such an idea of their sublime and towering height. . . .

At Monza we visited the cathedral, saw the iron crown, and other treasures of the church, passed over the bridge of Lodi, with less of bloodshed than Bonaparte occasioned there, to Placentia and Bologna. At Placentia we had a tremendous storm of thunder, lightning, and rain. It began in the night, and lasted through the next day. I could not have believed that the country could have been so flooded in the time. Some of the rivers which we crossed—and many thanks to the bridges by which we crossed them!—were rolling down their beds with magnificent force. After full twenty-four hours of storm we entered Bologna in sunshine, to an eight o'clock dinner.

We cross the Apennines to-morrow, and thence to Florence.

Your affectionate father,   R. T.

THE APENNINES.

Nearly the whole way from Bologna to Florence, seventy miles, is along the Apennines. Groups of peasants in their long dark cloaks as we passed them reminded us of figures of banditti in the pictures of Salvator Rosa. At Pianoro, .the first relay from Bologna, the ascent of the Apennines begins; we, therefore, had six horses to the carriage, and a short distance farther, stopped at a house to have two oxen attached in front of the horses. The ascent is not in any part very steep; but long hills make it tedious travelling. On looking back we saw the towers of Modena, and a glimpse of the Adriatic, whilst to the north, the long line of the Alps bounded the horizon. At Pietramala we left the Papal Dominions, and entered Tuscany. We had no trouble at the Dogana; but one carriage in the road was entirely unpacked and examined. The Apennines are very different from the Alps; the valleys not so deep, the mountains of gradual slope, and with firs instead of bare rocks, the ground being cultivated nearly to the summit; luxuriant vines and olives in great abundance. The fruit of the olives is not gathered till after a frost. The vintage had begun, and the grapes were being gathered into large casks, each drawn by oxen. Snow was on top of the mountains. Descending towards the south, flowers by the roadside, and views extensive and beautiful. Having dismissed the oxen and four of the horses we proceeded slowly down a long hill, passed a fine villa with an avenue of dark, taper cypress; then a large convent came in sight; but after leaving Fontebuona (the last *poste*) the sun being set, no twilight there, it became too dark to see the beautiful Val d'Arno.

FLORENCE IN 1827.

The windows of our hotel on the Lung' Arno commanded a good view of the Arno and of several noble palaces on its banks. Directly opposite is that of the Corsini family, the magnificent dome of the cathedral and its 'campanile' rising behind it; farther to the right the lofty tower of the Palazzo Vecchio and the Ponte di Trinità with statues of the four seasons at each end. The quays and principal streets are paved with flat stones, which is very pleasant; and a clear sky overhead showed all to advantage as we drove about. The Duomo, or 'Santa Maria dei fiori,' is a grand pile, encrusted with black, white, and red marbles. It was begun in 1298; the dome is said to have been the first on so lofty a scale in Europe. It was erected by Brunellesco in 1472. The pavement within is entirely of various marbles; near the entrance is a monument of Giotto, the celebrated painter and architect; a portrait of Dante, and several other monuments and bas-reliefs. Close to the Duomo at the east end is the campanile erected by Giotto in 1334, an elegant square tower, 294 feet high, covered with marble and ornamented with statues. Opposite is the ancient baptistry, likewise of marble, and the lofty bronze doors with bas-reliefs so beautiful that Michael Angelo said they were fit for the gates of Paradise; the artists were Andrea Pisano and Lorenzo Ghiberti. At the entrance are two fine columns of porphyry. The roof and pavement are covered with mosaics in marble, but within it is richly adorned ; near the entrance is the tomb of Michael Angelo, who died in 1570, aged 88. Three figures of painting, sculpture, and architecture are at the base of the monument, and a bust of Michael Angelo is on the top. There is also a monument of Alfieri by Canova : Italy mourning over the tomb of the poet, with his bust ; many other monuments of historians and great men are there also. The Church of the Annunciation is the most magnificent of all ; even the ceiling covered with painting and gilding in patterns. The chapel of the Virgin is enclosed with a silver balustrade and richly decorated with silver throughout. In the cloisters is the celebrated fresco, well known by engravings, called the Madonna del Sacco. It is said that in a time of famine Andrea del Sarto borrowed a sack of corn from the monks of the convent, and afterwards repaid them by painting this fresco in their cloisters. S. Joseph is represented sitting on a sack reading to the Blessed Virgin. In the spacious piazza is an equestrian statue of Ferdinand I., Grand Duke of Tuscany by Giovanni di Bologna, and it is ornamented by two fine fountains. The most interesting building in Florence is the Palazzo Vecchio, which together with the beautiful ' Loggia,' the statues and fountains and the long arcades of the picture gallery, form the finest and most attractive part of what was once the chief city of Etruria. In the Loggia is a group in bronze of Judith with the head of Holofernes, by Donatello; Perseus with the head of Medusa, likewise in bronze, by Benvenuto Cellini ; a Roman soldier with a Sabine woman, by Giovanni di Bologna, of one entire block of marble, displaying marvellous power in the turning of the limbs—with the Rape of the Sabines in bas-relief on the pedestal. The celebrated ' Galleria' was founded and enriched by the House of Medici, and a more precious collection of statues and pictures cannot be seen. It requires days, or even weeks, to examine each and all. In the vestibule at the top of the stairs is the wonderful group of Niobe and her children—she endeavouring to shield her last loved one is very touching and noble. In the Tribune are some of the choicest pictures, and in the centre stands the famous ' Venus de' Medici.' It is impossible to de- scribe the rare beauty and grace of this incomparable statue. It was found in the Villa Adriana at Tivoli in 1680, amongst other works of ancient Grecian art. The Apollini, the Arolini, and the Wrestlers are all remarkable, and the Dancing Faun, said to be the work of Praxiteles. Of the numerous choice paint- ings it is not possible to give a full idea. Each room is devoted to a certain school. In one of them we found a portrait of Sir Joshua Reynolds and one of the

Honourable Mrs. Damer. In the grand hall of the Palazzo Vecchio Bonaparte once held a magnificent reception, and in one saloon is a portrait of himself in the modern French style. In the cloisters of San Spirito are the arms of the Bonapartes, showing that the family was 700 years old.

The Palazzo Pitti is a majestic, dull, reddish-brown building, with two rows of arcades built by Pitti, a merchant of Florence, and, for a time, the rival of Cosmo de' Medici ; but since 1743 it has belonged to the sovereigns of Tuscany, a change which reminded us of Cardinal Wolsey and Hampton Court. The apartments are spacious, and embellished with choice paintings and specimens of Florentine and Roman mosaics in tables and even pictures. Amidst the numerous pictures worthy of note is one of the Three Fatal Sisters of Old, with their Distaff, Spindle, and Shears, by Michael Angelo. In San Lorenzo is the beautiful chapel, with the tombs of the noble Medici, whose name and fame will long be held in honour. On one monument are four remarkable statues of Twilight, Darkness, Day, and Night, by Michael Angelo Buonarroti, in the grandest and most noble style, worthy commemorations of that family which, during three centuries, bore so conspicuous a part among the sovereigns of Europe.

Having seen all the principal churches and palaces, we took the advice of our guide, and drove up to a vine-covered hill at a short distance from the city, called ' Bello Sguardo,' from whence is a lovely view

of the city and of the Val d'Arno, with the distant
Apennines, and olives and vines in the foreground.
To the right the Palazzo Pitti, with its extensive
gardens and taper cypresses, which add so much to
the beauty of Italian scenery.   All the towers and
objects so clear and distinct under the serene blue
sky, amply vindicating its claim to the old title of
'Florence the fair,' all in such perfect beauty and
harmony, the noble Duomo rising grandly in the
midst, with its graceful campanile, high above all the
other churches.   The walls of the city are six miles
in extent.

In the evening, from the windows of our hotel, we
observed a striking instance of the purity of the atmosphere : the moon being a week old, we saw distinctly
the unenlightened portion of it.

E. T.

Richard Twining to R. T. junior.

Beauvoisin, Sunday evening, Oct. 7, 1827.

Here we are in France, having passed for the *last*
time over the mighty Alps, and for the *first* time
through a French custom-house, the latter, in some
instances, the more troublesome undertaking.   I must,
however, do the officers the justice to acknowledge
that they gave us very little trouble.   Indeed, I
scarcely know how they could have given less, if they
had any duty of inspection to discharge.   They didn't
even take a slice of Mayor's Bologna sausage, which

he is taking home to his friends, perhaps for a 'bonne bouche' at Christmas. We begin to think ourselves *at home*, and are happy in the recollection of the pleasures we have enjoyed, and in the forecast of soon seeing those from whom we have been so long separated.

Since we quitted Turin we have made good progress; one stage, indeed, was a longer one than we liked, chiefly because we grudged the loss of any of the beauties which daylight would have displayed. The moon, indeed, did all she could to supply the place of the 'greater light,' and, where her powers failed, imagination was at hand to 'picture forth' the forms of 'things dimly seen.' We trusted for our night's lodging to a house, which is not one of the usual *sleeping* places, and had no reason to regret having taken our chance of what accommodation we could get. We had excellent beds, which was well-nigh all the accommodation we required. There is sometimes amusement in the variety of style in which one is received in the course of a long journey, especially if, as has uniformly been our lot, the worst has not been without comfort. At the summit of Mont Cenis everything was in a rough style, except the cheerful attention of the landlord and his good wife. They seemed to be aware that warmth was the chief desideratum for the comfort of their guests in that wild region, and we had not been in the house many minutes before our hearths were smiling with a cheerful blaze, and our active host—'ligna super foco, largè reponens.   At Genoa the style had been very different. There most of the hotels were formerly palaces, inhabited by great nobles or wealthy merchants—ranks then not unfrequently united in the same person—and there they lived in a situation overlooking the port, so that from the windows of their stately apartments they could watch the arrival or departure of their proud argosies, and devise means of successful rivalry with the rich Venetians.   In such-like rooms we were lodged, having to ascend to them, though no higher than the second floor, by no less than eighty-seven stone steps ; but, once there, we had to admire all the splendour of bygone days in lofty ceilings, profusion of gilding, and marble balconies.   How shall we drop down, think you, from such magnificence ?

> Non ebur neque aureum
> Meâ renidet in domo lacunar !

Lyons, Oct. 8.—We expect to be in Paris in five days.

Your affectionate father,   R. T.

From the same to the same.

Paris, Oct. 23, 1827.

Our 'business' yesterday was to dine at the Café de Paris and to adjourn to the ' Feydeau ;' to-day to pay some visits, to entertain Mr. and Mrs. Woodcock at dinner, and to adjourn to a *soirée* at Mrs. Mayne's in the evening.   One must not talk of 'business' on a Sunday; so I will only hint at the *pleasures* of Baron Rothschild's princely table on that day. Friday for the coast—and the shorter and the smoother the passage which is to convey us to our long-deserted native land, the better. R. T.

'VOITURIERS.'— OSNABRÜCK.—ROYAL REVIEW AT HANOVER.

Richard Twining to R. T., junior.

Hanover, April 26, 1834.

.   .   .   .   .   .

I am writing from our most *northern* point, at which we arrived about 5 o'clock, and we stop not without feeling an attraction to move forwards, as we are anxious to see Mary, who, we know, is looking out for *us*. It would not be wise, however, to proceed without seeing at least a good portion of what Hanover has to offer to the notice of strangers; but we shall probably take half the distance between this place and Brunswick to-morrow afternoon so as to arrive there in good time on Monday. A letter which I left at Osnabrück will have informed you of our river adventure, and you will not be surprised that your sisters, who are never partial to steamers, should be in favour of quitting the evident uncertainty of water for the better chances of land. We should have felt more regret in parting from our new and agreeable friends had there been any apprehension other than that of delay to them in prosecuting their

U

journey by steam, for I never saw a finer or more vigilant crew on board of any vessel than in that in which they proceeded, and I am sure that they had no reason to fear any such mishap as that which they had already experienced.   Having reached Deventer we found that we must have waited a day for the *diligence* to put us forward, and we therefore determined to make trial of the *voiturier* system for the day, and, having found it to answer well we have continued it for three days, which brought us hither.   We accomplished forty to fifty miles a day ; slow work, you will say ; but indeed it is as much as can be done pleasantly by this mode of travelling, and it suits us perfectly well, unless perhaps that it threatens us with some extra hurry at last.   If we come to a bit of bad road—as, you know, *has* happened to us—we get out and walk a bit, easing the horses, and enabling Elizabeth to botanise,[9] when she generally contrives to pick up something.   For my part I am by no means indifferent to that important point in travelling, good food, for I am particularly anxious to have my companions well supported in order to go through the pleasant labours of the day, and for that matter our drivers have been ready enough to take a hint as to stopping to bait their horses at the right time for our 'baiting' also.   At Rheine, a Prussian town (now a railway station) on the Ems, we were too early, as we thought, but the landlord was so agreeable that I did not like to wait so long as our horses required (they

* An opportunity of which she has made good use through life. --R. T.

never stop but once) without calling for something, and so we had some wine and bread and butter ; but after I had paid him he was not satisfied that we should not take more, as we should not see another house for thirty miles, which proved to be the fact— at least nothing deserving the name of a house. The next day we reached· our halting-place just as the *table d'hôte* was being served, and fared capitally— some *vin de grave* inclusive—for little more than one shilling per head, after which the landlord's gentlemanly son escorted us round the town. Yesterday we stopped at an extremely pretty watering-place, Neudorff, where great preparations were in progress to receive the company expected for the season, commencing June 1, when large numbers may be, and we understand are, accommodated there. While we walked about the extensive and nicely laid-out grounds a good dinner was provided for us at the seasonable hour of a quarter to one, we having breakfasted at six o'clock: The country from the time of our quitting Osnabrück formed a welcome contrast to the specimens, or ' the bad specimens,' which the preceding days had afforded, for it was an uninterrupted succession of highly cultivated lands and farms and neat villages. The fields are almost without exception open and arable, and we seldom saw any grazing, unless here and there a solitary cow or calf in leading strings, under the care of a poor girl whom the frolicsome animal seemed to lead a tiresome life. It was very interesting to see the number of fine horses employed

in the plough, or the harrow, or in the waggon teams.
In the districts through which we have passed and
which nature has treated with a sparing hand, the inhabitants have striven to bring every spot into cultivation which would admit of it, and it was gratifying
to see the good effects of their labour.   In these parts
the spade is much employed, and often by women.

Sunday Evening.—It occurred to us that Randle
Ford [1] was in the neighbourhood of Hanover, and on
describing the institution in which he was studying to
the landlord of the hotel, he thought he knew where
he was likely to be, and it was confirmed by some one
in the public room, of whom he made enquiry.   I
therefore sent a messenger, at six this morning (the
distance being only three miles) to request the
pleasure of his company, and he promised to join us
at noon. . . . . I may go back a stage or so to tell you
one unusual sight we had on Saturday morning while
the horses were watering.   The obliging landlord—we
have found them all obliging hereabouts—seeing us
prying into the entrance of an old *château*, came to
us, and sent to his wife for the keys, as she had charge
of the Prince of Steinfurth's venerable place.   It was
a fine specimen of the ancient time, and we were
surprised to see some old prints in the dining-room,
of 'Clarke' Tillotson, Wake, Tennison, and Addison :
that was one unusual sight.   Another was the escorting
of two young men (with limbs unscathed) who had
been fighting a duel, and had a mounted dragoon to

[1] First cousin of my wife.—R. T.

bring them before a magistrate. At noon Randle
Ford arrived in good health and spirits, and we all
went to the parade on the 'Waterloo Place,' with its
Waterloo pillar and figure of fame on tiptoe on the
globe at the top of it, to see a parade of the Hano-
verian cavalry, rifles, and grenadiers, all of whom
presented a fine appearance on that noble parade-
ground. After a short time the Duke,[2] with the
Duchess, Princess, and their suite made their appearance; but we were in the crowd at a distance from
the centre. The troops were inspected by His Royal
Highness, who also looked well, and they afterwards passed him in the usual order. My military
ardour,[3] I suppose, made me bold, and having two
English ladies under my care raised my pride a little,
and I led Elizabeth and beckoned Fanny and Randle
to follow towards the centre, and we stood at the end
of the staff, suite, &c. ; but soon others followed, and
an old general officer sent them back ; but did not
interfere with us, a courtesy which I acknowledged
with a bow. He came up, and I told him in French
that we were English, and wished to see as much as
we could of our Prince. He asked in English, if we
were acquainted with him. I said I could not absolutely claim that honour; but that I believed my
name was familiar to His Royal Highness. 'Will
you not call upon him: he will be so glad to see you?'

[2] H.R.H. the Duke of Cambridge, then Viceroy of Hanover.

[3] An allusion to the old times of the Royal Westminster Volunteers,
of which my father was lieut.-colonel, *circa* 1805.—R. T., 1885.

I explained that we were doing little more than passing through Hanover; but that I should esteem it a great honour to be introduced to His Royal Highness, if that would not be an impropriety. 'Oh, no!' replied the General, 'I will speak to one of the equerries ; that is the best way,' and away he posted. The parade was ended, and the royal party passed us on their return ; but not before the General by a quick movement had put our name in train to the Duchess, who looked round and bowed, and presently the Duke stopped, and we heard him say, 'Where is he?' when His Royal Highness seeing me with my hat off, came back, and most kindly said he was glad to see me; should I make any stay? how long had I been in Hanover? very happy to make acquaintance with me; spoke most affectionately of Dr. Hughes, and referred to his friendship for my father. 'Where do you live continually?' 'In London, sir?' 'Do you carry on the same concern?' 'Well, what do you say to these great changes?'[4] I said it was a great experiment, and the change was certainly not in accordance with my wishes. 'No, no, I suppose you had rather things had remained as they were,' to which I assented.[5] His Royal Highness then asked if the ladies with me were of my family, &c. ; and, indeed, stopped much longer than I could

[4] The abolition of the East India Company's trading charter.

[5] The outlook has certainly been a very different one from what was anticipated, looking to the reduction in the prices of, and enormous increase in the consumption of, tea in Great Britain since that time.—R. T., 1885.

have presumed to have expected, and then left us most graciously. Our good friend the General came up afterwards and seemed quite pleased at the complete success of his assistance and gave me his name —General Behrends. I was very glad of the opportunity of thanking him for his kindness, and the gratification which he had been the means of affording me. By the time we returned to our hotel, we had a carriage ready to take us to the palace and gardens of Herrenhausen. At four o'clock we dined at the *table d'hôte*, and soon after five we took leave of Randle Ford, and proceeded to the singular, antiquated town of Hildesheim, about one-third of the distance from Hanover, to the long wished-for Brunswick, arriving there the next day by noon, when we found our dear Mary looking quite well. It was a happy meeting after a long absence. Mrs. Cole and her daughters received us with the warmest hospitality. We all talk of the pleasure it would have afforded our good friend Mr. Cole [6] to have received us. . . .

Yesterday was really summer, and the sun shines bright this morning. We all but see the foliage grow. The trees are said to be more backward than in England. We leave on Thursday for Göttingen, Cassel, &c., embarking at Rotterdam by the 'Batavier' for London.

Your affectionate father,   R. T.

---

[6] Mr. Cole had been a merchant at Brunswick, and suffered considerably during its occupation by Bonaparte.

THE MOLDAU.—PRAGUE

Weltrus on the Moldau, Thursday evening, Sept. 19, 1844.

My dear Daniel,—If I had dated my letter from Prague (from whence it will most likely be forwarded), you would have known precisely where we were without turning to your maps; but as I like to be sent to those sources of information myself, I will invite you to turn to a map of Germany and look how near we are to that ancient and celebrated city, which I used to consider at an inaccessible distance; but which we find it no difficulty to approach, at least; and which we hope to carry to-morrow morning, having ordered horses at six o'clock. The banks of the Moldau! To be sure Thomas in his widely extended travels may have been here, but I rather think we are the first of the family who have ever crossed it. We did so this evening, seated in our carriage and *three*, and followed, rather to my surprise, by a huge loaded waggon and four which drove down the bank and took its station by our side on the flying bridge. The horses were probably pretty well accustomed to the operation, for they all stood very quietly, and ours brought us to our inn, which we entered by a large farm-yard, where we found a range of building of considerable extent, with much of the appearance of an old monastery —judging by the long passages into which the numerous bed-rooms open. It has ceased, however, to be monastic in its habits, for we found under the arched entrance, some noble Bohemians, deep in their potations of their favourite beverage, beer. One went away as happy as a prince, though not walking quite so upright as princes generally do. It is the only place where we have had any perplexity about money —but I had been rather too inconsiderate in parting from Austrian money, which I had provided for the purpose of paying the *poste*, &c., where I could have exchanged Napoleons without any difficulty, but *here* and at the preceding station, the poste-master was out, so was the master of the Farm Inn; the postilion could speak nothing but Bohemian, and looked at the *little bit of gold* which was to represent so many small pieces of *his* currency. He shook his head and we could do nothing with him. I got my trunk, secretly to take from it some French five-franc pieces—for I never like to make a display of money, though I really believe there is as large a share of honesty in the country through which we have travelled as can be found anywhere—when a traveller came up who could speak Bohemian, and he explained to the postilion, that at the rate at which we reckoned the Napoleon he would get more for his 'trinkgelt' than he would otherwise have after accounting to his master, and he was content to take it with a smile upon his rough countenance: and so we retired to our cells (pretty capacious ones) trusting that Napolleon will set us free at six o'clock! And so he did.

Prague, Saturday, September 21.—After a night of continued hard rain. We had hoped that the violent storm of the preceding day—Wednesday—would have cleared the air and restored fine weather to us. It was such a storm of thunder, lightning, and rain as I have never been in, except when we quitted the steam-boat on the Danube, when we went to Vienna. The lightning really seemed to be playing all around us, and the appearance of the storm upon the ranges of mountains, at nearly the foot of which we were (and which we crossed on Thursday), before it swept down to us, was awful and magnificent. Our carriage from the inn was a very nice one, but open at the sides; our vigilant driver, however, saw what was coming, and *taking the windows from the boot*, fixed them just in time to protect us.

We have been at Töplitz, it's true, but I suppose that fact will not be admitted by the frequenters of that celebrated place, for all the gay world had quitted it, as they usually do after August is past: and this year in particular there has been such an abundance of rain and of unsummerlike weather, that perhaps there were fewer stragglers left than might sometimes be the case; but we could imagine the sort of concourse that there must be in a fine season, when it appears that there are sixty hotels in the place, and almost every house is prepared for the reception of visitors. It is finely situated as to surrounding country, which comprises a range of lofty mountains. The first three miles generally takes three hours, but we did it in less time, for our carriage is rather light and we allow three horses to it; but they—the poste-master—gave us four good ones—

charging us for only three, for which we paid about one shilling per mile and they took us over the mountain capitally.

We were off at six, and arrived here at half-past nine (two stages), so that we have had a whole day to commence operations in this fine old city, which contains a great deal to see and to admire. I did *not* admire the immediate neighbourhood, not the quarter by which we entered, for after the rain all the roads were deep, and footpaths there were none; and it was really painful to see the many poor shoeless creatures, young and old, male and female, in great proportion wading through the dirt with heavy loads, and with wheelbarrows so large and so loaded that even the young who often had them in charge, trembled in their efforts to keep them level ; and the suburb through which we passed was but little better. To be sure the scene changed within the gates of Prague, and, therefore, to keep you no longer on the more cheerless part of the picture, let me hope that you will find yourself more comfortable when you accompany us through the principal street to the Hotel of the ' Three Lime Trees.' Indeed it is a fine and interesting place, and we shall stay a few days to enjoy the many objects of attraction. The Moldau divides it into two parts—the old being on the right bank, and the new on the left bank, which is lofty and rather abrupt, and upon which there are many buildings of commanding aspect : the cathedral, the royal palace,— a vast range of buildings, from whence the view is singularly fine. To write about such things is, I fear, but idle work, for how can one convey any adequate idea, yet it may serve to show that those whom we have left in our glorious England are still in our minds. We are all well, and unite in kind love to you and cousins, of course including both generations at Hull.

We quit this on Tuesday morning, going—never mind! We hope to be home by Christmas.

Ever your affectionate brother,

R. TWINING.

APPENDIX.

ΧΑΡΑΚΤΗΡΕΣ.
Κεφ. δ.

Ετι δε τις ὀν καλως διωρισασθαι ܀κ ευμαρες. ἁπασιν γαρ τοις ἀλλοις ἀνομοιυς ὠν, ἀυτος ἀυτῳ ἀνομοιοτατα κ, λεγων κ, πραττων φανερος ετιν. Αμελει τοιܟτος ἐτι τις ὁιος σωφρων περ και μετριος ων ὁμως χλιδῃ παντοδαπῃ κ, τρυφῃ ἐξαιρετως ἀγαλλεσθαι, κ, τܟ ὁινܟ πιειν ὁσα ἑιδη τιμαλφεστατα, κ, των πλακܟντων φαγειν ὁσܟς ἡδιστܟς, κ, καθευδειν μαλακως, κ, λεχος κοκκινοβαφες ἀντι τܟ ἀ᾿βαπτܟ προαιρεσθαι, κ, δυܟ ἀνθ' ενος. Και πραܟς ὠν ἠθει ἐρεχελειν κ, φιλονεικος ἐχειν, κ, ἐριζειν, τας δε ἐριδας ἀγαθην κοινωνιαν ονομαζειν. Και προς τον βασιλεα ἑννοικωτατως ἐχων, ομως παμπονηρῳ τινι κ, προς τον βασιλεα δυσμενεστατῳ συνηγορειν κ, συναπολογεισθαι κ, συνεπιψηφιζειν. Και λεγειν ὡς χρη τܟς βαρβαρܟς ἀπαντας, ὡσπερ φαλαγγια, σαρωθρῳ απωθεισθαι κ, εξ ἀνθρωπων ἀφανισθηναι, κ, ὡς δει ἁπαξ των πεντε ἑτων τ ἐν πολιτειᾳ πρωτευοντα πελεκιζεσθαι, ܟκ ὡς πονηρον ὀντα, αλλ' ὁτι πρωτευει. ἡ δη κ, πλειܟς ἡ τετταρακοντα ανδρας μνημονευειν, ὡς αποπνιγεσθαι φησι δειν. κ, επιτριπτܟ τινος δενδρωνα ἑτηκως συνθεωρειν, κ, λογειζεσθαι προς ἑαυτ܍ν ἐκ τινος ἀν δενδρܟ ὁ κεκτημενος ευχημονετατως κρεμαθῃ. κ, τον βροχον φαναι παντων νοσηματων ιασιν ποιεισθαι. κ, την τܟ δημοκοινܟ τεχνην ἀκριβεϛατως ἐπιϛαϛαι, κ, περι των πεπελεκισμενων κ, κεκρεμασμενων ὀνομαϛι μεμνῃϛαι, κ, τα τܟ δημιܟ απομνημονευματα συχνακις αναγινωσκειν—και δικην οφληκως ἢ δικαϛην βꙋλεσθαι κρεμαννυειν. κϳ περι τꙋς λογꙋς δεινος ὠν, τραγικον τι τῇ δεξιᾳ κρꙋτειν κϳ σοβαρον λαλειν, κϳ μεταξυ ἱππαζομενος διαγωνιζεσθαι κϳ διαμφισβητειν, κϳ ἱππῳ τῳ τεταλαιπωρημενῳ δια την εν τῳ λεγειν δεινοτητα πληγας ἐκτεινειν. κϳ των ἑαυτꙋ ὁμοφυλων τꙋς πολλꙋς τιμασθαι πλειϛꙋ, ὁι δε ꙋδενι ἀλλῳ τꙋς ἑτερꙋς ὑπερβαλλꙋσι πλην τολμῃ τε κϳ μοχθηριᾳ. κϳ το ὁλον, κωδωνιζειν δυνατος κϳ παρονομαζειν, κϳ δισκενειν, κϳ ταυροκοπειν, κϳ τραγηματιζεσθαι, κϳ ἀιλꙋρον θρεψαι, κϳ τριγγισμον τριγγιζειν κϳ ἑαυτον λανθανειν των ἀλλων διαφερων.

TRANSLATION FROM THE GREEK.

A character written playfully in imitation of Theophrastus by Mr., afterwards Sir, William Jones, and sent by him to his friend Dr. Parr.

There is another sort of man whose character is not easily drawn, for not only is he very unlike everybody else : but is strikingly inconsistent with himself in everything he says or does.

He is a man of great prudence and moderation, yet delights beyond measure in every kind of luxury and indulgence, drinking the choicest wine, eating the most luscious sweetmeats, and sleeping in the largest and softest beds, and in a crimson bed rather than a plain one. His disposition is gentle, yet he contradicts, cavils, and disputes, saying that without contradiction there is no good fellowship. He is well affected towards his sovereign, yet sides with the meanest and most inveterate of his enemies, vindicating their conduct and supporting their measures. He maintains that all disagreeable people should be swept away like spiders with a broom, and not be suffered to infest society ; and that every five years the Prime Minister should lose his head, not for any fault, but because he *is* minister ; then he runs over a list of above forty persons, who, he thinks, ought to be strangled, and, when he comes to a wood stops to consider with him-self which tree would serve best to hang the worth-less owner upon ; a halter being, as he says, the cure of all mischiefs. He thoroughly understands the office of an executioner, and has the names of all who have been brought to the block or the gallows, and frequently repeats their last dying speeches : but if a verdict is given against himself nothing less will satisfy him than hanging the judge. His manner of speaking is vehement, smacking his hands with a kind of stage effect ; his tone of voice is deep and hollow ; even on horseback he enters into debate, and in the heat of argumentation inflicts a heavy blow upon the sorry jade which carries him. He pays the highest compliments to those of his own party, though they are pre-eminent only in effrontery and baseness. In short he can ring a peal, pun and quibble, pitch a quoit, fell an ox, eat sugar-plums, nurse a cat, and live all the while unconscious how much he excels other men !   D. T.

1848.

SIR WILLIAM JONES.

*From the Journals of Thomas Twining, Esq., in
India.   Bengal Civil Service.*

I had a very favourable introduction to the celebrated Oriental scholar, Sir William Jones, one of the
judges of the King's Court at Calcutta.   It was given to
me by his friend Dr. Parr, who was also the intimate
friend of my uncle Thomas Twining of Colchester,
and the doctor recommended me to accompany his
letter with a handsomely bound copy of my uncle's
late work, a translation of the poetics of Aristotle.
Sir William received me and my introduction and
present most politely.   Meeting me at a public entertainment a few evenings after he again spoke to me
very kindly, expressing the great pleasure which a
cursory look into my uncle's book had afforded him,
and his regret that he was not able for the present
to read it more regularly, his time being entirely taken
up with his public duties.   It was on that account, he
said, that he saw scarcely anybody, and that he never
had company to dinner.   After this observation I was
agreeably surprised at receiving a few days subsequently an invitation to dine with him.   The party
consisted of Sir William and Lady Jones, another
gentleman and myself.   Sir William was very cheerful and agreeable.   He made some observations on
certain mysterious words of the Hindoos and other
Indian subjects.   While sitting after dinner he sud-

denly called out with a loud voice, 'Othello, Othello!'
Waiting a minute or two, and 'Othello' not coming,
he repeated his summons, 'Othello, Othello!' His
particularly fine voice, his white Indian dress sur-
mounted by a small black wig, his cheerfulness and
great celebrity, rendered this scene extremely interesting. I was surprised that no one—Mussulman
or Hindoo—answered his call. At last I saw a black
turtle of very large size, crawling slowly towards us
from an adjoining room. It made its way to the side
of Sir William's chair, where it remained, he giving
it something it seemed to like. Sir William observed
that he was fond of birds, but had little pleasure in
seeing or hearing them unless they were at liberty;
and, he, no doubt, would have liberated Othello, if he
had not considered that he was safer by the side of
his table than he would be in the Ganges. There
could be no doubt that the place intended for
'Othello' by the captain was not *under* Sir William's
table but *on* it.

I passed a most pleasant day in the company of
this distinguished and amiable man. He was so good
as to express some approbation of my Persian studies
and repeated two lines, in that language, of Ferdousi,
the Persian poet, and also his translation of them :—

> Kill not the ant that steals a little grain ;
> It lives with pleasure, and it dies with pain.

T. T.

X

OBITUARY.

In the hot season of this year (1794) India deplored the loss of one of the most distinguished men that had ever visited her shores, and I lost in that event one of my kindest friends. Sir William Jones died at Calcutta after a short illness. His death was deeply lamented by all classes, European and native, and was, indeed, a public misfortune, interrupting literary labours for which it was scarcely possible to find another individual uniting similar qualifications— such a knowledge of Asiatic languages, so refined a judgment, and such indefatigable zeal. All his time, public and private, when on the bench as a judge, or when amidst the Brahmins of Nuddea he 'explored the vast extent of ages past,' was devoted to the public good. His private hours, at the time of his death, were employed upon a translation of the Institutes of Menu, a work as important as curious, being the Justinian code of Hindostan.

Sir William intended to have returned to England as soon as the work should be completed, proceeding, it was said, first to China, thence to Bencoolen and Bombay, and so up the Red Sea and overland to Europe. Lady Jones had left India the year before. Sir William was buried at Calcutta and on his tomb was placed the following

EPITAPH WRITTEN BY HIMSELF.

Here lies deposited
The mortal part of a man
Who feared GOD but not death ;
And maintained independence
But sought not riches ;
Who thought none below him
But the base and unjust,
None above him but the wise and virtuous ;
Who loved his parents, kindred, friends, and country,
And having devoted his life to their service
Resigned it calmly,
Giving glory to his Creator,
Wishing peace on earth,
And goodwill to all His creatures,
On the 27th April,
In the year of our Blessed Redeemer
1794.[7]

'WE ARE SEVEN.'—WORDSWORTH.

I.

A simple child, dear brother Jim,
That lightly draws its breath,
And feels its life in every limb,
What should it know of death ?

II.

I met a little cottage girl,
She was eight years old, she said ;
Her hair was thick with many a curl
That clustered round her head.

---

[7] Sir William Jones was only forty-eight years of age at the time of his death, having been born in London in 1746.

III.

She had a rustic, woodland air,
  And she was wildly clad ;
Her eyes were fair, yea, very fair,
  Her beauty made me glad.

IV.

' Sisters and brothers, little maid,
  How many may you be ? '
' How many ? seven in all,' she said,
  And wondering, looked on me.

V.

' And where are they ?   I pray you, tell '—
  She answered, ' Seven are we,
And two of us at Conway dwell,
  And two are gone to sea.

VI.

' Two of us in the churchyard lie—
  My sister and my brother—
And in the churchyard cottage, I
  Dwell near them with my mother.'

VII.

' You say that two at Conway dwell,
  And two are gone to sea,
Yet you are seven ; I pray you tell,
  Sweet maid, how this may be ? '

VIII.

Then did the little maid reply,
  ' Seven boys and girls are we ;
Two of us in the churchyard lie,
  Beneath the churchyard tree.'

IX.

' You run about, my little maid,
  Your limbs they are alive ;
If two are in the churchyard laid
  Then are ye only five.'

X.

'Their graves are green, they may be seen,'
  The little maid replied,
'Twelve steps or more from my mother's door,
  And they are side by side.

XI.

'My stockings there I often knit,
  My kerchief there I hem ;
And there upon the ground I sit—
  I sit and sing to them.

XII.

'And often after sunset, sir,
  When it is light and fair,
I take my little porringer
  And eat my supper there.

XIII.

'The first that died was little Jane;
  In bed she moaning lay,
Till God released her from her pain,
  And then she went away.

XIV.

'So in the churchyard she was laid,
  And all the summer dry
Together round her grave we played,
  My brother John and I.

XV.

'And when the ground was white with snow,
  And I could run and slide,
My brother John was forced to go,
  And he lies by her side.'

SEPTEM SUMUS.

I.

Dum calet, et totos sentitur vita per artus,
  Quid tum de gelidâ morte puella sapit?

II.

' Annum nunc perago,' mihi dixit parvula, ' nonum ; '
Pulchra fuit crispis implicitisque comis.

III.

Vestitus nullâ gestusve decebat ab arte ;
Lumina luminibus quam placuere meis !

IV.

' Quot fratres,' inquam, ' quot habesque, puella, sorores ?
' Septem, si velis scire quot esse, sumus ! '

V.

' Ast ubi sunt omnes ? ' ' Septem certe sumus omnes.
In ratibus duo sunt, sunt et in urbe duo.

VI.

' Atque duos nostrûm templi sacrata sepultos
Terra tegit ; cura est unica matris—ego.'

VII.

' Urbe duos, memorasque duos super æquora vectos ;
Dic mihi, quid septem vos tamen esse putas ? '

VIII.

' Nos septem,' dixit, ' pueri sumus atque puellæ,
Atque duos nostrûm funebris arbor habet.'

IX.

' Integra sed tua vis, pedibus tu currere gestis ;
Si duo sub terrâ corpora, quinque manent.'

X.

' Aspice sed virides tumulos ubi cespite vivo,
Ante fores lateri conseruere latus.

XI.

' Hic super est cordi deducere stamine lanam
Hic sedeo, atque illis hic operosa cano.

XII.

' Sæpius hic, postquam sol occidit, æthere puro,
　　Gramineâ in mensâ cæna parata mea est.

XIII.

' Post longos primùm soror est abrepta dolores,
　　Parcentis miseræ voce vocata Dei.

XIV.

' Jamque Dei juxta templum jacet ; ipsa Petrusque,
　　Dum licuit, positæ lusimus ad tumulum.

XV.

' Venit hyems, glaciesque tulit mihi lubrica ludos,
　　Occidit ille !—soror qua jacet, ille jacet.'

D. T.

FAREWELL TO BITTESWELL.

Farewell Bitteswell—long farewell !
　　Happy hours I've spent in thee ;
Thoughts—that may hence my bosom swell
　　With joy—if they reverted be.

The quiet cot, the blessed dream
　　That creeps o'er earth's more wandering son,
Would in thy lovely village seem
　　To him—he had Elysium won.

For all so calm, that to one's breast
　　We feel we've found a home at last ;
And all who meet this halcyon rest
　　Are soothed from trouble—sorrows past.

The tempest of the world unknown,
　　Sweet village ! ever calm with thee ;
Kingdoms are lost—the world o'erthrown—
　　But ever thine, Tranquillity.

W. H. L., Bitteswell, June 1790.

Spottiswoode & Co., Printers, New-street Square, London.

50 Albemarle Street, London,

November 1886.

MR. MURRAY'S

LIST OF WORKS

IN

GENERAL LITERATURE,

CONTAINING

THE SPEAKER'S COMMENTARY ON THE BIBLE.

HISTORY, ANCIENT & MODERN.

BIOGRAPHY, MEMOIRS, &C.

GEOGRAPHY, VOYAGES, AND TRAVELS.

HANDBOOKS FOR TRAVELLERS.

THEOLOGY, RELIGION, &C.

SCIENCE, NATURAL HISTORY, GEOLOGY, &C.

ART, ARCHITECTURE, AND ANTIQUITIES.

EDUCATIONAL WORKS.

POETRY, THE DRAMA, &C.

NAVAL AND MILITARY WORKS.

PHILOSOPHY, LAW, AND POLITICS.

RURAL & DOMESTIC ECONOMY.

FIELD SPORTS, &C.

MISCELLANEOUS LITERATURE AND PHILOLOGY.

HOME AND COLONIAL LIBRARY.

DR. WM. SMITH'S ATLAS OF ANCIENT GEOGRAPHY.

THE SPEAKER'S COMMENTARY.

Now Ready, Medium 8vo.

THE HOLY BIBLE, according to the Authorised Version, A.D. 1611, with an EXPLANATORY and CRITICAL COMMENTARY, and a REVISION of the TRANSLATION. By BISHOPS and CLERGY of the ANGLICAN CHURCH. Edited by F. C. COOK, M.A., Canon of Exeter, and Chaplain in Ordinary to the Queen.

THE OLD TESTAMENT. 6 VOLS. 135s.

Vol. I.—30s.

GENESIS—Bishop of Winchester.
EXODUS—Canon Cook and Rev. Samuel Clark.

LEVITICUS—Rev. Samuel Clark.
NUMBERS—Canon Espin and Rev. J. F. Thrupp.
DEUTERONOMY—Canon Espin.

Vols. II. and III.—36s.

JOSHUA—Canon Espin.
JUDGES, RUTH, SAMUEL—Bishop of Bath and Wells.

KINGS, CHRONICLES, EZRA, NEHEMIAH, ESTHER—Canon Rawlinson.

Vol. IV.—24s.

JOB—Canon Cook.
PSALMS—Dean Johnson, Canon Elliott, and the Editor.

PROVERBS—Dean of Wells.
ECCLESIASTES—Rev. W. T. Bullock.
SONG OF SOLOMON—Canon Kingsbury.

Vol. V.—20s.

ISAIAH—Rev. Dr. Kay.

JEREMIAH AND LAMENTATIONS — Dean of Canterbury.

Vol. VI.—25s.

EZEKIEL—Rev. Dr. Currey.
DANIEL—Archdeacon Rose and Prof. J. M. Fuller.
HOSEA and JONAH—Rev. E. Huxtable.
AMOS, NAHUM, and ZEPHANIAH—Rev. R. Gandell.

JOEL and OBADIAH—Rev. F. Meyrick.
MICAH and HABAKKUK—Rev. Samuel Clark and Canon Cook.
HAGGAI, ZECHARIAH, and MALACHI—Canon Drake.

THE NEW TESTAMENT. 4 VOLS. 94s.

Vols. I. and II.—38s.

INTRODUCTION—The Archbishop of York.

ST. MATTHEW and ST. MARK—Dean Mansel and Canon Cook.

ST. LUKE—Bishop of St. David's.
ST. JOHN—Canon Westcott.
THE ACTS—Bishop Jacobson.

Vol. III.—28s.

ROMANS—Rev. Dr. Gifford.
CORINTHIANS—Canon Evans and Rev. J. Waite.
GALATIANS—Dean of Chester.
PHILIPPIANS, EPHESIANS, COLOSSIANS, THESSALONIANS, and PHILEMON —

Rev. F. Meyrick, Bishop of Derry, and Dean of Raphoe.
PASTORAL EPISTLES—Bishop of London and Rev. Dr. Wace.
HEBREWS—Rev. Dr. Kay.

Vol. IV.—28s.

EPISTLE OF ST. JAMES—Dean of Rochester.
ST. PETER and ST. JUDE — Prof. T. R. Lumby, D.D.

EPISTLES OF ST. JOHN—Bishop of Derry.
REVELATION of ST. JOHN—Archdeacon Lee.

₊ The BOOK OF PSALMS and the GOSPEL ACCORDING TO ST. JOHN are sold separately, 10s. 6d. each, and the EPISTLES TO THE ROMANS, 7s. 6d.

HISTORY ANCIENT AND MODERN.

Ancient History.

History of Greece, from the Earliest Period to the close of the Generation contemporary with Alexander the Great. By GEORGE GROTE. Portrait and Plans. 12 vols. post 8vo, 40s. each.

Student's Ancient History of the East. From the Earliest Times to the Conquest of Alexander the Great; including Egypt, Assyria, Babylonia, Media, Persia, Asia Minor, and Phœnicia. By PHILIP SMITH. Woodcuts. Post 8vo, 7s. 6d.

Manners and Customs of the Ancient Egyptians: their Religion, Arts, Laws, Manufactures, etc. By Sir J. GARDNER WILKINSON. Revised by SAMUEL BIRCH, LL.D. Illustrations. 3 vols. 8vo, £4:4s.

Popular Account of the AN-CIENT EGYPTIANS. By Sir J. G. WILKINSON. Illustrations. 2 vols. post 8vo, 12s.

The Five Great Monarchies of the ANCIENT EASTERN WORLD; or the History, Geography, and Antiquities of Chaldea, Assyria, Babylonia, Media, and Persia. By Canon RAWLINSON. Illustrations. 3 vols. 8vo, 42s.

Herodotus: A new English version. With notes and essays, historical and ethnographical. By Canon RAWLINSON, Sir HENRY RAWLINSON, and Sir J. G. WILKINSON. Illustrations. 4 vols. 8vo, 48s.

Greece. Pictorial, Descriptive, and Historical. By CHRISTOPHER WORDSWORTH, D.D. New Edition. Edited by H. F. TOZER, M.A. With 400 Illustrations. Royal 8vo, 31s. 6d.

History of the Ancient World; from the earliest Records to the fall of the Western Empire, A.D. 476. By PHILIP SMITH. Plans. 3 vols. 8vo, 31s. 6d.

Villiers Stuart's Egypt, &c. *See p. 19.*

History of Egypt under the Pharaohs. Derived from the Monuments. With Memoir on the Exodus of the Israelites. By Dr. BRUGSCH. Maps. 2 vols. 8vo, 32s.

Student's History of Greece, from the Earliest Times to the Roman Conquest, with the History of Literature and Art. By Dr. WM. SMITH. Maps and Woodcuts. Post 8vo, 7s. 6d.

Student's History of Rome, from the Earliest Times to the Establishment of the Empire. With the History of Literature and Art. By Dean LIDDELL. Maps and Woodcuts. Post 8vo, 7s. 6d.

History of the Decline and Fall of the ROMAN EMPIRE. By EDWARD GIBBON, with Notes by MILMAN and GUIZOT. Edited by Dr. WM. SMITH. Maps. 8 vols. 8vo, £3.

Student's Gibbon; an Epi-tome of the History of the Decline and Fall of the Roman Empire. By EDWARD GIBBON. Woodcuts. Post 8vo, 7s. 6d.

Dictionary of Greek and Roman ANTIQUITIES. Edited by Dr. WM. SMITH. Illustrations. Royal 8vo, 28s.

Dictionary of Greek and Roman BIOGRAPHY and MYTHOLOGY. Edited by Dr. WM. SMITH. Illustrations. 3 vols. royal 8vo, 84s.

Classical Dictionary of Bio-GRAPHY, MYTHOLOGY, and GEOGRAPHY, for the Higher Forms. By Dr. WM. SMITH. Illustrations. 8vo, 18s.

Smaller Classical Dictionary of Mythology, Biography, and Geography. Woodcuts. Crown 8vo, 7s. 6d.

Smaller Dictionary of Greek and Roman Antiquities. Abridged from the large work. By Dr. WM. SMITH. Woodcuts. Crown 8vo, 7s. 6d.

Scripture and Church History.

Student's Old Testament His-tory; from the Creation to the Return of the Jews from Captivity. By PHILIP SMITH. Woodcuts. Post 8vo, 7s. 6d.

Student's New Testament His-tory. With an Introduction connecting the History of the Old and New Testaments. By PHILIP SMITH. Woodcuts. Post 8vo, 7s. 6d.

History of the Jews, from the Earliest Period to Modern Times. By Dean MILMAN. 3 vols. post 8vo, 12s.

History of the Jewish Church. By Dean STANLEY. From Abraham to the Christian Era. New Edition. With Portrait and Maps. 3 vols. Cr. 8vo, 18s.

History of Christianity, from the Birth of Christ to the Extinction of Paganism in the Roman Empire. By Dean MILMAN. 3 vols. post 8vo, 12s.

History of the Christian Church from the Apostolic Age to the Reformation, A.D. 64-1517. By Canon ROBERTSON. 8 vols. post 8vo, 6s. each.

Student's Manual of Ecclesiastical History. PART I.—From the Time of the Apostles to the Full Establishment of the Holy Roman Empire and the Papal Power. PART II.—The Middle Ages and the Reformation. By PHILIP SMITH. Woodcuts. 2 vols. post 8vo, 7s. 6d. each.

History of the Gallican Church, from the Concordat at Bologna, 1516, to the Revolution. By Rev. W. H. JERVIS. Portraits. 2 vols. 8vo, 28s.

History of the Eastern Church. By Dean STANLEY. New Edition. Plans. Crown 8vo, 6s.

Student's Manual of English Church History. FIRST PERIOD—Down to the Accession of Henry VIII. SECOND PERIOD—Henry VIII. to the Silencing of Convocation in the 18th Century. By Canon PERRY. 2 vols. post 8vo, 7s. 6d. each.

History of the Church of SCOTLAND. By Dean STANLEY. 8vo, 7s. 6d.

Dictionary of Christian Antiquities, comprising the History, Institutions, and Antiquities of the Christian Church. Edited by Dr. WM. SMITH and Archdeacon CHEETHAM. Illustrations. 2 vols. med. 8vo, £3:13:6.

Dictionary of Christian Biography, Literature, Sects, and Doctrines, during the first eight centuries. Edited by Dr. WM. SMITH and Rev. H. WACE, D.D. Vols. I. II. and III. Medium 8vo, 31s. 6d. each.

The Jesuits, their Constitution and Teaching. An Historical Sketch. By W. C. CARTWRIGHT. 8vo, 9s.

History of Latin Christianity and of the Popes to Nicholas V. By Dean MILMAN. With Portrait. 9 vols. post 8vo, 36s.

Mediæval and Modern History.

An Account of the Modern Egyptians. By E. W. LANE. Illustrations. 2 vols. crown 8vo, 12s.

History of Europe during the MIDDLE AGES. By HENRY HALLAM. Library Edition. 3 vols. 8vo, 30s.; Cabinet Edition. 3 vols. post 8vo, 12s. Student's Edition. Post 8vo, 7s. 6d.

Student's History of France. From the Earliest Times to the Fall of the Second Empire. With Notes on the Institutions of the Country. By W. H. JERVIS. Woodcuts. Post 8vo, 7s. 6d.

Student's Hume; a History of ENGLAND, from the Earliest Times to the Revolution of 1688. Revised and continued to the Treaty of Berlin, 1878, by J. S. BREWER. With 7 Coloured Maps and 70 Woodcuts. Post 8vo, 7s. 6d. Or in Three Parts. Price 2s. 6d. each.

History of England, from the Accession of Henry VII. to the Death of George II. By HENRY HALLAM. 3 vols. 8vo, 30s.; or Cabinet Edition, 3 vols. post 8vo, 12s. Student's Edition. Post 8vo, 7s. 6d.

History of Charles the Bold, Duke of Burgundy. By J. FOSTER KIRK. Portraits. 3 vols. 8vo, 45s.

Literary History of Europe during the 15th, 16th, and 17th Centuries. Library Edn., 3 vols. 8vo, 36s. Cabinet Edn., 4 vols. post 8vo, 16s.

The Reign of Henry VIII.; From his Accession till the Death of Wolsey. Reviewed and illustrated from Original Documents. By the late Professor BREWER. Edited by JAMES GAIRDNER, of the Record Office. With Portrait. 2 vols. 8vo, 30s.

Historical Memorials of Canterbury. 1. Landing of Augustine—2. Murder of Becket—3. Edward the Black Prince—4. Becket's Shrine. By Dean STANLEY. Woodcuts. Crown 8vo, 6s.

History of the United Netherlands, from the Death of William the Silent to the Twelve Years' Truce, 1609. By J. L. MOTLEY. Portraits. 4 vols post 8vo, 6s. each.

Life and Death of John of BARNEVELD. With a view of the primary causes and movements of the Thirty Years' War. By J. L. MOTLEY. Illustrations. 2 vols. post 8vo, 12s.

Student's History of Modern Europe, from the End of the Middle Ages to the Treaty of Berlin, 1878. Post 8vo, 7s. 6d.

LIFE OF CHARLES DARWIN

AND

NEW EDITIONS OF HIS WORKS.

THE LIFE AND LETTERS OF CHARLES DARWIN, F.R.S. With an Autobiographical Chapter. Edited by his Son, FRANCIS DARWIN, F.R.S. With Portraits. 3 Vols. 8vo. 36s.

NEW LIBRARY EDITIONS.

THE ORIGIN OF SPECIES BY MEANS OF NATURAL SELECTION; or the Preservation of Favoured Races in the Struggle for Life. *Large Type Edition.* (760 pp.) 2 Vols. 12s.

THE DESCENT OF MAN, AND SELECTION IN RELATION TO SEX. *Large Type Edition.* (900 pp.) 2 Vols. 15s.

CHEAPER, AND UNIFORM EDITIONS.

A NATURALIST'S VOYAGE ROUND THE WORLD. 7s. 6d.

THE ORIGIN OF SPECIES BY MEANS OF NATURAL SELECTION. 6s.

THE VARIOUS CONTRIVANCES BY WHICH ORCHIDS ARE FERTILISED BY INSECTS. 7s. 6d.

VARIATION OF ANIMALS AND PLANTS UNDER DOMESTICATION. 2 Vols. 15s.

THE DESCENT OF MAN, AND SELECTION IN RELATION TO SEX. 7s. 6d.

EXPRESSION OF THE EMOTIONS IN MAN AND ANIMALS. Illustrations. [*In the Press.*

MOVEMENTS AND HABITS OF CLIMBING PLANTS. 6s.

EFFECTS OF CROSS AND SELF-FERTILIZATION IN THE VEGETABLE KINGDOM. 9s.

INSECTIVOROUS PLANTS. 9s. [*In the Press.*

DIFFERENT FORMS OF FLOWERS ON PLANTS OF THE SAME SPECIES. 7s. 6d.

POWER OF MOVEMENT IN PLANTS. [*In the Press.*

FORMATION OF VEGETABLE MOULD THROUGH THE ACTION OF WORMS. 6s.

LIFE OF ERASMUS DARWIN. New Edition. Portrait. 7s. 6d.

Sir John Northcote's Note-book during the Long Parliament. From the Original MS. Edited by A. H. A. HAMILTON. Crown 8vo, 9s.

Historic Peerage of England, Exhibiting the Origin, Descent, and Present State of every Title of Peerage which has existed since the Conquest. By Sir HARRIS NICOLAS. 8vo, 30s.

History of India—The Hindoo and Mohammedan Periods. By the Hon. MOUNTSTUART ELPHINSTONE. Edited by Professor COWELL. Map. 8vo, 18s.

Two Sieges of Vienna by the TURKS. From the German. By Lord ELLESMERE. Post 8vo, 2s.

British India from its origin to 1783. By Earl STANHOPE. Post 8vo, 3s. 6d.

History of England, from the Reign of Queen Anne (1701) to the Peace of Versailles (1783). By Earl STANHOPE. 9 vols. post 8vo, 5s. each.

"The Forty-Five;" or, the Rebellion in Scotland in 1745. By Earl STANHOPE. Post 8vo, 3s. 6d.

Historical Essays. By Earl STANHOPE. Post 8vo, 3s. 6d.

French Retreat from Moscow, and other Essays. By Earl STANHOPE. Post 8vo, 7s. 6d.

King William IV.'s Correspondence with the late Earl GREY, 1830-1832. Edited by his SON. 2 vols. 8vo, 30s.

Scenes from the War of Liberation in Germany. From the German. By Sir A. GORDON. Post 8vo, 3s. 6d.

The Siege of Gibraltar, 1772-1780. By JOHN DRINKWATER. Post 8vo, 2s.

Annals of the Wars of the 18th and 19th Centuries, 1700-1815. By Sir EDWARD CUST. Maps. 9 vols. 16mo, 5s. each.

State of Society in France BEFORE THE REVOLUTION, 1789. By ALEXIS DE TOCQUEVILLE. Translated by HENRY REEVE. 8vo, 14s.

History of Europe during the FRENCH REVOLUTION, 1789-95. From the Secret Archives of Germany. By Professor VON SYBEL. 4 vols. 8vo, 48s.

English Battles and Sieges of the Peninsular War. By Sir W. NAPIER. Portrait. Post 8vo, 9s.

The Story of the Battle of WATERLOO. By Rev. G. R. GLEIG. Post 8vo, 3s. 6d.

Wellington's Civil and Political Despatches, 1819-1831. Edited by his SON. 8 vols. 8vo, 20s. each.

Wellington's Supplementary Despatches and Correspondence. Edited by his SON. 15 vols. 8vo, 20s. each. An index. 8vo, 20s.

Campaigns at Washington and NEW ORLEANS. By Rev. G. R. GLEIG. Post 8vo, 2s.

Sale's Brigade in Affghanistan. By Rev. G. R. GLEIG. Post 8vo, 2s.

French in Algiers; the Soldier of the Foreign Legion—and Prisoners of Abd-el-Kadir. Translated by Lady DUFF GORDON. Post 8vo, 2s.

History of the Fall of the Jesuits in the XIXth Century. Post 8vo, 2s.

English in Spain; the Civil War between Christinos and Carlists in 1834, 1840. By Col. F. DUNCAN, R.A. With plates. 8vo, 16s.

Personal Narrative of Events in China during Lord Elgin's Second Embassy. By Sir H. B. LOCH. Illustrations. Post 8vo, 9s.

History of the Royal Artillery. Compiled from the original Records. By Col. F. DUNCAN, R.A. Portraits. 2 vols. 8vo, 18s.

A Magistrate's Experiences of the Indian Mutiny. By MARK THORNHILL. Crown 8vo.

The Huguenots in England & Ireland, their Settlements, Churches, and Industries. By SAMUEL SMILES. Crown 8vo, 7s. 6d.

Historical Memorials of Westminster Abbey, from its Foundation to the Present Time. By Dean STANLEY. Illustrations. 8vo, 15s.

Notices of the Historic Persons buried in the Chapel of St. Peter, in the Tower of London, with an Account of the Discovery of the Remains of Queen Anne Boleyn. By DOYNE C. BELL. Illustrations. Crown 8vo, 14s.

Handbook to St. Paul's Cathedral. By Dean MILMAN. Illustrations. Crown 8vo, 10s. 6d.

Collections towards the History and Antiquities of the County of Hereford. Vol. III. In continuation of Duncumb's History. By W. H. COOKE, Q.C. Illustrations. 4to, 52s. 6d.

BIOGRAPHY AND MEMOIRS.

Ecclesiastical and Missionary.

Dictionary of Christian Bio-graphy, Literature, Sects, and Doctrines. Vols. I. II. and III. Med. 8vo, 31s. 6d. each.

Life of St. Hugh of Avalon, Bishop of Lincoln. By Canon PERRY. Portrait. Post 8vo, 10s. 6d.

Personal Life of Dr. Living-stone. By W. G. BLAIKIE, D.D. With Portrait and Map. Post 8vo, 6s.

Memoir of Bishop Milman, Metropolitan of India. By his SISTER. Map. 8vo, 12s.

Memoir of William Ellis, the Missionary. Portrait. 8vo, 10s. 6d.

Life of John Wilson, D.D. (of Bombay); Fifty Years a Philanthropist and Scholar in the East. By GEORGE SMITH. Illustrations. Post 8vo, 9s.

Life of Bishop SUMNER. By Rev. G. H. SUMNER. Portrait. 8vo, 14s.

Life and Times of St. John Chrysostom. By Rev. W. R. W. STEPHENS. With Portrait. 8vo, 7s. 6d.

Life of Samuel Wilberforce, Bishop of Oxford and Winchester. By Canon ASHWELL and R. G. WILBER-FORCE. 3 vols. Portraits. 8vo, 15s. each.

Recollections of Arthur Pen-rhyn Stanley. By G. G. BRADLEY, Dean of Westminster. Cr. 8vo. 3s. 6d.

Political and Social.

Princess Alice, Grand Duchess of Hesse. Biographical Sketch and Letters. Portrait. Crown 8vo, 7s. 6d.

Memoirs of James Hope Scott, of Abbotsford, Q.C. With Selections from his Correspondence. By Prof. R. ORNSBY. 2 vols. 8vo, 24s.

Memoirs, Diaries, and Corre-spondence of Right Hon. J. W. CROKER (Sec. to Admiralty 1809-1830). Comprising Documents relating to Chief Events first half of present century. Edited by L. J. JENNINGS. Portrait. 3 vols. 8vo. 45s.

Memoir of the Public Life of Rt. Hon. J. C. HERRIES during the reigns of George III., George IV., William IV., and Victoria. By his Son, Ed. HERRIES, C.B. 2 vols. 8vo, 24s.

Life of the Hon. Mountstuart Elphinstone. By SIR E. COLEBROOKE Bt. Portrait and Plans. 2 vols. 8vo, 26s.

James and Philip Van Arteveld. With a Description of the State of Society in Flanders in the 14th Cent. By JAMES HUTTON. Crown 8vo, 10s. 6d.

Memoirs of Sir Fowell Buxton. By CHARLES BUXTON. Portrait. 8vo, 16s. ; or post 8vo, 5s.

Sketches of Eminent Statesmen and Writers. By A. HAYWARD, Q.C. 2 vols. 8vo, 28s. CONTENTS:—Thiers, Bismarck, Cavour, Metternich, Melbourne, Wellesley, Byron, Tennyson, St. Simon, Sévigné, etc.

Life and Death of John of BARNEVELD. With a View of the Primary Causes and Movements of " The Thirty Years' War." By J. L. MOTLEY. Illustrations. 2 vols. post 8vo, 12s.

Bolingbroke : an Historical Study; to which is added an Essay on Voltaire in England, by J. CHURTON COLLINS. Crown 8vo, 7s. 6d.

Brief Memoir of the Princess CHARLOTTE OF WALES. By Lady ROSE WEIGALL. Portrait. Crown 8vo, 8s. 6d.

Life of William Pitt. By Earl STANHOPE. Portraits. 3 vols. 8vo, 36s.

Life of William Wilberforce. By his SON. Portrait. Post 8vo, 6s.

Memoirs; By Sir Robert Peel. Edited by Earl STANHOPE and Lord CARDWELL. 2 vols. post 8vo, 15s.

Monographs : Personal and So-cial. By Lord HOUGHTON. Portraits. Crown 8vo, 10s. 6d.

Rheinsberg; Memorials of Frederick the Great and Prince Henry. By A. HAMILTON. 2 vols. crown 8vo, 21s.

Life and Correspondence of Dr. Arnold of Rugby. By Dean STANLEY. Portrait. 2 vols. cr. 8vo, 12s.

Memoir of Edward, Catherine, and Mary Stanley. By Dean STANLEY. Post 8vo, 6s.

Life of Theodore Hook. By J. G. LOCKHART. Fcap. 8vo, 1s.

Memoir of Hon. Julian Fane. By Lord LYTTON. Portrait. Post 8vo, 5s.

Selection from the Familiar Correspondence of Sir CHARLES BELL. Portrait. Post 8vo, 12s.

Literary and Artistic.

Dictionary of Greek & Roman Biography and Mythology. Edited by Dr. Wm. Smith. 3 vols. 8vo, 84s.

Personal Life of George Grote, the Historian of Greece. Compiled from Family Documents. By Mrs. Grote. Portrait. 8vo, 12s.

Mrs. Grote; a Sketch. By Lady Eastlake. Crown 8vo, 6s.

Life of Horace. By Dean Milman. 8vo, 9s.

Michel Angelo, Sculptor, Painter, and Architect; including Documents from the Buonarroti Archives. By C. Heath Wilson. Plates. 8vo, 15s.

Raphael; His Life and Works, with particular reference to recently discovered Records, and an exhaustive Study of Extant Drawings and Pictures. By J. A. Crowe and G. B. Cavalcaselle. 2 vols. 8vo.

Titian: his Life and Times, with some Account of his Family from Unpublished Documents. By J. A. Crowe and G. B. Cavalcaselle. Illustrations. 2 vols. 8vo, 21s.

The Early Life of Jonathan Swift. By John Forster. 1667-1711. Portrait. 8vo, 15s.

Life of Jonathan Swift. By Henry Craik. With Portrait. 8vo, 18s.

Life of Dr. Samuel Johnson. By James Boswell. Edited by J. W. Croker. With Notes by Sir Walter Scott, Disraeli, Markland, Lockhart, &c. Portraits. Medium 8vo, 12s.

Life and Letters of Lord Byron. By Thomas Moore. Portraits. Royal 8vo, 7s. 6d.; or 6 vols. fcap. 8vo, 18s.

Lives of the British Poets. By Thomas Campbell. Post 8vo, 3s. 6d.

Memoir of Sir Charles Eastlake. By Lady Eastlake. Prefixed to his Contributions to the Literature of the Fine Arts. 2 vols. 8vo, 24s.

Popular Biographies—Bunyan, Cromwell, Clive, Conde, Drake, Munro. See *Home and Colonial Library*, p. 30.

Life and Times of Sir Joshua Reynolds. With Notes of his Contemporaries. By C. R. Leslie and Tom Taylor. Portraits. 2 vols. 8vo, 42s.

Lives of the Early Italian Painters; illustrating the Progress of Painting in Italy from Cimabue to Bassano. By Mrs. Jameson. Illustrations. Post 8vo, 12s.

Lives of the Early Flemish Painters, and Notices of their Works. By Crowe and Cavalcaselle. Illustrations. Post 8vo, 7s. 6d.; or large paper, 15s.

Life and Works of Albert Dürer. By Moriz Thausing. Edited by F. A. Eaton, Sec. Royal Academy. Illustrations. 2 vols. 8vo, 42s.

Life and Works of Sir Charles Barry, R.A. By Canon Barry, D.D. Portrait and Illustrations. 8vo, 15s.

Naval and Military.

Lives of the Warriors of the 17th Century. By Sir Edward Cust, D.C.L. 6 vols. crown 8vo, 50s.

Memoir of Capt. Gill, R.E. By Col. Yule. Prefixed to Gill's River of Golden Sand. *See p. 8.*

Letters and Journals of F.-M. Sir Wm. Gomm, G.C.B., 1799-1815. The Helder, Bergen, Copenhagen, Rolica, Vimera, Corunna, Walcheren, Busaco, Torres Vedras, Fuentes d'Oñor, Albuera, Badajos, Salamanca, Burgos, Vittoria, Pyrenees, Waterloo, &c. &c. By F. C. Carr Gomm. Portraits. 8vo, 12s.

Napoleon at Fontainebleau and Elba. Being a Journal of Occurrences and Notes of Conversations, &c. By Sir Neil Campbell. Portrait. 8vo, 15s.

Life of Belisarius. By Lord Mahon. Post 8vo, 10s. 6d.

Letters and Journals of the Earl of Elgin, Governor-General of India. Edited by Theodore Walrond. 8vo, 14s.

Memoirs and Correspondence of the Duke of Saldanha, Soldier and Statesman. By Conde da Carnota. With Portrait and Maps. 2 vols. 8vo, 32s.

Memoir of Sir John Burgoyne. By Sir Francis Head. Post 8vo, 1s.

Autobiography of Sir John Barrow, Bart. Portrait. 8vo, 16s.

Private Diary of General Sir Robert Wilson: during Missions and Employments with the European Armies in 1812-1814. Map. 2 vols. 8vo, 26s.

Character, Actions, and Writings of Wellington. By Jules Maurel. Fcap. 8vo, 1s. 6d.

Legal and Scientific.

Lives of the Lord Chancellors and KEEPERS of the GREAT SEAL of ENGLAND, from the Earliest Times to the death of Lord Eldon, 1838. By Lord CAMPBELL. 10 vols. post 8vo, 6s. each.

Lives of the Chief Justices of ENGLAND, from the Norman Conquest till the death of Lord Tenterden. By Lord CAMPBELL. 4 vols. cr. 8vo, 6s. each.

Life and Letters of Lord Campbell. Based on his Autobiography, Journals, and Correspondence. Edited by Hon. Mrs. HARDCASTLE. With Portrait. 2 vols. 8vo, 30s.

Life of Lord Lyndhurst, three times Lord Chancellor of England. From Letters and Papers in possession of his family. By Sir THEODORE MARTIN, K.C.B. With portraits. 8vo, 16s.

Biographia Juridica. A Biographical Dictionary of the Judges of England, from the Conquest to 1870. By EDWARD FOSS. Medium 8vo, 21s.

Life, Letters, and Journals of Sir CHARLES LYELL. Edited by his Sister-in-Law, Mrs. LYELL. Portraits. 2 vols. 8vo, 30s.

Life of Lord Chancellor Eldon. By HORACE TWISS. Portrait. 2 vols. post 8vo, 21s.

Life of Erasmus Darwin. By CHARLES DARWIN. With a Study of his Scientific Works by Dr. KRAUSE. Portrait, 8vo, 7s. 6d.

Lives of the Engineers. From the Earliest Times to the Death of the Stephensons. By SAMUEL SMILES, LL.D. 9 Portraits and 340 Woodcuts, 5 vols. Crown 8vo, 7s. 6d. each.

Industrial Biography; or, Iron-Workers and Tool-Makers. By SAMUEL SMILES. Post 8vo, 6s.

Life of Thomas Edward (Shoemaker, of Banff), Scotch Naturalist. By S. SMILES. Illustrated. Crown 8vo, 6s.

James Nasmyth, Engineer: An Autobiography. Edited by S. SMILES, LL.D. With portrait and 90 Illustrations. Crown 8vo, 16s.; or post 8vo, 6s.

Life of Robert Dick (Baker, of Thurso), Geologist and Botanist. By S. SMILES. Illustrations. Cr. 8vo, 12s.

Memoir of Sir Roderick Murchison. By Professor GEIKIE. Portraits. 2 vols. 8vo, 30s.

Memoir and Correspondence of Caroline Herschel. Portraits. Crown 8vo, 7s. 6d.

Personal Recollections, from Early Life to Old Age. By MARY SOMERVILLE. Portrait. Crown 8vo, 12s.

Memorials of John Flint South, Surgeon to St. Thomas's Hospital (1841-63). By the Rev. C. L. FELTOE. Portrait. Crown 8vo, 7s. 6d.

GEOGRAPHY, VOYAGES, AND TRAVELS.

The East Indies, China, &c.

India in 1880. By Sir RICHARD TEMPLE, Bart. 8vo, 16s. *See p. 21.*

The Student's Geography of British India—Political and Physical. By GEORGE SMITH, LL.D. Maps. Post 8vo, 7s. 6d.

The River of Golden Sand. A Narrative of a Journey through China to Burmah. By the late Capt. Gill. An Abridged Edition. By E. COLBORNE BABER. With Memoir and Introductory Essay by Col. H. YULE, C.B. With Portraits, Map, and Illustrations. Post 8vo, 7s. 6d.

Travels of Marco Polo. A new English version. Illustrated with copious Notes. By Col. YULE, C.B. Illustrations. 2 vols. 8vo, 63s.

A Cruise in the Eastern Seas, from the Corea to the River Amur. With an Account of Russian Siberia, Japan, and Formosa. By Capt. B. W. BAX. Illustrations. Crown 8vo, 12s.

A Visit to High Tartary, Yarkand, and KASHGAR, and over the Karakorum Pass. By ROBERT SHAW. Illustrations. 8vo, 16s.

British Burma and its People: Sketches of Native Manners, Customs, and Religion. By Capt. FORBES. Crown 8vo, 10s. 6d.

New Japan; The Land of the Rising Sun. By SAMUEL MOSSMAN. Map. 8vo, 15s.

The Satsuma Rebellion. An Episode of Modern Japanese History. By AUGUSTUS H. MOUNSEY. Map. Crown 8vo, 10s. 6d.

Letters from Madras. By a LADY. Post 8vo, 2s.

Thirteen Years' Residence at the Court of China, in the Service of the Emperor. By Father RIPA. Post 8vo, 2s.

Popular Account of the Manners and Customs of India. By Rev. CHAS. ACLAND. Post 8vo, 2s.

Journey to the Source of the River Oxus, by the Indus, Kabul, and Badakhshan. By Capt. Wood. With the Geography of the Valley of the Oxus, by Col. Yule. Map. 8vo, 12s.

The Golden Chersonese and the Way Thither. By Isabella L. Bird (Mrs. Bishop). With Map and Illustrations. Post 8vo, 14s.

Unbeaten Tracks in Japan. Including Visits to the Aborigines of Yezo and the Shrines of Nikko and Isé. By Isabella L. Bird. Map and Illustrations. Crown 8vo, 7s. 6d.

Japan; Its History, Traditions, and Religions. By Sir E. J. Reed, K.C.B. With Map and Illustrations. 2 vols. 8vo, 28s.

Africa—Egypt.

The Wild Tribes of the Soudan: An Account of Travel and Sport chiefly in the Basé Country. Being Personal Experiences and Adventures during Three Winters in the Soudan. By F. L. James. With Maps, 40 Illustrations, and 6 Etchings. 8vo, 21s.; or post 8vo, 7s. 6d.

A Popular Account of Dr. Livingstone's Travels and Adventures in South Africa, 1840-56. Illustrations. Post 8vo, 7s. 6d.

A Popular Account of Dr. Livingstone's Expedition to the Zambesi, Lakes Shirwa and Nyassa, 1858-64. Illustrations. Post 8vo, 7s. 6d.

Dr. Livingstone's Last Journals in Central Africa, 1865-73. By Rev. Horace Waller. Illustrations. 2 vols. 8vo, 15s.

Livingstonia; Journal of Adventures in Exploring Lake Nyassa, and Establishing a Settlement there. By E. D. Young, R.N. Map. Post 8vo, 7s. 6d.

Journey to Ashango Land, and Further Penetration into Equatorial Africa. By P. B. du Chaillu. Illustrations. 8vo, 21s.

Adventures and Discoveries among the Lakes and Mountains of Eastern Africa. By Captain Elton and H. B. Cotterill. With Map and Illustrations. 8vo, 21s.

Wanderings South of the Atlas Mountains, in the Great Sahara. By Canon Tristram. Illustrations. Post 8vo, 15s.

Six Months in Ascension. An Unscientific Account of a Scientific Expedition. By Mrs. Gill. Map. Crown 8vo, 9s.

A Residence in Sierra Leone, described from a Journal kept on the Spot. By a Lady. Post 8vo, 3s. 6d.

Five Years' Adventures in the far Interior of S. Africa with the Wild Beasts of the Forests. By R. Gordon Cumming. Woodcuts. Post 8vo, 6s.

Recollections of Fighting and Hunting in South Africa, 1834-67. By Gen. Sir John Bisset, C.B. Illustrations. Crown 8vo, 14s.

Egypt after the War, &c. By Villiers Stuart. *See p. 19.*

The Country of the Moors. A Journey from Tripoli in Barbary to the Holy City of Kairwan. By Edward Rae. Illustrations. Crown 8vo, 12s.

British Mission to Abyssinia. With Notices of the Countries traversed. By Hormuzd Rassam. Illustrations. 2 vols. 30s.

Sport in Abyssinia. By Earl of Mayo. Illustrations. Crown 8vo, 12s.

Abyssinia during a Three Years' Residence. By Mansfield Parkyns. Woodcuts. Post 8vo, 7s. 6d.

Adventures in the Libyan Desert. By B. St. John. Post 8vo, 2s.

Travels in Egypt, Nubia, Syria, and the Holy Land. By Captains Irby and Mangles. Post 8vo, 2s.

The Cradle of the Blue Nile. A Visit to the Court of King John of Ethiopia. By E. A. de Cosson. Illustrations. 2 vols. post 8vo, 21s.

An Account of the Manners and Customs of the Modern Egyptians. By Edward Wm. Lane. Woodcuts. 2 vols. post 8vo, 12s.

Madagascar Revisited; Describing the Persecutions endured by the Christian Converts. By Rev. W. Ellis. Illustrations, 8vo, 16s.

Mediterranean—Greece, Turkey in Europe.

Travels in Asia Minor: With Antiquarian Researches and Discoveries, and Illustrations of Biblical Literature and Archæology. By H. Van Lennep. Illustrations. 2 vols. post 8vo, 24s.

Troja, Ilios, Mycenæ, &c. By Dr. Schliemann. *See p. 18.*

Cyprus; its Ancient Cities, Tombs, Temples, &c. By Gen. di Cesnola. Illustrations. Medium 8vo, 50s.

Bulgaria before the War: a Seven Years' Experience of European Turkey and its Inhabitants. By H. C. Barkley. Post 8vo, 10s. 6d.

Between the Danube and the Black Sea; or, Five Years in Bulgaria. By H. C. Barkley. Post 8vo, 10s. 6d.

Researches in the Highlands
of Turkey. By Rev. H. F. Tozer. Illustrations. 2 vols. crown 8vo, 24s.

Lectures on the Geography of
Greece. By Rev. H. F. Tozer. Map. Post 8vo, 9s.

Twenty Years' Residence
among the Bulgarians, Greeks, Albanians, Turks, and Armenians. By a Consul's Wife. 2 vols. crown 8vo, 21s.

Reminiscences of Athens and
the Morea, during Travels in Greece. By Lord Carnarvon. Crown 8vo, 7s. 6d.

Asia, Syria, Holy Land.

England and Russia in the East.
A Series of Papers on the Political and Geographical Condition of Central Asia. By Sir H. Rawlinson. Map. 8vo, 12s.

Siberia in Asia. A Visit to
the Valley of the Yenesay in East Siberia. With Description of the Natural History, Migration of Birds, &c. By Henry Seebohm. With Map and 60 Illustrations. Crown 8vo, 14s.

The Caucasus, Persia and Tur-
key in Asia. A journey to Tabreez, Kurdistan, down the Tigris and Euphrates to Nineveh and Babylon, and across the Desert to Palmyra. By Baron Thielmann. Illustrations. 2 vols. post 8vo, 18s.

Sketches of the Manners and
Customs of Persia. By Sir John Malcolm. Post 8vo, 3s. 6d.

Sinai and Palestine ; in Con-
nection with their History. By Dean Stanley. Plans. 8vo, 14s.

The Bible in the Holy Land.
Extracts from the above Work. Woodcuts. Fcap. 8vo, 2s. 6d.

Researches in the Holy Land
in 1838 and 1852. By E. Robinson, D.D. Maps. 3 vols. 8vo, 42s.

Damascus, Palmyra, Lebanon ;
with Travels among the Giant Cities of Bashan and the Hauran. By Rev. J. L. Porter. Woodcuts. Post 8vo, 7s. 6d.

Nineveh and its Remains.
With an Account of a Visit to the Chaldean Christians of Kurdistan, and the Yezedis or Devil Worshippers, &c. By Sir H. Layard. Illustrations. 2 vols. 8vo, 36s.; or post 8vo, 7s. 6d.

Nineveh and Babylon ; a Nar-
rative of a Second Expedition to the Ruins of Assyria, with Travels in Armenia. By Sir H. Layard. Illustrations. 8vo, 21s. ; or post 8vo, 7s. 6d.

The Jordan, the Nile, Red Sea,
Lake of Gennesareth, etc. The Cruise of the Rob Roy in Palestine, Egypt, &c. By John Macgregor. Illustrations. Post 8vo, 7s. 6d.

The Land of Moab. Travels
and Discoveries on the East Side of the Dead Sea and the Jordan. By Canon Tristram. Illustrations. Cr. 8vo, 15s.

The Bedouins of the Euphrates
Valley. By Lady Anne Blunt. Illustrations. 2 vols. crown 8vo, 24s.

A Pilgrimage to Nejd, the
Cradle of the Arab Race, and a Visit to the Court of the Arab Emir. By Lady Anne Blunt. With Illustrations. 2 vols. post 8vo, 24s.

Visits to the Monasteries of the
Levant. By the Hon. Robert Curzon (Lord Zouche). With Illustrations. Post 8vo, 7s. 6d.

Australia, Polynesia, &c.

Winters Abroad : Australia —
Melbourne, Tasmania, Sydney, Queensland ; the Riverina, Algiers, Egypt, Cape of Good Hope, Davos. By R. H. Otter, M.A. Crown 8vo, 7s. 6d.

The Gardens of the Sun ; or a
Naturalist's Journal on the Mountains and in the Forests and Swamps of Borneo and the Sulu Archipelago. By F. W. Burbidge. With Illustrations. Crown 8vo, 14s.

A Boy's Voyage Round the
World. Edited by Samuel Smiles. Woodcuts. Small 8vo, 6s.

Hawaiian Archipelago ; Six
Months among the Palm Groves, Coral Reefs, and Volcanoes of the Sandwich Islands. By Isabella Bird. Illustrations. Crown 8vo, 7s. 6d.

Typee and Omoo ; or the
Marquesas and South Sea Islanders. By H. Melville. 2 vols. post 8vo, 7s.

Notes and Sketches of New
South Wales. By Mrs. Meredith. Post 8vo, 2s.

America, West Indies, Arctic Regions.

Mexico To-Day : A Country
with a Great Future. With a Glance at the Prehistoric Remains and Antiquities of the Montezumas. By T. U. Brocklehurst. With 18 Coloured Plates and 37 Woodcuts. Medium 8vo, 21s.

Mexico and the Rocky Moun-
tains. By George F. Ruxton. Post 8vo, 3s. 6d.

A Lady's Life in the Rocky Mountains. By ISABELLA BIRD. Illustrations. Post 8vo, 7s. 6d.

Pioneering in South Brazil. Three Years of Forest and Prairie Life By T. P. BIGG WITHER. Illustrations. 2 vols. Crown 8vo, 24s.

Voyage of a Naturalist round the World. By CHAS. DARWIN. Post 8vo, 9s.

The Naturalist on the River AMAZON, with Adventures during Eleven Years of Travel. By H. W. BATES. Illustrations. Post 8vo, 7s. 6d.

Voyage up the River Amazon and a visit to Para. By WILLIAM H. EDWARDS. Post 8vo, 2s.

The Patagonians; Wanderings over Untrodden Ground from the Straits of Magellan to the Rio Negro. By Capt. MUSTERS. Illustrations. Post 8vo, 7s. 6d.

Voyage of the "Fox" in the ARCTIC SEAS, and the Discovery of the Fate of Sir John Franklin and his Companions. By Sir LEOPOLD M'CLINTOCK. Illustrations. Post 8vo, 7s. 6d.

Perils of the Polar Seas. True Stories of Arctic Discovery and Adventure. By Mrs. CHISHOLM. Illustrations. Small 8vo, 6s.

Communistic Societies of the UNITED STATES; their Creeds, Social Practices, and Present Condition. By C. NORDHOFF. Illustrations. 8vo, 15s.

Europe.

The White Sea Peninsula. A Journey to the White Sea. By EDWARD RAE. With Map, 12 Etchings, and 14 Woodcuts. Crown 8vo, 15s.

Summer Travelling in Iceland. The Narrative of Two Journeys across the Island by Unfrequented Routes. With Hints for a Tour. By JOHN COLES. With a Chapter on Askja by E. D. MORGAN. Map and Illustrations. 8vo, 18s.

The Land of the Midnight Sun. Summer and Winter Journeys through Sweden, Norway, Lapland, and Northern Finland. With descriptions of the Inner Life of the People, their Manners, Customs, Primitive Antiquities, etc. By PAUL B. DU CHAILLU. Map and 235 Illustrations. 2 vols. 8vo, 36s.

Etchings on the Mosel: a Series of 20 Plates, with Descriptive Letterpress. By ERNEST GEORGE. Folio, 42s.

Twenty Years in the Wild West of Ireland; or, Life in Connaught. By Mrs. HOUSTOUN. Crown 8vo, 9s.

Greece. By Bishop WORDSWORTH. *See p. 3.*

Etchings from the Loire and South of France. In a Series of Twenty Plates, with Descriptive Text. By ERNEST GEORGE. Folio, 42s.

Rambles among the Hills; or, Walks on the Peak of Derbyshire and in the South Downs. By L. J. JENNINGS. With Illustrations. Post 8vo, 12s.

The Ascent of the Matterhorn. By EDWARD WHYMPER. 100 Illustrations. Medium 8vo, 10s. 6d.

A Month in Norway. By J. G. HOLLWAY. Fcap. 8vo, 2s.

Letters from the Shores of the Baltic. By a LADY. Post 8vo, 2s.

Letters from High Latitudes: An Account of a Yacht Voyage to Iceland, Jan Mayen, and Spitzbergen. By Lord DUFFERIN. Illustrations. Crown 8vo, 7s. 6d.

The Bible in Spain; or, the Journeys, Adventures, and Imprisonments of an Englishman in the Peninsula. By GEORGE BORROW. Post 8vo, 5s.

The Gypsies of Spain; their Manners, Customs, Religion, and Language. By GEO. BORROW. Post 8vo, 5s.

Gatherings from Spain. By RICHARD FORD. Post 8vo, 3s. 6d.

Bubbles from the Brunnen of NASSAU. By Sir FRANCIS HEAD. Woodcuts. Post 8vo, 7s. 6d.

General Geography and Travels.

A History of Ancient Geography among the Greeks and Romans, from the Earliest Ages. By E. H. BUNBURY. 2 vols. 8vo, 21s.

The Journal of a Lady's Travels Round the World: Including Visits to Japan, Thibet, Yarkand, Kashmir, Java, the Straits of Malacca, Vancouver's Island, etc. By F. D. BRIDGES. With Illustrations. Crown 8vo, 15s.

Art of Travel; or, Hints on the Shifts and Contrivances available in Wild Countries. By FRANCIS GALTON. Woodcuts. Post 8vo, 7s. 6d.

Dictionary of Greek and Roman Geography. 2 vols. royal 8vo, 56s.

Atlas of Ancient Geography. *See p. 30.*

Journal of the Royal Geographical Society. 8vo. From 1831 to 1880.

See also SCHOOL BOOKS, *pp. 26, 27, 28, 29.*

HANDBOOKS FOR TRAVELLERS.

Foreign.

Handbook—Holland and Belgium. Maps and Plans. Post 8vo, 6s.

Handbook—North Germany; the Rhine, the Black Forest, the Hartz, Thüringerwald, Saxon Switzerland, Rügen, the Giant Mountains, Taunus, Odenwald, Elass, and Lothringen. Map and Plans. Post 8vo, 10s.

Handbook—Switzerland; The Alps of Savoy and Piedmont. Maps and Plans. In Two Parts. Post 8vo, 10s.

Handbook—South Germany; Tyrol, Bavaria, Austria, Salzburg, Styria, Hungary, the Danube, etc. Maps and Plans. Post 8vo, 10s.

Handbook—France. Part I. Normandy, Brittany, the French Alps, the Loire, Seine, Garonne, and Pyrenees. Maps and Plans. Post 8vo, 7s. 6d.

Handbook—France. Part II. Auvergne, the Cevennes, Burgundy, the Rhone and Saone, Provence, Nimes, Arles, Marseilles, the French Alps, Alsace, Lorraine, Champagne, etc. Maps and Plans. Post 8vo, 7s. 6d.

Handbook—Paris and its Environs. Maps and Plans. 16mo, 3s. 6d.

Handbook — Mediterranean : Its principal Islands, Cities, Seaports, Harbours, and Borderlands. With nearly 50 Maps and Plans. Post 8vo, 20s.

Handbook—Algeria and Tunis; Algiers, Constantin, Oran, Atlas Mts., etc. Maps and Plans. Post 8vo, 10s.

Handbook — Spain ; Madrid, The Castiles, Basque, Asturias, Galicia, Estremadura, Andalusia, Ronda, Granada, Murcia, Valencia, Catalonia, Aragon, Navarre, Balearic Islands. Maps and Plans. Post 8vo, 20s.

Handbook—Portugal ; Lisbon, Oporto, Cintra, etc. Map. Post 8vo, 12s.

Handbook—North Italy; Piedmont, Nice, Lombardy, Venice, Parma, Modena, and Romagna. Maps and Plans. Post 8vo, 10s.

Handbook—Central Italy; Tuscany, Florence, Lucca, Umbria, The Marches, and the Patrimony of St. Peter. Maps and Plans. Post 8vo, 10s.

Handbook—Egypt ; the Nile, Nubia, Alexandria, Cairo, The Pyramids, Thebes, Suez Canal, Peninsula of Sinai, The Oases, the Fyoom. Map and Plans. In Two Parts. Post 8vo, 15s.

Handbook — Greece ; Ionian Islands, Athens, Peloponnesus, Ægæan Sea, Albania, Thessaly, and Macedonia. Maps and Plans. Post 8vo.

Handbook—Rome and its Environs. Map and Plans. Post 8vo, 10s.

Handbook — South Italy ; Naples, Pompeii, Herculaneum, Vesuvius, Abruzzi. Maps and Plans. Post 8vo, 10s.

Handbook—Turkey in Asia ; Constantinople, The Bosphorus, Brousa, Troy, Crete, Cyprus, Smyrna, Ephesus, the Seven Churches, the Black Sea, Armenia, ¶ Mesopotamia. Maps and Plans. Post 8vo, 15s.

Handbook—Denmark ; Sleswig-Holstein, Copenhagen, Jutland, Iceland. Maps and Plans. Post 8vo.

Handbook—Sweden ; Stockholm, Upsala, Gothenburg, the Shores of the Baltic, etc. Maps and Plans. Post 8vo.

Handbook—Norway ; Christiania, Bergen, Trondhjem, the Fjelds, Iceland. Maps and Plans. Post 8vo, 9s.

Handbook—Russia; St. Petersburg, Moscow, Poland, Finland, The Crimea, Caucasus, Siberia, and Central Asia. Maps and Plans. Post 8vo, 18s.

Handbook—Bombay, Poonah, Beejapoor, Kolapoor, Indore, Surat, Baroda, Ahmedabad, Somnauth, Kurrachee, etc. Map and Plans. Post 8vo, 15s.

Handbook—Madras, Trichinopoli, Madura, Tinnevelly, Tuticorin, Bangalore, Mysore, the Nilgiris, Wynaad, Ootacamund, Calicut, Hyderabad, Ajanta, Elura Caves, etc. Maps and Plans. Post 8vo, 15s.

Handbook—Bengal, Calcutta, Orissa, British Burmah, Darjiling, Dacca, Patna, Gaya, Benares, N.-W. Provinces, Allahabad, Cawnpore, Lucknow, Agra, Gwalior, Naini, Tal, Delhi, Khatmandu, etc. Maps and Plans. Post 8vo, 20s.

Handbook — The Punjab. Amraoti, Indore, Ajmir, Jaypur, Rohtak, Saharanpur, Ambala, Lodiana, Lahore, Kulu, Simla, Sialkot, Peshawar, Rawul Pindi, Attock, Karachi, Sibi, etc. Maps. 15s.

Handbook—Holy Land; Sinai, Edom and the Syrian Deserts, Jerusalem, Petra, Damascus, and Palmyra. Maps and Plans. Post 8vo, 20s.

Travelling Map of Palestine, Mounted and in a Case. 12s.

Handbook — Japan. Tokio, Kisto, Ozaka, Hakodate, Nagasaki, and other Cities. With an Account of the most Interesting Parts of the Main Island ; and of the Ascents of the Principal Mountains ; and Descriptions of Temples. With Historical Notes and Legends. By ERNEST M. SATOW, C.M.G., and Lt. A. G. S. HAWES, R.M. With Maps and Plans. Post 8vo.

Languages.

Handbook Dictionary: English, French, and German. Containing all the words and idiomatic phrases likely to be required by a traveller. Bound in leather. 16mo, 6s.

Handbook — Travel Talk;— English, French, German, and Italian. 16mo, 3s. 6d.

English.

Handbook—London as it is. Map and Plans. 16mo, 3s. 6d.

Handbook—Environs of London, within 20 miles round of the Metropolis. 2 vols. Post 8vo, 21s.

Handbook—England & Wales. Condensed in one Volume. Forming a Companion to Bradshaw's Railway Tables. Map. Post 8vo, 10s.

Handbook—Eastern Counties; Chelmsford, Harwich, Colchester, Maldon, Cambridge, Ely, Newmarket, Bury, Ipswich, Woodbridge, Felixstowe, Lowestoft, Norwich, Yarmouth, Cromer. Map and Plans. Post 8vo, 12s.

Handbook — Kent; Canterbury, Dover, Ramsgate, Rochester, Chatham. Map and Plans. Post 8vo, 7s. 6d.

Handbook—Sussex; Brighton, Eastbourne, Chichester, Hastings, Lewes, Arundel, etc. Map. Post 8vo, 6s.

Handbook—Surrey and Hants; Kingston, Croydon, Reigate, Guildford, Dorking, Boxhill, Winchester, Southampton, New Forest, Portsmouth, Isle of Wight. Maps and Plans. Post 8vo, 10s.

Handbook—Berks, Bucks, and Oxon; Windsor, Eton, Reading, Aylesbury, Henley, Oxford, Blenheim, and the Thames. Map and Plans. Post 8vo, 9s.

Handbook—Wilts, Dorset, and Somerset; Salisbury, Stonehenge, Chippenham, Weymouth, Sherborne, Wells, Bath, Bristol, etc. Map. Post 8vo, 12s.

Handbook—Devon; Exeter, Ilfracombe, Linton, Sidmouth, Dawlish, Teignmouth, Plymouth, Devonport, Torquay. Maps and Plans. Post 8vo, 7s. 6d.

Handbook—Cornwall; Launceston, Penzance, Falmouth, The Lizard, Land's End. Maps. Post 8vo, 6s.

Handbook—Gloucester, Hereford, and Worcester; Cirencester, Cheltenham, Stroud, Tewkesbury, Leominster, Ross, Malvern, Kidderminster, Dudley, Evesham. Map. Post 8vo.

Handbook — North Wales; Bangor, Carnarvon, Beaumaris, Snowdon, Llanberis, Dolgelly, Cader Idris, Conway. Map. Post 8vo, 7s.

Handbook — South Wales; Monmouth, Llandaff, Merthyr, Vale of Neath, Pembroke, Carmarthen, Tenby, Swansea, the Wye. Map. Post 8vo, 7s.

Handbook—Derby, Notts, Leicester, and Stafford; Matlock, Bakewell, Chatsworth, The Peak, Buxton, Hardwick, Dovedale, Ashbourn, Southwell, Mansfield, Retford, Burton, Belvoir, Melton Mowbray, Wolverhampton, Lichfield, Tamworth. Map. Post 8vo, 9s.

Handbook—Shropshire & Cheshire, Shrewsbury, Ludlow, Bridgnorth, Oswestry, Chester, Crewe, Alderley, Stockport, Birkenhead. Maps and Plans. Post 8vo, 6s.

Handbook—Lancashire; Warrington, Bury, Manchester, Liverpool, Burnley, Clitheroe, Bolton, Blackburn, Wigan, Preston, Rochdale, Lancaster, Southport, Blackpool. Map. Post 8vo, 7s. 6d.

Handbook—Northamptonshire and Rutland; Northampton, Peterborough, Towcester, Daventry, Market Harborough, Kettering, Wallingborough, Thrapston, Stamford, Uppingham, Oakham. Maps. Post 8vo, 7s. 6d.

Handbook—Yorkshire; Doncaster, Hull, Selby, Beverley, Scarborough, Whitby, Harrogate, Ripon, Leeds, Wakefield, Bradford, Halifax, Huddersfield, Sheffield. Map and Plans. Post 8vo, 12s.

Handbook—Durham and Northumberland; Newcastle, Darlington, Bishop Auckland, Stockton, Hartlepool, Sunderland, Shields, Berwick, Tynemouth, Alnwick. Map. Post 8vo, 9s.

Handbook—Westmorland and Cumberland; Lancaster, Furness Abbey, Ambleside, Kendal, Windermere, Coniston, Keswick, Grasmere, Ulswater, Carlisle, Cockermouth, Penrith, Appleby. Map. Post 8vo.

Travelling Map of the Lake District, 3s. 6d.

Handbook—Scotland; Edinburgh, Melrose, Abbotsford, Glasgow, Dumfries, Galloway, Ayr, Stirling, Arran, The Clyde, Oban, Inverary, Loch Lomond, Loch Katrine and Trossachs, Caledonian Canal, Inverness, Perth, Dundee, Aberdeen, Braemar, Skye, Caithness, Ross, and Sutherland. Maps and Plans. Post 8vo, 9s.

Handbook—Ireland; Dublin, Belfast, The Giant's Causeway, Bantry, Glengariff, etc., Donegal, Galway, Wexford, Cork, Limerick, Waterford, Killarney. Maps and Plans. Post 8vo, 10s.
[In preparation.

Handbook—Herts, Beds, Warwick. Map. Post 8vo.

Handbook — Huntingdon and Lincoln. Map. Post 8vo.

ENGLISH CATHEDRALS.

Handbook — Southern Cathedrals. Winchester, Salisbury, Exeter, Wells, Rochester, Canterbury, Chichester, and St. Albans. Illustrations. 2 vols. Crown 8vo, 36s.

Handbook — Eastern Cathedrals. Oxford, Peterborough, Ely, Norwich, and Lincoln. Illustrations. Crown 8vo, 21s.

Handbook — Western Cathedrals. Bristol, Gloucester, Hereford, Worcester, and Lichfield. With 60 Illustrations. Crown 8vo, 16s.

Handbook — Northern Cathedrals. York, Ripon, Durham, Carlisle, Chester, and Manchester. Illustrations. 2 vols. crown 8vo, 21s.

Handbook—Welsh Cathedrals. Llandaff, St. David's, Bangor, and St. Asaph's. Illustrations. Crown 8vo, 15s.

Handbook—St. Alban's Cathedral. Illustrations. Crown 8vo, 6s.

Handbook—St. Paul's. Illustrations. Crown 8vo, 10s. 6d.

RELIGION AND THEOLOGY.

The Speaker's Commentary on THE BIBLE. Explanatory and Critical, With a Revision of the Translation. By Bishops and Clergy of the Anglican Church. Edited by Canon COOK. Medium 8vo. Old Test. : 6 vols., 135s. New Test. : 4 vols., 94s. *See p. 2, ante.*

The Apocrypha ; with a Commentary, Explanatory and Critical, by various writers. Edited by Professor H. WACE, D.D. 2 vols. medium 8vo. Uniform with the Speaker's Commentary.

The New Testament : Edited, with a short Practical Commentary, by Archdeacon CHURTON and Bishop BASIL JONES. With 100 Illustrations. 2 vols. crown 8vo, 21s.

The Student's Edition of the Speaker's Commentary on the Bible. By J. M. FULLER, M.A. 4 vols. cr. 8vo, 7s. 6d. each. *See inside of Wrapper.*

Dictionary of the Bible ; its Antiquities, Biography, Geography, and Natural History. By various Writers. Edited by Dr. WM. SMITH. Illustrations. 3 vols. 8vo, 105s.

Concise Bible Dictionary. For the use of Students and Families. Condensed from the above. Maps and 300 Illustrations. 8vo, 21s.

Smaller Bible Dictionary ; for Schools and Young Persons. Abridged from the above. Maps and Woodcuts. Crown 8vo, 7s. 6d.

Dictionary of Christian Antiquities ; comprising the History, Institutions, and Antiquities of the Christian Church. Edited by Dr. WM. SMITH, and Archdeacon CHEETHAM. Illustrations. 2 vols. 8vo, £3 : 13 : 6.

Church Dictionary. By Dean HOOK. Medium 8vo.

Dictionary of Christian Biography, Literature, Sects, and Doctrines ; from the Times of the Apostles to the Age of Charlemagne. Edited by Dr. WM. SMITH and H. WACE, D.D. Vols. I., II., & III. 8vo, 31s. 6d. each.

A Dictionary of Hymnology ; A Companion to existing Hymn Books. Setting forth the Origin and History of the Hymns in the most popular Hymnals, together with Biographical Notices of their Authors and Translators, and their Sources and Origins. By Rev. JOHN JULIAN. 8vo.

See STUDENTS' MANUALS, *p. 27.*

History of Latin Christianity, including that of the Popes to the Pontificate of NICHOLAS V. By Dean MILMAN. 9 vols. crown 8vo, 36s.

Some of the Chief Facts in the Life of our Lord ; and the Authority of the Evangelical Narratives. Lectures preached in St. James's, Westminster. By HENRY WACE, D.D. Crown 8vo. 6s.

Book of Common Prayer ; with Historical Notes. With Initial Letters, Vignettes, etc. 8vo, 18s.

A Book of Family Prayers : Selected from the Liturgy of the English Church. With Preface. By CHARLES E. POLLOCK. 16mo, 3s. 6d.

Signs and Wonders in the Land of HAM. With Ancient and Modern Parallels and Illustrations. By Rev. T. S. MILLINGTON. Woodcuts. 8vo, 7s. 6d.

The Talmud : Selected Extracts, chiefly Illustrating the Teaching of the Bible. With an Introduction. By Bishop BARCLAY. Illustrations. 8vo, 14s.

History of the Christian Church from the Apostolic Age to the Reformation, A.D. 64-1517. By Canon ROBERTSON. 8 vols. post 8vo, 6s. each.

Undesigned Scriptural Coincidences in the Old and New Testaments ; a Test of their Veracity. By Rev. J. J. BLUNT. Post 8vo, 6s.

History of the Christian Church in the First Three Centuries. By Rev. J. J. BLUNT. Post 8vo, 6s.

The Parish Priest; His Duties, Acquirements, and Obligations. By Rev. J. J. BLUNT. Post 8vo, 6s.

Biblical Researches in Palestine and the Adjacent Regions. A Journal of Travels and Researches. With Historical Illustrations. By EDWARD ROBINSON, D.D. Maps. 3 vols. 8vo, 42s.

Should the Revised New Testament be Authorised? By Sir EDMUND BECKETT, Q.C. Post 8vo, 6s.

The Revision Revised. Three Articles Reprinted from the *Quarterly Review*: (I.) The New Greek Text; (II.) The New English Version; (III.) Westcott and Hort's Textual Theory. With a Reply to Bishop Ellicott. By JOHN W. BURGON, B.D., Dean of Chichester. 8vo, 14s.

The Revised Version of the Three First Gospels, Considered in its Bearings upon the Record of our Lord's Words and Incidents in His Life. By Canon F. C. COOK. 8vo, 9s.

The Origins of Language and Religion. Considered in Five Essays. By Canon F. C. COOK, M.A. 8vo, 15s.

Psalms of David; with Notes, Explanatory and Critical. By Dean JOHNSON, Canon ELLIOTT, and Canon COOK. Medium 8vo, 10s. 6d.

The Gospel According to St. John. With Notes and Dissertations by Canon B. F. WESTCOTT, D.D. Medium 8vo, 10s. 6d.

Manual of Family Prayer; arranged on a card. 8vo, 2s.

The First Principles of the Reformation, Illustrated in the Ninety-five Theses and the Three Primary Works of Martin Luther. Edited by HENRY WACE, D.D., and Professor BUCHHEIM. Portrait. 8vo, 12s.

Church and the Age: a Series of Essays on the Principles and Present Position of the Anglican Church. By various Writers. 2 vols. 8vo, 26s.

The Synoptic Gospels,—The Death of Christ,—The Worth of Life,— Design in Nature, and other Essays. By Archbishop THOMSON. Cr. 8vo, 9s.

Companions for the Devout Life. Lectures delivered at St. James's Church. 1875-76. Post 8vo, 6s.

Classic Preachers of the English Church.
FIRST SERIES. 1877. Donne, Barrow, South, Beveridge, Wilson, Butler. With Introduction. Post 8vo, 7s. 6d.
SECOND SERIES. 1878. Bull, Horsley, Taylor, Sanderson, Tillotson, Andrewes. Post 8vo, 7s. 6d.

Masters in English Theology. Lectures delivered at King's College, London. By Canon BARRY, Dean of St. Paul's, Prof. PLUMPTRE, Canons WESTCOTT and FARRAR, and Archdeacon CHEETHAM. Post 8vo, 7s. 6d.

Essays on Cathedrals. By various Authors. Edited, with an Introduction, by Dean HOWSON. 8vo, 12s.

The Cathedral: its Necessary Place in the Life and Work of the Church. By the Archbishop of CANTERBURY. Crown 8vo, 6s.

The Gallican Church. From the Concordat of Bologna, 1516, to the Revolution. With an introduction. By W. H. JERVIS. Portraits. 2 vols. 8vo, 28s.

Continuity of Scripture, as declared by the Testimony of Our Lord and of the Evangelists and Apostles. By Lord HATHERLEY. 2s. 6d.

Bible Lands: their Modern Customs and Manners, illustrative of Scripture. By HENRY VAN LENNEP, D.D. Illustrations. 8vo, 21s.

The Shadows of a Sick Room. With Preface by Canon LIDDON. 16mo, 2s. 6d.

An Argument for the Divinity of Jesus Christ. From "Le Christianisme et les temps presents." By ABBE EM. BOUGAUD. Translated by C. L. CURRIE. Fcap. 8vo, 6s.

The Witness of the Psalms to Christ and Christianity. The Bampton Lectures for 1876. By the Bishop of DERRY. 8vo, 14s.

Treatise on the Augustinian Doctrine of Predestination. By Canon MOZLEY. With Index and Analysis. Crown 8vo, 9s.

Foundations of Religion in the Mind and Heart of Man. By Sir JOHN BYLES. Post 8vo, 6s.

Hymns adapted to the Church Service. By Bishop HEBER. 16mo, 1s. 6d.

The Nicene and Apostles' CREEDS. With some account of "The Creed of St. Athanasius." By Canon SWAINSON. 8vo, 16s.

Religious Thought and Life in India. An Account of the Religions of the Indian Peoples, based on a Life's Study of their Literature. By Sir MONIER WILLIAMS. Part I. Vedism, Brahmanism, and Hinduism. 8vo, 18s.

Christian Institutions; Essays on Ecclesiastical Subjects. By Dean STANLEY. 8vo. 12s.

Epistles of St. Paul to the Corinthians. The Greek Text; with Critical Notes and Dissertations. By Dean STANLEY. 8vo, 18s.

Lectures on the History of the EASTERN CHURCH. By Dean STANLEY. With Plans. Crown 8vo, 6s.

Lectures on the History of the JEWISH CHURCH, from the time of Abraham to the Christian Era. By Dean STANLEY. Maps and Portrait. 3 vols. Crown 8vo, 18s.

Sermons preached during the Tour of the Prince of Wales in the East. By Dean STANLEY. With Notices of the Localities visited. 8vo, 9s.

Sermons Preached in Westminster Abbey on Public Occasions. By the late Dean STANLEY. 8vo, 12s.

The Jesuits : their Constitution and Teaching ; an Historical Sketch. By W. C. CARTWRIGHT. 8vo, 9s.

Life in the Light of God's Word. By Archbp. THOMSON. Post 8vo, 5s.

Sermons preached in Lincoln's-Inn. By Canon COOK. 8vo, 9s.

Benedicite ; or, Song of the Three Children. Being Illustrations of the Power, Beneficence, and Design manifested by the Creator in His Works. By G. C. CHILD CHAPLIN, M.D. Post 8vo, 6s.

Life in Faith. School Sermons. By T. W. JEX-BLAKE, D.D. Small 8vo, 3s. 6d.

A History of Christianity, from the Birth of Christ to the Abolition of Paganism in the Roman Empire. By Dean MILMAN. 3 vols. post 8vo, 12s.

History of the Jews, from the earliest period, continued to Modern Times. By Dean MILMAN. 3 vols. post 8vo, 12s.

A Smaller Scripture History of the Old and New Testaments. Edited by Dr. W. SMITH. Maps and Woodcuts. 16mo, 3s. 6d.

Sermons preached at Lincoln's-Inn. By Archbp. THOMSON. 8vo, 10s. 6d.

Rome and the Newest Fashions in Religion. By the Right Hon. W. E. GLADSTONE. Containing The Vatican Decrees—Vaticanism—Speeches of Pius IX. 8vo, 7s. 6d.

Eight Months at Rome, during the Vatican Council, with a Daily Account of the Proceedings. By POMPONIO LETO. 8vo, 12s.

Worship in the Church of ENGLAND. By A. J. B. BERESFORD-HOPE. 8vo, 9s.; or, *Popular Edition*, 8vo, 2s. 6d.

Worship and Order. By A. J. B. BERESFORD-HOPE, M.P. 8vo, 9s.

SCIENCE, NATURAL HISTORY, GEOLOGY, ETC.

Science.

Connexion of the Physical Sciences. By MARY SOMERVILLE. New Edition revised. Plates. Post 8vo, 9s.

Molecular and Microscopic Science. By MARY SOMERVILLE. Illustrations. 2 vols. post 8vo, 21s.

Ironclad Ships; their Qualities, Performances, and Cost, with Chapters on Turret Ships, Rams, etc. By Sir E. J. REED, K.C.B. Illustrations. 8vo, 12s.

Six Months in Ascension ; an Unscientific Account of a Scientific Expedition. By Mrs. GILL. Map. Crown 8vo, 9s.

The Admiralty Manual of Scientific Inquiry, prepared for the use of Officers, and Travellers in General. Map. Post 8vo, 3s. 6d.

Reports of the British Association for the Advancement of Science, from 1831 to the present time. 8vo.

Philosophy in Sport made Science in Earnest ; or, the First Principles of Natural Philosophy explained by aid of the Toys and Sports of Youth. By Dr. PARIS. Woodcuts. Post 8vo, 7s. 6d.

Metallurgy ; The Art of Extracting Metals from their Ores. By JOHN PERCY. With Illustrations. 8vo. FUEL, WOOD, PEAT, COAL, &c. 30s. LEAD, and Part of SILVER. 30s. SILVER and GOLD. 30s.

The Manufacture of Russian Sheet-iron. By JOHN PERCY, 8vo, 2s. 6d.

A Manual of Naval Architecture for the Use of Officers of the Royal Navy, Mercantile Marine, Yachtsmen, Shipbuilders, and others. By W. H. WHITE. 150 Illustrations. 8vo, 24s.

Hydrographical Surveying. A Description of the Means and Methods Employed in Constructing Marine Charts. By Capt. W. J. L. WHARTON, R.N. With Illustrations. 8vo, 15s.

Walks in the Regions of Science and Faith : Essays by the Bishop of CARLISLE. Crown 8vo, 7s. 6d.

A Practical Treatise on Ship-Building in Iron and Steel. By Sir E. J. REED, K.C.B., M.P. Second and Revised Edition. With Plans and Woodcuts. 8vo.

Natural Philosophy; an Introduction to the study of Statics, Dynamics, Hydrostatics, Light, Heat, and Sound ; with numerous Examples. By SAMUEL NEWTH. Small 8vo, 3s. 6d.

Mathematical Examples. A Graduated Series of Elementary Examples in Arithmetic, Algebra, Logarithms, Trigonometry, and Mechanics. By SAMUEL NEWTH. Small 8vo, 8s. 6d.

Patterns for Turning; to be cut on the Lathe *without* the use of *any* Ornamental Chuck. By W. H. ELPHINSTONE. Illustrations. Small 4to, 15s.

Elements of Mechanics, including Hydrostatics, with numerous Examples. By SAMUEL NEWTH. Small 8vo, 8s. 6d.

The Freedom of Science in the Modern State. By RUDOLF VIRCHOW. Fcp. 8vo, 2s.

Natural History and Medicine.

Siberia in Asia. A Visit to the Valley of the Yenesay in East Siberia. With Description of the Natural History, Migration of Birds, &c. By HENRY SEEBOHM. Map and Illustrations. Crown 8vo, 14s.

Life of a Scotch Naturalist (THOMAS EDWARD). By S. SMILES. Illustrations. Post 8vo, 6s.

The Cat; an Introduction to the Study of Backboned Animals, especially Mammals. By ST. GEORGE MIVART. With 200 Illustrations. 8vo, 30s.

Lessons from Nature ; as manifested in Mind and Matter. By ST. GEORGE MIVART, F.R.S. 8vo, 15s.

The Origin of Species, by MEANS OF NATURAL SELECTION ; or the Preservation of Favoured Races in the Struggle for Life. By CHARLES DARWIN. Post 8vo, 7s. 6d.

Voyage of a Naturalist ; a Journal of Researches into the Natural History and Geology of the Countries visited during a Voyage round the World. By CHARLES DARWIN. Illustrations. Post 8vo, 9s.

Variation of Animals and Plants UNDER DOMESTICATION. By C. DARWIN. Illustrations. 2 vols. cr. 8vo, 18s.

The Various Contrivances by which ORCHIDS are FERTILISED by INSECTS. By CHARLES DARWIN. Woodcuts. Post 8vo, 9s.

The Effects of Cross and Self Fertilisation in the Vegetable Kingdom. By CHARLES DARWIN. Crown 8vo, 12s.

Expression of the Emotions in Man and Animals. By CHARLES DARWIN. Illustrations. Crown 8vo, 12s.

Descent of Man and Selection in Relation to Sex. By CHARLES DARWIN. Illustrations. Crown 8vo, 9s.

Insectivorous Plants. By CHARLES DARWIN. Post 8vo, 14s.

The Movements and Habits of Climbing Plants. By CHAS. DARWIN. Post 8vo, 6s.

The Different Forms of Flowers on Plants of the same Species. By CHARLES DARWIN. Woodcuts. Crown 8vo, 10s. 6d.

The Power of Movement in Plants. By CHARLES DARWIN, assisted by FRANCIS DARWIN. Woodcuts. Crown 8vo, 15s.

The Formation of Vegetable Mould through the Action of Worms. With Observations on their Habits. By CHARLES DARWIN. Woodcuts. Post 8vo, 9s.

Facts and Arguments for Darwin. By FRITZ MULLER. Illustrations. Post 8vo, 6s.

Geographical Handbook of all the known Ferns, with Tables to show their Distribution. By K. M. LYELL. Post 8vo, 7s. 6d.

The Gardens of the Sun ; or, a Naturalist's Journal on the Mountains and in the Forests and Swamps of Borneo and the Sulu Archipelago. By F. W. BURBIDGE. With Illustrations. Crown 8vo, 14s.

Harvest of the Sea. An Account of the British Food Fishes. With Sketches of Fisheries and Fisher-Folk. By JAMES G. BERTRAM. Illustrations. Post 8vo, 9s.

Household Surgery; or, Hints for Emergencies. By JOHN F. SOUTH. With new Preface and Additions. Woodcuts. Fcap. 8vo, 3s. 6d.

Winters Abroad : Some Information Respecting Places Visited by the Author on Account of his Health. Intended for the Use and Guidance of Invalids. By R. H. OTTER, M.A. Crown 8vo, 7s. 6d.

Kirkes' Handbook of Physiology. By W. MORRANT BAKER. 420 Woodcuts. Post 8vo, 14s.

Gleanings in Natural History. By EDWARD JESSE. Woodcuts. Fcap. 3s. 6d.

Geography and Geology.

Student's Elements of Geo- logy. By Sir CHARLES LYELL. A new Edition, entirely revised by Prof. P. M. DUNCAN. Woodcuts. Post 8vo.

Principles of Geology ; or, the Modern Changes of the Earth and its Inhabitants, as Illustrative of Geology. By Sir CHARLES LYELL. Woodcuts. 2 vols. 8vo.

Physical Geography. By MARY SOMERVILLE. New Edition, Revised by Rev. J. RICHARDSON. Portrait. Post 8vo, 9s.

Physical Geography of the Holy Land. By EDWARD ROBINSON, Post 8vo, 10s. 6d.

A History of Ancient Geo- graphy among the Greeks and Romans, from the Earliest Ages to the Fall of the Roman Empire. By E. H. BUNBURY. With 20 Maps. 2 vols. 8vo, 21s.

Siluria ; a History of the Oldest Rocks in the British Isles and other Countries; with Sketches of the Origin and Distribution of Native Gold, the general succession of Geological Formations and changes of the Earth's surface. By Sir RODERICK MURCHISON. Illustrations. 2 vols. 8vo, 18s.

Records of the Rocks ; or, Notes on the Geology, Natural History, and Antiquities of North and South Wales, Devon, &c. By Rev. W. S. SYMONDS. Illustrations. Crown 8vo, 12s.

Life of a Scotch Geologist and Botanist (ROBERT DICK). By S. SMILES. Illustrations. Crown 8vo, 12s.

Scepticism in Geology, and the Reasons for it. An assemblage of Facts from Nature opposed to the Theory of " Causes now in Action," and refuting it. By VERIFIER. Post 8vo, 6s.

See also STUDENT'S MANUALS, *p. 27.*

FINE ARTS, ARCHITECTURE, & ANTIQUITIES.

The National Memorial to the PRINCE CONSORT at KENSINGTON. A Descriptive and Illustrated Account, consisting of Coloured Views and Engravings of the Monument and its Decorations, its Groups, Statues, Mosaics, Architecture, and Metalwork. With descriptive text by DOYNE C. BELL. Folio, £12 : 12s.

Greece : Pictorial, Descriptive, and Historical. By CHRISTOPHER WORDSWORTH, D.D., Bishop of Lincoln. With an Introduction on the Characters of Greek Art by GEORGE SCHARF, F.S.A. A Revised Edition. Edited by H. F. TOZER, M.A. With 400 Illustrations of Scenery, Architecture, and the Fine Arts of the Country. Royal 8vo, 31s. 6d.

A Handbook to the Albert Memorial. Fcap. 8vo, 1s. ; or with Illustrations, 2s. 6d.

Mediæval and Modern Pottery and PORCELAIN. By JOSEPH MARRYAT. Illustrations. Medium 8vo, 42s.

Old English Plate : Ecclesias- tical, Decorative, and Domestic; its Makers and Marks. With Illustrations and Improved Tables of the Date Letters used in England, Scotland, and Ireland. By WILFRED J. CRIPPS. With 70 Illustrations. Medium 8vo, 16s.

Old French Plate : Furnishing Tables of the Paris Date Letters, and Facsimiles of other marks. By W. J. CRIPPS. With Illustrations. 8vo, 8s. 6d.

Cyprus ; its Ancient Cities, Tombs, and Temples. A Narrative of Researches and Excavations during Ten Years' Residence in that Island. By LOUIS P. DI CESNOLA. 400 Illustrations. Medium 8vo, 50s.

A History of Greek Sculpture. By A. S. MURRAY, of the British Museum. With 130 Illustrations. 2 vols. Medium 8vo. Vol. I. From the Earliest times to the Age of Pheidias. 21s.

Vol. II. Under Pheidias and his Successors. 31s. 6d.

Ancient Mycenæ ; Discoveries and Researches on the Sites of Mycenæ and Tiryns. By Dr. SCHLIEMANN. With Preface by the Right Hon. W. E. GLADSTONE. 500 Illustrations. Medium 8vo, 50s.

Troja : Results of the Latest Researches and Discoveries on the Site of Homer's Troy, and in the Heroic Tumuli and other Sites, made in 1882 ; with a Journey to the Troad in 1881. By Dr. SCHLIEMANN. With Preface and Notes. With Map, Plans, and Illustrations. Medium 8vo, 42s.

Ilios ; a Complete History of the City and Country of the Trojans, including all Recent Discoveries and Researches made on the Site of Troy and the Troad in 1871-3 and 1878-9. With an Autobiography of the Author. By Dr. SCHLIEMANN. With nearly 2000 Illustrations. Imperial 8vo, 50s.

Egypt after the War. Being Notes made during a Tour of Inspection, including Experiences and Adventures among the Natives. With Descriptions of their Homes and Customs, to which are added Notes of the latest Archæological Discoveries. By VILLIERS STUART, of Dromana, M.P., Author of "Nile Gleanings." With Coloured Illustrations and Woodcuts. Royal 8vo, 31s. 6d.

The Funeral Tent of an Egyptian Queen (contemporary with Solomon), lately discovered nearly perfect at Thebes. Printed in facsimile. With Translations and Explanatory Notices. By VILLIERS STUART, of Dromana, M.P. With 30 Plates. Royal 8vo, 18s.

The Cities and Cemeteries of Etruria. By GEORGE DENNIS. 200 Illustrations. 2 vols. medium 8vo, 21s.

History of Painting in North Italy, 14th to 16th Century. Venice, Padua, Vicenza, Verona, Ferrara, Milan, Friuli, Breschia. By CROWE and CAVALCASELLE. Illustrations. 2 vols. 8vo, 21s.

Raphael : His Life and Works, with Particular Reference to Recently Discovered Records, and an Exhaustive Study of Extant Drawings and Pictures. By J. A. CROWE, and G. B. CAVALCASELLE. Vol. I. 8vo, 15s.

Titian : his Life and Times. By CROWE and CAVALCASELLE. Illustrations. 2 vols. 8vo, 21s.

Handbook to the Italian Schools of Painting; Based on the work of Kugler. Revised by Lady EASTLAKE. 140 Illustrations. 2 vols. crown 8vo, 30s.

Handbook to the German, Dutch, and Flemish Schools of Painting. Based on the work of Kugler. Revised by J. A. CROWE. 60 Illustrations. 2 vols. post 8vo, 24s.

Lives of the Italian Painters ; and the Progress of Painting in Italy. Cimabue to Bassano. By Mrs. JAMESON. Illustrations. Post 8vo, 12s.

Lives of the Early Flemish Painters, with Notices of their Works. By CROWE and CAVALCASELLE. Illustrations. Post 8vo, 7s. 6d. ; or large paper, 8vo, 15s.

The Cicerone ; or, Art Guide to Painting in Italy. By Dr. BURCKHARDT. Post 8vo, 6s.

History of Architecture in all COUNTRIES, from the Earliest Times to the Present Day. By JAMES FERGUSSON. With 1600 Illustrations. 4 vols. Medium 8vo.
   I. & II. Ancient and Mediæval. 63s.
   III. Indian and Eastern. 42s.
   IV. Modern. 31s. 6d.

Landscape Art : down to the time of Claude and Salvator. By JOSIAH GILBERT. With numerous Illustrations. Crown 8vo.

Albert Dürer ; a History of his Life and Works. By MORIZ THAUSING, Vienna. Edited by F. A. EATON, Secretary of the Royal Academy. With Portrait and Illustrations. 2 vols. med. 8vo, 42s.

Rude Stone Monuments in all COUNTRIES : their Age and Uses. By JAMES FERGUSSON. Illustrations. Medium 8vo, 24s.

The Temples of the Jews and other Buildings in the Haram Area at Jerusalem. By JAMES FERGUSSON. Illustrations. 4to, 42s.

The Parthenon. An Essay on the Mode in which Light was introduced into Greek and Roman Temples. By JAMES FERGUSSON. 4to, 21s.

The Holy Sepulchre and the Temple at Jerusalem. By JAS. FERGUSSON. Woodcuts. 8vo, 7s. 6d.

Leaves from My Sketch-Book, By E. W. COOKE, R.A. 50 Plates. With Descriptive Text. 2 vols. Small folio, 31s. 6d. each. 1st SERIES—Paris, Arles, Monaco, Nuremberg, Switzerland, Rome, Egypt, etc. 2d SERIES—Venice, Naples, Pompeii, Poestum, the Nile, etc.

Life of Michel Angelo, Sculptor, Painter, and Architect, including unedited Documents in the Buonarroti Archives, by C. HEATH WILSON. With Index and Illustrations. 8vo, 15s.

A Descriptive Catalogue of the Etched Work of Rembrandt ; with Life and Introductions. By CHAS. H. MIDDLETON. Plates. Medium 8vo, 31s. 6d.

The Rise and Development of Mediæval Architecture. By Sir G. GILBERT SCOTT. 450 Illustrations. 2 vols. medium 8vo, 42s.

Secular and Domestic Architecture. By Sir G. SCOTT, R.A. 8vo, 9s.

The Gothic Architecture of ITALY. By G. E. STREET, R.A. Illustrations. Royal 8vo, 26s.

The Gothic Architecture of SPAIN. By G. E. STREET, R.A. Illustrations. Royal 8vo, 30s.

Collections Towards the History and Antiquities of the County of Hereford. In continuation of Duncumb's History. By W. H. COOKE, Q.C. With Map and 11 Illustrations. 4to, 52s. 6d.

Notes on the Churches of Kent. By Sir STEPHEN GLYNNE. With a Preface by W. H. GLADSTONE. Illustrations. 8vo, 12s.

Handbooks to English Cathedrals. *See p. 14.*

Purity in Musical Art. By A. F. J. THIBAUT. With Memoir by W. H. GLADSTONE. Post 8vo, 7s. 6d.

Handbook for Young Painters. By C. R. LESLIE. Illust. Post 8vo, 7s. 6d.

Life and Times of Sir Joshua Reynolds, with notices of his Contemporaries. By C. R. LESLIE and TOM TAYLOR. Portraits. 2 vols. 8vo, 42s.

Lectures on Architecture. Delivered before the Royal Academy. By EDWARD M. BARRY, R.A. Edited with Memoir by Canon BARRY. Portrait and Illustrations. 8vo, 16s.

London : its History—Antiquarian and Modern. Alphabetically arranged. By PETER CUNNINGHAM. A new and revised edition by JAMES THORNE and H. B. WHEATLEY. 3 vols. 8vo. [*In the Press.*]

Mexico To-Day : A Country with a Great Future. With a Glance at the Prehistoric Remains and Antiquities of the Montezumas. By T. U. BROCKLEHURST. With Coloured Plates and Woodcuts. Medium 8vo, 21s.

School Architecture. Practical Information on the Planning, Designing, Building, and Furnishing of Schoolhouses, etc. By E. R. ROBSON. Illustrations. Medium 8vo, 18s.

Contributions to the Literature OF THE FINE ARTS. By Sir C. LOCK EASTLAKE, R.A. With a Memoir by Lady EASTLAKE. 2 vols. 8vo, 24s.

The Choice of a Dwelling ; a Practical Handbook of useful information on all points connected with a House. Plans. Post 8vo, 7s. 6d.

Life of Sir Charles Barry, R.A., Architect. By Canon BARRY. Illustrations. Medium 8vo, 15s.

PHILOSOPHY, LAW, AND POLITICS.

The Rise and Growth of the Law of Nations, as Established by General Usage and by Treaties, from the Earliest Time to the Treaty of Utrecht. By JOHN HOSACK. 8vo, 12s.

The Eastern Question. By Viscount STRATFORD DE REDCLIFFE, Being a Selection from his Recent Writings. With a Preface by Dean STANLEY. Post 8vo, 9s.

Property and Progress ; or, Facts against Fallacies. A reprint of three Articles from the *Quarterly Review*. Containing a brief enquiry into contemporary Social Agitation in England. By W. H. MALLOCK. Post 8vo, 6s.

Letters on the Politics of Switzerland, pending the outbreak of the Civil War in 1847. By GEORGE GROTE. 8vo, 6s.

Constitutional Progress. By MONTAGUE BURROWS. Post 8vo, 5s.

Constitution and Practice of Courts-Martial. By Capt. SIMMONS. 8vo, 15s.

The Laws of Copyright. An Examination of the Principles which should Regulate Literary and Artistic Property in England and other Countries. By Prof. T. E. SCRUTTON. 8vo, 10s. 6d.

Administration of Justice under Military and Martial Law, as applicable to the Regular and Auxiliary Forces. By C. M. CLODE. 8vo, 12s.

A Handbook to the Political Questions of the day, with the Arguments on Either Side. By SYDNEY C. BUXTON. 8vo, 6s.

The English Constitution ; its Rise, Growth, and Present State. By DAVID ROWLAND. Post 8vo, 10s. 6d.

Laws of Nature the Foundation of Morals. By D. ROWLAND. Post 8vo, 6s.

A Manual of Moral Philosophy. With Quotations and References. By WILLIAM FLEMING. Post 8vo, 7s. 6d.

Gleanings of Past Years, 1843-78. By the Rt. Hon. W. E. GLADSTONE. Small 8vo, 2s. 6d. each. *See p. 22.*

Speeches and Addresses on Political, Literary, and Social Subjects. By the EARL OF DUFFERIN. 8vo, 12s.

Philosophy of the Moral Feelings. By JOHN ABERCROMBIE. Fcap. 8vo, 2s. 6d.

The Intellectual Powers, and the Investigation of Truth. By JOHN ABERCROMBIE. Fcap. 8vo, 3s. 6d.

Hortensius ; an Historical Essay on the Office and Duties of an Advocate. By WILLIAM FORSYTH. Illustrations. 8vo, 7s. 6d.

Lectures on General Jurisprudence ; or, the Philosophy of Positive Law. By JOHN AUSTIN. Edited by ROBERT CAMPBELL. 2 vols. 8vo, 32s.

Student's Edition of Austin's Lectures on Jurisprudence. Compiled from the larger work. By ROBERT CAMPBELL. Post 8vo, 12s.

An Analysis of Austin's Jurisprudence for the Use of Students. By GORDON CAMPBELL. Post 8vo, 6s.

England and Russia in the East.
A Series of Papers on the Political and Geographical Condition of Central Asia. By Sir H. RAWLINSON. Map. 8vo, 12s.

Asiatic Studies—Religious and
Social. By Sir ALFRED C. LYALL, K.C.B. Second Edition. 8vo, 12s.

Ancient Law: its Connection
with the Early History of Society, and its Relation to Modern Ideas. By Sir HENRY S. MAINE. 8vo, 12s.

Village Communities in the
East and West. By Sir HENRY S. MAINE. 8vo, 12s.

The Early History of Institu-
tions. By Sir HENRY MAINE. 8vo, 12s.

Dissertations on Early Law and
Custom; Being a Selection from Oxford Lectures. By Sir H. MAINE. 8vo, 12s.

Local Taxation of Great Britain
and Ireland. By R. H. I. PALGRAVE. 8vo, 5s.

Plato and other Companions
of Socrates. By GEORGE GROTE. 3 vols. 8vo, 45s.

Aristotle. By GEORGE GROTE.
Second Edition. With Additions. 8vo, 18s.

Minor Works of George Grote.
With Critical Remarks on his Intellectual Character, Writings, and Speeches. By ALEX. BAIN. Portrait. 8vo, 14s.

The Bengal Famine. How it
will be Met, and how to Prevent Future Famines. By Sir BARTLE FRERE. Maps. Crown 8vo, 5s.

Results of Indian Missions.
By Sir BARTLE FRERE. Small 8vo, 2s. 6d.

India in 1880. By Sir R.
TEMPLE. 8vo, 16s.

Men and Events of my Time
in India. By Sir RICHARD TEMPLE, Bart. 8vo, 16s.

Oriental Experience: a Selec-
tion of Essays and Addresses delivered on Various Occasions. By Sir RICHARD TEMPLE. With Woodcuts and Maps. 8vo, 16s.

Researches into the Early
History of Mankind, and the Development of Civilisation. By E. B. TYLOR. 8vo, 12s.

Eastern Africa viewed as a
Field for Mission Labour. By Sir BARTLE FRERE. Crown 8vo, 5s.

The Lex Salica; The Ten
Texts, With the Glosses and the Lex Emendata. Synoptically Edited by J. H. HESSELS. With Notes on the Frankish Words in the Lex Salica by Professor KERN. 4to, 42s.

Primitive Culture : Researches
into the Development of Mythology, Philosophy, Religion, Art, and Custom. By E. B. TYLOR. 2 vols. 8vo, 24s.

Ricardo's Political Works.
With a Biographical Sketch. By J. R. M'CULLOCH. 8vo, 16s.

The Moral Philosophy of Aris-
totle. Consisting of a Translation of the Nicomachean Ethics, and of the Paraphrase attributed to Andronicus of Rhodes; with Introductory Analysis of each Book. By the late WALTER M. HATCH, M.A. 8vo, 18s.

History of British Commerce,
and of the Economic Progress of the Nation, 1763–1878. By LEONE LEVI. 8vo, 18s.

Notes of Thought: by the Late
CHARLES BUXTON, M.P. With a Biographical Sketch by the Rev. J. LLEWELLYN DAVIES. Second Edition. Post 8vo, 5s.

Ideas of the Day on Policy.
By CHARLES BUXTON. 8vo, 6s.

Judgments of the Privy Council,
with an Historical Account of the Appellate Jurisdiction in the Church of England. By G. C. BRODRICK and W. H. FREMANTLE. 8vo, 10s. 6d.

A Little Light on the Cretan
Question. By A. F. YULE. Post 8vo, 2s. 6d.

History of the English Poor
Laws. By Sir G. NICHOLLS. 2 vols. 8vo.

Method in Almsgiving. A
Handbook for Helpers. By M. W. MOGGRIDGE, Hon. Secretary of the St. James's and Soho Charity Organisation Society. Post 8vo, 3s. 6d.

Consolation in Travel; or, the
Last Days of a Philosopher. By Sir HUMPHRY DAVY. Woodcuts. Fcap. 8vo, 3s. 6d.

GENERAL LITERATURE AND PHILOLOGY.

A Practical and Conversational
Pocket Dictionary of the English, French, and German Languages. Designed for the Use of Travellers and Students Generally. By GEORGE F. CHAMBERS. Small 8vo. 6s.

Recreations and Studies of a
Country Clergyman of the Last Century, being Selections from the Correspondence of THOMAS TWINING, M.A., Sometime Fellow of Sidney Sussex College, Crown 8vo, 9s.

The Quarterly Review. 8vo, 6s.

The Origins of Language and Religion, considered in Five Essays. By Canon F. C. Cook. 8vo, 15s.

The Talmud and other Literary Remains of Emanuel Deutsch. With a Memoir. 8vo, 12s.

Letters, Lectures, and Reviews, including Phrontisterion, or Oxford in the 19th Cent. By Dean Mansel. 8vo, 12s.

The Novels and Novelists of the 18th Century; in Illustration of the Manners and Morals of the Age. By Wm. Forsyth. Post 8vo, 10s. 6d.

Principles of Greek Etymology. By Professor Curtius. Translated by A. S. Wilkins, M.A., and E. B. England, M.A. 2 vols. 8vo.

The Greek Verb. Its Structure and Development. By Professor Curtius. Translated by A. S. Wilkins and E. B. England. 8vo, 12s.

Miscellanies. By Earl Stanhope. 2 vols. post 8vo, 13s.

Historical Essays. By Earl Stanhope. Post 8vo, 3s. 6d.

French Retreat from Moscow, and other Essays. By the late Earl Stanhope. Post 8vo, 7s. 6d.

The Papers of a Critic. Selected from the Writings of the late C. W. Dilke. 2 vols. 8vo, 24s.

Gleanings of Past Years. I. The Throne, Prince Consort, Cabinet, and Constitution. II. Personal and Literary. III. Historical and Speculative. IV. Foreign. V. and VI. Ecclesiastical. VII. Miscellaneous. By the Right Hon. W. E. Gladstone, M.P. Small 8vo. 2s. 6d. each.

Lavengro : the Scholar— the Gipsy—and the Priest. By George Borrow. Post 8vo, 5s.

The Romany Rye : a Sequel to 'Lavengro.' By George Borrow. Post 8vo, 5s.

A Glossary of Peculiar Anglo-Indian Colloquial Words and Phrases. Etymological, Historical, and Geographical. By Col. Yule, C.B., and the late Arthur Burnell, Ph.D. 8vo.

Old Deccan Days : Hindoo Fairy Legends current in Southern India. Collected by Mary Frere. With Introduction by Sir Bartle Frere. Illustrations. Post 8vo, 7s. 6d.

Æsop's Fables. A new Version. With Historical Preface. By Rev. Thomas James. Woodcuts, by Tenniel. Post 8vo, 2s. 6d.

Livonian Tales. By a Lady. Post 8vo, 2s.

Wild Wales : its People, Language, and Scenery. By George Borrow. Post 8vo, 5s.

Romano Lavo-Lil ; Word-Book of the Romany, or English Gypsy Language ; with an Account of certain Gypsyries. By George Borrow. Post 8vo, 10s. 6d.

The Handwriting of Junius. Professionally investigated by C. Chabot. Edited by the Hon. Edward Twisleton. With Facsimiles. 4to, 63s.

The Literary History of Europe. By Henry Hallam. Library edition, 3 vols. 8vo, 36s. ; or Cabinet edition, 4 vols. post 8vo, 16s.

Stokers and Pokers, or the London and North - Western Railway. By Sir F. Head. Post 8vo, 2s.

Specimens of the Table-Talk of Samuel Taylor Coleridge. Portrait. Fcap. 8vo, 3s. 6d.

The Remains in Prose and Verse of Arthur Hallam. With Memoir. Portrait. Fcap. 8vo, 3s. 6d.

Self-Help. With Illustrations of Conduct and Perseverance. By Dr. Smiles. Small 8vo, 6s.

Character. A Book of Noble Characteristics. By Dr. Smiles. Small 8vo, 6s.

Thrift. A Book of Domestic Counsel. By Dr. Smiles. Post 8vo, 6s.

Duty, with Illustrations of Courage, Patience, and Endurance. By Dr. S. Smiles. Post 8vo, 6s.

Mottoes for Monuments. By Mrs. Palliser. Illust. Cr. 8vo, 7s. 6d.

Words of Human Wisdom. Collected by E. S. With Preface by Canon Liddon. Fcap. 8vo, 3s. 6d.

The Amber-Witch : a Trial for Witchcraft. Translated by Lady Duff Gordon. Post 8vo, 2s.

Letters from the Baltic. By a Lady. Post 8vo, 2s.

Literary Essays from the 'Times.' By Samuel Phillips. Portrait. 2 vols. fcap. 8vo, 7s.

Rejected Addresses. By James and Horace Smith. Woodcuts. Post 8vo, 3s. 6d. ; or fcap. 8vo, 1s.

Lispings from Low Latitudes ; or, the Journal of the Hon. Impulsia Gushington. Edited by Lord Dufferin. Plates. 4to, 21s.

An English Grammar. Methodical, Analytical, and Historical. With a Treatise on Orthography, Prosody, Inflections, and Syntax. By Professor Maetzner. 3 vols. 8vo, 36s.

POETRY, THE DRAMA, ETC.

The Prose and Poetical Works of Lord Byron. With Notes by SCOTT, JEFFREY, WILSON, GIFFORD, CRABBE, HEBER, LOCKHART, etc., and Notices of his Life. By THOMAS MOORE. Illustrations. 2 vols. royal 8vo, 15s.

Poetical Works of Lord Byron. Library Edition. Portrait. 6 vols. 8vo, 45s.

Poetical Works of Lord Byron. Cabinet Edition. Plates. 10 vols. fcap. 8vo, 30s.

Poetical Works of Lord Byron. Pocket Edition. 8 vols. bound and in a case. 18mo, 21s.

Poetical Works of Lord Byron. Popular Edition. Plates. Royal 8vo, 7s. 6d.

Poetical Works of Lord Byron. Pearl Edition. Post 8vo, 2s. 6d.

Childe Harold. By Lord Byron. 80 Engravings. Crown 8vo, 12s.

Childe Harold. By Lord Byron. 2s. 6d., 1s., and 6d. each.

Tales and Poems. By Lord Byron. 24mo, 2s. 6d.

Miscellanies. By Lord Byron. 2 vols. 24mo, 5s.

Dramas. By Lord Byron. 2 vols. 24mo, 5s.

Don Juan and Beppo. By Lord Byron. 2 vols. 24mo, 5s.

Beauties of Byron. Prose and Verse. Portrait. Fcap. 8vo, 3s. 6d.

Oliver Goldsmith's Works, edited by PETER CUNNINGHAM. Vignettes. 4 vols. 8vo, 30s.

Agamemnon. Translated from Æschylus. By the Earl of CARNARVON. Small 8vo, 6s.

Argo ; or, the Quest of the Golden Fleece, a Metrical Tale in ten books. By the late Earl of CRAWFORD and BALCARRES. 8vo, 10s. 6d.

The Vaux-de-Vire of Maistre Jean le Houx, Advocate of Vire. Translated by J. P. MUIRHEAD. Illustrations. 8vo, 21s.

Life and Poetical Works fo George Crabbe. Plates, royal 8vo, 7s.

Life and Works of Alexander Pope. Edited by Rev. W. ELWIN and W. J. COURTHOPE. Portraits. Vols. 1, 2, 3, 4, 6, 7, 8. 8vo, 10s. 6d. each.

Iliad of Homer. Translated into English blank verse. By the Earl of DERBY. Portrait. 2 vols. post 8vo, 10s.

The Odyssey of Homer. Rendered into English Verse. By General SCHOMBERG, C.B. 2 vols. 8vo, 12s. each.

Poetical Works of Bishop Heber. Portrait. Fcap. 8vo, 3s. 6d.

Hymns adapted to the Church Service. By Bishop HEBER. 16mo, 1s. 6d.

The Sonnet; its Origin, Struc- ture, and Place in Poetry. With Translations from Dante and Petrarch. By CHARLES TOMLINSON. Post 8vo, 9s.

The Fall of Jerusalem. By Dean MILMAN. Fcap. 8vo, 1s.

Horace. By Dean MILMAN. Illustrated with 100 Woodcuts. Post 8vo, 7s. 6d.

Ancient Spanish Ballads. Historical and Romantic. Translated by J. G. LOCKHART. Woodcuts. Crown 8vo, 5s.

Remains in Prose and Verse of Arthur Hallam. With Memoir. Portrait. Fcap. 8vo, 3s. 6d.

Rejected Addresses. By JAMES and HORACE SMITH. With Biographical Notices. Portraits. Post 8vo, 3s. 6d. ; or fcap. 8vo, 1s.

An Essay on English Poetry. With short lives of the British Poets. By THOMAS CAMPBELL. Post 8vo, 3s. 6d.

Poems and Fragments of Ca- tullus. Translated in the Metres of the Original. By ROBINSON ELLIS. 16mo, 5s.

Poetical Works of Lord Houghton. New Edition. 2 vols. fcap. 8vo, 12s.

Gongora's Poetical Works. With an Historical Essay on the Age of Philip III. and IV. of Spain. By Archdeacon CHURTON. Portrait. 2 vols. small 8vo, 12s.

Poetical Remains of the late Archdeacon Churton. Post 8vo, 2s. 6d.

NAVAL AND MILITARY WORKS.

Hart's Army List. 8vo. Quarterly, 10s. 6d.; and Annual, 21s.

A Dictionary of Naval and Military Technical Terms. English-French, French-English. By Colonel BURN. Crown 8vo, 15s.

Our Ironclad Ships: their Qualities, Performances, and Cost, including Chapters on Turret Ships, Ironclad Rams, etc. By E. J. REED, C.B. Illustrations. 8vo, 12s.

Manual of Naval Architecture for Officers of the Royal Navy, Mercantile Marine, Yachtsmen, Shipowners, and Shipbuilders. By W. H. WHITE. Second Edition, revised. With 150 Woodcuts. 8vo, 24s.

A Practical Treatise on Ship- building in Iron and Steel. By Sir E. J. REED. Second and Revised Edition. With Plans and Woodcuts. 8vo.

Hydrographical Surveying. A Description of the Means and Methods Employed in Constructing Marine Charts. By Capt. W. J. L. WHARTON, R.N. With Illustrations. 8vo, 15s.

Modern Warfare as Influenced by Modern Artillery. By Col. P. L. MACDOUGALL. Plans. Post 8vo, 12s.

Naval Gunnery; for the Use of Officers and the Training of Seaman Gunners. By Sir HOWARD DOUGLAS. 8vo, 21s.

The Royal Engineer and the Royal Establishments at Woolwich and Chatham. By Sir FRANCIS B. HEAD. Illustrations. 8vo, 12s.

The Principles and Practice of Modern Artillery, including Artillery Material, Gunnery, and Organisation and Use of Artillery in Warfare. By Lieut.-Col. C. H. OWEN. Illustrations. 8vo, 15s.

The Administration of Justice under Military and Martial Law, as applicable to the Army, Navy, Marine, and Auxiliary Forces. By C. M. CLODE. 8vo, 12s.

History of the Administration and Government of the British Army from the Revolution of 1688. By C. M. CLODE. 2 vols. 8vo, 21s. each.

Constitution and Practice of Courts-Martial, with a Summary of the Law of Evidence, and some Notice of the Criminal Law of England with reference to the Trial of Civil Offences. By Capt. T. F. SIMMONS, R.A. 8vo, 15s.

History of the Royal Artil- lery. Compiled from the Original Records. By Col. FRANCIS DUNCAN, R.A. 2 vols. 8vo, 18s.

The English in Spain. The True Story of the War of the Succession in 1834-1840. By Colonel FRANCIS DUNCAN, R.A. Illustrations. 8vo, 16s.

Wellington's Supplementary Despatches and Correspondence. Edited by his SON. 15 vols. 8vo, 20s. each. An index. 8vo, 20s.

Wellington's Civil and Political Correspondence, 1819-1831. 8 vols. 8vo, 20s. each.

The Light Cavalry Brigade in the Crimea: Extracts from Letters and Journals during the Crimean War. By General Lord GEORGE PAGET. With Map. Crown 8vo, 10s. 6d.

Lives of the Warriors of the Seventeenth Century. By Gen. Sir EDWARD CUST. 4 vols. post 8vo. THE CIVIL WARS OF FRANCE AND ENGLAND. 1611-75. 2 vols. 16s. COMMANDERS OF FLEETS AND ARMIES, 1648-1704. 2 vols. 18s.

Annals of the Wars of the 18th and 19th Centuries, 1700-1815. Compiled from the most Authentic Histories of the Period. By Gen. Sir E. CUST. Maps. 9 vols. fcap. 8vo, 5s. each.

Deeds of Naval Daring; or, Anecdotes of the British Navy. By EDWARD GIFFARD. Fcap. 8vo, 3s. 6d.

RURAL AND DOMESTIC ECONOMY, ETC.

The English Flower Garden. Its Style and Position. With an Illustrated Dictionary of all the Plants used, and Directions for their Culture and Arrangement. By various Writers. By WILLIAM ROBINSON, F.L.S. With numerous Illustrations. Medium 8vo, 15s.

Hardy Flowers. Descriptions of upwards of 1300 of the most Ornamental Species; with Directions for their Arrangement, Culture, etc. By WM. ROBINSON. Post 8vo, 3s. 6d.

God's Acre Beautiful; or, the Cemeteries of the Future. By WM. ROBINSON. 8 Illustrations. 8vo, 7s. 6d.

The Illustrated Wild Garden; or, Our Groves and Gardens made Beautiful by the Naturalisation of Hardy Exotic Plants. By W. ROBINSON. With 90 Woodcuts. 8vo, 10s. 6d.

The Parks and Gardens of Paris, considered in relation to the wants of other Cities and of Public and Private Gardens; being Notes on a Study of Paris Gardens. By W. ROBINSON, With 350 Illustrations. 8vo, 18s.

Alpine Flowers for English GARDENS. How they may be grown in all parts of the British Islands. By W. ROBINSON. Illustrations. Crown 8vo, 7s. 6d.

A Popular Account of the In-troduction of Peruvian Bark from South America into British India and Ceylon, and of the Progress of its Cultivation. By CLEMENTS R. MARKHAM. With Maps and Woodcuts. Post 8vo, 14s.

Plain Instructions in Gardening; with a Calendar of Operations and Directions for every Month. By Mrs. LOUDON. Woodcuts. Fcap. 8vo, 3s. 6d.

Modern Domestic Cookery, Founded on Principles of Economy and Practice, and adapted for private families. By a LADY. Fcap. 8vo, 5s.

A Geographical Handbook of FERNS. By K. M. LYELL. Post 8vo, 7s. 6d.

Sub-Tropical Garden; or, Beauty of Form in the Flower Garden, with Illustrations of all the finer Plants used for this purpose. By W. ROBINSON. Illustrations. Small 8vo, 5s.

Thrift: a Book of Domestic Counsel. By SAMUEL SMILES. Small 8vo, 6s.

Duty: With Illustrations of Courage, Patience, and Endurance. By SAMUEL SMILES. Small 8vo, 6s.

Royal Agricultural Journal (published half-yearly). 8vo.

Bees and Flowers. By Rev. THOMAS JAMES. Fcap. 8vo, 1s. each.

Music and Dress. By a LADY. Fcap. 8vo, 1s.

Choice of a Dwelling; a Practical Handbook of Useful Information on all Points connected with Hiring, Buying, or Building a House. Plans. Post 8vo, 7s. 6d.

The Art of Dining; or, Gas-tronomy and Gastronomers. By A. HAYWARD, Q.C. Post 8vo, 2s.

Household Surgery; or Hints for Emergencies. By JOHN F. SOUTH. Woodcuts. Fcap. 8vo, 3s. 6d.

Methods in Almsgiving. A Handbook for Helpers. By M. W. MOGGRIDGE, of the Charity Organisation Society. Post 8vo, 3s. 6d.

FIELD SPORTS.

Dog-breaking; the most Ex-peditious, Certain, and Easy Method. By General HUTCHINSON. Woodcuts. 8vo, 7s. 6d.
*** A Summary of the Rules, for Gamekeepers, &c. 1s.

My Boyhood: a Story of Country Life and Sport for Boys. By H. C. BARKLEY, Civil Engineer. With Illustrations. Post 8vo, 6s.

Wild Sports and Natural His-tory of the Highlands. By CHARLES ST. JOHN. New and Beautifully Illustrated Edition. Crown 8vo. 15s.; or cheap ed., post 8vo, 3s. 6d.

The Chase—The Turf—and the ROAD. By NIMROD. Illustrations. Crown 8vo, 5s.; or coloured plates, 7s. 6d.

Sport in the Soudan. By F. L. JAMES. *See p. 9.*

Salmonia; or Days of Fly-Fish-ing. By Sir HUMPHRY DAVY. Woodcuts. Fcap. 8vo, 3s. 6d.

Five Years' Adventures in the far Interior of South Africa with the Wild Beasts and Wild Tribes of the Forests. By R. GORDON CUMMING. Woodcuts. Post 8vo, 6s.

Sport and War. Recollections of Fighting and Hunting in South Africa, from 1834-67, with an Account of the Duke of Edinburgh's Visit. By General Sir JOHN BISSET, C.B. Illustrations. Crown 8vo, 14s.

Western Barbary, its Wild Tribes and Savage Animals. By Sir JOHN DRUMMOND HAY. Post 8vo, 2s.

Sport in Abyssinia. By Earl of MAYO. Illustrations. Crown 8vo, 12s.

EDUCATIONAL WORKS.

DR. WM. SMITH'S DICTIONARIES.

A Dictionary of the Bible ; Its Antiquities, Biography, Geography, and Natural History. Illustrations. 3 vols. 8vo, 105s.

A Concise Bible Dictionary. For the use of Students and Families. Condensed from the above. With Maps and 300 Illustrations. 8vo, 21s.

A Smaller Bible Dictionary. For Schools and Young Persons. Abridged from the above. With Maps and Woodcuts. Crown 8vo, 7s. 6d.

A Dictionary of Christian Antiquities. The History, Institutions, and Antiquities of the Christian Church. With Illustrations. 2 vols. medium 8vo, £3 : 13 : 6.

A Dictionary of Christian Biography, Literature, Sects, and Doctrines. From the Time of the Apostles to the Age of Charlemagne. Vols. I. II. and III. Medium 8vo, 31s. 6d. each.

A Dictionary of Greek and Roman Antiquities. Comprising the Laws, Institutions, Domestic Usages, Painting, Sculpture, Music, the Drama, etc. With 500 Illustrations. Medium 8vo, 28s.

A Dictionary of Greek and Roman Biography and Mythology, containing a History of the Ancient World, Civil, Literary, and Ecclesiastical, from the earliest times to the capture of Constantinople by the Turks. With 564 Illustrations. 3 vols. medium 8vo, 84s.

A Dictionary of Greek and Roman Geography, showing the Researches of modern Scholars and Travellers, including an account of the Political History of both Countries and Cities, as well as of their Geography. With 530 Illustrations. 2 vols. medium 8vo, 56s.

A Classical Dictionary of Mythology, Biography, and Geography. With 750 Woodcuts. 8vo, 18s.

A Smaller Classical Dictionary. Abridged from the above. With 200 Woodcuts. Crown 8vo, 7s. 6d.

A Smaller Dictionary of Greek and Roman Antiquities. Abridged from the larger work. With 200 Woodcuts. Crown 8vo, 7s. 6d.

A Latin - English Dictionary. Based on the works of Forcellini and Freund. With Tables of the Roman Calendar, Measures, Weights, and Monies. Medium 8vo, 21s.

A Smaller Latin-English Dictionary. With Dictionary of Proper Names, and Tables of Roman Calendar, etc. A New and thoroughly Revised Edition. Square 12mo, 7s. 6d.

An English-Latin Dictionary, Copious and Critical. Medium 8vo, 21s.

A Smaller English-Latin Dictionary. Abridged from the above. Square 12mo, 7s. 6d.

DR. WM. SMITH'S SMALLER HISTORIES.

A Smaller Scripture History of the Old and New Testaments. With Coloured Map and 40 Woodcuts. 16mo, 3s. 6d.

A Smaller Ancient History of the East, from the Earliest Times to the Conquest of Alexander the Great. With 70 Woodcuts. 16mo, 3s. 6d.

A Smaller History of Greece, from the Earliest Times to the Roman Conquest. With Coloured Maps and 74 Woodcuts. 16mo, 3s. 6d.

A Smaller History of Rome, from the Earliest Times to the Establishment of the Empire. With Coloured Map and Woodcuts. 16mo, 3s. 6d.

A Smaller Classical Mythology. With Translations from the Ancient Poets, and Questions on the Work. With 90 Woodcuts. 16mo, 3s. 6d.

A Smaller Manual of Ancient Geography. 36 Woodcuts. 16mo, 3s. 6d.

A Smaller Manual of Modern Geography. Physical and Political. 16mo, 2s. 6d.

A Smaller History of England, from the Earliest Times to the year 1880. With Coloured Maps and 68 Woodcuts. 16mo, 3s. 6d.

A Smaller History of English Literature ; giving a Sketch of the Lives of our chief Writers. 16mo, 3s. 6d.

Short Specimens of English Literature. Selected from the chief Authors, and arranged chronologically. 16mo, 3s. 6d.

MURRAY'S STUDENT'S MANUALS.

A Series of Historical Class Books for advanced Scholars. Forming a complete chain of History from the earliest ages to modern times.

Student's Old Testament History, from the Creation to the Return of the Jews from Captivity. With an Introduction by PHILIP SMITH. Maps and Woodcuts. Post 8vo, 7s. 6d.

Student's New Testament History. With an Introduction connecting the History of the Old and New Testaments. By PHILIP SMITH. Maps and Woodcuts. Post 8vo, 7s. 6d.

Student's Ecclesiastical History PART I.—From the Times of the Apostles to the full Establishment of the Holy Roman Empire and the Papal Power. PART II.—The Middle Ages and the Reformation. By PHILIP SMITH. Woodcuts. 2 vols. post 8vo, 7s. 6d. each.

Student's English Church History. FIRST PERIOD—From the Planting of the Church in Britain to the Accession of Henry VIII. SECOND PERIOD—From the Time of Henry VIII. to the Silencing of Convocation in the 18th Century. By Canon PERRY. 2 vls. post 8vo, 7s. 6d. each.

Student's Ancient History of the East. Egypt, Assyria, Babylonia, Media, Persia, Phœnicia, &c. By PHILIP SMITH. Post 8vo, 7s. 6d.

Student's History of Greece, from the Earliest Times to the Roman Conquest; with the History of Literature and Art. With coloured Maps and Woodcuts. Post 8vo, 7s. 6d.

Student's History of Rome, down to the Establishment of the Empire; with the History of Literature and Art. By Dean LIDDELL. With coloured Map and Woodcuts. Post 8vo, 7s. 6d.

Student's History of the Decline and Fall of the Roman Empire. By ED. GIBBON. Woodcuts. Post 8vo, 7s. 6d.

Student's History of Modern Europe. From the End of the Middle Ages to the Treaty of Berlin, 1878. Post 8vo. *[In Preparation.*

Student's Hume: a History of ENGLAND from the Roman Invasion to the Revolution in 1688. New Edition. Continued to the Treaty of Berlin, 1878. By J. S. BREWER. With 7 Coloured Maps and Woodcuts. Post 8vo, 7s. 6d. Or in 3 Parts. Price 2s. 6d. each.

Student's History of France, from the Earliest Times to the Fall of the Second Empire. By Rev. W. H. JERVIS. Coloured Maps and Woodcuts. Post 8vo, 7s. 6d.

Student's History of England from the Accession of Henry VII. to the Death of George II. By HENRY HALLAM. Post 8vo, 7s. 6d.

Student's History of Europe during the MIDDLE AGES. By HENRY HALLAM. Post 8vo, 7s. 6d.

Student's Ancient Geography. By Canon BEVAN. Woodcuts. Post 8vo, 7s. 6d.

Student's Modern Geography. Mathematical, Physical, and Descriptive. By Canon BEVAN. Woodcuts. Post 8vo, 7s. 6d.

Student's Geography of British India, Political and Physical. By GEO. SMITH, LL.D. Maps. Post 8vo. 7s. 6d.

Student's Manual of the English Language. By GEORGE P. MARSH. Post 8vo, 7s. 6d.

Student's Manual of English Literature. By T. B. SHAW. Post 8vo, 7s. 6d.

Student's Specimens of English LITERATURE. By T. B. SHAW. Post 8vo, 7s. 6d.

Student's Manual of Moral Philosophy. By W. FLEMING. Post 8vo, 7s. 6d.

Student's Manual of the Evidences of Christianity. By H. WACE, D.D. Post 8vo.

Student's History of the Roman Empire, from the Establishment of the Empire to the Accession of Commodus, A.D. 180. Post 8vo.

*** This Work will form a connecting link between the Student's Rome and Student's Gibbon.

MARKHAM'S HISTORIES.

(With Conversations at the end of each Chapter.)

A History of England, from the First Invasion by the Romans to 1880. With 100 Woodcuts. 12mo, 3s. 6d.

A History of France, from the Conquest of Gaul by Julius Cæsar to 1878. Woodcuts. 12mo, 3s. 6d.

A History of Germany, from the Invasion by Marius to 1880. With 50 Woodcuts. 12mo, 3s. 6d.

Little Arthur's History of England. By Lady CALLCOTT. Continued down to the year 1878. With 36 Woodcuts. 16mo, 1s. 6d.

Little Arthur's History of France, from the Earliest Times to the Fall of the Second Empire. On the Plan of 'Little Arthur's England.' With Woodcuts. Foolscap 8vo.

DR. WM. SMITH'S EDUCATIONAL WORKS.

ENGLISH COURSE.

A Primary History of Britain for Elementary Schools. 12mo, 2s. 6d.

A School Manual of English Grammar, with Illustrations and Practical Exercises. By T. D. HALL. Post 8vo, 3s. 6d.

A Primary English Grammar for Elementary Schools. With Numerous Exercises and Carefully Graduated Parsing Lessons. By T. D. HALL. 16mo, 1s.

A Manual of English Composition. With Copious Illustrations and Practical Exercises. By T. D. HALL. 12mo, 3s. 6d.

A School Manual of Modern Geography, Physical and Political. By JOHN RICHARDSON. Post 8vo, 5s.

A Smaller Manual of Modern Geography, for Schools and Young Persons. 16mo, 2s. 6d.

LATIN COURSE.

The Young Beginner's First Latin Book ; Containing the Rudiments of Grammar, Easy Grammatical Questions and Exercises, with Vocabularies. Being Introductory to Principia Latina, Part I. 12mo, 2s.

The Young Beginner's Second Latin Book ; Containing an Easy Latin Reading Book, with an Analysis of the Sentences, Notes, and a Dictionary. Being Introductory to Principia Latina, Part II. 12mo, 2s.

Principia Latina, Part I. A First Latin Course, comprehending Grammar, Delectus, and Exercise Book, with Vocabularies. With Accidence adapted to the Ordinary Grammars, as well as the Public School Latin Primer. 12mo, 3s. 6d.

Appendix to Principia Latina, Part I. ; Additional Exercises, with Examination Papers. 12mo, 2s. 6d.

Principia Latina, Part II. A Latin Reading Book, an Introduction to Ancient Mythology, Geography, Roman Antiquities, and History. With Notes and Dictionary. 12mo, 3s. 6d.

Principia Latina, Part III. A Latin Poetry Book, containing Easy Hexameters and Pentameters, Eclogæ Ovidianæ, Latin Prosody, First Latin Verse Book. 12mo, 3s. 6d.

Principia Latina, Part IV. Latin Prose Composition, containing the Rules of Syntax, with copious Examples and Exercises. 12mo, 3s. 6d.

Principia Latina, Part V. Short Tales and Anecdotes from Ancient History, for Translation into Latin Prose. 12mo, 3s.

A Latin-English Vocabulary : arranged according to subjects and etymology ; with a Latin-English Dictionary to Phædrus, Cornelius Nepos, and Cæsar's "Gallic War." 12mo, 3s. 6d.

The Student's Latin Grammar. Post 8vo, 6s.

A Smaller Latin Grammar. Abridged from the above. 12mo, 3s. 6d.

GREEK COURSE.

Initia Græca, Part I. A First Greek Course : comprehending Grammar Delectus, and Exercise-book. With Vocabularies. 12mo, 3s. 6d.

Appendix to Initia Græca, Part I.—Additional Exercises, with Examination Papers and Easy Reading Lessons, with the Sentences analysed, serving as an Introduction to Part II. 12mo, 2s. 6d.

Initia Græca, Part II. A Greek Reading Book, containing Short Tales, Anecdotes, Fables, Mythology, and Grecian History. Arranged in a systematic progression, with Lexicon. 12mo, 3s. 6d.

Initia Græca. Part III. Greek Prose Composition : containing a Systematic Course of Exercises on the Syntax, with the Principal Rules of Syntax, and an English-Greek Vocabulary to the Exercises. 12mo, 3s. 6d.

The Student's Greek Grammar. By Professor CURTIUS. Post 8vo, 6s.

A Smaller Greek Grammar. Abridged from the above. 12mo, 3s. 6d.

Greek Accidence. Extracted from the above work. 12mo, 2s. 6d.

Elucidations of Curtius's Greek Grammar. Translated by EVELYN ABBOTT. Post 8vo, 7s. 6d.

Plato. The Apology of Socrates, the Crito, and Part of the Phædo ; with Notes in English from Stallbaum, and Schleiermacher's Introductions. 12mo, 3s. 6d.

FRENCH, GERMAN, AND ITALIAN COURSE.

French Principia, Part I. A First French Course, containing Grammar, Delectus, and Exercises, with Vocabularies and materials for French Conversation. 12mo, 3s. 6d.

Appendix to French Principia, Part I. Being Additional Exercises and Examination Papers. 12mo, 2s. 6d.

French Principia, Part II. A Reading Book, with Notes, and a Dictionary. 12mo, 4s. 6d.

Student's French Grammar: Practical and Historical. By C. HERON-WALL. With Introduction by M. Littré. Post 8vo, 6s.

A Smaller Grammar of the French Language. Abridged from the above. 12mo, 3s. 6d.

German Principia, Part I. A First German Course, containing Grammar, Delectus, Exercises, and Vocabulary. 12mo, 3s. 6d.

German Principia. Part II. A Reading Book, with Notes and a Dictionary. 12mo, 3s. 6d.

Practical German Grammar. With an Historical development of the Language. Post 8vo, 3s. 6d.

Italian Principia, Part I. A First Course, containing a Grammar, Delectus, Exercise Book, with Vocabularies, and Materials for Italian Conversation. By Signor RICCI. 12mo, 3s. 6d.

Italian Principia, Part II. A Reading-Book, containing Fables, Anecdotes, History, and Passages from the best Italian Authors, with Grammatical Questions, Notes, and a Copious Etymological Dictionary. 12mo, 3s. 6d.

SCHOOL AND PRIZE BOOKS.

Æsop's Fables, chiefly from Original Sources, by Rev. THOS. JAMES. With 100 Woodcuts. Post 8vo, 2s. 6d.

King Edward VI.'s Latin Accidence. 12mo, 2s. 6d.

King Edward VI.'s Latin Grammar. 12mo, 3s. 6d.

Oxenham's English Notes for Latin Elegiacs. Designed for early proficients in the art of Latin Versification. 12mo, 3s. 6d.

Hutton's Principia Græca : an Introduction to the study of Greek, comprehending Grammar, Delectus, and Exercise Book, with Vocabularies. 12mo, 3s. 6d.

Buttmann's Lexilogus; a Critical Examination of the Meaning and Etymology of Passages in Greek Writers. 8vo, 12s.

Matthiæ's Greek Grammar. Revised by CROOKE. Post 8vo, 4s.

Horace. With 100 Vignettes. Post 8vo, 7s. 6d.

Practical Hebrew Grammar ; with an Appendix, containing the Hebrew Text of Genesis I. VI. and Psalms I. VI. Grammatical Analysis and Vocabulary. By Rev. STANLEY LEATHES. Post 8vo, 7s. 6d.

Elements of Mechanics, including Hydrostatics. By Prof. NEWTH. Sm. 8vo, 8s. 6d.

First Book of Natural Philosophy : an Introduction to the Study of Statics, Dynamics, Hydrostatics, Light, Heat, and Sound. By Prof. NEWTH. Sm. 8vo, 3s. 6d.

Mathematical Examples. A Graduated Series of Elementary Examples in Arithmetic, Algebra, Logarithms, Trigonometry, and Mechanics. By Professor NEWTH. Small 8vo, 8s. 6d.

Progressive Geography. By J. W. CROKER. 18mo, 1s. 6d.

A Child's First Latin Book, comprising a full Praxis of Nouns, Adjectives, and Pronouns, with Active Verbs. By T. D. HALL. 16mo, 2s.

Gleanings in Natural History. By EDWARD JESSE. Fcap. 8vo, 3s. 6d.

Philosophy in Sport made Science in Earnest: or Natural Philosophy inculcated by the Toys and Sports of Youth. By Dr. PARIS. Woodcuts. Fcap. 8vo, 7s. 6d.

Puss in Boots. By OTTO SPECK-TER. Illustrations. 16mo, 1s. 6d.

The Charmed Roe. By OTTO SPECKTER. Illustrations. 16mo, 5s.

A Boy's Voyage Round the World. By SAMUEL SMILES. Illustrations. Small 8vo, 6s.

The Home & Colonial Library.

Class A—BIOGRAPHY, HISTORY, &c.

1. DRINKWATER's Gibraltar. 2s.
2. The Amber Witch. 2s.
3. SOUTHEY's Cromwell and Bunyan. 2s.
4. BARROW's Sir Francis Drake. 2s.
5. British Army at Washington. 2s.
6. French in Algiers. 2s.
7. Fall of the Jesuits. 2s.
8. Livonian Tales. 2s.
9. Condé. By Lord MAHON. 3s. 6d.
10. Sale's Brigade in Affghanistan. 2s.
11. Sieges of Vienna. 2s.
12. MILMAN's Wayside Cross. 2s.
13. Liberation War in Germany. 3s. 6d.
14. GLEIG's Battle of Waterloo. 3s. 6d.
15. STEFFENS' Adventures. 2s.
16. CAMPBELL's British Poets. 3s. 6d.
17. Essays. By Lord MAHON. 3s. 6d.
18. GLEIG's Life of Lord Clive. 3s. 6d.
19. Stokers and Pokers. By Sir FRANCIS HEAD. 2s.
20. GLEIG's Life of Munro. 3s. 6d.

Class B—VOYAGES and TRAVEL.

1. BORROW's Bible in Spain. 3s. 6d.
2. BORROW's Gipsies of Spain. 3s. 6d.
3. 4. HEBER's Indian Journals. 7s.
5. Holy Land. IRBY & MANGLES. 2s.
6. HAY's Western Barbary. 2s.
7. Letters from the Baltic. 2s.
8. MEREDITH's New S. Wales. 2s.
9. LEWIS' West Indies. 2s.
10. MALCOLM's Persia. 3s. 6d.
11. Father Ripa at Pekin. 2s.
12, 13. MELVILLE's Marquesas 7s.
14. ABBOTT's Missionary in Canada 2s.
15. Letters from Madras. 2s.
16. ST. JOHN's Highland Sports. 3s. 6d.
17. The Pampas. Sir F. HEAD. 2s.
18. FORD's Spanish Gatherings. 3s. 6d.
19. EDWARDS' River Amazon. 2s.
20. ACLAND's India. 2s.
21. RUXTON's Rocky Mountains. 3s 6d
22. CARNARVON's Portugal. 3s. 6d.
23. HAYGARTH's Bush Life. 2s.
24. ST. JOHN's Libyan Desert. 2s.
25. Letters from Sierra Leone. 3s. 6d.

DR. WM. SMITH'S ANCIENT ATLAS.

AN ATLAS OF ANCIENT GEOGRAPHY, BIBLICAL AND CLASSICAL. Intended to illustrate the 'Dictionary of the Bible,' and the 'Dictionaries of Classical Antiquity.' Compiled under the superintendence of WM. SMITH, D.C.L., and SIR GEORGE GROVE, LL.D. Folio, half-bound, £6 : 6s.

1. Geographical Systems of the Ancients.
2. The World as known to the Ancients.
3. Empires of the Babylonians, Lydians, Medes, and Persians.
4. Empire of Alexander the Great.
5, 6. Kingdoms of the Successors of Alexander the Great.
7. The Roman Empire in its greatest extent.
8. The Roman Empire after its division into the Eastern and Western Empires.
9. Greek and Phœnician Colonies.
10. Britannia.
11. Hispania.
12. Gallia.
13. Germania, Rhætia, Noricum.
14. Pæonia, Thracia, Mœsia, Illyria, Dacia.
15. Italy, Sardinia, and Corsica.
16. Italia Superior.
17. Italia Inferior.
18. Plan of Rome.
19. Environs of Rome.
20. Greece after the Doric Migration.
21. Greece during the Persian Wars.
22. Greece during the Peloponnesian War.
23. Greece during the Achæan League.
24. Northern Greece.
25. Central Greece—Athens.
26. Peloponnesus.—With Plan of Sparta.
27. Shores and Islands of the Ægean Sea.
28. Historical Maps of Asia Minor.
29. Asia Minor.
30. Arabia.
31. India.
32. Northern Part of Africa.
33. Ægypt and Æthiopia.
34. Historical Maps of the Holy Land.
35, 36. The Holy Land. North and South.
37. Jerusalem, Ancient and Modern.
38. Environs of Jerusalem.
39. Sinai.
40. Asia, to illustrate the Old Testament.
41. Map, to illustrate the New Testament.
42, 43. Plans of Babylon, Nineveh, Troy, Alexandria, and Byzantium.

INDEX.